DHARMAKSHETRA

EPIC Television Channel is the flagship factual entertainment offering from IN10 Media—a network with diverse interests in the media and entertainment sector. It is an India-centric, content-driven destination that has redefined the genre by being the only native Hindi-language infotainment channel. With a reputation for excellence in showcasing premium factual content that celebrates, explores, discovers and inspires India through untold stories, facts and possibilities, over the years, EPIC Television Channel has been bestowed with several accolades, including the prestigious PromaxBDA Award across various categories, the Indian Television Academy Award for the show *Stories by Rabindranath Tagore* and the Asian Rainbow Television Award for the show *Umeed India.*

Based on the popular TV show 'Dharmakshetra'

DHARMAKSHETRA

The Great Trial after
KURUKSHETRA

Published by
Rupa Publications India Pvt. Ltd 2019
7/16, Ansari Road, Daryaganj
New Delhi 110002

Sales centres:
Allahabad Bengaluru Chennai
Hyderabad Jaipur Kathmandu
Kolkata Mumbai

ISBN: 978-93-5333-620-2

First impression 2019

10 9 8 7 6 5 4 3 2 1

Transcription and translation by Malobika Chatterjee

CONTENTS

PROLOGUE

The Great War of Mahabharata is over. The battlefield of Kurukshetra lies barren, sans its great warriors and mighty kings, sans justice. The vicious battle saw the end of the world as it was known at the time. While the war decimated the Kauravas, the alleged villains, the Pandavas or the professed heroes renounced their kingdom and departed on a journey to Heaven. The war erased everything, including the thin line between the just and the unjust, deceit and loyalty, betrayal and duty. Never had the line been questioned before; the world had chosen to bury the answers to these unasked questions in the ruins of history.

But beyond the mortal world, up in the court of Maharaj Chitragupta, a post-apocalyptic trial is in progress.

Maharaj Chitragupta is the God of Justice, who keeps complete records of the actions of human beings and, upon their death, decides whether they deserve the glory of Heaven or the damnation of Hell. It is in his court that the Kauravas and the Pandavas now question each other, attempting to justify their actions to themselves, to each other, and to the God who will decide their final fate. After hearing all the arguments made by the prosecution and the defence, Chitragupta will deliver his final verdict.

This book asks primeval questions about the nature of

humanity, questions that have rarely been voiced before. Who, indeed, were the villains responsible for the ghastly bloodshed on the grounds of Kurukshetra? Who were the heroes? While attempting to ask and answer intriguing questions that determine the behaviour of human beings, this book also puts together forgotten pieces of the story we thought we knew.

Based on the television serial *Dharmakshetra*, this book is purely a work of fiction and not adapted from the original text of the Mahabharata by Ved Vyasa.

1

DRAUPADI

The Kurukshetra War had raged for eighteen days. It left behind a gaping hole, a silence where the survivors stood unsure. In this combat between 'the good' and 'the bad', who had truly emerged victorious? Who stood for the truth and who for falsehood? Who was irreligious and who the protector of religion? The eighteen-day-long bloodshed had changed our culture and history drastically; perhaps it would never be the same again. The warfare had now ended, but so had the era. Kurukshetra lay muted in the ruins of the past. It was now the dawn of Dharmakshetra.

It was the coveted throne of Hastinapur—gleaming with riches and glory—that had been so bitterly contested on the grounds of Kurukshetra. But now, all the stalwarts had left behind their earthly possessions in search of eternal freedom. It was salvation they sought, the *moksha* that would free their souls and let them rest in the tranquility of paradise. However, one final test remained.

In this great epic, the world had categorized people into heroes and villains. It had seemed straightforward enough:

the ones with fantastic sagas of valour, ideology and honesty should necessarily be regarded as heroes, right? But all that was back in the mortal world, not in the Court of Maharaj Chitragupta—the God who takes stock of everyone's deeds and seals the fate of their souls. Here, in the last stop before entering Heaven or being thrown into hellfire, it isn't hearsay that makes decisions; it is a trial.

This epic of great eminence will now unfold in the presence of Maharaj Chitragupta. The protagonists of the Mahabharata will attempt to explain their deeds on Earth. Charges will be levied, questions will be asked, and answers will be given, unearthing realities that have forever remained hidden from sight.

Chitragupta: I extend my salutations to all the revered persons in this assembly. Today, we have with us Bhishma, the son of Ganga; the erudite Vidura; and Maharaj Dhritarashtra with his sons Suyodhana and Sushasana. On the other side of the assembly are Karna, the eldest son of Rani Kunti; Yudhishthira, a man of religion; Bhima; Arjuna; Nakula and Sahadeva. Today, in front of this assembly, I would like to summon—

Karna: I beg your forgiveness, Maharaj. It is because of my birth that I have been thus seated. If you permit me, I would like to sit with my friends over there. (*Karna points to the opposite side of the assembly where Duryodhana sits with his father and brother.*)

Chitragupta: Angaraj Karna, this is not the classroom of Guru Drona. You are free to sit anywhere you please.

Yudhishthira: Karna, I thought we had closed this subject. Matashree has also acknowledged you as her firstborn son.

Your place is here with us, not there.

Karna: I am not your brother! My place is not here with you but with the people I have lived with all my life. Today, too, I would like to be by their side.

Chitragupta: Please drop this matter. We need to get on with the first accusation; I have an entire list of charges to go through!

To commence the first session of this Dharmakshetra, the Assembly of Religion, I would request Maharani Gandhari to come forward. She is the one who has made the first accusation. Maharani Gandhari, please introduce yourself to all the attendees. It's not that you warrant any introduction, but I need it for the records.

Gandhari: I am Gandhari, the daughter of Maharaj Gandhar, a wife of the Kuru clan, the consort of Maharaj Dhritarashtra, and the mother of one hundred sons and a daughter. But my children are not the ones I want to present before today's assembly. My accusation is against someone who is not even here.

Yudhishthira: Who is it, Badi Ma?

Gandhari: She is the one to whose apron strings all five of you have remained tied. Her ego and pride wrested all my sons from me. Our entire kingdom was razed to the ground; everything I ever held dear went up in flames and smoke! Where is that Panchali? I need that Yagyaseni Draupadi, that woman born of fire!

Sri Krishna: Draupadi, my friend, you have been summoned to the Assembly of Religion.

Draupadi: When will my trial come to an end, Keshava? Will it ever end at all? In the Battle of Kurukshetra, they questioned my circumstances and my motives, never once stopping to think what I had been through. Now, in the Dharmakshetra, will they raise questions about my entire life?

Sri Krishna: Panchali, you have answered questions in the past. You will do so again today. Many shameful allegations may be cast. I advise you to keep calm, my friend.

Draupadi: My patience is you. My calm is you. I will keep glancing at you, Keshava, and the answers—no matter how devastating—will come.

Chitragupta: Rani Draupadi, please approach in this direction and not towards Sri Krishna. The Assembly of Religion has begun, and you are the first one to be charged. I must say, there are a lot of accusations to go through.

Draupadi: I am ready, Maharaj. Please read out the first accusation.

Chitragupta: Rani Draupadi, the first allegation against you pertains to your marriage with the five Pandavas. You're accused of entering into marriage with the Pandavas only to further a conspiracy and fructify a carefully thought-out plan.

Draupadi: Conspiracy, Maharaj? Everyone present in the assembly today knows that my marriage took place at a *swayamvar*. My father had set out an archery test, and only the one who was successful in clearing it could ask for my hand in marriage. What kind of conspiracy are you talking about?

Gandhari: Let me answer that, Draupadi! But before I do,

I want you to tell me something. Do you remember your swayamvar?

Draupadi: Indeed I do.

Gandhari: Okay. Then you'll also remember that all the seven princes seated here today were present at your swayamvar. All of them wanted to prove their prowess at archery and win your hand in marriage. Do you remember?

Draupadi: Yes.

Gandhari: So, tell me Draupadi, of everyone present at your swayamvar that day, who was the prince who first caught your attention? Speak only the truth, Draupadi, for this is the Assembly of Maharaj Chitragupta. I, for one, am certain that it was not my son Duryodhana. Was it Dharmaraj Yudhishthira?

Draupadi: No.

Gandhari: Vayuputra Bhima?

Draupadi: Bhima is very dear to me.

Gandhari: That is not the answer to my question, Draupadi.

Draupadi: No, it wasn't Bhima.

Gandhari: Then it must be Nakula or Sahadeva, the sons of the Ashwini Kumaras, the Vedic twin-Gods.

Draupadi: No.

Gandhari: I see. The answer is now evident. It was Arjuna who caught your eye, that valiant victor who eventually won your swayamvar.

Draupadi: No, it wasn't him!

Gandhari: Ah, by some uncanny happenstance, it wasn't the feisty Angaraj Karna, was it?

Chitragupta: Well, Rani Draupadi, is this true?

Draupadi: Yes, Maharaj, it is true.

Chitragupta: I don't understand. Angaraj Karna was the one who first caught your eye. He was also the first one to reach the target, even before Arjuna. Then why didn't you put your wedding garland around his neck?

Draupadi: Well, at that time Karna was seen as a low-caste scion. I was not permitted even to think of marrying such a person.

Gandhari: That is untrue, Draupadi. You very well know you're lying! Let me share the truth with this assembly. Oh, don't worry—praise for you also lies hidden in the truth that I'm going to share.

You, my dear daughter-in-law, were born only so you could seek vengeance for what Guru Dronacharya had done to your father, the King Drupad. In fact, that was also why your brother—Prince Dhrishtadyumna—was born. Your father conducted a special *yajna* and offered to the sacred fire all his resentment for Guru Drona—someone he had thought was his true friend. It was from the fiery embers of this *yajna* that you and Dhrishtadyumna emerged. Your very birth was fuelled by fire, and throughout your life, an infernal fire of revenge continued to burn in your heart. Your father knew of your suffering but did little to help you. All his attention was focused on Dhrishtadyumna—the son he thought would fight for his father's honour. Even though you too had emerged from the flames of vengeance, what could a hapless woman really do to redeem her father's lost pride? The desire for attention and the need to singlehandedly seek revenge for your father grew so much within you that your ego overpowered your sense of reason!

FLASHBACK (Dhrishtadyumna, Draupadi's brother, practising warfare as a child)

King Drupad: Well done, son! Keep practising hard. Remember—you have to asunder Drona's breast. You have to take vengeance for your father. I am counting on you, son.

END OF FLASHBACK

Gandhari: Tell me, Draupadi, isn't this true? Your ego was what compelled you to marry Arjuna even though it was Karna who had captured your heart. You wanted to take vengeance for your father!

Sri Krishna: Badi Ma, I urge you to stop. Even if we accept what you say and agree that Draupadi wanted to help her father, where was the sense in marrying Arjuna? Everyone knew that Arjuna was Guru Drona's favourite disciple. If there was anyone who nurtured feelings of loathing against Guru Drona, it was Karna! Guru Drona had refused to make Karna his student and teach him the art of wielding the Brahmastra. Not only that, but he had also insulted Karna publicly. If Draupadi indeed wanted to seek revenge, it would have been wiser to marry Karna, not Arjuna.

Gandhari: Draupadi is not a fool, nor does she lack foresight. She has always been conversant with royal politics. She knew well that one day war was sure to break out between the Pandavas and the Kauravas. Karna, renowned for his sense of duty and fairness, would side with the Kauravas. He would hold his friendship with Duryodhana above everything else. Naturally, then, Karna and Drona would be far from enemies. They would be on the same team!

Sri Krishna: That seems far-fetched. How can you be sure that Draupadi indeed thought all this out?

Gandhari: What she thought, and who was responsible for what ensued, is not hidden from you, Keshava.

FLASHBACK (before the swayamvar)

Draupadi: Who is he, my friend?

Sri Krishna: He is your destiny.

Draupadi: There are many valiant warriors around. Why is he my destiny?

Sri Krishna: I cannot answer your question today, Draupadi. But I assure you, you will get your answer when the time comes.

END OF FLASHBACK

Gandhari: Why are you silent, Draupadi? You know that I speak the truth! The hatred from which you were born, the great ambition of vengeance that you always nurtured—they inflated your ego so much that you didn't hesitate even for a moment before sowing the seeds of a war that would decimate my entire family.

Chitragupta: Devi Gandhari, I can understand your pain. But it never serves any purpose to base one's accusations on hatred and disgust instead of logic and reason. I would request you not to get carried away by rage.

Draupadi: It's all right, Maharaj; I am used to being the target of hatred and apathy. I will respond to Mata Gandhari's accusation. Yes, I admit that I aspired to help my father. What is wrong in that? Do only men have the right to yearn for great things? At my swayamvar, my eyes did fall on Karna; he looked as powerful as the Sun God himself, and it did cross my mind that marrying a man like him would bring me great joy. But, for me, nothing supersedes my duty. And I will not allow anyone to cast aspersions on a decision that I took to fulfil my responsibilities as a daughter.

Chitragupta: Let's move on to the next accusation cast against Rani Draupadi—

Karna: Excuse me, Maharaj. May I be allowed to pose a question to Draupadi?

Bhima: Karna, don't forget that I, Draupadi's husband, am sitting here in this assembly today. She is my beloved wife and will always remain so. Be careful not to direct a single word of disgust or disgrace at my wife. I will protect her at all costs.

Karna: Bhima, this is not the right place for wrestling. Nor is it your bedroom.

Chitragupta: Angaraj, Bhima, this is not Kurukshetra! This is the Dharmakshetra, and I will not allow my courtroom to be insulted like this. I am warning both of you to remain within your limits. Angaraj, you may ask your question.

Karna: Yes, Maharaj. Draupadi, you admitted that I was the one who sent your heart aflutter in the swayamvar. You toyed with the idea of marrying me but chose Arjuna instead for reasons of duty. Have you ever thought about how it was your ever-so 'dutiful' decision that led to the Battle of Kurukshetra? If you hadn't married Arjuna that day and, instead, told me that you sought revenge on Guru Drona, I would have willingly given up everything to fulfil your wish. Ask Duryodhana; I always fulfilled his desires, even when the price was death. I would have done the same for you in return for your love. Why didn't you listen to your heart?

Draupadi: You are right, Karna. You are someone who adored his friend so much that you spent your entire life fulfilling his heinous wishes. What hope did a wife have of earning your favours? Your friend would say, 'Get rid of Draupadi.' You would. Your friend would say, 'Strip Draupadi of her clothing in full view of the assembly.' You, buried deep under your friend's debt, would wag your tail like a pup and disrobe me like a rapist! No, Karna, you would never have made a good husband for me. Even after all that has happened, I maintain that not marrying you was the right decision.

Chitragupta: Angaraj Karna, please take your seat. Devi Gandhari, I request you too to be seated with your family, for someone else is now coming forward to lay the next charge against Rani Draupadi. Please come forward, Devi Kunti.

Bhima: Arjuna, what is happening? Has our mother also accused Draupadi of something? What can it possibly be?

Arjuna: I don't know, Bhima. But I do know that our mother never speaks untruths.

Chitragupta: Devi Kunti, before you press charges against Rani Draupadi, I want to ask you one question.

Kunti: Yes, Maharaj.

Chitragupta: Devi Kunti, there were always undercurrents of enmity between your sons and the Kauravas—the sons of Devi Gandhari. Everybody was aware of this, including you and Devi Gandhari. But did you ever think that this hostility would snowball into the bloodiest battle known to humankind?

Kunti: No, Maharaj.

Chitragupta: Well, as we all know, it did. And yet, you, the mother of the Pandavas, claim never to have expected it. Tell me this: after your sons got married, did you then start feeling that the enmity between the Pandavas and the Kauravas could take a horrible turn?

(Kunti remains silent.)

Chitragupta: If this question seems hard to answer, let me simplify it. You were the mother-in-law of Rani Draupadi. How were her behaviour and demeanour as a daughter-in-law?

Kunti: I was blessed to have a daughter-in-law like her, Maharaj. I think my five sons were also extremely fortunate to have found a woman like her as their bride.

Chitragupta: What about the time when you started living with your sons in Indraprastha, the capital city of Khandavaprastha? Was Rani Draupadi's behaviour in line with the conduct expected from a bride of your dynasty? Did anything happen in Khandavaprastha that brought out her simmering soul and exposed the feelings she had long smothered inside her heart?

Kunti: Maharaj, I find myself unable to answer your question.

Draupadi: Yes, Maharaj, I too cannot imagine what you're talking about.

Duryodhana: Oh, so you don't remember anything, do you? You're the perfect queen, incapable of vice, are you? Let me tell you, Draupadi—your demeaning laughter still rings in my ears.

FLASHBACK (in the palace at Indraprastha)

Draupadi: What is the matter, brother Duryodhana? Are you also blind like your father? I find it hilarious what a true son of your father you indeed are, brother Duryodhana! Blind father, blind son!

END OF FLASHBACK

Chitragupta: Devi Kunti, since you did not answer my

question, let me voice the next allegation against Rani Draupadi for you. She, a daughter-in-law of the Kuru family, insulted the senior members of her clan. Is that true, Devi Kunti?

Arjuna: No, Matashree, do not answer his question.

Kunti: Yes, it is true.

Bhima: Matashree, what are you saying? You are supporting the allegations made against your daughter-in-law! This is Draupadi we are talking about, the woman who has never disregarded anything you have said. She left behind all the luxuries she had been used to and lived in the harsh forest with us. How can you have the heart to accuse her of being disrespectful to her elders?

Kunti: Bhima, don't interrupt me. It doesn't delight me to press such charges against my daughter-in-law, but I cannot deny that it was her vanity that led to that ghastly battle. It doesn't matter how much hostility you and the Kauravas shared. You were—and always will be—brothers. This woman entered your lives, and everything changed for the worse.

Sri Krishna: Choti Ma, I am stunned at the way you have let your feelings come to the fore! Have you always secretly nurtured these prejudiced feelings for your daughter-in-law? Tell me this, Choti Ma. Right since they were little children, the Kauravas conspired to kill your sons. It was your sons' good fortunes that helped them escape each time. How did you react to these deathtraps that the Kauravas set for your children? Let me recount what you did: nothing! You did not utter a word—not to the Kauravas, not to their mother,

Devi Gandhari. For some indiscernible reason, you chose to remain silent. Following your example, your sons remained silent too. Then, one day, their bride entered the household and carried out every duty that a bride is expected to fulfil. Never did she make a mistake, except for the time she committed the biggest folly of her life. She broke her silence. She resented the injustice being meted out to her and her husbands, and she did not hesitate to raise her voice against it.

Draupadi: Matashree, if your sons have been meted out injustice so many times—and God knows, they have—why did you never take any steps to stop it? If you had taught a lesson to Duryodhana and his brothers while they were still children, they would have remembered it and not dared to entrap your sons again. What was the use of getting your sons trained in warfare if they had to run from their enemies continually?

Sri Krishna: Choti Ma, your sons are warriors. They have always been warriors, ever since their childhood. But, if anybody pointed them in the direction where they could use their skills to defend their honour and that of their family, it was your daughter-in-law. If you talk of insult—and excuse me for saying this—I think no one has insulted Panchali more grievously than you have, Choti Ma.

Draupadi: Matashree, forgive me. I accept all the charges you have laid against me. If you think I was unworthy of being a bride of this clan, perhaps that is the truth.

Chitragupta: Devi Kunti, you may go back to your seat. Let's move to the next allegation laid against Rani Draupadi, this time by Suyodhana. He has claimed that Rani Draupadi became thirsty for vengeance after being insulted during the game of dice between the Pandavas and the Kauravas. The craze for vengeance went to her head, but she directed her rage against the wrong people. Suyodhana claims that Draupadi should have avenged her honour from the Pandavas, her husbands, instead of the Kauravas. If she had done so, she could have averted the horrifying Kurukshetra War.

FLASHBACK

Servitor: Excuse me, Rani Draupadi?

Draupadi: What is the matter? Did no one tell you that I was resting?

Servitor: Yes, Rani Draupadi. But Prince Duryodhana has summoned you to be present at the court.

Draupadi: Does your prince not know that the bride of a prestigious clan cannot be publicly summoned like this in a courtroom full of men?

Servitor: He has said that you are no longer the bride of a royal clan. You, he said, are nothing more than his maidservant with whom he can do as he chooses.

END OF FLASHBACK

Duryodhana: I was right, wasn't I? You were nothing but a maid! Dharmaraj had lost you in the game of dice.

Yudhishthira: Please do not make us recollect that terrible day. This is my earnest request to you, Duryodhana.

Arjuna: Bhaiya, what are you saying? Why are you pleading with that dirty man?

Duryodhana: Come on, Arjuna; do not overreact. What right have you to abuse me? If this hurts you so much, shouldn't you have stopped Dharmaraj that day when he, so enthusiastically, put his wife's honour at stake? He was the one who traded Draupadi like a commodity, and I am dirty for treating her like one?

Draupadi: The only one who was left feeling like trash that day was me. My soul was shattered into pieces, and I never recovered.

FLASHBACK

Draupadi: Dushasana, don't commit this sin!

Dushasana: Otherwise? What will you do? Laugh at me? Go ahead, make fun of me. Insult me all you like. I'd like to see the insults that a filthy maidservant is capable of.

Draupadi: You don't know what you're doing! I will—

Dushasana: Shhhhh! Your problem is that you talk too much, maid! Today I will put an end to all your troubles. I will take you with love—oh, so much love—that you will be quiet for good.

END OF FLASHBACK

Draupadi: I kept crying and screaming. I couldn't believe that I had been so unceremoniously dragged into this assembly of men. I couldn't believe that Dushasana could dare to use such foul words for me or touch my skin with his filthy hands. And yet it was happening. All of you know what happened after that.

Duryodhana: Before you narrate any more of your woeful tales and attempt to make this assembly sentimental, answer one question. When you were brought into that court, what were you?

Draupadi: I wasn't a 'what'! I was a bride of the Kuru clan, the wife of your brothers. Your father and mother addressed me as the bride of the clan. I was a queen!

Duryodhana: No! You were neither the bride of any clan nor were you anybody's wife. Those nincompoop husbands of yours had lost you in a game. You were one thing and one thing only: my maid!

Draupadi: Duryodhana, it is gold and silver that is staked in a game of dice, not the wife of a respected clan.

Duryodhana: Your husbands should have known that before losing you; you can't blame me. I am not questioning either your rage or your desire for vengeance, but they should have been directed at your husbands and not at my brothers and me. We only behaved as we would with our maidservant.

Karna: Panchali, you said earlier that I was so submerged in the pool of my friend's generosities that I could never rise and defend you if the need arose. Well, what did your five husbands do to protect you? One lost you in a game, and the rest stood like chickens, watching in silence as someone destroyed all your pride.

FLASHBACK

Duryodhana: Behold Draupadi, the daughter of Maharaj Drupad, born of fire with the kind of beauty that even heavenly danseuses cannot match. And yet, here she stands, reduced to nothing but my maidservant! Ha, what did you think? You could laugh at the prince of the Kuru clan without any repercussions? Look around yourself: you have not one but five husbands. And yet, all your husbands are now my slaves, helpless and incapable of claiming you back. This reminds me, you too are my slave. So let me think, what can I do to you? Where should I begin?

END OF FLASHBACK

Bhima: Enough, that's enough! I cannot hear more.

Duryodhana: Bhima, where was this rage when your brother lost you in a game? Remember that this is the Dharmakshetra; your noisy fury will not bend a single hair on my head. Maharaj Chitragupta, I have had my say on this subject. I blame Draupadi entirely for her misdirected anger that led to the battle, killing all of us and destroying everything in its wake.

Chitragupta: Rani Draupadi, what do you want to say in your defence? Suyodhana claims that the insult you faced was the fault of your husbands, and it is against them that you should have rallied. Instead, you showed poor judgement and decided to bring down the Kauravas.

Draupadi: Maharaj, this allegation is false. Yes, I do admit that I have struggled with one question for years. It is a question that has left me heartbroken and shattered, and will perhaps continue to haunt anyone who supports me for aeons to come. It first came to me when I was forced to lie on the floor in the courtroom that day—helpless, lacerated. I asked myself constantly: When was it that Dharmaraj put me at stake? Was it after losing himself? If he staked me after he had lost himself, then he had *no right* to gamble me! I was not an ornament of Indraprastha to be put on a decorative platter when guests came for drinks. I wasn't a toy that kids lost to each other while playing. I got married after a swayamvar, for God's sake! I had the right to choose my fate, my partner. The moment my husband lost his standing was the instant he also lost all rights over me. Once my husband became someone's slave, it was only Maharaj Drupad, my father, who could exercise any right or control over me. Maharaj, you are renowned for your sense of fairness. You tell me—am I not telling the truth?

Chitragupta: You are right, Rani Draupadi. But your argument is not enough to refute Suyodhana's allegations.

Duryodhana: I do not want to discuss this matter any further. First, Draupadi insulted both my father and me. Then, she overreacted to the entire incident that happened during the game, blamed my brothers and me for sins that weren't ours, and delighted in the battle that ensued. I did not make or break any promises; it was this woman's wrath and the oaths she forced her husbands to take that brought on the war!

Gandhari: Panchali, I agree with my son. Why did you do it?

Kunti: Didi, what are you saying? How can you blame Draupadi for reacting to everything that happened on the fateful day of the game?

Gandhari: I am merely speaking the truth, Kunti. Your sons savoured the beauties and riches of life. And my sons? Even as I lived, they were burnt to ashes. What can be more painful for a mother than seeing her sons breathe their last? It all happened because this daughter of fire willed it to happen. Answer me, Panchali, for such a minor offence, why did you take such a fearful oath?

Sri Krishna: Badi Ma, you shock me! Being a woman, how can you call Draupadi's insult a minor offence? It seems that none of you here today—except Draupadi—remembers the appalling incident as it really happened.

FLASHBACK

Duryodhana: Get up, Draupadi. The floor is not your place; your place is here, on my thigh.

END OF FLASHBACK

Sri Krishna: If her insult was a minor offence, then her oath, too, was inconsequential. If it was acceptable for the soil of Hastinapur to be thus moistened with Draupadi's tears, then, surely, it was also acceptable for the Earth to be sullied under the chariot wheels in Kurukshetra.

You, Prince Duryodhana, tell me this: You may have won Draupadi in the game of dice, and she may have become your maid. But if what you sought was vengeance for your insult, wasn't this victory adequate? Did you have to drag her to the assembly, pulling her along by her tresses?

Badi Ma, I sympathize with you, but do you know why? Before the Battle of Kurukshetra, you were the eldest queen of Hastinapur. Your husband, Maharaj Dhritarashtra, was the King of Hastinapur. Despite this, you could never really be the reigning queen. Do you know why? Oh, you probably do. Mata Kunti's sons *listened* to her. They obeyed all her commands. And your sons? Forget about obeying you; they didn't even listen to you.

Duryodhana: That is a lie. I have obeyed every command of my mother.

Sri Krishna: Badi Ma, is that the truth?

Gandhari: Yes, Keshava, it is the truth.

Sri Krishna: So, that means, Panchali was dragged to the court by her tresses on your orders. Isn't that right? Don't attempt to deny it, Badi Ma, for I will then ask: If you had forbidden your sons to disrespect Draupadi, why didn't they obey your order?

FLASHBACK (Dushasana pulling at Draupadi's sari, trying to disrobe her)

Draupadi: I was born of fire. All my life, until now, I have endured the heat that dwells in other people's hearts—without a word of complaint. But today, you have dared to lay your dirty hands on me, a chaste woman devoted to her husbands! Neither will I forget this insult, nor will I let it be ignored in the annals of history. I promise that this court will see corpses everywhere—bloodied, grotesque corpses of those who insulted me and laughed while I cried. I swear that the thigh that was offered to me as a seat will be shattered to pieces. Blood will flow, and my tresses will set everything on fire!

END OF FLASHBACK

Sri Krishna: The truth, Badi Ma, is that you had lost that very day. You had wanted to come even with your sister-in-law—Mata Kunti, the mother of the Pandavas—but your desire was smashed to smithereens by your eldest son. A queen had lost to a crown prince; a wife had lost to a mother. I don't deny that your son was devoted to you, but he didn't stop to think how his actions left you burning and writhing in pain. Perhaps he, too, inherited your subliminal pangs of sorrow at not being the reigning queen despite being the oldest. He wanted to secure a victory for his helpless mother. When he sensed that victory was not possible, he attempted to find sadistic pleasure in the loss of others.

Duryodhana: I refuse to listen to another word about my mother!

Sri Krishna: I merely posed a few questions to your mother, and you could not control your rage. And yet, you perpetrated this terrible insult on the wife of the Pandavas. Your elder brother's wife is also like your mother. If her insult became the cause of war, where is the injustice in that?

Chitragupta: So, coming back to the allegations cast against Rani Draupadi—

Draupadi: May I say something, Maharaj, before you pass your judgement?

Chitragupta: Yes, Rani Draupadi.

Draupadi: I grew up following my father, and then, after I got married, my husbands. My actions emanated from my sense of duty and loyalty towards my father, my husbands and the prestige of the clan I was married into. And yet, in this magnificent epic, I have turned out to be the villain. All that I have lost, no one else has. Yes, Mata Gandhari, I too have lost—my pride, my peace, all my sons. Perhaps, for years to come, people will blame me for the lives lost in the great war of the Mahabharata. They will forget my insults and my trauma; all they will remember me as is the vengeful woman who slaughtered thousands of people. And I will stand here, stunned into silence.

Gandhari: You are right, my child. This band around my eyes—the band that I have worn since the day of my marriage—has blinded me. My love for my sons has blinded me. If I hold you responsible for the carnage in the Kurukshetra War, I hold myself equally accountable. And look at the games that fate has played with me! When I was alive, I could see everything that was going on, despite being blindfolded. But I never said a word. Today, too, I see everything clearly, but cannot say anything. Nothing I say can make a difference or change the horrors that have been forever imprinted in our history. Child, I urge you to consider my silence as my apology.

Duryodhana: But, Matashree—

Gandhari: Enough, son, enough! Today, at least, listen to me. For once!

Chitragupta: In this Assembly of Religion, the Dharmakshetra, I have listened to all the allegations levied against Rani Draupadi. I have also listened to everything that was said to extenuate them. It is my duty now to decide which allegations are true and which are not.

Rani Draupadi, I sympathize with you. Tragic were your losses and grave were your insults. However, in the Dharmakshetra, there is no room for love, empathy or sympathy; there is only room for judgement. Rani Draupadi, you will remain an example for the generations to come. Your thoughts, your desire to fulfil your duties toward your loved ones, and your irrepressible passion will live on for aeons. However, you will also be remembered as a grim warning. From you the world will learn never to allow desires to overpower the sense of reason. If the desire for anything at all—for greatness, revenge or attention—clouds our mind, only darkness can ensue.

2

SHAKUNI

FLASHBACK

Unknown: Shakuni, your brothers have sent you food.

Shakuni: How many of my brothers are still alive?

Unknown: The last ten of your brothers remain. In the next few days, probably, they too will be gone.

END OF FLASHBACK

In the Mahabharata, the epic of vengeance, it wasn't just Draupadi who emerged from the flames to avenge her father's pride. There was a man who developed a tortuous conspiracy more infernal than any fire, and it was this maze that largely materialized into the bloodiest battle known to humankind. So cunning was he in hiding behind elaborate ruses of his own creation that this man's motives never came to the fore. But what Shakuni did not realize was that the Assembly of

Dharmakshetra would be the one test he couldn't hope to win only with guile.

Chitragupta: I welcome all of you to today's Assembly of Dharmakshetra. Let me call the next person on trial— Shakuni, the Prince of Gandhar and son of Maharaj Subal.

FLASHBACK

Shakuni: What is happening today? I have won again! Bhanje Yudhishthira, I bet you will win at the next turn.

END OF FLASHBACK

Chitragupta: Shakuni, today, in the Dharmakshetra, you will have to answer the allegations levied against you. Before we begin, is there anything you want to tell the assembly?

Shakuni: Maharaj, in your Assembly of Religion, my trial is unique. This is the first time that the defendant is equally looked down upon by both the sides. Do I have anything to say to these people? Well, the two fearless brothers of Yudhishthira—Bhima and Arjuna—did not even find me worthy of being killed. It was Sahadeva, this child, who did not find any other warrior to battle with, who finally killed me. My sister's husband didn't speak to me in years— actually, he never did. Maharaj, I am a very petty individual. It is your greatness that compelled you to call me to this Dharmakshetra. Otherwise, who am I? What am I? Does anyone care to remember?

Nakula: No! No one cares to remember you. You don't *deserve* to be acknowledged by anyone at all! It is because of your wicked scheming that the Kuru clan got divided. It was you who planted the seed of enmity between brothers. You sweet-talked on the surface, but the poison in your heart made you commit terrible deeds I feel ashamed to even talk about!

Sahadeva: I agree. I killed you only because our victory would have been incomplete as long as you were alive.

Shakuni: Oh my, oh my, even these little children can get angry! Sahadeva, I did you a favour. You were unable to find any warrior to kill; you were too naive to contest anyone on that battlefield. I gave you the chance to become a hero. So, stop behaving like a know-it-all and step forward to seek the forgiveness of your maternal uncle. Come, my nephews, I am willing to forgive you if you apologize.

Chitragupta: Shakuni, you have just arrived. Isn't it a bit early to start weaving your infamous webs of words? And no, I didn't invite you here as a favour; you were summoned here because it was my duty. You aren't quite as inconsequential to the scheme of things as you're trying to make yourself out to be. There are a number of serious allegations against you.

Shakuni: Maharaj, this is your Assembly of Religion. You are at liberty to do what you want. I am—

Chitragupta: Stop, Gandhar Kumar! Your skill with words and hypocritical sweetness will not make any difference to my judgement. I make my decisions based on reason and fairness, and you're incapable of swaying me with your gift of the gab. Remember, I too can play with words, and arguably better than you—so it would be in your best interests not to wage a match.

Shakuni: Maharaj, I want to spend a few days with you in this assembly. I can learn a lot from you. Forgive me, please, and begin levying your allegations.

Chitragupta: The first allegation against you, Shakuni, is that you were the reason behind the horrific battle of the Mahabharata. It is because of you that brothers went to war against each other. Vidur, I ask you to come forth, please.

Duryodhana: Where are you going, Vidur Kaka? You don't even know our uncle well.

Vidur: Son, it may surprise you, but it is only me who knows him.

Shakuni: Maharaj, I admit that I am a petty person. But am I so trivial as to be questioned by the son of a maid?

Vidur: Shakuni, I know that you can probably guess the allegation I am going to bring up against you. It is possible that you also have your answer ready. That is why I don't want to go there just yet. I want to ask you something that has been eternally hidden from everyone present in the assembly today. Tell me, Shakuni, the day you first found out that your sister, Devi Gandhari, had married a sightless king, how did you feel?

Shakuni: What kind of an absurd question is that? Naturally, I was unhappy.

Vidur: What about the time when you saw how Devi

Gandhari, a devoted wife, had wrapped a blindfold around her eyes, unwilling to see a world that her husband could not?

Shakuni: Oh, I was thrilled. Of course I was unhappy!

Vidur: Well, how unhappy?

Shakuni: Maharaj, what kind of idiotic questions is this maid's son asking me? What connection do his questions have with the allegation laid against me?

Chitragupta: Answer the question, Shakuni.

Shakuni: Haven't I answered it already? I was *miserable*. My sister would miss out on enjoying all the grandeur, all the splendour of the world. She would be unable to soak in the luxuries of the palace, unable to see her children. Which brother wouldn't feel heartbroken at such a fate of his sister?

Vidur: So, what did you do about it?

Shakuni: What could I possibly do? I just came to Hastinapur so I could at least stay by my sister's side and spend time with my beloved nephew.

Vidur: Was that really your motive? Didn't you come to Hastinapur seeking revenge for your sister's misfortune?

Shakuni: You son of a maid! What are you insinuating?

Vidur: You very well know that I am speaking the truth. So, tell me, Shakuni, what was this convoluted plan of revenge you concocted? Didn't you find it sick to push your beloved sister's sons towards their deaths?

Shakuni: Shut up, you lowborn son of a maid!

Duryodhana: Vidur Kaka, what are you saying? Have you lost your mind? How could our maternal uncle, the one who doted on us, possibly want us dead?

Vidur: Your mother is blindfolded, Duryodhana, but can you too see nothing? If there was one person who single-handedly orchestrated the Kurukshetra War, it was your dear maternal uncle. He was so obsessed with taking revenge that he burnt Hastinapur to ashes!

Duryodhana: That is impossible, Kakashree. The only people responsible for destroying Hastinapur were your beloved Pandavas. Our maternal uncle has always been on our side.

Vidur: You've always been a fool, Duryodhana.

Duryodhana: Watch your words, Kakashree!

Vidur: I am done watching everything I say, Duryodhana. I have always tried to speak to you and your brothers without any resentment or agitation even though you never listened to me. But here, in this Dharmakshetra, I, Vyasa's son, will not remain mute. I will tell you expressly why and how Shakuni destroyed your entire clan. And if you have even a shred of sense, you'll see your Mama Shakuni's true colours.

Shakuni: Yes, of course, go right ahead. I am curious to see the story that the erudite Vidur has manufactured.

Dushasana: Mamashree, please do not pay any attention to what Vidur is saying. He is just plain jealous. We always heeded your advice—all our lives—and the poor man probably felt sidelined.

Vidur: Ha! It is because you heeded Shakuni's advice that your entire dynasty was destroyed! Your Mamashree never forgot what happened to his sister; he could not bear to see her hidden from the world, deprived of her sight even though she wasn't blind. He begged her not to blindfold her eyes, but she was committed to siding with her husband. It was then that Shakuni hatched his evil plan to seek revenge on your father. He started laying the foundation of his disgusting and dangerous plan early in your childhood; he began poisoning your young minds against the Pandava princes. Think and you will remember! Everything about this man was contrary to religion and rightfulness, and that is the path he compelled all of you to follow.

FLASHBACK

Shakuni: Everyone is blind here. No one can bear to see the sorrow of anyone else. But I will soon change that. In this very house, living amongst its people, I will infuse poison. I will poison everyone's minds to the extent that they will begin striking each other. With every roll of the dice—the dice I can so easily charm to do my bidding—I will erase the dynasty that cheated my sister. Happy togetherness is a thing of the past; now, the game will begin!

END OF FLASHBACK

Vidur: You planned well, Shakuni. But you could never have won. For you, both defeat and death were foretold.

Shakuni: Vidur, blessed be your intellect and your storytelling skills! What a horribly fascinating but grossly untrue story you have narrated!

Duryodhana: This is nonsense. Vidur Kaka, I refuse to accept this. You're lying.

Vidur: Oh, my son, how do I make you understand? I do not lie; it is your blind faith in this deceitful man that has blinded you to his hideous face. Tell me, do you remember what your Mamashree said to you the very first time you had met him?

Duryodhana: He said what he always did. He assured me that the stars predicted kingship for me, that one day I would become the king of the whole of Bharatvarsh. He was the only one whose faith in my capabilities never dwindled.

Vidur: If this were indeed true, why didn't it happen? Why couldn't you become the king? Why did you die on the battlefield?

Shakuni: It was because of you, you son of a maid! You were always the biggest obstacle standing in my nephew's path to success. My brother-in-law did you a great favour by making you his counsellor. It was your duty to have given him sound counsel. But no, right from the outset, you harboured feelings of disgust for Duryodhana. You always planted hurdles in his life, hurdles he couldn't trace back to you. Whenever I tried to help him, you stood like a mountain in our path, never failing to shield those Pandavas. Today, in this Dharmakshetra, the real accusation shouldn't be against me; it should be against you, Vidur! Why did you sow the seeds of hatred in the minds of the Kauravas? Why did you continually instigate hatred among the brothers, egging them on to kill each other?

Vidur: Maharaj, Shakuni forgets himself. He is rambling on without making an iota of sense! He doesn't even remember what he did in the House of Wax—the death trap where the Pandavas were virtually certain to burn to their deaths. But does anybody know what happened *before* that fateful night?

Shakuni: I do!

FLASHBACK (Duryodhana maltreats a slave and angrily questions him: 'Am I blind?')

Shakuni: Duryodhana! What is the matter? Why are you so agitated?

Duryodhana: Who does he think he is?! He has constructed a palace on those ruins and now he believes he has conquered the world! Let me tell you—I am neither blind nor will I take this insult sitting down!

Shakuni: Calm down! I had feared that something like this might happen. That is why I had asked the Maharaj not to allow the Pandavas back in Hastinapur. But he never listens to me. He doesn't know that he is jeopardizing his own family.

Duryodhana: I will speak to him!

Shakuni: A fat lot of good that would do; the Maharaj doesn't listen to you either.

Duryodhana: Then what do I do, Mamashree? I can't stand those Pandavas! I hope they—

Shakuni: No, you must not curse your brothers. What does it matter if they have changed Khandavaprastha into Indraprastha? It is Hastinapur that truly matters. Ask the Pandavas to return to Hastinapur. Trust me; they will come as royalty but return home as hapless servants.

END OF FLASHBACK

Shakuni: I don't deny this, Maharaj. My nephew was greatly disturbed. Those brothers of his were ruining his mental peace, and he could not figure out what to do. He begged me several times to help him uproot the Pandavas from his life. I dearly loved my nephew and felt compelled to do something. So, I devised a scheme.

FLASHBACK

Shakuni: Duryodhana, do you know what this material is? It is wax. Wax ignites immediately upon coming in contact with fire.

Duryodhana: Why are you showing me this, Mamashree? I am not interested in anything that doesn't relate to eliminating those dratted Pandavas.

Shakuni: Don't jump the gun, nephew. Do you remember that I had asked the Pandavas to be sent to the Lakshagraha—the palace in the forest of Varnavrat? And you had been restless about sending them to a mansion, demanding to know the reason?

Duryodhana: Yes, I remember.

Shakuni: Well, the palace in which your beloved Pandavas are residing is made of wax. Tonight, when the Pandavas are asleep in their chambers, Prochan, the builder of the palace, will set his handiwork on fire. Come morning, neither will the palace remain, nor the five thorns in your side!

Duryodhana: Mamashree, I can't believe this! What would I do if you weren't there for me? Who else would take such good care of me?

Shakuni: Duryodhana, I will always be there for you. I have promised myself this, and my promise is my reason for living.

END OF FLASHBACK

Duryodhana: Vidur Kaka, I am getting confused here. What are you trying to say? It is true that I had conspired with Mamashree to kill the Pandavas in the House of Wax. Mamashree devised this plan because he had genuinely been concerned about me all my life—and he wanted to help me become the King of Hastinapur. You, on the other hand, couldn't stand the prospect of my success. Wasn't it you who helped the Pandavas emerge from Varnavrat alive? Wasn't it you who told them how to save themselves?

Vidur: Yes, it was me. I told the Pandavas how to emerge unscathed from your Mamashree's House of Death. But tell me, Duryodhana, do you know how I found out about your uncle's plan? I did not have a vivid dream that forecasted the death of the Pandavas in Varnavrat; it was your uncle who told me!

Duryodhana: What? Mamashree?

Vidur: Yes, Duryodhana, your dear Mamashree. Oh, he didn't do it upfront; your uncle is a smart man. But he made sure that the news reached my ears.

Shakuni: Indeed, I didn't! You lived in Hastinapur. You were probably a spy for the Pandavas. Maybe you had a network of spies working for you—people who filled your ears every day about the goings-on in the lives of your lords!

Duryodhana: This doesn't make any sense, Vidur Kaka. Mama Shakuni hatched the plan to kill the Pandavas. Why would he circulate the news to you? He very well knew that you loved those Pandavas, God knows why. I cannot believe that he would jeopardise his plans by telling you of them.

Vidur: I will tell you why he did it, Duryodhana. Shakuni didn't hatch the plan to kill the Pandavas; no, he *wanted* them to emerge alive from the wax palace. He longed to see the Pandavas furious—raging with anger at the behaviour meted out to them, burning with the desire to decimate the one who had executed the plan—you, Duryodhana!

Shakuni: Wonderful. Wonderful! You are truly erudite, Vidur. You, who have remained under the aegis of Maharaj Dhritarashtra all your life and yet always sided with the enemies of his sons, are casting allegations against me! You set your spies to work to uncover all our plans and stop Duryodhana from being crowned the king. You double-crossed the one who sheltered you—my sister's husband and his sons—and you dare to stand here, accusing me of double-crossing my beloved nephew?

Vidur: I knew you'd say something absurd like that, which is why I have kept my answer ready. Maharaj, when someone shelters you at their house, it is your duty to ensure the happiness of your hosts. You never say or do anything that could offend the house owners and make them throw you out. Shakuni, too, knew that I cared for the welfare of all the princes of Hastinapur—the Pandavas as well as the Kauravas. He knew that if I ever heard about a conspiracy against any of the princes, I would do my best to avert it. With Shakuni present in Hastinapur, I never had to spy. He *told* me everything I needed to know! It wouldn't be an exaggeration to say that he was the true protector of the Pandavas. He wanted them to murder all the Kauravas and help him complete his revenge.

Shakuni: Stop right now, Vidur! Just ask him, Duryodhana, if I truly wanted you defeated at the hands of the Pandavas, then why did I not instigate you to go to war right from the beginning? If I wanted to kill you and your brothers to take revenge for my sister, I could have sided with the Pandavas. But did I? No! I continually asked you to refrain from warfare! I left behind my roots, my Gandhar, and remained in Hastinapur, choosing to stay among people who regarded me as a villain!

Maharaj, my nephew was the first one who genuinely loved me; I cradled him in my arms since he was a baby. Is it wrong if I wanted him to become the Maharaj of Hastinapur? When those Pandavas came in the path, trying to wrest away rights that were my nephew's, I could not stand it. I admit I used deception and wile, but it was only to see my dear nephew's face light up with a smile.

Bhanje Duryodhana, nobody here will ever know just how much I love you. All I wanted was for you to become the King of Hastinapur, for my sister to be the mother of the king. The darkness of her life would be erased with the glory of your success. But I failed to fulfil my mission. If there is anybody against whom I have committed a crime, it is you, my nephew. I could not give you the happiness, the riches and the glories that I so badly wanted to.

Duryodhana: Vidur Kaka, forgive me, but I forbid you from casting any further allegations against Mamashree. I cannot see him breaking down like this. Mamashree, I know how much you love me; you sided with me even when the entire world was against me. It was only you who said, 'Duryodhana, you are a good person; you deserve to be king.' It doesn't matter what they say, Mamashree, I know you could never even *think* of harming me!

Vidur: Duryodhana, I am sorry to see that his crocodile tears have once again deceived you. But if you have shut your mind to the truth—as you have, most of your life—I see no point in going on. Your Mamashree well knows that every word I've spoken here today is the truth. Look underneath those tears, and you will see the spiteful, vengeful man for what he is.

Shakuni: Maharaj, Vidur is making my head pound. If the allegations against me have come to an end, may I have your permission to leave?

Chitragupta: Stop crying, Shakuni, for your tears will take you nowhere. You do not have permission to leave yet.

Vidur may have withdrawn, but there are other people in this assembly—people whose great troubles may well be attributed to you. Pandavas, if any of you want to address Shakuni, please go ahead.

Yudhishthira: Maharaj, we know that Mama Shakuni devised multiple plans to have us killed. He was also the reason for our intense humiliation during the game of dice. But we do not have any accusations to make against him, Maharaj.

Bhima: What are you saying?! Here is the man who constantly provoked Duryodhana to have us killed, whose deceptions forced us to wander through forests, whose evil mind turned the grounds of Kurukshetra bloody. He deceived you, Bhaiya, and humiliated all of us, including our wife. How can you let him go?

Arjuna: I agree with Bhima. Shakuni deserves to be severely penalized. In that game of dice, he let us start. The stars were in our favour; we were winning. And then, suddenly, everything changed. We began losing—once, twice, countless times—over and over. What was that if not deception?

Draupadi: Dharmaraj, I have never asked you about that game of dice. Never. I kept silent even though that day ended my life as I knew it. And yet today, when this filthy, disgusting man is in front of us, you will not address him even if it is to set things straight for your wife?

Shakuni: Dharmaraj will not say a word because he is not an ignoramus like all of you. He knows that after you have lost at a game, you cannot stand up and claim you were cheated. It's not magic that determines the outcome of a game of dice; it is fate. Fate! When the game started, Dharmaraj was winning. So much so that Duryodhana lost almost all his treasures. But then, fate did an about-turn, and he started losing. If Duryodhana's losses were not deception or trickery, then neither were yours! Isn't that so, Dharmaraj?

FLASHBACK

Yudhishthira: It is your turn, Mama Shakuni.

Duryodhana: Mamashree, are you waiting for next year to win?

Shakuni: Patience is a virtue, Bhanje. At the game of dice, if you cannot be patient, you cannot win. So, Duryodhana, tell me what you want. Five?

(*The dice rolls, coming up with six.*)

Duryodhana: Oh no! What on Earth is wrong with you, Mamashree? Are you playing on my behalf or his?

Shakuni: Patience, Bhanje, patience!

END OF FLASHBACK

Shakuni: The tables turned then; Lady Luck shone down on us. If anyone played a game of deception with the Pandavas, it was fate and not me.

Chitragupta: It seems to me that it is impossible to prove the veracity of this allegation against Shakuni.

Sri Krishna: No, Maharaj, if you will allow me, there is something I need to ask Shakuni. It is something I have heard all my life, but find extremely unsettling.

Chitragupta: Please proceed, Sri Krishna.

Sri Krishna: Shakuni, people keep telling me that if there is anyone as beguiling as me, anyone as crafty, then it is you. The insinuation seems to be that I am deceptive. Do you also think so?

Shakuni: Keshava, there is no one like you when it comes to getting people to do your bidding. You can deceive anyone with your sugar-coated words.

Sri Krishna: Maharaj, with your permission, I would like to test what Shakuni is saying. I want to engage him in a quick test of guile.

Chitragupta: Is this related to the allegation levied against Shakuni?

Sri Krishna: Indeed, Maharaj.

Chitragupta: Then you have my permission.

Sri Krishna: Thank you, Maharaj. Shakuni, let me begin with a simple question. Are you ready?

Shakuni: Yes, Keshava. You know that I am always ready for a game.

Sri Krishna: Tell me, Shakuni. How does one win against an enemy?

Shakuni: By vanquishing him, Keshava.

Sri Krishna: What happens if the enemy is more powerful than you?

Shakuni: In that case, the enemy's strength must be weakened. If that's not possible, it is best to strike when the enemy least suspects it.

Sri Krishna: So, for example, what you did with the Pandavas in the House of Wax.

Shakuni: Yes, I planned to set the house on fire when the Pandavas were asleep in their chambers. No one would be around to rescue them at night, and they wouldn't live to see the light of day.

Sri Krishna: But your plan failed. Vidur Kaka rescued the Pandavas and put your intentions to dust.

Shakuni: Keshava, haven't we already discussed all that?

Sri Krishna: Tell me, Shakuni. If there are two enemies, how should one tackle them?

Shakuni: The weaker enemy should be vanquished first.

Sri Krishna: Or one can sow seeds of enmity between the two.

Shakuni: Yes, Keshava.

Sri Krishna: Look at all the people present in the Dharmakshetra today. If I ask you who your greatest enemy is, what will your answer be? The Pandavas?

Shakuni: Yes, Keshava.

Sri Krishna: Are you sure? Are the Pandavas your only enemies or is there someone else too?

Shakuni: Who else can it be, Keshava?

Sri Krishna: How about Maharaj Dhritarashtra?

Shakuni: Maharaj Dhritarashtra? Oh no. No, Keshava. I agree that it was because of him that my sister remained deprived of eyesight all her life but he isn't my enemy. Maybe I don't like him much, but calling him my enemy would be an untruth.

Sri Krishna: Let's change the subject. Tell me, how many siblings did you have?

Shakuni: My father had a hundred sons.

Sri Krishna: Ah, just like Maharaj Dhritarashtra. Well, what happened to them?

Shakuni: They died.

Sri Krishna: All of them? Where?

Shakuni: In the dungeons of Hastinapur.

Sri Krishna: How did your brothers reach the dungeons of Hastinapur? Were you with them too? Was your father?

Shakuni: My father was there too.

Sri Krishna: So, your father and brothers died in Hastinapur. How did you survive?

FLASHBACK

Maharaj Subal: Salutations, Maharaj.

Dhritarashtra: What do you want?

Maharaj Gandhar: I have come to beg for your forgiveness. My sons and I made the shameful mistake of attacking Hastinapur. I should never have done so.

Dhritarashtra: But why did you do it?

Maharaj Subal: Please try to understand things from my perspective, Maharaj. I felt that my daughter Gandhari had suffered a terrible injustice. She was compelled to remain blind all her life—even though she could see perfectly well— only to fulfil her duty towards you, her husband. It angered and upset me. But I should have remembered that as your wife, her first duty was towards you.

When my sons and I attacked Hastinapur, it was only justified that you imprisoned us. You punished all of us by handing out only one grain of rice every day. I am not complaining, but Maharaj, my ninety-nine sons gave their rice grains to their youngest brother, my last-born son, Shakuni. They couldn't see their little brother die. Today, all my sons but Shakuni are dead. I beg you to please forgive him and let him live. Let him stay by his sister's side. I promise that for his entire life, he will remain a servitor of Hastinapur. This is the last wish of a man on the brink of death; please spare my son his life.

Dhritarashtra: Your last wish will, of course, be granted.

END OF FLASHBACK

Sri Krishna: So, even though Maharaj Dhritarashtra killed your father and all your brothers, you persist in claiming that he wasn't your enemy?

Shakuni: He wasn't!

Sri Krishna: Quit lying, Shakuni! How long will you continue to act? Bring out your favourite dice; tell the assembly what it is made of. Don't the dice continually remind you of your father and your brothers? Nothing is hidden from me, Shakuni. Look at your favourite dice, that I now hold in my hands. They are made from the embers of your father's funeral pyre, aren't they? That is why they always obey what you say!

FLASHBACK (The game of dice is on, and Duryodhana is winning—unfailingly.)

Shakuni: Ask, Duryodhana, and it shall be yours! What is it that you want? Riches, servants, the entire kingdom?

END OF FLASHBACK

Shakuni: Yes, Keshava, the dice did obey my orders. The dice decided the destiny of the game, leading Duryodhana to victory. I always wanted Duryodhana to be victorious, in everything.

Sri Krishna: If you always wanted his victory, then why did he get defeated in battle? Why did he lose everything—and everyone—he owned before losing his life? Duryodhana, will you remain adamant and ignorant even now?

Duryodhana: Mamashree, is all this true? Was your alleged love for me a mere facade to your real intentions?

Shakuni: Duryodhana, don't believe that Krishna—

Duryodhana: If all this is true, then you have conspired against me more murderously than even the Pandavas. You trapped me under your insincere emotions and blarney and led me down a road that could only take me to my death. You're more vicious than those I considered my worst enemies—

Shakuni: That's enough! All my life, I have endeavoured to make you victorious. All my years went by in supporting you, dreaming that you'd one day become the King of Hastinapur. And today, you get ensnared by this charlatan and that son of a maid and stop believing in me?! I knew this conman of a Krishna would bring up something irrelevant and try to present it as false evidence of crimes I have never committed. Tell me, Duryodhana, if what he claims is true, why did I let myself be killed in the battlefield, and that too by this Sahadev? I continued battling for your victory until my last breath. Do you have an answer? You brothers waged an ugly war among yourselves and carved permanent places in the history of Bharatvarsh. And I, who supported you and fought for you—even though I am no warrior—became a villain? The truth is simple: your family is messed up. You are the killers! My only weapon was my dice, and that, too, I used only for your well-being.

Dhritarashtra: It's all my fault, son. I committed a colossal folly that cost me the lives of my entire family. I never did tell you how your Mama Shakuni came to be a part of Hastinapur. I had to fulfil the last wish of his father, Maharaj Subal. But it is now evident that letting him live was a dangerous, lethal mistake. He ate into my family like a canker! I should have killed him just like I killed his brothers.

Shakuni: Maharaj, your words break my heart. I always wished the best for your sons. Never did I wish evil upon them, not once!

Gandhari: Really? How did you wish the best for my sons? By giving in to all their whims, no matter how misplaced? Making them a part of your abominable conspiracies? Encouraging them to insult the bride of the clan? Let me also be privy to the good that you wanted for my children.

Shakuni: Didi, how can you talk like this? Have you forgotten all that happened to you? It is because of this sightless prince, this man who stands here blaming your brother, that your life was propelled into darkness. It is because of him that our father and brothers were butchered. Have you not listened to anything?

Gandhari: I have, Shakuni. Just when I thought my heart couldn't shatter any further, it did. You are a sick man, Shakuni, and you infected my sons with the sickness of envy and loathing. So what if I had blindfolded myself? As my brother, you should have become my eyes! You should have helped bring up my sons! But no, all you did was drive my sons away from me. You cast such a heinous spell on them that they stopped listening to me and obeyed everything you said. If only my sons had listened to me instead, if they had sought my advice, they would be alive and well today.

Duryodhana: For once, I agree with Matashree, Mama Shakuni. You don't deserve to be called a brother or an uncle! What kind of uncle conspires to kill his nephews? You claim to have been driven by the love for your sister, but look, whatever you did only threw her deeper into sorrow! What could be worse for a mother than seeing her sons slaughtered on the battlefield, all because of her conniving brother? You are a monster! I always wondered why Yudhishthira and his brothers managed to defeat us in the war. Now I know—it was because of you! You stood between me and the throne of Hastinapur, and it was your dirty magic that stopped me from achieving anything in life. Forgive me, Matashree, for disregarding you and listening to this fraud of a man.

Shakuni: Even if you had listened to your mother, Duryodhana, you would never have become king. As soon as I first saw you, it became evident to me that you were a gullible man without a sense of right and wrong. If you had realized your strengths and weaknesses, perhaps you could have hoped to rule the kingdom one day. But no, I don't think you would have succeeded even then. You don't have the mental faculty to become an emperor, Duryodhana, so don't humour yourself by blaming me for your failures.

Duryodhana: Well, Mamashree, I admit I have failed. And how! You led us into fighting, and we fell headlong into your trap. We killed each other mercilessly. Even the victors were left with nightmares that would haunt them all their lives. The Kurukshetra War had only one true victor: you. You wanted the extermination of our clan, and you got it.

Chitragupta: After listening to all the arguments and the case put together by Vidur and Keshava, I have concluded that Shakuni deserves to be singlehandedly held responsible for the Battle of Kurukshetra. It was the seeds of hatred he sowed that sprouted into an all-consuming, fatal antagonism. In this Dharmakshetra, I declare Shakuni guilty. Heaven has no place for a man whose scheming destroyed a family. Shakuni, do you accept this judgement?

Shakuni: I accept your judgement, Maharaj. In this Dharmakshetra, I might have lost. But I am thankful that at least in the world below, I did as I pleased. Yes, it was unpleasant at times—terrible enough to be in Hell on Earth—so I don't mind living in Hell again. If nothing else, I will forever be a warning to future generations. People will think a million times before perpetrating such injustice to somebody's daughter or sister! Keshava, before I go, could I have my dice back?

Sri Krishna: Shakuni, have dice ever belonged to anybody? They don't listen to anyone but the dictum of destiny. You believed you could control destiny once, and you lost. That is precisely what will happen to anyone who commits the folly of thinking that he can change fate.

3

DURYODHANA

In this Bharatvarsh, we grow up to believe that good always wins against evil, and those on the path of religion vanquish the irreligious. Valiant heroes become part of our lives; indeed, children are named after these men and women with their glorious, courageous deeds. But what about the people who are forgotten as soon as their funeral pyres are burnt? Have we done right by them, or have we judged them, driven by prejudice and ignorance?

After the Kurukshetra War, as time made a steep turn, an era breathed its last. The protagonists of the Mahabharata set off for their ultimate destination—in search of salvation for their souls. They arrived in the assembly of Maharaj Chitragupta, for it was here that they'd have to take stock of their deeds on Earth. One by one, everyone would have to address the allegations against their names; they would have to recount and justify their human actions before their souls could find eternal peace.

Chitragupta: My greetings to everyone present in the assembly today. On one side we have Bhishma, the son of

Ganga; Maharaj Dhritarashtra and Maharani Gandhari; and their son Dushasana. Along with them is Karna, Rani Kunti's eldest son. On the other side are Rani Kunti and all the sons of Pandu—Dharmaraj Yudhishthira, Bhima, Arjuna, Nakula and Sahadev. Joining them are Rani Draupadi and Sri Vasudeva Krishna. Before we begin, I would like to request all of you: keep your cool. Remember that this is my court, and I urge you to maintain its honour.

Bhishma: Who is being judged here today, Maharaj Chitragupta?

Chitragupta: I am afraid the person coming on the stand today might make many of you lose your sanity. He might make your wounds fester or agitate you. But Kurukshetra was incomplete without him, and so is the Dharmakshetra.

Duryodhana: I am ready, Maharaj. I hope the assembly is ready for me too.

Chitragupta: Rajkumar, please introduce yourself.

Duryodhana: I am a member of the Kuru clan, the eldest son of Maharaj Dhritarashtra and Maharani Gandhari. I am Suyodhana, the true King of Hastinapur.

Bhima: Ha, the true King of Hastinapur is my brother, Dharmaraj Yudhishthira. You lost! You're no king! Or have you forgotten that already, Duryodhana?

Duryodhana: Bhima, I have reminded you a million times not to interrupt your elders. Keep him on a leash, Dharmaraj! Or else there will be another battle here in the Dharmakshetra, and guess what, the outcome won't be one he can gloat over!

Chitragupta: Bhima, see this as a request or a warning, but henceforth, you will not speak unless I ask you to. Suyodhana, there are some serious allegations against you to be levied in today's court. Will you be defending yourself?

Duryodhana: Yes, Maharaj. I don't want the assistance of someone else's words; I detest it when someone speaks on my behalf. I am not a coward like these people who need to depend on others to protect their pride and honour.

Chitragupta: I would like to ask Dharmaraj Yudhishthira to come forward.

Duryodhana: Oh! I thought you said you didn't want to press any charges against me? Come, Yudhishthira, come, this is the first time we are confronting each other. All your life, you have either remained hidden behind your pseudo-valiant brothers Bhima and Arjuna or asked Keshava to protect you. Come along now; I am keen to hear the allegations you have against me.

Arjuna: Keshava, I don't like what is happening here. I don't trust this Duryodhana at all. What if he cooks up a ruckus here and cheats our brother again?

Sri Krishna: Don't worry, Arjuna. This is the Dharmakshetra. Here Yudhishthira can conquer anyone, even the mighty Yamraj.

Chitragupta: Suyodhana, the first allegation against you is that you were overpowered by your greed. You were so obsessed with becoming the King of Hastinapur that you denied your brothers what was rightfully theirs.

Duryodhana: What greed, Maharaj? What rights? The Pandavas did not have any authority over Hastinapur. I have no idea why this Dharmaraj started considering himself the rightful heir of Hastinapur.

Kunti: What are you saying, son?

Duryodhana: I am only telling the truth, Choti Ma. The obsession for kingly power and riches ruled your sons, not me. And I think it is you who embedded this obsession deep into their brains. My brothers and I were happily spending our childhood in Hastinapur. These five people joined us from nowhere and claimed they were our brothers. We were made to share our toys with our new 'brothers'. But the greedy men couldn't be content with that, could they?

FLASHBACK

Gandhari: My sister, henceforth this section of the palace belongs to you.

Kunti: Thank you, Didi. My sons and I are lucky to have found someone who loves us so much. My sons found a hundred brothers too!

Gandhari: Duryodhana, this is your elder brother Yudhishthira. Let him play with your toys. Remember, one must always share, right?

END OF FLASHBACK

Duryodhana: First, it was the toys, and then you wanted my entire kingdom! Nobody has ever wrested anything from you, so naturally, you have no idea what I went through.

Yudhishthira: Duryodhana, brother, you know that we had as much right over Hastinapur as you did.

Duryodhana: If the sun is hidden by clouds, it is not necessarily night-time! Before all of you came to my kingdom, everything was going just fine. But no, you and your brothers had to plant yourself in my palace, win people over with your deceitful charm, and make it appear that Hastinapur was yours. The message you circulated was that everything would be overcast with sin if I became king. But you and your brothers, you paragons of virtue who had never even lived in a palace before, would turn around the fate of Hastinapur, and how! Tell me, between Maharaj Dhritarashtra and Maharaj Pandu, who is older?

Yudhishthira: Maharaj Dhritarashtra, of course.

Duryodhana: Yes, *my* father! He was older, but it was Maharaj Pandu who ascended the throne. He was followed by my father. As the eldest son of the King of Hastinapur, wasn't it natural that I would be the one to inherit the throne?

Yudhishthira: Duryodhana, we were also part of the Kuru clan.

Duryodhana: So? Why are you called the Pandavas while my brothers and I are called the Kauravas? Let me tell you why—it is because you have never thought of yourselves as Kauravas! Why would you think so anyway? None of you had a human father; one is the son of Indra, another of Vayu, the God of wind. The oldest is the son of Yamraj, while the two youngest brothers are Ashwiniputras. How can people like you, without any clear identities of your own, become princes and kings? I am a true-blue Kaurava, the real heir, and Hastinapur should have been mine.

Bhishma: Son, why don't you ask your father, Dhritarashtra, about this? I am sure that even he won't be able to lie about the worthiest prince among all of you. Yudhishthira, the Crown Prince of Hastinapur, deserved to become the king.

Duryodhana: What is wrong with all of you? My head is whirling! I keep asking myself: Who are these people? What kind of illusory net have they woven? How did they trap everyone in this fraudulent web, making all the elders of my family devoted to them? Oh, don't attempt to deny it—do you think I didn't notice? Since my childhood, you and Guru Drona never loved me or valued my capabilities. All your attention would be focused on Bhima's skill with the mace, Arjuna's archery or this Dharmaraj's so-called wisdom! Was I not a pupil of yours? If you had given me a chance, maybe I would have grown up to become far more valiant than all of them combined!

Yudhishthira: No, Duryodhana. I am not questioning your capabilities, but no amount of attention would have made you a more valiant warrior or more deserving of kingship than us. Do you know why? Well, here's your answer: it was you who didn't pay attention. Guru Drona and Bhishma Pitamaha never discriminated; you received the same education and training that we did. But your attention lay elsewhere—perhaps on usurping the kingdom and revelling in gold and diamonds. You claim that we never considered ourselves Kauravas. But Duryodhana, the truth is that *you* never considered *us* Kauravas. Our claim over Hastinapur was established the very day Bhishma Pitamaha enthroned Maharaj Pandu, our father, as the King of Hastinapur. He may have died early, but he was the first to sit on the throne. As his eldest son, it was my birthright to take the throne after Maharaj Dhritarashtra.

Duryodhana: Your birthright, or something your mother constantly droned into your ears?

Yudhishthira: Don't speak ill of Matashree, Duryodhana. Do you know that it is this woman you stand here blaming today who never thought ill of you? She told me: 'Duryodhana is your brother. You must share with him.' It was because of her that I agreed to divide the kingdom into two. We would have been satisfied with half the kingdom, but your spiralling greed had no limits. Our elders had to cajole and urge you to part with even half the kingdom—

Duryodhana: They forced me! Why should I have divided a kingdom that was mine in entirety? I could not sleep at night. If I had my way, and if our elders had stopped meddling in my affairs, I would have sent all five of you to your true fathers, whoever they were!

Bhima: Duryodhana, haven't you been taught to think before you speak? Only filth and garbage come out of your mouth!

Duryodhana: Don't you dare shout at me! I was not afraid of you then, and I am not scared of you now.

Chitragupta: Suyodhana and Bhima, I told you this before, and I am repeating it for the last time: this is neither your home nor your Gurukul. It isn't a wrestling arena or the battlefield. It isn't Hastinapur, but the Dharmakshetra. Stop behaving like children trying to outdo each other in a foolish fit of temper. In my court I will not tolerate such childish behaviour. All I want is answers, so if you stir up an uproar again, I will be compelled to take my decisions without letting you speak!

Suyodhana, the next allegation against you is even more serious: conspiring to murder. It has been alleged that you planned to kill your brothers—not once, but several times. Is this true, Suyodhana?

FLASHBACK

Dushasana: What are we doing, Bhaiya?

Duryodhana: I am mixing poison in the food of that monster Bhima. I wish that glutton eats all this up; it will be his last meal on Earth!

Dushasana: But—

Duryodhana: But what, Dushasana? If Bhima does not die today, pretty soon he will kick us out of the house. Haven't you seen how those Pandavas are trying to capture everything we own?

Dushasana: But Bhaiya, Matashree says they are our brothers.

Duryodhana: Brothers, eh? They don't deserve to be our brothers! Do you want this entire world to know that Suyodhana's brothers are slaves of sages and saints? Do you want such people to be your family members? No, Dushasana, they will all have to die.

END OF FLASHBACK

Chitragupta: Suyodhana, is this true?

Duryodhana: Wait, Maharaj. I am trying to remember how many times I tried to kill the Pandavas.

Chitragupta: So, you accept that you tried to kill your brothers?

Duryodhana: If someone fills your life with poison—right up to the brim—what can you do? The Pandavas were like termites inflicting my home; slowly, they hollowed everything out, making my life empty and eating away all my valuable possessions. I had no option but to uproot them from my life. Tell me, Maharaj, shouldn't a mad elephant be put to sleep?

My poison failed to kill Bhima. After ensuring that he ate the poisoned food, I tied him up and threw him into the ocean. But somehow he lived. I sent the Pandavas to the House of Wax and had it set on fire, but they survived that too.

FLASHBACK

Yudhishthira: Now I know why Duryodhana was so keen on sending us to this palace in the woods. He wanted to have us all killed! Matashree, were you aware of this conspiracy?

Bhima: What are you saying? Matashree, did you know about this?

Kunti: Yes, son.

Bhima: Then why did we come here? You should have told us!

Yudhishthira: No, Bhima. If we had refused to come to the palace, Duryodhana would have guessed that we had got wind of his plans.

Arjuna: Those darned Kauravas have always hatched conspiracies to spoil our lives. But trying to kill us all in cold blood? What they have done today is unforgivable.

Kunti: No, Arjuna. This conspiracy was not the machination of the Kauravas, but the well-thought-out scheme of another. What he failed to realize was that the strength of the saviour is far greater than that of the killer.

Sahadeva: But Matashree, who informed you about the conspiracy?

Kunti: It was your Kaka Vidur.

END OF FLASHBACK

Bhishma: Vidur, your conscience and intellect prevented a terrible disaster from taking place. I know you have averted a tragedy, not once, but many times. Please accept my gratitude.

Duryodhana: Ha, he should have looked after my welfare, not theirs! When he always stood by the sidelines, waiting to destroy my plans, how could I possibly be successful?

Chitragupta: Let the assembly be aware that Suyodhana has accepted this allegation. Suyodhana, the next allegation against you is—

Duryodhana: Maharaj, I have accepted this allegation to be true, yes, but I have a few questions. If you permit me, I would like to ask Dharmaraj about some religious dictums. I don't have the vast knowledge that he has, and where again will I get the opportunity to increase my knowledge?

Chitragupta: Go ahead, Suyodhana.

Duryodhana: Yudhishthira, tell me this: when a warrior realizes that his enemy is planning to strike, what should he do?

Yudhishthira: He should bolster his strength so that he can vanquish his enemy.

Duryodhana: Okay, does that mean a warrior should always be ready for war?

Yudhishthira: No, Duryodhana. A true warrior should always strive for peace.

Duryodhana: That is what I was doing, Dharmaraj. I did not want to bring about a war. My enmity was with all of you, so I wanted to have you killed. Then, there would be no question of war. Many innocent people who were annihilated at Kurukshetra would still be alive.

Bhishma: What is this you are saying, son?

Duryodhana: Pitamaha, maybe you never noticed, but I carefully observed all the Pandavas in the Gurukul. The brothers were so engrossed in learning that it appeared as if they were perpetually ready for warfare. First, they come to our Gurukul and start learning from our Guru. Then, in front of our eyes, they become the star students, the favourites! Why were they working so hard? Against whom were they preparing to fight? What was the imminent crisis threatening

Hastinapur that required them to train so very vigorously?

Yudhishthira: Yes, there was a crisis, Duryodhana. And if there wasn't, it could appear out of the blue at any time. Right from your childhood, you always remained in the palace, never having to move from place to place like us. You grew up believing that what was yours would always be yours. No one could extort it from you. Neither did you lack anything, nor did you learn to share. If you had wanted to, Duryodhana, you could have embraced your brothers and ensured that we got similar comforts and luxuries. But you didn't. If we were becoming skilled at warfare, you should have been proud. It should have pleased you that Hastinapur was becoming stronger; in your brothers' strength lay your strength too! But look what you did—you misconstrued the whole situation and assumed that we were preparing to go to war against you. You have never grasped the norms of warfare, Duryodhana. Don't you know that true warriors are permitted to use their weapons, their strength and their intellect, but not deception?

Duryodhana: You talk of deception? Your victory in Kurukshetra is cradled in the black mesh of fraud, and you accuse me?

Yudhishthira: *You* began the war with deception, Duryodhana, not me. You tried to kill us when we were mere children. With you, ethics has never been important, neither on the battlefield nor outside it.

Duryodhana: A-ha! My elder brother gets furious too! You don't sound so wise and highbrow now, do you? Maharaj, please read the next allegation, or else these Pandavas will continue to waste the time of everyone in the assembly.

Chitragupta: Suyodhana, before reading out the next allegation, I want to summon Angaraj Karna.

Duryodhana: Maharaj, what kind of allegation is this? Why do you need my best friend as a witness?

Chitragupta: You will know very soon.

Karna: Maharaj, I don't know why I am being called, but I'd like to repeat: I have been and always will be at my friend Duryodhana's side. I have nothing to say against him.

Chitragupta: Angaraj Karna, tell me this: was your friend Suyodhana responsible for giving you the position of Angaraj and crowning you King of Anga?

Karna: Yes, Maharaj. Not only did Duryodhana make me Angaraj, but he also gave me recognition and social standing. Whatever I was, it was only because of you, my friend.

Duryodhana: Karna, you are Surya. You don't need any recognition or introduction. Even if I hadn't made you Angaraj, your power and strength would have shone on as brightly. It is my good fortune that you acknowledged and accepted my friendship.

Karna: No, my friend, I owe everything to you. You befriended me when nobody called me their own and everyone picked on me for being the son of a low-caste charioteer. You were the one who embraced me in front of everyone and accepted me as your own. The debt I owe to you can never be repaid.

Chitragupta: If this display of friendship is over, can I ask some questions? Suyodhana, why did you bestow upon Karna the title of Angaraj?

Duryodhana: There wasn't a specific reason, Maharaj. I liked Karna. I wanted to give him a gift, and so I did.

Chitragupta: You aren't answering my question adequately. What were your real motives behind making Karna the King of Anga?

Duryodhana: Maharaj, trust me. It is true that I liked Karna as soon as I saw him.

Chitragupta: And the Pandavas had nothing to do with it?

Duryodhana: Well, okay, I admit that they were part of the reason. Those Pandavas always believed that they were better than me at everything. It was during a public show of our warfare skills that Karna came to me and requested permission to display his prowess at archery. Bhima called out then, declaring that a low-caste man had no right even to hold a bow, let alone shoot an arrow in front of royalty. I hated Bhima for saying that. A prince becomes one not by birth but through his deeds! I couldn't endure the injustice being meted out to this potentially great archer. That is why I made him Angaraj. I wanted to free him from the humiliation of having to narrate the story of his birth at every gathering.

FLASHBACK

Duryodhana: Welcome, Karna. Sorry, Angaraj! Please be seated.

Karna: Duryodhana, you crowned me Angaraj in front of everybody. You made me—a low-caste man—your friend.

For this honour you have bestowed upon me, I can probably never repay you. Even offering my life wouldn't quite be enough.

Duryodhana: Oh, you most certainly can repay me, my friend.

Karna: I am willing to do anything you want me to.

Duryodhana: So, do this: from today onwards, never see our friendship as a favour I have done to you. We are friends, and that's all you need to remember.

Karna: Absolutely. But, Duryodhana, a question has been bothering me. I don't know what to think. Why—

Duryodhana: Why did I make you Angaraj? Karna, you are special and worthier of becoming a king than anyone else I know. You, my friend, are neither lowborn nor a Kshatriya; you are a bright, glowing flame whose time to shine has begun. Come, Angaraj, let me show you your royal quarters.

END OF FLASHBACK

Chitragupta: Now that we have listened to your reasons for making Karna the King of Anga, I will move on to reading the allegation.

Duryodhana: Forgive me, Maharaj, but I don't think that will be necessary. Since the moment I stepped into your assembly, I seem to have been blessed with divine powers. I can portend, Maharaj, and I know the next allegation against me.

Chitragupta: Is that so?

Duryodhana: Yes, Maharaj. In this Assembly of Dharmakshetra, Suyodhana will now be accused of harbouring ulterior motives behind crowning Karna as Angaraj. He will be blamed for doing it only to submerge Karna in an ocean of debt—one that Karna would struggle to emerge from throughout his life. And what could be a better way of repayment for an archer as skilled as Karna than going to war for his friend? Tell me, Maharaj, aren't these the allegations?

Chitragupta: Yes, Suyodhana. That is the allegation.

Karna: What kind of allegation is this, Maharaj? What answer can my friend possibly give?

Arjuna: Your so-called friend knows that this allegation is legitimate. That is why he is trying to use sarcasm as a shield to avoid answering the question.

Duryodhana: You seem to know it all, Arjuna. Why don't you answer the question instead of me?

Arjuna: Of course, it would be my pleasure to unmask you, Duryodhana. I am sick of your constant hiding behind that facade of friendship. The truth, Karna, is that Duryodhana befriended you at the Dikshan Ceremony only because he thought you could equal me at archery. He wanted someone by his side to protect him when I cast my arrows.

Duryodhana: That's your conceit speaking, Arjuna. Karna is not as adept as you are at archery; he is far better! As for befriending anyone to help me deal with you, I have never needed to do that. I would have been enough for you, had you not employed deceit and trickery to win.

Bhima: Well, all I can say is that you made the right decision by not making more bodyguard-friends like Karna. They would all have been killed in battle.

Duryodhana: Bhima, I have no regrets about my death. I died battling you, and boy, was it worth it! But do not ridicule the deaths of my friends. I'd happily take you on again, right in this Dharmakshetra!

Chitragupta: Please answer the question put to you, Suyodhana. Did you befriend Karna only to get back at the Pandavas?

Duryodhana: No, Maharaj. This is all make-believe.

Chitragupta: Do you have evidence to prove what you say?

Duryodhana: How can I offer proof of the respect and love I have for my friend? You have to take my word for it. Anyhow, if anyone can raise fingers at my friendship with Karna, it can only be him. If Karna levies an accusation against me, claiming that my friendship was based on selfish motives, I won't say a word in defence. I will accept every allegation.

Chitragupta: Suyodhana, I too have mystical powers; I too can prophesize. When I asked you to provide proof, I was sure you would ask me to question Karna. In fact, I also know what Karna will say. He will declare that your friendship with him was absolutely selfless; it was the purest thing in the mortal world. Isn't that right, Karna?

Karna: Yes, it was, Maharaj.

Chitragupta: This is why I dislike allegations based on intangible emotions. I am not omniscient or someone who can pass judgement based on intuition. Is there anyone in this assembly who can provide any evidence in favour of or against this allegation?

Bhishma: Yes, Maharaj. I can.

Duryodhana: You?! It would be better if you stay quiet, Pitamaha. You could never tolerate my friendship with Karna. It is obvious that you will concoct some biased, untruthful story in the name of proof.

Bhishma: Yes, Duryodhana, I don't deny that I disliked your friendship with Karna. But it isn't from personal wrath of any sort that I speak today. I want to share something with the assembly that might shake everyone present. But in this Dharmakshetra, I think it needs to be said.

Chitragupta: What is it, Son of Ganga? Please hurry up; I have a long list of allegations to get through!

Bhishma: Maharaj, I have known Duryodhana since he was an infant. For as long as he lived, he never committed a single selfless act. But, even so, the allegation that has been levelled against him today is untrue. I will prove it.

Duryodhana: You are taking my side, Pitamaha? I cannot believe my ears!

Arjuna: Pitamaha, what are you saying? How can you support this unethical, vicious man?

Bhishma: I am supporting true friendship, Arjuna—perhaps the rarest thing in the world. Maharaj, I frequently advised

Duryodhana to follow the right path, to distinguish between the ethical and the unethical. But he never listened to me. I asked him to give half the kingdom to the Pandavas; he disobeyed. I asked him to stop the game of dice on that fateful day; he disobeyed. But I will never forget the one time he did obey my wishes—when I told him that as long as I was the Chieftain of his army, Karna would not lead the troops in battle.

Karna: Yes, Pitamaha, as long as you were the Chieftain, I did not pick up arms.

Bhishma: Do you know why Duryodhana obeyed me and forbade Karna from picking up arms, Arjuna? It wasn't because he honoured and respected me. It was because he feared for Karna's life. He was afraid that Karna would be decimated, and he wanted to do everything he could to save his friend from any danger. If Duryodhana had regarded Karna as a mere, albeit brave, soldier, he would have disobeyed me again. Karna would have battled from the very first day. But this time, Duryodhana listened to me.

Karna: Duryodhana, my friend, is this true?

FLASHBACK

Duryodhana: You sent for me, Pitamaha?

Bhishma: Yes, my son.

Duryodhana: You should now address me as the Crown Prince. I am not a child anymore.

Bhishma: I have something important to tell you,

Duryodhana. I hope you will pay heed to what I am about to say.

Duryodhana: Well, if the Chief of my Army has sent for me at this time of the night, it must be something important.

Bhishma: I am pleased to hear that you regard me as the Chieftain of your army. I hope you also know the first rule of war: you must follow your Chieftain's commands.

Duryodhana: What do you want, Pitamaha?

Bhishma: I don't want Karna to participate in this battle.

Duryodhana: What? Pitamaha, are you insane? Karna is one of our strongest warriors!

Bhishma: It is not as your Pitamaha that I give this command; it is as the Senapati of your army. You just regarded me as the Chieftain, and the very next moment you question my authority?

Duryodhana: I know you're the Chieftain; I am the one who elected you to the post! There's no need to remind me. But I fail to understand the reason behind this odd command of yours. Why can't Karna fight in this battle? Why should my friend be denied the honour when he is easily the best archer and the most courageous man I know?

Bhishma: As the Chieftain, I am entitled to make my own decisions. I don't need to answer your questions. If you want me to continue serving as the Chieftain of your army, Karna cannot participate in the warfare.

Duryodhana: Pitamaha, you know that Karna is a great

warrior. He has been longing to take part in this battle so that he can help me, his friend, win. If he fights for us, I think our chances of winning will increase manifold.

Bhishma: I have said what I had to say.

Duryodhana: But Pitamaha—

Bhishma: Enough! As long as I am the Chieftain, Karna cannot take part in this battle. You're free to do as you please if and when I am no more.

Duryodhana: Okay, Senapati. I accept what you say—not because I am giving in to your unreasonable demand, but because it might bode better for my friend.

END OF FLASHBACK

Duryodhana: I don't know why you made that curious demand, Pitamaha. But I am glad I decided to obey you. It helped my friend live longer and be by my side in turbulent times.

Chitragupta: Gangaputra Bhishma, what you have said proves that this allegation against Suyodhana is false. I will proceed to the next accusation.

Duryodhana: There are more?

Chitragupta: Suyodhana, the next allegation against you is one of cheating and fraud. During the game of dice, you allegedly took recourse to deception to defeat Yudhishthira.

Duryodhana: I won through cheating, did I? How is that,

Maharaj? The only reason for Yudhishthira's loss was his dismal fate. He has no one to blame but himself!

Bhima: You're lying, Duryodhana! You *did* cheat. Tell me, when you invited my brother for the game, why did you not play?

FLASHBACK

Duryodhana: Welcome, Maharaj! Welcome to my gambling room.

Yudhishthira: Thank you, Duryodhana, but I am afraid we cannot stay long. We have to return to Indraprastha.

Duryodhana: Yes, of course. But first, we must play. Dharmaraj, I have a small request to make.

Yudhishthira: What is it, Duryodhana?

Duryodhana: Well, everyone knows you're highly skilled at the game of dice. But I am far less competent. If you don't mind, I'd like to ask someone else to play on my behalf so it can be a game of equals.

Yudhishthira: Whom do you want to ask?

Duryodhana: My maternal uncle, Shakuni.

END OF FLASHBACK

Duryodhana: It was my house and my space, wasn't it? I had every right to ask someone else to take my place. What's wrong in that, Maharaj?

Chitragupta: Nothing, Suyodhana. But the one you asked to take your place was neither an ordinary nor an honest player.

Yudhishthira: You asked Mama Shakuni to play on your behalf because you knew he would charm the dice and make you win. It was your planning, Duryodhana.

Duryodhana: I like that! I called you for a spot of gambling, and you arrived. First, you lost your kingdom, which I generously returned. But you played again and lost it again! Where was my fault in this? If my trickery had made you lose the first time, why did you play over? Had you lost your mind? Why did you accept my invitation in the first place?

Yudhishthira: Duryodhana, I don't think you know it, but it is the protocol among kings not to refuse an invitation, irrespective of who has extended it.

Duryodhana: Oh, and is it also protocol to place one's brothers as pawns?

FLASHBACK

Shakuni: What number do you want, Bhanje?

Duryodhana: Seven!

Shakuni: Look, there comes seven!

Duryodhana: That's splendid, Mamashree. The dice is throwing up exactly what I want!

Shakuni: What can I say? The orders of the Crown Prince have to be obeyed, even by the inanimate.

Duryodhana: What is the matter, Bhaiya? You have lost once again! Your magical and divine Indraprastha now belongs to me. What will you stake now? Look, let me give you another chance. If you win this time, I will return everything you have lost. But if you lose, you'll have to give up something very precious to you—your four brothers.

Bhishma: Duryodhana, stop this game now. Immediately.

Duryodhana: Pitamaha, I do not need your unsolicited advice. As for Dharmaraj, he knows what he is doing. What do you say, King of Indraprastha? Oh, I forgot, I am the king now! Do you agree to one final wager? It is a fabulous chance to try to retrieve your lost kingdom.

Yudhishthira: Yes.

END OF FLASHBACK

Duryodhana: When I asked you if you had anything else to wager, why didn't you accept defeat and leave? You kept losing the wager each time. If I won, how does that make me the villain of the game? Two play at a game, don't they? None of these people who now claim I cheated tried to stop the game. What about you, Vidur Kaka? Wasn't Yudhishthira your great favourite? You were right there in the room, but you let the game continue. If the game indeed reeked of cheating, why did you allow Yudhishthira to keep playing?

Vidur: I did try to stop both of you, multiple times. But nobody paid any attention to me.

FLASHBACK

Vidur: Maharaj Dhritarashtra, please stop this. Whatever is going on here is no game. Stop it, or there will be disastrous consequences!

Dhritarashtra: Vidur, do you think I can stop it? No one listens to me. I am a blind man whose word doesn't make the slightest difference. I urge you to please go out there and bring things under control.

Vidur: Duryodhana, stop it. This is no longer a game. What is going on is completely irreligious and utterly wrong. You have won Indraprastha already; now end this obnoxious game and let your brothers leave.

Duryodhana: Oh no, Kakashree! The game has just begun. Plus, these men are no longer my brothers, they are my slaves! They can leave only when I tell them to. But don't worry; perhaps they will win the next game.

Vidur: Son, you have got what you wanted. Please stop now. If this goes on, it won't matter who wins. It will be a terrible loss for our entire kingdom.

Duryodhana: What rubbish! I am winning, not losing—or haven't you noticed, Kakashree?

Vidur: Yudhishthira, even if Duryodhana is adamant, at least you listen to me. Put an end to this game.

Duryodhana: Vidur Kaka, he is no longer the King of Indraprastha, but my slave. He will obey my orders, not yours. I am giving your beloved Yudhishthira a last opportunity to win. What do you say, slave-man, one more game? If you win, I will return everything. Everything! But wait, you have nothing left to stake. Let me think, what can you stake?

Vidur: Duryodhana, stop it now.

Duryodhana: I've got it! You can stake Draupadi, your wife. What do you say? One last gamble?

Yudhishthira: Okay.

END OF FLASHBACK

Duryodhana: I admit you lost everything at that game— your kingdom, your brothers, your wife—but it was you who pawned them in the first place. I have already accepted that I wanted all of you to disappear from my life, but why did you, the great propagator of all things righteous, stake your family members and even your wife? How can I be blamed for this disgusting decision you made?

Dushasana: Now watch, Karna, Dharmaraj will have no answer to this question.

Karna: I don't think this Kuntiputra will lose so quickly.

Yudhishthira: Duryodhana, you want to know why I pawned my brothers at a game, right? Why I pawned my beloved Panchali? I will answer all your questions, brother, and in my answer is your defeat.

I pawned my family members because I loved them. Surprised? Let me tell you the first rule of the game of dice: you can only pawn something on which you can exercise your rights. I could pawn my brothers because they were my own. You will never understand the agony I felt when I lost them. But my brothers were with me; even in our sorrow, we were together.

There was someone else who was with us through thick and thin, someone else who was truly ours. Yes, I talk of Draupadi. She was the one who always bound us together. The pain I went through upon losing her was no less than the agony of losing my kin. Draupadi and my relationship was through marriage—an unbreakable bond singed by fire. After that day, replete with losses more heart-rending than anyone has ever experienced, we were left with only one mission: to get revenge for the heinous crime and extreme humiliation you had subjected us to.

You ask me how my losses that day could be your fault. Let me tell you how. Duryodhana, you lost all self-control that day in the sheer joy of crowing over us. A person who has no patience or self-control cannot be trusted with anything, let alone a kingdom. That day you humiliated us; you shamed our beloved wife. But in truth, the only one who was shamed and who publicly demonstrated his incapacity to become a king was you, Duryodhana! What kind of Kshatriya does the dastardly act of insulting the bride of a clan? Making his brothers his slaves? That day, Duryodhana, you made the battle inevitable. All the discord and murder that followed was your responsibility—yours alone.

Duryodhana: If the night is dark, is it the coal's fault for being black? Dharmaraj, strip off your facade of religion! You have masqueraded as a righteous, pious man all your life, but you cannot deny that you treated your family members as objects. You are a fraud, Dharmaraj, and yet you dare to call me blasphemous?

Chitragupta: Suyodhana, don't forget that the charges are being levied against you today, not Yudhishthira. Get a grip over your anger, for I will not tolerate displays of rage in my court.

Duryodhana: I am sorry, Maharaj. Please read aloud the next allegation.

Chitragupta: The last allegation against you is that you rejected the proposal for a truce, despite knowing that all the elders of your clan were against the war. You insulted your clan and refused to avert a war that went on to destroy an entire generation.

Duryodhana: Ah, this was all that was left for me to hear! And may I know who has levied this allegation? My father, grandfather, great-grandfather—people who played with me when I was a baby, claiming to love me and support me in everything? The truce proposal was a joke! It was a mockery that the Pandavas put up, pretending to be 'kind' to me. No, thank you, a warrior like me did not need anybody's pity!

Bhishma: No, son, you misconstrued it then, and you're repeating your folly. Have you forgotten that Keshava himself came with the peace proposal? What more evidence do you need that it wasn't mockery but a genuine, heartfelt proposal?

Duryodhana: Yes, I remember that Keshava had come with the proposal. Of course I remember! I can still recall the sting in his words, the belittling attitude of extending mercy to someone who cannot protect himself.

FLASHBACK

Sri Krishna: My respectful salutations, Maharaj Dhritarashtra. I am glad that all the venerable elders of Hastinapur are present here today. I hope that my proposal will be heard and reflected upon carefully.

Vidur: Keshava, everybody has always listened to you.

Sri Krishna: I sincerely hope that they will continue to do so today. Maharaj, I have brought a proposal on behalf of the Pandavas—a proposal of peace. The Pandavas don't want warfare. Going to war is a path that can only lead to disaster. There is still time for us to halt and reconsider.

Vidur: Keshava, you have voiced aloud what has been in my heart for a very long time. I completely agree with you. The Kaurava clan doesn't want this battle either. No good can come of it except mass killing. Maharaj, Keshava himself has come with a proposal of peace. This is our last chance to save ourselves from this potentially disastrous war. I strongly advise you to accept it.

Bhishma: Yes, Vidur. I agree with you. We should accept this peace proposal.

Dhritarashtra: Thank you for your counsel, Pitamaha and Vidur. I think we are all in agreement that this peace proposal must be accepted. Since the Pandavas have extended the hand of friendship, we must reciprocate.

Duryodhana: Don't be daft, all of you! We have come so far, how can we retreat? Pitashree, all the preparations have been made already; this peace proposal has come too late. I refuse to accept any peace treaty whatsoever.

Vidur: Son, I implore you to listen to what Keshava is saying.

Duryodhana: No. Kakashree, not today.

Sri Krishna: Duryodhana, you are the eldest of your brothers, but you are also a brother to the Pandavas. Why do want to enter into a war with your brothers? Why are you choosing a path that will render the Earth bloody and dead? If you accept this peace proposal, I assure you that I will persuade the Pandavas never to bring up the war again. They will be content with the half-kingdom that they have. It is only you who must decide; it is only you who can choose either to stop or to bring about the destruction of the Kuru clan.

END OF FLASHBACK

Duryodhana: Keshava, I know that you had come with a peace proposal. But the way you spoke was so demeaning that it seemed I was the only one eager to fight. You were sure that the war would kill my brothers and me; it insinuated that we weren't as valiant warriors as your beloved Pandavas. My pride was hurt, Keshava! As for the elders present in court that day, they were so blinded by their love and admiration for the Pandavas that they didn't hear or feel the scorn in your words.

Vidur: Son, do not talk in this manner. You are not only insulting the elders of your clan but also Sri Krishna.

Sri Krishna: No, Vidur Kaka, don't stop him; let him talk. I want to understand how he noted a non-existent sting in my words but failed to recognize that I only desired the welfare of Hastinapur.

Duryodhana: Keshava, your melodious flute plays only for the Pandavas; you have never given me either thought or concern. Don't attempt to fool the Dharmakshetra by talking about your overwhelming desire to save the Kuru clan. You know you wanted no such thing! Your proposal had one purpose only: to demonstrate that we, the Kauravas, were weak and would be destroyed.

FLASHBACK

Sri Krishna: Duryodhana, listen to my proposal before you reject it outright. If you go to war, no one can predict the victors. But if you accept my peace proposal today, I assure you that Yudhishthira will never become the King of Hastinapur. He will continue to be the King of Indraprastha. All the riches and glories of Hastinapur—the fertile land, the palaces, the chariot in which Arjuna rides, this entire Bharatvarsh—will be yours. All you need to do is call off the warfare. Duryodhana, do not start this battle, for you know not of the tragedy it hides in its breast.

Duryodhana: But what if I win this war? I will not give even half the kingdom to those Pandavas. They have no right over my land! No, Keshava, I want a complete victory. There will be no compulsory sharing, for we aren't children anymore.

Sri Krishna: Okay, the Pandavas will accept this demand of yours. You don't have to give them half your kingdom. Just give them five villages. Haven't you always complained that you want them away from you? Give them five villages, and I promise you they will never demand the throne you so dearly desire.

END OF FLASHBACK

Sri Krishna: Tell me, Duryodhana. Couldn't you have given your brothers even five villages? Five villages from the entire kingdom of Hastinapur? You were so crazed for power and kingship that sensible advice bounced off of your ears like water off a duck's back. You saw and heard only what you *wanted* to see and hear. The sting wasn't in my words; the scorn was in your head! Maharaj Chitragupta, I have one question to ask you.

Chitragupta: Please proceed, Keshava.

Sri Krishna: If, before the commencement of a war, one king goes to visit another, is there any danger to his life?

Chitragupta: Of course not, Keshava. You know as well as I do that kings are expected to be civil towards each other before the war has officially begun.

Sri Krishna: Then, doesn't the emissary of one of these kings also expect similar civility? Duryodhana, do you remember what you did? You behaved in a manner that would shame any Kshatriya and make him cry out in agony.

FLASHBACK

Duryodhana: Keshava, I am grateful to you for coming to visit us today. I am a petty person, am I not, and you spent your valuable time on me. You talked a lot—like you usually do—and the elders of my household liked what you said. Let me take a minute to think—actually, no. No! Your so-called peace proposal remains unacceptable. It is a good proposal, you say? Well, what can I do, Keshava? Anything that is good has, supposedly, never appealed to me.

Vidur: Son, you don't know what you are saying! Don't talk in this infuriating manner with Keshava.

Duryodhana: I will do as I please, Vidur Kaka. By rejecting this proposal, I am rejecting the Pandavas' hidden agenda to belittle and humiliate me. Keshava, please convey to the Pandavas that they will get nothing from me. Not half the kingdom, not five villages, not the ground on which they are standing! I refuse to give them land equivalent to the space on the tip of a needle. In this birth, at least, they will get nothing at all.

Sri Krishna: As you will, Duryodhana. Maharaj Dhritarashtra, I request your permission to leave. I should convey this unfortunate news to the Pandavas as soon as possible.

Duryodhana: Just a minute, Keshava. Where are you going? It will be some days before the war begins. Why not accord me a small victory until then?

Sri Krishna: What victory, Duryodhana?

Duryodhana: I have been thinking about you. You, Keshava, have always sided with the Pandavas, and a lot of their strength emanates from your support. You will do your best to help them win the battle to come. So, I was considering inaugurating the war right here by capturing you as my prisoner! What do you say? That, to me, seems only fair.

Bhishma: Duryodhana, have you lost your mind? This is Keshava! He is the emissary of the Pandavas and has come here with a proposal of peace.

Duryodhana: If he were a mere emissary, Pitamaha, I would have let him go. But no, he is far more than that. If I apprehend him today, the Pandavas will also get a strong message that I mean business. It will be the beginning of the golden trail of victory I will chart for myself at Kurukshetra. Don't be afraid, Keshava, I will not kill you. You will merely remain my prisoner until the end of the battle. We will look after you well.

Dhritarashtra: Son, what is this you are doing?

Duryodhana: Keshava, my soldiers are right behind you. They know that they mustn't cause you any discomfort. After all, you are an emissary of peace, aren't you? So, why don't you go with them peacefully and set a good example?

Sri Krishna: Duryodhana, I came here with a peace proposal. It saddened me that you didn't accept a proposal that could have saved your clan. But this is not the time for sorrow and regret. You want war, don't you? Well, war is what you will now get. Prepare for a battle that will shake you down to your roots! As for imprisoning me, don't be absurd. How can someone like you, a prisoner himself of pettiness and conceit, possibly have the power to detain Vasudeva Krishna?

END OF FLASHBACK

Yudhishthira: Duryodhana, did you know that Keshava went to you with the peace proposal without telling me first? How could there have been any scorn in what Vasudeva Krishna said to you? If you had agreed to Keshava's proposal, I, in turn, would have accepted whatever he asked me to do. But you didn't have the sense to listen to him. Forget sense; you had the impropriety to try to capture him! Does respecting and obeying elders hold no meaning for you at all?

Duryodhana: Why should I obey my elders? They have never considered my needs and desires. For them, I have always remained a child—in intelligence, judgement and promise. All my life they have told me 'Do this!' or 'Don't do that!' as if I couldn't make my own decisions even as an adult. Is this how you bring up children? My elders promised me that when I grew up, the entire kingdom would be mine. And then one day, out of the blue, I am asked to 'share everything' with random strangers parading about as my brothers! If it was always destined for me to exercise such inhuman generosity, why did my elders make grandiose promises in the first place? If I am indeed as spoiled as all of you claim I am, it was entirely the fault of those who raised me—yes, these hallowed elders I am supposed to stoop to!

Bhishma: Quit blaming other people, Duryodhana. You have the heart to remind your parents and the senior members of your clan of their teachings, but have you ever thought about yourself? When have you ever fulfilled the duties of a son? A son who couldn't even obey his parents now stands here in the Dharmakshetra, casting aspersions on his elders! Are you doing it out of a guilty conscience, Duryodhana? Don't you, deep down, know that if you had listened to your elders, the Kurukshetra War would never have taken place?

Yudhishthira: I hardly think so, Pitamaha. For Duryodhana, being irreligious is second nature. He followed this path of treachery even during the battle.

Duryodhana: Are you kidding me, Dharmaraj? You have the temerity to say this when you let your greed for victory overpower all the wisdom you're falsely renowned for? It was you who adopted every kind of wile only to win the war!

Bhishma: That is untrue, son.

Duryodhana: Oh, come on, Pitamaha! You have suffered the trickery of these Pandavas yourself; they killed you through a dirty conspiracy! Have you forgotten how, hiding behind a eunuch, this beloved Arjuna of yours shot an avalanche of arrows at you? He forced you to lie down on an entire bed of arrows! If this is untrue, Pitamaha, then accept that this Dharmakshetra is as hollow as Kurukshetra was, and victory will again side with the irreligious.

Arjuna: Enough, Duryodhana! If you speak another word, I will—

Duryodhana: What will you do? Get your charioteer to spin a magical web? Or try to slay a far better, more skilled archer than you the moment he steps down from his chariot? You knew, Arjuna, that I valued Karna and his friendship more than my own life. He knew that he was a Pandava, but he still sided with me, a Kaurava. You killed that friend of mine—a friend more selfless than Bharatvarsh will ever know. Was it ethical to kill a warrior when he was trying to extract his chariot wheel from the mire? Every arrow that struck Karna hurts me even today; they are more painful than the injuries Bhima inflicted upon my thigh.

Maharaj, compared to the sins these Pandavas committed during the Battle of Kurukshetra, I fought more fairly than humanly possible! No charges can be levied against me.

Chitragupta: Allow me to decide that, Suyodhana, for this is my court.

Duryodhana: Forgive me, Maharaj, but I am convinced that I haven't committed a single felony in the Battle of Kurukshetra that can lead to an allegation in your assembly.

Arjuna: What kind of a man are you, Duryodhana? How conveniently you have forgotten Abhimanyu, my young son! The world will forever be haunted by the atrocious, unethical manner in which all of you surrounded a child and slaughtered him! Wasn't it you who got Karna to set Ghatotkach, my brother Bhima's son, on fire? Didn't you make King Shalya, the maternal uncle of my brothers Nakula and Sahadeva, a charioteer? Do you want me to remind you of all the other sins you committed? I have a ready list with me.

Duryodhana: I am enjoying seeing you roar like this, Arjuna; you would-be-great archer! I had thought it was only the glutton Bhima who could roar.

Chitragupta: Suyodhana, stop beating around the bush and address the allegation. Do you have any justification for using deceit and trickery during the Battle of Kurukshetra?

Duryodhana: Maharaj, you shock me! I always knew that many people in my household hate me. They falsely believe that I would be cowardly enough to use trickery in battle.

But you too? How did a wise man like you get trapped in this web of untruths constructed by the Pandavas?

Chitragupta: There are limits to the level of audacity I can endure in my court, Suyodhana. Let me warn you that your behaviour is dangerously close to the ceiling of my patience. If I hear another word of chiding or disregard from your mouth—even a monosyllabic word—I will instantly disband the assembly and consider every allegation levelled against you to be ture.

Duryodhana: I beg your forgiveness, Maharaj.

Chitragupta: So, answer me, Suyodhana. Did you order Abhimanyu's death? Did you sanction the release of the Indrastra—the most destructive weapon known to humankind, and forbidden in battle—against Ghatotkach? Did you treat a king as a mere charioteer out of spite? All these actions are against the norms of war, Suyodhana.

Duryodhana: Maharaj, I don't know how to answer your questions. I accept that as the Crown Prince, the responsibility of whatever transpired in the war was mine. Whether it was religious or not, I do not know. All that I do know is, to the best of my knowledge, I did not initiate any step that went against the norms of war.

Arjuna: He is lying through his hat, Maharaj! He is sidestepping your questions, not answering them.

Duryodhana: Maharaj, this Arjuna may scream as much as he wants to, but I maintain my stand. I did not take the first step in deviating from the norms of war. It was they who did! In the first eleven days of the war, everything went as per war protocol. But then the Pandavas started fearing that they would lose. And thus began their elaborate game of deceit, which managed to fool everyone—even you, Maharaj! What Arjuna did to Pitamaha was only the first deception. After that, with every passing day, they became more and more shameless. If I retaliated, it was only in self-defence.

Yudhishthira: Maharaj, my brothers and I cannot endure his guff and bluster any more. If this is all that Duryodhana has to say in response to the allegation, I, too, rest my case.

Duryodhana: Why, Yudhishthira? This is the first time you are facing home truths that no one dared to voice to you before. It isn't pretty, eh? Isn't it music to your ears? Now you know what I have gone through night and day. Welcome to Hell, brother.

Gandhari: Son, if your brothers don't want to hear anything further, I request you to stay quiet. It is not too late, son. You can still bow your head and acknowledge your wrongs. You can still be forgiven.

Duryodhana: Forgiven for what, Matashree? And why should I stay quiet when they accuse me of wrongdoings I haven't committed? I have to answer their asinine questions, haven't I?

Sri Krishna: You have no answers to give, son of Gandhari; you're just trying to erase these allegations with fury, similar to what you did on the battlefield. The world burnt because of you, Duryodhana! I cannot count your sins on my fingers, even if Maharaj Chitragupta can enlist them in his book. From the Royal Palace to Kurukshetra, you sowed the seeds of hatred. How can you blame others if the fruits now taste bitter?

Duryodhana: You think you know everything, don't you, Keshava? You can read minds very well—I grant you that. Perhaps you have always been aware of my motives, which is why the Pandavas have always been victorious. In any battle, it is critical to gauge what your enemy is planning. With you by their side, the Pandavas were blessed with excellent inside knowledge of my war tactics. But Keshava, this is the Dharmakshetra and not the mortal world. No longer can you read my mind, so don't pretend to speculate. Maharaj, what is the next allegation against me?

Chitragupta: There are no further allegations against Suyodhana. If anyone among you wants to question him, please proceed.

Duryodhana: What? More questions? Haven't I answered everything? It is my turn to ask some questions now.

Vidur: Duryodhana, I want to ask you something. I hope you will answer me truthfully.

Duryodhana: Vidur Kaka, what do you want now? Haven't your beloved Pandavas tortured me enough with their unfair questions and accusations? What remains?

Vidur: I have been listening to your responses, Duryodhana. And I have been wondering: why are your vanity and ego so inflated? Why do you have this impression of being the best? I cannot understand why you think so highly of yourself when you neither displayed any great show of valour during the battle nor ever followed the path of righteousness. And yet you stand here, reiterating your hypothetical greatness over and over. Have you thought about the life you led back on Earth? I don't see anything at all that can give you pride.

Gandhari: Vidur, you forget yourself! I agree that my son is no man of principles, but I won't tolerate everyone in this assembly pointing accusing fingers towards him. Didn't you see that both Maharaj and I remained silent? Do you think we didn't have any questions to ask our son? But we refrained. How much more will Duryodhana handle? Don't you think he deserves to have at least some of his people by his side?

Duryodhana: No, Matashree; don't stop Vidur Kaka. He is a wise man. Perhaps there is a lot of truth in what he just said. In fact, I was surprised that he didn't speak up before. I have been used to hearing him say: 'Suyodhana, that's not right.' 'Suyodhana, they are your brothers.' 'Suyodhana, your life is pointless.' Go on, Kakashree; say some more. My heart is pining for more words of appreciation and support from your erudite mouth!

Bhishma: Duryodhana, don't speak to Vidur in this manner.

Duryodhana: I am sorry, Pitamaha. Okay, let me very 'respectfully' answer Vidur Kaka's questions. Kakashree, I have been like this since childhood. I have always been vain and egoistic. Whenever I demanded something, I would get it instantly. You and Pitamaha never let my demands go unfulfilled; you bent over double trying to please the prince. I enjoyed seeing you worried; making demands of you was an amusing pastime.

Bhishma: That's enough, Duryodhana. You haven't answered a single question adequately, ever since you first started talking. You're making me feel ill.

Duryodhana: I feel ill inside, Pitamaha! I have been speaking the truth, but none of you has been listening. Vidur Kaka, didn't you ask me why I thought so highly of myself when I hadn't displayed any glowing acts of valour or intelligence? Well, Kakashree, tell me honestly: have you ever *wanted* to see my good side? When I was the Crown Prince of Hastinapur, did you ever hear my subjects complaining about me? Did anyone tell you that Suyodhana was a heartless ruler? Was there ever a revolt or rebellion against me? No! I was quite capable of managing the affairs of the kingdom, Kakashree. I was also capable of looking after my brothers. I raised Sushasana with a lot of affection. If he didn't love me, wouldn't he be sitting with the Pandavas, what with all their reputed valour and intelligence? I also knew how to respect friends, Kakashree, and how to be affectionate. Is all this not true?

Dushasana: Kakashree, our enmity was with the Pandavas. They can accuse my brother as much as they want, but I won't accept anything against his character. He was a loving brother and never shirked his duties towards the family. If anyone here wants to dispute that, talk to me, not my brother. I have excellent ways of silencing such wayward accusations.

Duryodhana: Save your anger, little brother. Your turn will also come, and knowing these people, you too will have to suffer unfairly. Maharaj, if the allegations against me are over—

Sri Krishna: I must say, Duryodhana, the arguments you have presented are excellent. We levied allegations against you—

serious accusations of fraud and murder—but you tackled them all with considerable self-control. I know that restraint doesn't come easily to you, which is why I am surprised and pleased. I could even sense some kindness and affection in you, especially in your response to Vidur Kaka.

Duryodhana: Thank you, Keshava. I had hoped that my answers would please you.

Sri Krishna: Yes, Duryodhana. But I have to pinpoint a fatal flaw in all your arguments.

Duryodhana: Well, I am not surprised.

Sri Krishna: Duryodhana, when charges are levied against a killer, do the members of his family come forward and sing praises of his family life? No. But in your arguments, this is what you did. By recounting deeds of kindness and empathy, you portrayed a humane image in front of this assembly. But we both know the reality of that image, don't we, Duryodhana?

Duryodhana: Keshava, I am what I am. I may not be a saint, but I am not the villain the Pandavas are portraying me to be. Maharaj Chitragupta, as the allegations are at a close, am I permitted to ask a question?

Chitragupta: Yes.

Duryodhana: I would like to summon to this court someone who knows me for what I am. If you know what the Pandavas think and feel, Keshava, this man knows me and admires me. In his presence, the false bravado of your doting Pandavas will disappear like smoke.

Chitragupta: Who would you like to summon, Suyodhana? Why wasn't I informed of this?

Duryodhana: I am sorry, Maharaj. Please allow me to call forth my Gurudev Balarama.

Dushasana: Karna, now you will see how Bhaiya refutes every charge levied against him.

Duryodhana: Gurudev, thank you for coming forward to speak for me.

Balarama: Suyodhana, you don't have to thank me. I am blessed to have a disciple like you, and I will always stand in your support. But where is that unworthy bearer of the mace, that Bhima? I detest it that the world falsely recognizes him as the greatest wielder of a weapon he has thoroughly insulted! Bhima, don't sit there like a coward. You will have to pay for what you have done!

Duryodhana: Gurudev, I request you not to get worked up over that disgraceful man. Your presence here today is enough for me.

Balarama: If you say so, Suyodhana, I will spare him. But will this Assembly of Religion do the same?

Chitragupta: Balarama, in line with my court's protocol, please introduce yourself.

Balarama: I am Balarama from Vrindavan, the son of Vasudeva, the elder brother of Krishna, and Suyodhana's Guru.

Duryodhana: Gurudev, plenty of allegations have been levied against me in this Dharmakshetra. I am tired of fighting against these people and so-called elders of my clan who refuse to see the truth. But I know you won't be fooled by untruths, Gurudev, which is why I want to ask one last question in my defence. Guru Balarama, do you remember the last day of the battle?

Balarama: That day can never be forgotten.

FLASHBACK

Duryodhana: The war is not over, Yudhishthira. I, Suyodhana, the son of the Emperor of Hastinapur, stand here alive. None of you is strong enough to kill me, and as long as I am still breathing, the war goes on.

Yudhishthira: Duryodhana, nothing remains anymore. You have lost everything you owned, including your entire army and all your warriors. Let go of your ego now, brother, and surrender.

Duryodhana: Never, Yudhishthira! I am alive; can't you see? Vanquish me, and only then can you win. You will see today that I am a Kshatriya not only in name but also in might.

END OF FLASHBACK

Duryodhana: Gurudev, correct me if I am wrong: isn't the battle of maces supposed to be between two warriors?

Balarama: You are right, Suyodhana. Since you were alone, you could have chosen any one of the Pandavas to fight with.

Duryodhana: If I had wanted, I could have chosen Nakula or Sahadev. Or even Yudhishthira, for he only had the powers of debate at his disposal. But whom did I choose, Gurudev? I picked one of the mightiest mace warriors in Bharatvarsh. I chose Bhima! Why did I do so, Gurudev?

Balarama: You did so because you are a true Kshatriya, Suyodhana. The rules of warfare permit battling against only those who are equal in strength to you.

Duryodhana: Did you hear that, Dharmaraj? Then what happened, Gurudev? I was winning, wasn't I?

Balarama: Yes, Suyodhana. You have always been exceptional with the mace.

Duryodhana: What happened next, Dharmaraj? How did I lose? I had forced Bhima to fall on his knees; he could barely breathe. Dharmaraj is quiet, so let me see—how about you, Keshava? Do you have an answer to my question? I was the disciple of your elder brother, who is the greatest wrestler of this universe. And yet, I lost. Tell me: was what happened to me fair or remotely religious?

Balarama: I will answer that, Suyodhana. No, it wasn't! What happened to you was irreligious and disgusting. The rules of wrestling clearly dictate that no warrior can strike his opponent below the waist. And yet Bhima did just that, violating the rule in an act that deserves to be punished by hellfire. I don't care what the decision of this court is; I will see to it that Bhima gets punished!

Sri Krishna: No, Bhaiya!

Balarama: Move away, Keshava. I will find peace only when I grind this irreligious man and bury him in the ground.

Sri Krishna: Bhaiya, don't punish Bhima. He only did his duty. If you have to punish anyone, perhaps it should be me. It was I who gestured to Bhima to attack Duryodhana on his thigh.

Balarama: Keshava, stop defending the Pandavas. You know as well as I do that Bhima sinned.

Bhima: Forgive me, Gurudev.

Duryodhana: Didn't I tell you, Keshava, that you would be dumbstruck at my last question? What happened to me was unjust. The Pandavas won the war by deceit, period. Bhima struck my thigh even though he knew it wasn't permitted. He knew I was too strong and that he could never defeat me without defying ethics. I like how you are quiet now, Keshava. In your silence is my victory.

Yudhishthira: No, Duryodhana. What Bhima did may have been against the laws of wrestling, but it was inevitable. You inscribed the attack on your destiny the day you asked the bride of the clan to sit on your thigh.

FLASHBACK

Duryodhana: Draupadi, how did you fall? Your father is not blind, so you should be able to see, right? It pains me that your five husbands don't look after you. Never mind, henceforth, this new master of yours is your world. No longer will you live in that mystical palace. You will stay here with me, obeying all my orders. Get up, Draupadi. Your place is not down on the floor; it is here—on my thigh!

END OF FLASHBACK

Yudhishthira: It was you who started a dirty game, Duryodhana. To overpower your loathing, deception and trickery, we had to stoop down. Did you not realize the magnitude of the sin you committed on the day we played dice? How could you gesture so obscenely to the bride of a clan—the wife of your brothers? When Bhima smashed your thigh during the duel, it was in punishment for your heinous crime, possibly a crime more devastating than any that Bharatvarsh has ever known.

Your life has been a long, seemingly interminable series of sins, Duryodhana. You didn't deserve to be king, nor did you have any right to the throne. You didn't listen to Pitamaha, who had pledged to look after the well-being of Hastinapur. If he had believed that Hastinapur was safe in your hands, he could have ended the battle on the very first day. But he didn't. By not listening to his advice, you insulted Pitamaha— the selfless man who devoted his entire life to Hastinapur, never getting married, never aspiring to become an emperor.

Not only Pitamaha, but you also insulted the man you call your best friend! Guru Drona knew that while Arjuna could control his bow and arrow, Karna had been cursed by Guru Parashurama. He was destined to lose control of his weapons at the most crucial moment of his life. And yet, Karna went ahead and sacrificed his life for you. By calling his sacrifice trickery, you are insulting Karna. That, Duryodhana, is perhaps your most unforgivable sin.

Duryodhana: The intelligent and righteous Dharmaraj has answered my question. I wish to argue no more, Maharaj Chitragupta. But I am proud that I died with the same beliefs with which I lived. I was born a Kshatriya, lived the life of a Kshatriya, and died in battle. Wherever I go from here, I will be accompanied by my thoughts and the people who are dear to me. I have never deserted my loved ones like this Dharmaraj, and that, to me, matters more than being a stickler for religion.

Maharaj, I accept every allegation against me, just like I have accepted this loving name 'Duryodhana' that has stuck to me like a leech. I am not a man who believes in regrets, and I don't plan to change that now. I believe that Heaven should be my final abode, where I will meet no unwanted brothers. But whatever decision you take, Maharaj, I will willingly accept.

Chitragupta: In today's Dharmakshetra, several allegations were levelled against Suyodhana. He has accepted all the charges. However, in his sins, he wasn't alone. When a young man gets misguided and deviates from the path of religion, the elders must show him the light. Several questions have remained unanswered, which we will take up as the Dharmakshetra proceeds.

Duryodhana, I condemn you to Hell. No man in Bharatvarsh will ever be named after you. No father will want his son to grow up in your shadow. Only one Duryodhana was enough to trigger the greatest war the world has known, and never again shall the world be in need of a man like you.

Duryodhana: Bhima, look, you won. But the look of self-loathing I caught on your face not long ago was my victory. And I can assure you, it was the sweetest victory I have ever tasted.

4

ARJUN

FLASHBACK

Mayasura: Don't kill me! Oh, please don't kill me—

END OF FLASHBACK

The warrior who has remained etched in history as the greatest archer the world has ever known, whose proficiency with the bow and arrow determined the fate of the Battle of Kurukshetra, the Arjuna everyone recognizes as a straightforward, courageous and powerful man hides a shameful secret in his heart. There was a time—little known in the chronicles of history—when Arjuna wavered from the path of righteousness. The repercussions of that time were more far-reaching than he thought, and will reverberate in today's session of the Dharmakshetra. The line between religion and irreligion will grow even fainter as Arjuna battles not with his bow and arrow, but with the truth.

Chitragupta: I welcome you to today's hearing of the Dharmakshetra. I summon before the court an obedient son, an ideal brother, a skilful warrior. Most people fail to fulfil even one of these roles adequately in a lifetime, but there is someone who did it all. Arjuna, son of Kunti, please come forward.

FLASHBACK

Draupadi: Do you have to go?

Arjuna: Yes, Draupadi, I have to go. In a war, one can never be too prepared. My brothers have already gone, and so must I.

Draupadi: When will you return?

Arjuna: I don't know.

Draupadi: But why must *you* go? Can't someone else take your place?

Arjuna: No, Draupadi. I must go because it is my duty. I must go because I long for victory.

Draupadi: And me? Don't you ever long for me? Won't you even ask me what I want?

END OF FLASHBACK

Duryodhana: Behold the brave warrior! As soon as he steps forward, he glances at his friend. Dear brother Arjuna cannot stand without divine protection! Today, in this assembly, even his words won't be his own.

Arjuna: Duryodhana, Krishna is my friend. I can look up to him for support whenever I want. If you have any objections, you may leave the assembly.

Sri Krishna: You are right, Duryodhana; I have frequently spoken on Arjuna's behalf. But you forget that this is the Dharmakshetra. Arjuna must speak for himself; I cannot help him.

Arjuna: Keshava, you are an integral part of my existence. Even if you don't say a word, even if you weren't here at all, I know you would still be looking out for me.

Duryodhana: Ah, the assembly should be fun today. For the first time, I will see the Pandavas learning to speak without Keshava's witticisms.

Chitragupta: Suyodhana, the court is not held for your amusement. We are here to judge the allegations laid against Arjuna. Let me begin—

Karna: Maharaj, shouldn't you introduce Arjuna to the assembly? If you allow me, I would like to do it.

Arjuna: That is interesting. Maharaj, please allow him to introduce me. He could not harm a single hair on my head during battle; what can he possibly do to me now? Go on, Karna. Let me see the kind of poison you store against me in your case of arrows.

Karna: Today, in this assembly, stands a skilled archer and courageous warrior—a Kshatriya whose praise is sung in ballads, after whom children are named. But there's only one thing that the songs overlook: the fact that this hero is, in reality, a coward.

Arjuna: That's amazing, Karna. What a magnificent

introduction you have given for me! I don't deny that you, too, are a highly skilled archer, perhaps equivalent to me in valour. But the only difference between us is that I don't make excuses for my failings. You, on the other hand, keep droning on about the great deceptions and tragedies in your life. I defeated you in battle, and you blame it on 'injustice'.

Karna: The truth remains the truth, doesn't it, Arjuna?

Arjuna: What is the truth, Karna?

Chitragupta: Karna doesn't get to decide the truth, Arjuna. Neither do you make the judgement here. It is only I who decide. Karna, take your seat, please, and don't interrupt the proceedings again.

Karna: Forgive me, Maharaj.

Chitragupta: Arjuna, if you are ready, I would like to ask you a question before we begin your trial.

Arjuna: I am ready, Maharaj.

Chitragupta: The animosity between you and the Kauravas was hardly a state secret; everyone present here knew about it. But the Kauravas never displayed their enmity in public. When was it that the simmering hatred in Suyodhana's heart came to the fore, incapable of being concealed any longer?

Arjuna: I would say it was on the day we played dice with Duryodhana. When we were invited to Hastinapur for the game, no one could have imagined the horrors that would ensue. I think, on that day, everyone in Hastinapur saw that there was little love lost between us.

Chitragupta: Suyodhana, why did you call your brothers for the game of dice? We all know it wasn't for the sake of sport.

Duryodhana: Maharaj, I thought my trial was over. Anyhow, I will repeat: I wanted to insult the Pandavas. They were completely blinded by the glamour and razzmatazz of their kingdom Indraprastha. I wanted to put them into such a horrifying plight that they would forget they had ever been kings!

Chitragupta: What is the matter, Suyodhana? Why has the colour left your face at the very mention of Indraprastha?

Duryodhana: Maharaj, I detested Indraprastha. It was the palace where Draupadi had insulted me. I have never forgotten that insult; I don't think I ever will.

FLASHBACK

Draupadi: What happened, Suyodhana Bhaiya? Your father is blind, but can you not see either? Like father, like son!

END OF FLASHBACK

Chitragupta: To take revenge for your insult, you set up that charade of a game of dice—didn't you, Suyodhana? The game changed everything. The Pandavas and Draupadi, raging under a grievous insult, left to spend twelve years in the forest, followed by a year in anonymity. They sacrificed all their royal pleasures, and the brunt of the insult kept them up every night. When they returned, war was inevitable.

Arjuna: Excuse me, Maharaj, but I didn't understand the charge levelled against me.

Chitragupta: Tell me, Arjuna, wasn't the insult that Suyodhana faced in the mystical Indraprastha a prime catalyst for the Kurukshetra War?

Arjuna: Yes, Maharaj.

Chitragupta: Then isn't the one responsible for constructing the mystical palace also, in some way, responsible for the disaster?

Arjuna: I didn't get you, Maharaj.

Chitragupta: Think about the time when, after marrying Draupadi, the five of you returned to Hastinapur. Maharaj Dhritarashtra gave Yudhishthira a segment of Hastinapur; it was called Khandavprastha. What happened then, Arjuna? What did you do to orchestrate the construction of the mystical palace that eventually became the trigger of tragedy?

FLASHBACK

Yudhishthira: Look around, Arjuna. Maharaj Dhritarashtra did give us half the kingdom, but forgot to tell us that it was thickly forested. Even if we start cutting down trees right now, it will take us several years to build a city.

Arjuna: Don't worry, Bhaiya. In a very short while, there won't be any sign of a forest. There will only be ground for us to build upon.

END OF FLASHBACK

Chitragupta: You're not telling me, Arjuna, but you forget that I must take stock of all your deeds on Earth. In this Dharmakshetra, I am now calling upon Mayasura. Mayasura, please come forward and introduce yourself.

Mayasura: I am Mayasura, the architect of the Maya Bhawan or the palace of the Pandavas in Indraprastha. I used to have three beautiful children.

Chitragupta: What happened to them, Mayasur?

Mayasura: They were killed, Maharaj. In front of my eyes, all my three children were taken away from me.

Chitragupta: Who killed them, Mayasur?

Mayasura: Arjuna! This great warrior killed my innocent children!

Chitragupta: And that, Arjuna, is the first allegation against you. You committed a felony—an irreligious act that not only killed children but also went on to become the cause of a great and tragic war. Mayasura, please tell the assembly why you call Arjuna a killer.

Mayasura: Maharaj, I lived with my family in the forest of Khandav. We were a poor but happy family. One day, the forest caught fire. I tried my best to save my family and my house, but I could not. Helpless and distraught, I ran out of the forest trying to protect myself from the flames. But a shock awaited me. In front of me stood a warrior, appearing ready to kill me if I didn't fall at his feet and beg for mercy.

FLASHBACK

Arjuna: Who are you?

Mayasura: I am an ordinary man who just lost his beloved wife and three children in the fire. Somehow, I managed to save my life. Dev, I don't know why you set my home on fire but please do not kill me. I have run far and long to save my life; I do not wish to die. Please spare me!

Arjuna: What do you do in the forest? How do you make a living?

Mayasura: I am an architect, Dev—an architect who is now at your mercy. I beg you to let me go.

Arjuna: Don't worry. You have come under the protection of a Kshatriya. I will not kill you. But you have to do something for me.

Mayasura: What, Dev?

Arjuna: Construct for me a palace that is beautiful beyond imagination, whose beauty and grandeur are incomparable to anything that anyone has ever seen on Earth. I want a palace that will leave people gaping.

Mayasura: I will do whatever you say, Dev. You have spared my life, for which I am indebted to you. I will construct a palace that will change the entire course of history. This is my promise to you, Dev.

END OF FLASHBACK

Mayasura: I kept my word, Maharaj. Didn't I? There will never be any palace quite like Indraprastha. It was magical and beautiful beyond what words can describe.

FLASHBACK

Yudhishthira: Bhima, why did you stop? Come, walk with me.

Bhima: Stop teasing me, Bhaiya. How can I walk on water?

Yudhishthira: Draupadi, please explain to Bhima what this is.

Draupadi: I think it deserves to be experienced, not explained. Come along, Bhima.

Arjuna: Are you scared, Bhima? Since when have you been afraid of water?

Nakula: Bhima Bhaiya, they are only teasing you. This isn't water but a regular pathway! Look, anyone can easily walk on this.

Arjuna: Haha, Bhima! You too got deceived, didn't you? Mayasura has indeed spun a spell of magic in every corner of this palace. The architectural and artistic skills he has demonstrated are incomparable.

Draupadi: I agree. Doors cannot be seen in the walls of this palace, yet they exist. Once you go deeper inside, you may suddenly find hidden chambers and concealed walls of stone. It is the most enthralling palace in the world.

Bhima: Truly, Arjuna, our Indraprastha is incredible. I

am glad you entrusted Mayasura with the responsibility of constructing our palace. Now, I long for the Kauravas to come visit. Won't they be taken aback to see the beautiful palace we have built among the ruins and the forests?

END OF FLASHBACK

Chitragupta: Mayasura, you lived up to your promise. There is no doubt that your work was incredible. But it was based on a precarious foundation: vengeance. You knew, didn't you, that the palace could, and probably would, become the cause of the destruction of the Kuru clan?

Mayasura: Yes, Maharaj, I accept. I built the palace well knowing that it would lead to the annihilation of the Kauravas. If Arjuna hadn't killed my family by starting the forest fire, I wouldn't have constructed the palace. Duryodhana wouldn't have been insulted, Rani Draupadi wouldn't have been humiliated, and Bhima wouldn't have made such a horrific pledge to avenge his wife's insult. Maharaj Dhritarashtra and Rani Gandhari wouldn't have lost their hundred sons. The entire chain of events wouldn't have begun if Arjuna hadn't killed my family. If anyone has truly sinned, it is this great archer, this man that Vasudeva Krishna lovingly calls Partha.

Chitragupta: Well, Arjuna, is this true?

Arjuna: Maharaj, this is an unreasonable allegation. What if I said that it was Pitamaha who started the war? Had he not promised to remain a bachelor all his life, he could have become the king. The prospect of enmity between the Kauravas and the Pandavas over potential kingship wouldn't have arisen! I find it unfair to be blamed for events that were beyond my control at the time.

Mayasura: It wasn't beyond your control, Arjuna. You started the fire that took the lives of my wife and little children.

Arjuna: Mayasura, when I promised my brother Yudhishthira that I would raze the Khandav forest to the ground and clear the area to construct our palace, I wasn't aware that you inhabited it with your family. If I had known, I would have escorted you to safety first.

Mayasura: I cannot accept your ignorance as the justification for murders, Arjuna.

Arjuna: Mayasura, please try to understand. I was merely obeying the orders of my elder brother.

Duryodhana: How feeble your argument is, Arjuna—as ineffective and powerless as your arrows! My younger brother Dushasana was also obeying the orders of his elder brother when he attempted to disrobe Draupadi. But look around, and you will see him present in the assembly, waiting for his punishment. Didn't your wise friend Sri Krishna enlighten the gathering only some time ago that those who give an irreligious order and those who carry it out are both deserving of punishment?

Arjuna: Vasudeva Krishna was correct. But Duryodhana, you must remember that punishment is meted out depending on the order in question. Dushasana was carrying out a disgraceful command, one that should make you feel so ashamed that you never open your mouth again! But my brother had ordered me only to clear the forests so we could construct a palace and start a new life.

Maharaj, this accusation is like a convoluted thread extending from the erstwhile Khandav forest to Kurukshetra. Mayasura tugs at it from one end, while Duryodhana tugs at it from another, trying to prove I am wrong. But the real reason behind the battle does not lie in this thread; it lies elsewhere.

Maharaj, when we returned to Hastinapur from Panchal, Draupadi's maiden home, we were given half the kingdom. This was what the elders of the family consented to, and we happily accepted it, not once protesting that our segment was densely forested. It was a massive challenge to build a habitable city in Khandavaprastha, but we took this responsibility without complaint. If the allegation is that our palace triggered the war, then it is Duryodhana who should be blamed for forcing us to build it!

Chitragupta: Suyodhana, do you have anything to say in response?

Arjuna: Duryodhana does not have an answer to this, Maharaj. He knows he gave us the ruined, overgrown part of the kingdom on purpose, hoping that we'd never be able to turn it into a progressive and magical city.

Mayasura: Arjuna, this doesn't negate the fact that you killed my family in cold blood. Was it ethical to kill innocent people and build a palace on their dead bodies?

Arjuna: Mayasura, I repeat once again: I was ignorant of your inhabitation in the forest. It was never my motive to kill your family. If I had wanted to kill people in cold blood, why would I have spared you? Do you know what one of my friends once told me? He said that an arrow once released can never be withdrawn; it carries with it a missive for the target. But the archer can be responsible only for the direction in which the arrow is headed, not any unintended targets it ends up hitting in its path.

FLASHBACK

Arjuna: My respectful salutations, Sri Krishna.

Sri Krishna: Partha, do you know that your Mata Kunti is my aunt?

Arjuna: Of course, Sri Krishna.

Sri Krishna: That makes me your brother. Please address me as Keshava, the one with the long, shiny hair. Henceforth, we are not only brothers but also friends. Do you now feel comfortable calling me by my name?

Arjuna: Okay, Keshava.

Sri Krishna: Great! Were you practising your archery when I arrived?

Arjuna: Yes.

Sri Krishna: Let me give you some unsolicited advice that I think will serve you well. From now on, whenever you release an arrow, do so with pure intentions and unwavering faith. Forget about the direction of the arrow or the outcome of your aim; remember only your motive. What eventually happens to the arrow is known only to the arrow. An archer cannot control the destiny of that which has left his bow.

Arjuna: I will keep that in mind, Keshava.

END OF FLASHBACK

Arjuna: Mayasura, as one of the Pandavas, I was merely doing my duty when I set the forest on fire. I apologize for the tragedy it set loose on your family, but that was never my motive. Hence, I refuse to accept this allegation.

Duryodhana: Even if we accept that you didn't want to kill Mayasura's family, but what about all the other lives you took without any thought or consideration? What about all the animals you killed?

Arjuna: Have you completely lost it, Duryodhana? Many men kill animals every day to fill their stomachs! I did not kill animals out of malice or because it delighted me to do it. I had to build a royal forest so my brother's subjects could feed themselves.

Mayasura: Maharaj, I want to leave the assembly now. Arjuna's words have put my allegations to dust. I don't wish to punish him for anything. However, I will say this: whenever someone builds their home upon the ruins of someone else's, whenever someone creates happiness by destroying someone else's family, the result will be a disaster. Sorrow will forever accompany the residents of such a house, and their battles will leave behind nothing but ashes.

Chitragupta: Mayasura, you may take your leave. Arjuna, we will proceed to the next allegation against you—that of deception in battle. In the Kurukshetra War, warriors on both sides carried out deception. But that doesn't make it ethical.

If the war had been fought according to the moral norms of warfare, perhaps the outcome would have been different.

Karna: You are right, Maharaj. Arjuna killed me by deception. I had stepped down from my chariot and was trying to free my chariot wheels from the mud. But this noble Partha attacked me from behind! Why, Arjuna, what will you do today? Your Gandiva, that invincible bow you brandish, is not with you today. How will you strike me from the rear?

Arjuna: That's enough, Karna.

Karna: Ha, this is only the beginning! Today I will not spare you. You will—

Chitragupta: Stop, Angaraj! Your greatest problem is that you assume everything to be about you. You may be the son of the Sun God, but that does not mean the world revolves around you.

Karna: I am sorry, Maharaj.

Chitragupta: Arjuna, there is no doubt that you are a great warrior. But the allegation of deception in battle is grave. In the Kurukshetra War, you were the first person to disobey the regulations of warfare. It was you who perpetrated the first deception when you killed Bhishma, the son of Ganga.

FLASHBACK

Shikhandi: Bhishma, pick up your bow and strike! Let us see how valiant you still are, how much strength remains in those old muscles!

Bhishma: Not today, Shikhandi.

Arjuna: Please forgive me, Pitamaha.

END OF FLASHBACK

Duryodhana: Weren't you ashamed, Arjuna? How could you strike at Pitamaha—the one who brought you up with so much love and affection? You shot at him from behind that eunuch Shikhandi! I don't know what Maharaj Chitragupta's judgement will be, but I am sure no Kshatriya will forgive you for what you did to Pitamaha.

Sri Krishna: Duryodhana, since when have you started feeling bad for what happened to Gangaputra Bhishma? I know he headed your army, but didn't you always think that his heart wasn't in the battle? You must have been happy when he passed away, for that meant someone else—someone more enthusiastic about slaying the Pandavas—could now take part in the war.

Duryodhana: Keshava, you said earlier that you wouldn't be speaking on behalf of Arjuna. You are breaking your promise.

Sri Krishna: Oh no, my words have nothing to do with the allegation against Partha. I am merely praising your acting prowess. You said with such conviction that you were upset when Arjuna attacked Pitamaha, when deep down you were excited at the prospect of finally enrolling a more aggressive warrior into your army.

Arjuna: You can't deceive my friend with your acting, Duryodhana. He is privy to everything that transpires, whether or not it is spoken aloud.

Chitragupta: Arjuna, tell me this: could you have vanquished Gangaputra Bhishma? Do you think you had the wherewithal to defeat him in battle?

Arjuna: No, Maharaj.

Chitragupta: Do you know why I asked you this?

Arjuna: No, Maharaj.

Chitragupta: I asked you this so that Keshava could not rise to your defence and claim that you shot at Gangaputra to vanquish him. We all know that nobody in either army had the strength or the skill to defeat Gangaputra Bhishma. But we also know that for you to win the war, his defeat was essential. It adds up that you could only take recourse to deception to overpower Bhishma and inundate him with arrows, so much so that he couldn't rise from the arrow-bed you skilfully created. Tell me, Arjuna, was that your motivation?

Arjuna: I don't know how to answer, Maharaj.

Chitragupta: Since you don't seem to have an answer, should I assume that you accept this allegation? Well, I will note down in my book that you have accepted the accusation of deception. It was you who committed the first infringement during the Kurukshetra War.

Bhishma: Just a moment, Maharaj.

Arjuna: Pitamaha?

Bhishma: Don't interrupt me, Arjuna. I have remained silent all this while, but I cannot do it any longer. It is stifling me.

Arjuna: No, Pitamaha!

Bhishma: I will not stop, son, for the assembly needs to know the truth. Maharaj, you levelled an accusation against Arjuna today and debated whether or not it was true. But won't you consult with the person who was killed?

Duryodhana: Pitamaha, now that Keshava has not come to Arjuna's rescue, you did?! There is no dearth of people to help him out. Haven't you consistently claimed you were the protector of Hastinapur? Was I not a part—the principal part—of Hastinapur?

Bhishma: Duryodhana, I have always sided with religion. In the Battle of Kurukshetra, I was compelled to fight for you because of my oath to protect Hastinapur forever. But here in this Dharmakshetra, away from the mortal world, I am free of my promise. My words will be founded only in truth, even if it goes against you, son.

Maharaj, it was impossible for anyone to defeat me in archery—yes, even for a great warrior like Arjuna. Whatever Arjuna did, he did because there was no other way for religion to be victorious over irreligion. It was the only solution, the means to a righteous end.

Dhritarashtra: What are you doing, Pitamaha? Your words are painting all my sons in the light of darkness and deceit, while the Pandavas seem to be divine entities and blessings in human form! The allegation of deception is against Arjuna, isn't it? Why do you have to speak for him? If he has no answer, then let Maharaj Chitragupta read out the next allegation.

Duryodhana: Thank you, father. For the first time, you have spoken as a monarch should. Well, great archer Arjuna, have you eaten all your words as gluttonously as Bhima? Or are you incapable of talking without Keshava there to prompt you?

Bhima: Duryodhana, Arjuna is my brother. Whenever he has used his bow, the arrow has hit the target. Whenever he speaks, you will be thrown into silence.

Duryodhana: Really? Do we need to wait until the cows come home for Arjuna to start speaking? I don't think we should waste the time of this assembly any further. It has been proved that Arjuna is the lord of deception and trickery, not me! Yes, I accept that I wasn't particularly unhappy about what happened to Pitamaha. But that does not excuse Arjuna's deceptions, that only got worse with each passing day. They brought me no joy! Speak up, Arjuna, or admit that you've sinned.

Chitragupta: Arjuna, this is your last opportunity to answer this allegation.

Sri Krishna: Arjuna, I cannot stay silent any longer. I am going to reveal something that has, to date, remained between you and Pitamaha. Concealing it anymore would come in the way of justice, and I cannot let that happen.

Bhishma: Yes, Arjuna, my son. This allegation, of which you are accused today—my alleged defeat, which is being called deceitful—all of this lies shrouded in a secret that I have never shared with anyone. Neither have you. But the time has now come to let everyone know. I will be unable to live with myself if my secret leads to your condemnation.

FLASHBACK

Bhishma: Arjuna, the moment for which every warrior waits is here. The war begins tomorrow.

Arjuna: I hadn't waited for this moment, Pitamaha. Do you realize what this war will mean for us?

Bhishma: I know, son. It will mean that we will be pitted against each other.

Arjuna: Pitamaha, I cannot do it. How can I stand against you in war? How can I even think of shooting an arrow at the one who taught me how to walk? You raised me so lovingly that I didn't feel the vacuum that my father's loss left in my life.

Bhishma: Believe me, Arjuna, I am as devastated as you are. I am the Chieftain of Duryodhana's army. I have to ensure he wins. But Arjuna, this is not just a battle for me. It is something else.

Arjuna: What do you mean, Pitamaha?

Bhishma: Don't repeat to anyone what I am about to tell you, Arjuna. This battle will be my *moksha*—the doorway to leaving this world of sin and uniting with the Almighty. And it will be you who will grant me my *moksha*.

Arjuna: Me? No, Pitamaha! I cannot do that.

Bhishma: I know you are deeply disturbed, son. You are about to strike out against your brothers and the elders who have raised you since you were an infant. But, my son, it is only you who can bring me my salvation. Won't you do this for your Pitamaha?

Arjuna: I couldn't do it even if I wanted to, Pitamaha. No one can defeat you in battle.

Bhishma: You will know how to do it, Arjuna. Not today, but soon.

Arjuna: No! Pitamaha, if you tell me that, it will be unethical.

Bhishma: See this as the last request of an old, tired man, my son. Please grant me my *moksha*.

Arjuna: I cannot do it, Pitamaha. Please don't make me.

Bhishma: Do not weep, my son, do not weep. May you be victorious!

END OF FLASHBACK

Chitragupta: Gangaputra Bhishma, what are you saying? Arjuna has been accused of defeating you in battle through deception. But you claim that you *told* him to do so? You wanted to be beaten, and that too by Arjuna?

Bhishma: Yes, Maharaj.

Chitragupta: Gangaputra Bhishma, I can understand that you longed to achieve salvation after witnessing everything that transpired in Hastinapur. I can also accept that you wanted your beloved Arjuna to free your soul. But it was wrong to use such deceptive means. If Arjuna had killed you without resorting to trickery, salvation would have been yours. Possibly, you wouldn't even have been in this assembly today.

FLASHBACK

Bhishma: My last moments have arrived, Arjuna. I have seen a lot in life, much of which has disturbed me deeply. But I have also known and loved you, and it brings me great joy that you've been the one to free me from my earthly shackles.

Arjuna: I have committed a crime, Pitamaha. If I hadn't done it, you would still have been our protector; you'd be looking out for us like always.

Bhishma: No, my son; do not weep. I will forever be indebted to you for what you have done for me.

Arjuna: I cannot stop these tears, Pitamaha. I will never be able to forgive myself, but, if you can, please forgive me. Forgive me, Pitamaha.

END OF FLASHBACK

Chitragupta: Arjuna, Gangaputra Bhishma has placed me in a conundrum. I can see that you acted out of a sense of duty, for you had made a promise to Bhishma. But even so, I cannot be satisfied with your answer. Nothing can justify an act of deception on the battlefield.

Arjuna: Maharaj, can I ask you something?

Chitragupta: Go ahead.

Arjuna: Tell me, Maharaj, if a Kshatriya makes a promise to a dear friend—a commitment greater than even his duties— what should he do? Should he abide by his pledge during the war?

Chitragupta: If the promise was given before the war, then it is the warrior's duty to fulfil it.

Arjuna: What if deception must be undertaken to fulfil that promise? Should the warrior still proceed?

Chitragupta: Arjuna, I can see that you have learnt a great deal from Keshava. I refuse to answer this question until you tell me what the promise was.

Arjuna: Maharaj, I think Duryodhana will be able to recite it word by word.

FLASHBACK

Arjuna: Pranaam, Keshava.

Duryodhana: Pranaam, Keshava.

Sri Krishna: What a wonderful sight it is to see the son of Pandu and the son of Dhritarashtra together! What have I done this morning to be so fortunate?

Duryodhana: Keshava, it is likely that both Arjuna and I have come to you for the same reason. War is about to begin, and I am here to solicit your support. If you're by my side, I am convinced that victory will be mine.

Sri Krishna: Duryodhana, how gentle and mild you do sound! Where was this temperate behaviour when I had come to you with a peace proposal?

Duryodhana: I knew you would bring it up. You perhaps find this whole situation ridiculous, considering that you have always been outright in your support of the Pandavas. But Keshava, if you are a brother to the Pandavas, you are our brother too. I have every right to ask for your help. If you're still mad at me about—

Sri Krishna: Oh no, Duryodhana. I have forgiven you. But let me tell you—the Battle of Kurukshetra will be won by those on the side of religion, not necessarily by those with whom I side. I am willing to help you, but I am in a dilemma.

Duryodhana: What dilemma?

Sri Krishna: See, I am only one person; how can I support both you and Arjuna? What I can do is offer myself and my Narayani Army; it is a huge and powerful army and will be an excellent asset for either side. Remember, however, that if you choose me, I will never pick up arms.

Duryodhana: Keshava, I got here first. So, I should get the right to choose first.

Sri Krishna: But Duryodhana, my eyes fell on Arjuna first. So, the right to choose first is his. Tell me Arjuna—what do you want? My Narayani Army or just me?

Arjuna: Keshava, with you I get the entire world. You are the strength of the world; you are the light in this darkness that is enveloping us. I want nothing but you, Keshava. I give you my word: during the battle, I will never ask you to pick up any weapon.

Duryodhana: Keshava, this is what I had wanted too. But since Arjuna has already chosen you, I will make do with the Narayani Army.

Sri Krishna: Consider it yours, Duryodhana.

END OF FLASHBACK

Arjuna: Maharaj, I chose Keshava because I trusted his guidance. I knew that with his support, I would find the strength I needed to win this war that was splitting my heart in two. I kept my promise all through; I never let him take up any weapon during the war.

Sri Krishna: That is true, Maharaj. Arjuna never asked me to participate in the battle.

Chitragupta: Well, Keshava, you know as well as I do that Arjuna is a great warrior—perhaps among the greatest of all times. When he was fighting, what was the need for you to pick up weapons? I don't think we need to make a big deal out of this promise. It wasn't a difficult one to keep, was it?

Sri Krishna: I beg to disagree, Maharaj. During those initial days of battle, Bhishma Pitamaha slaughtered countless soldiers. If he had been allowed to continue the massacre, the Pandavas would have been left without an army! It was imperative to kill Pitamaha, yet seemingly impossible to stop him. Arjuna knew that I could stop Gangaputra Bhishma. I distinctly recall the day when I tested Partha and the strength of his promise.

FLASHBACK

Sri Krishna: Partha, look how ruthlessly Bhishma is killing your soldiers!

Arjuna: I can see that, Keshava.

Sri Krishna: So? Will you continue to observe his mass killing passively or do something to stop it?

Arjuna: What can I do, Keshava? How can I raise my Gandiva against my Pitamaha? And assuming I did, the chances of conquering him are slim to none.

Sri Krishna: If I had known you were such a coward, I would have thought twice about making you my friend. Forget it, Partha; you don't need to do anything. Let *me* see how valiant a warrior Gangaputra Bhishma is. Allow me to stop him.

Arjuna: No, Keshava!

Sri Krishna: Why are you stopping me, Partha? You know Pitamaha is the greatest warrior on this battlefield. He is the greatest warrior in Bharatvarsh! No one can defeat him. Do you have a plan to stop him? Do you have the heart even to try to stop him? No! But someone will have to do it, Partha, or else he will decimate our army.

Arjuna: No, Keshava, I cannot go against my word and allow you to take up arms.

Sri Krishna: If you want to keep your promise, you will have to defeat Pitamaha.

Arjuna: How, Keshava?

END OF FLASHBACK

Duryodhana: Well, all of us know the disgusting plan Arjuna and Keshava came up with to defeat Pitamaha.

Arjuna: Maharaj, you said that it was I who broke the first rule in the battle, that I committed the first act of deception. Well, if keeping my promise to Keshava equals deception, so be it.

Chitragupta: Arjuna, I can see now that keeping your promise to Keshava was indeed challenging. In abiding by your oath, you had to commit an act that was not only against the ethics of warfare but would also slay your beloved Pitamaha. This time, I cannot be the one to judge whether or not you made the right decision. I leave it to you, Gangaputra Bhishma, for it was you who were defeated by Arjuna's deceitful move.

Duryodhana: Maharaj, forgive me, but that is an entirely pointless decision you have made! We all know what Pitamaha will say. He will say, 'Please forgive my dear Arjuna. I told him to defeat me. He cannot do any wrong!' Come on, Pitamaha, speak up and free your beloved Arjuna!

Bhishma: Yes Duryodhana, you are right. In killing me, Arjuna did not sin. I had begged him to bring me *moksha*, and that's what he did. If he hadn't killed me when he did, I would have continued slaying the soldiers of the Pandavas. What Arjuna did cannot be called a wilful deception at all. If anyone deceived wilfully, it was me. Sometimes, Maharaj, one must deceive oneself to break free, and that's what I did.

But yes, Arjuna's actions did have an unfortunate result: after I left the battlefield and lay on my bed of arrows, waiting for death, the Kauravas got the golden opportunity to commence their own acts of deception!

Sri Krishna: I agree with Pitamaha. Even though Arjuna didn't perpetrate the deception of his own accord, we did have to pay the price for it. Both the Pandavas and the Kauravas faced the brunt of resorting to trickery on the battlefield.

Karna: What a joke! What price did the Pandavas pay, may I ask? I am appalled at the affection and love all of you have for those Pandavas—emotions that blind you to their grievous sins! Those brothers are indeed fortunate, especially this Arjuna. All his offences get forgiven as if they were a child's acts of mischief.

Chitragupta: What are you trying to say, Karna?

Karna: Maharaj, Arjuna's praises have been ringing in your court ever since he stepped on the stand. But has the assembly forgotten the cowardly way in which he killed *me*? I was unarmed; I wasn't even on my chariot. He shot at me from behind as no warrior worth his salt ever should. No one else may have noticed it, Arjuna, but I saw the fire in your eyes burn out the instant you killed me in that shameful manner. Deep inside, you knew you had sinned, and how! Do you have a well-thought-out explanation for why you murdered me like a coward? Why are you quiet, oh great archer?

Chitragupta: Have patience, Karna; I haven't forgotten it. Arjuna, this is the next allegation against you. The manner in which you killed Angaraj Karna appeared to have violated every ethic of warfare known to man.

Arjuna: Look, Karna, let me explain what happened—

Karna: Oh, don't bother, Arjuna. I know the gibberish you will utter: I *had* to do this. I had to win the war for my brothers. I had to win the kingdom. Isn't that right, Arjuna?

When have you ever thought about right and wrong before shooting your arrows? You killed Mayasura's family and fooled the court with some yarn about 'not holding the responsibility for the arrow's target'. What about me, Arjuna? Was I as inconsequential as Mayasura for you?

Arjuna: No, Karna.

Karna: Do you know why? There was only one difference between us, as far as you are concerned. While Mayasura joined his hands together, pleading not to be killed, I refused to bow down in front of you. I didn't want to die either, Arjuna, but I made a fatal mistake. If I had knelt before you and begged for my life, you wouldn't have killed me.

FLASHBACK

Karna: My bow is broken, Arjuna, and I don't have any arrows left. The wheels of my chariot have become embedded in the ground. This makes me unarmed and an easy target. You have two options: kill me now or let me come back with more arrows. So, which one do you pick?

Arjuna: I don't need to answer any of your questions, Karna.

Karna: Come on, Arjuna, tell me. You can see that I am unarmed right now. But I know you won't kill me in this state. You aren't a coward, are you? For years both of us have longed to face each other in battle. When the day is finally here, do you want to end it like a spineless weakling who attacks his competitor when he cannot defend himself?

END OF FLASHBACK

Karna: You know, Arjuna, I spoke the truth that day. I had indeed waited throughout my life to face you in battle. I think the entire country wanted to see us confront each other. When the day finally came, what did you do, Arjuna? Oh yes, you won, but who can call that a victory? How can you live with yourself or see your reflection in the mirror? Perhaps what you did was recommended by your charioteer, Sri Krishna. If that is so, I rest my case. I know, Keshava, what you say is the supreme truth. I have neither the energy nor the inclination to dispute it.

FLASHBACK

Sri Krishna: What is the matter, Partha? Why do you look disturbed?

Arjuna: Keshava, this war will be the death of me. My mind is a constant turmoil. How can I shoot Karna in this state? It might make me the victor, but I will never be able to consider myself an archer or even a Kshatriya again. It is unethical for a true warrior to attack an unarmed opponent.

Sri Krishna: Gaining victory over oneself is the most challenging battle of all, Partha. To feel victorious from within, you must calm your inner voice and listen to yourself. Rise above the admonishments and judgement of others around you. Tell me, Partha, can you afford to lose today? How will you quieten the voice within you that will blame you for changing the course of this battle? For pushing your brothers to defeat?

Arjuna: What do you suggest I do, Keshava? Please help me.

Sri Krishna: If you let Karna go today, you will still be the victor. If you kill him, triumph will be yours again. The decision rests with you. It is you who must decide the victory that you seek and the means you're willing to employ to reach it.

END OF FLASHBACK

Sri Krishna: Karna, it is possible that Arjuna didn't comprehend what I said that day. He was deeply disturbed; his mind was closed to anything besides his opponent on the battlefield and the decision that lay in front of him. The quandary was menacing and seemingly impossible to resolve. I did not instruct Partha to kill you. It was his decision, not mine.

Karna: Arjuna, even your charioteer and friend has refused to rescue you this time. He claims that he didn't instruct you to do the dastardly act of shooting at an unarmed warrior from the rear. So, why did you do it? You have to answer, Arjuna, for today I am not defenceless. The Gandiva is in my hands, and I demand justice.

Arjuna: You are mistaken, Karna. The Gandiva is and always has been in my hands. It was so in Kurukshetra and remains so in the Dharmakshetra. Don't worry, though, for I have your answer. It isn't an answer my friend has magically fed into my brain; it is an answer my soul knows to be true.

Karna: Is that so? Let us hear it then!

Arjuna: There are two reasons I decided to vanquish you that day, even though it meant violating the norms of war.

The first was your unpardonable behaviour during the game of dice—

Karna: What?! I did nothing at all during that game.

Arjuna: Precisely. You did nothing. You did nothing to stop the horrors that were unfurling in front of your eyes! The warrior who had been upholding 'ethics' and 'valour' sat mute when Duryodhana and Shakuni kept committing one unethical act after another. Aren't you known as the 'perpetual giver'? Don't you take pride in being righteous and never enduring injustice? How could you watch Draupadi—the bride of our clan—be insulted in a courtroom full of people? I know that Draupadi was not your wife, and Duryodhana was your best friend. But couldn't you have at least *tried* to stop him? Why should I have shown mercy on someone who could have protected a helpless woman but chose to remain a mute witness?

Duryodhana: That dratted game again! How many more of us will be held responsible for it? I am sick to death of the constant droning about that game of dice; it seems that all the ills of the world were set loose the moment Mama Shakuni rolled the dice on the board! I have already accepted that I am responsible for the deception that transpired during the game. I am responsible—and perhaps my brothers, my father and my mother too. But don't blame my friend Karna! He didn't do anything; he committed no sin. Arjuna, don't you have a thinner justification for your crimes than dragging in that game of dice so very senselessly?

Karna: Let it be, my friend. Arjuna, what was your other reason?

Arjuna: Maharaj, to explain the other reason, I want to summon someone to the court.

Chitragupta: You are permitted.

Arjuna: Today, before this Assembly of Religion, I want to call upon my dear son Abhimanyu.

Abhimanyu: Pranaam, Maharaj. Pranaam, Angaraj. You are my father's elder brother, and I greatly respect you.

Arjuna: Look, Karna, my son just sought your blessings. Abhimanyu, how do you know this man?

Abhimanyu: Pitashree, he is Karna, a great archer just like you. The entire world knows him as one of the most valiant warriors of all times.

Arjuna: And how did this great warrior behave with you?

Abhimanyu: It breaks my heart to repeat it, Pitashree.

Arjuna: Tell the assembly, son. What did he do to you?

Abhimanyu: He killed me inside the Chakravyuha, Pitashree. He was one of the warriors who surrounded me and tore me to shreds. I tried my best to fight all of them, but I couldn't defeat them single-handedly.

Arjuna: Maharaj, this young boy, my little son, who wasn't even an adult yet, was surrounded by the mighty warriors on Duryodhana's side and mercilessly killed. Since when does Kshatriya religion permit hounding a young boy and slaughtering him to death? How could you be a part of this, Karna?

Duryodhana: Maharaj, I ordered everything that happened inside the Chakravyuha. Abhimanyu was killed on my orders. It wasn't Karna's fault at all.

Sri Krishna: Duryodhana, for how long will you continue to shield your friend? He behaved unethically; he was party to the hideous sins of insulting the bride of a clan and murdering a minor on the battlefield. By killing him, Arjuna meted out punishment. That is all there is to the story.

Kunti: That is not the truth, Keshava.

Arjuna: Matashree! What are you saying?

Bhima: Yes, Matashree, what are you implying? What Arjuna did was absolutely right!

Kunti: No, son.

Chitragupta: Devi Kunti, what do you want to say? The allegation against Arjuna is that he broke every norm of warfare to kill Karna. Arjuna defends his actions by claiming that he only meted out punishment for Karna's wrongdoings. Are you saying Arjuna was wrong? Are you connected to the allegation in some way?

Kunti: Maharaj, I am the mother to both Arjuna and Karna. If I am not connected to the allegation, who is? I accept that Arjuna killed Karna only to punish him for his deeds. It is also true that if Arjuna hadn't murdered Karna, the Pandavas would have lost the war. Even so, what Arjuna did was unjust.

Arjuna: What do you mean, Matashree?

Kunti: Son, if it had been Karna in your place, he would never have done what you did. He would never have killed his brother.

Arjuna: But Matashree, that's not fair. I didn't *know* Karna was my brother! If I had, who can predict the decision I might have taken?

Kunti: No, Arjuna. I am convinced that even if Karna hadn't known that he was your brother, he wouldn't have behaved as you did.

Duryodhana: Karna, my friend, you have won today. Your mother is taking your side and that too in front of everyone!

Karna: No, Duryodhana. Devi Kunti is not taking my side; *she is merely repaying a debt.*

Chitragupta: What debt, Angaraj Karna? Please be specific.

Karna: Maharaj, Maharani Kunti had come to meet me before Arjuna and I had a faceoff in the battlefield. She had demanded a promise from me.

Duryodhana: And you, my friend, would have given the promise without a thought! I know you! What did she demand from you?

Karna: She demanded that I wouldn't kill any of the Pandavas, except Arjuna. That way, irrespective of what ensued, she would still have five sons. Her 'support' for me today is on account of that unfair promise. It is her way of repayment. No, Devi Kunti, I don't need your consolation or support. I lived all my life on Earth without a mother's love; my friend's love is all I had. In death too, it will be enough for me.

Arjuna, I thank you for answering my questions. I accept your response. Perhaps we will meet again in another birth. Maybe then I won't be accursed and will be able to confront you with nothing to hold me back.

Son Abhimanyu, I have done a great injustice against you. Forgive me, if you can. I bless you thus: the times may change, the Earth may stop revolving, and your father too may be forgotten—but you, oh great and courageous warrior, will never be forgotten.

Maharaj, if you now permit me, I would like to leave the assembly. I have absolutely no connection with any other allegation, and I cannot bear to face my so-called brothers and my estranged mother for a moment longer.

Chitragupta: Stop, Angaraj Karna. You cannot leave the assembly until I disband it. Devi Kunti and Arjuna may have had their say, but you forget that I make the final judgement in this court.

Arjuna: Maharaj, are there are any more allegations against me?

Chitragupta: Arjuna, I have heard a great deal about your courage and concentration. Rarely, if ever, has your focus wavered from your goal, and few can rival you on the battlefield. But there is one last allegation against you that you will be unable to address with your skill at archery or your knowledge of warfare. It is being levied by people who have always supported and loved you. I warn you to be strong, Arjuna.

Arjuna: Who is levying this last allegation, Maharaj?

Chitragupta: Sri Vasudeva Krishna and Rani Draupadi, please come forward.

Arjuna: What? Keshava? Draupadi? What allegations are you levying against me? When have I ever wronged you, my friend and my soulmate?

Chitragupta: Arjuna, Maharani Draupadi has alleged that in your pursuit to achieve glory and triumph, you disregarded your wife. You never fulfilled the duties of a husband.

Arjuna: Draupadi, my beloved, how can you say this? Keshava, do you also side with Draupadi in this allegation?

Sri Krishna: Yes, Partha. As your friend and confidante, I was always there for you. I did my best to help you whenever your mind was in turmoil. You are my closest friend, Partha, but so is Draupadi. I have a special place for her in my heart that cannot be contained in words or bracketed under relationships as we know them. Today, I will voice the feelings she has never been able to express—not to you, not to anyone else.

Arjuna: Keshava, you have always helped me and shown me the right path. Why didn't you ever discuss this with me?

Sri Krishna: I did not want to interfere in your personal life, Partha. I assumed you knew how to fulfil your duties as a husband, so I restricted my advice to your princely affairs and your role as a warrior. But in this Dharmakshetra, nothing can go unaccounted for. I am compelled to voice the questions that neither Draupadi nor I could ask you while on Earth.

Arjuna: I will answer all your questions truthfully, Keshava.

Sri Krishna: I know you will, Partha. So, tell me: when you saw Draupadi for the first time at her swayamvar, how did you feel?

FLASHBACK

Dhrishtadyumna: Brahmin, I do not know who you are or where you come from. But your prowess with the bow and the glow in your eyes make it evident that you're no ordinary man. Henceforth, my sister is your wife. Please look after her.

END OF FLASHBACK

Arjuna: Keshava, I thought that Draupadi—

Sri Krishna: No, don't tell me you fell in love at first sight. You were too overwhelmed by the victory to appreciate Draupadi for the beautiful and powerful woman she was. Perhaps you don't know the moment you started falling in love, Partha, but, surprisingly, I do. It was when your mother asked all five of you to consider her their wife.

Arjuna: I don't understand, Keshava.

Sri Krishna: You do, Partha. When you won Draupadi at the swayamvar, you accepted her as your wife. You could have had her as your very own. She could have been your wife and friend to lean on throughout your life. But then, Draupadi had to be shared among your brothers. You started fearing that the division would also split Draupadi's love in five, thereby diluting her love for you. Am I wrong, Partha?

Arjuna: No, Keshava. I did become afraid. I wanted Draupadi's love only for myself, but I could do nothing about it.

Sri Krishna: You accept that you realized the meaning Draupadi had in your life. You also admit that you started loving her deeply. But did you do anything to express your feelings to your wife?

Draupadi: Keshava, drop it. Don't tease your friend anymore.

Sri Krishna: I am not teasing, Draupadi. My friend must realize the mistake he made. Disrespecting one's duties towards the family is as serious a crime as turning one's back in battle out of cowardice. Tell me, Arjuna, why didn't you speak up for Draupadi? You didn't try to protect her when she had to get married to all five of you, against her wishes. You didn't defend her when she was insulted during the game of dice. Even during your Agyaat Vasa in Maharaj Virata's kingdom, when you were living in anonymity, and Kichaka, the king's brother-in-law, misbehaved with her, you remained silent. You could have fought to protect her in the way Bhima did, but you held back. You didn't consider it important enough.

Arjuna: Forgive me, Draupadi.

Sri Krishna: Partha, your unjust behaviour against Draupadi doesn't stop there. Tell me, when you had time to spare, did you ever spend it with your wife? No, you went to spruce up your skills at warfare! This princess married you and left everything behind, but you never considered her worthy of time or attention.

Arjuna: Keshava, I was preparing for war. It was essential at that time. Both you and Draupadi know this.

Sri Krishna: If you had paid more attention to your wife, it is possible that the war itself wouldn't have taken place.

Draupadi: Arjuna, my husband, you were blessed with a pair of eyes that no one else in the universe could rival. You had the eyes of a bird with a focus so sharp that no target was impossible for you to hit. You were the only one who succeeded in hitting the eye of the fish at my swayamvar while gazing only at its reflection in the water. It was because of you that my life got a new direction, a new meaning. But throughout your life, you never had the time for the pair of eyes that sought only you.

FLASHBACK

Bhima: Panchali! Finish your meal. You have to eat.

Draupadi: You finish eating, Bhima. I will have my meal when Arjuna returns.

Nakula: If you wait for him to come back, you might stay hungry for ages! Who knows when Bhaiya will return?

Draupadi: Never mind, I will wait.

END OF FLASHBACK

Chitragupta: Arjuna, are the allegations levied by Keshava and Rani Draupadi true?

Arjuna: Maharaj, many allegations have been levelled against me in your court. I have argued against them and tried my best to explain myself. But against this allegation I have no answer. I have wronged you, Draupadi, and I can only beg for your forgiveness. Keshava, I seek your forgiveness too, for I have caused untold pain to your dear friend. If it is any consolation to both of you, I am back now—

Draupadi: It is too late, Arjuna. I am no longer a princess who is deeply smitten with an archer. Our life is over; we await our final fate in the Dharmakshetra.

Arjuna: Maharaj, I have nothing more to say. I accept Draupadi's allegation and am deeply apologetic, even if my apology is now meaningless.

Chitragupta: In the Dharmakshetra today, many allegations were levelled against Arjuna—the warrior who has endeavoured to follow the path of religion throughout his life. Even though he wavered along the journey, there will be no one quite like Arjuna for demonstrating devotion, labour and commitment. I cannot pardon the unethical killing of Bhishma and Karna, no matter what his reasons were. But I do applaud the motives that drove Arjuna's decisions— motives that were always founded in righteousness. Arjuna, your name will forever be etched in history not only as a great warrior but also as a righteous man who did his best to be ethical even in the face of severe turmoil. Arjuna, you are the son of Indradev, and your deeds on Earth have proved that you'll always be the bearer of the Gandiva. No one can take that away from you.

For the last allegation against you, however, you will be punished. While labour and devotion to one's work are paramount, no man must disregard his duties towards his wife. I adjudge that while the world might regard Draupadi as the wife of Arjuna, he will have no right to be called her husband. Let this decision remind men for aeons to come that domestic duty must never be sacrificed in the name of work. The wife, the one who sides with you through thick and thin deserves not only your love but also your time and attention, and any man who disregards her is a sinner in his own right.

Arjuna: I accept your judgement, Maharaj. Keshava, before I get off the stand, I want to thank you once again for being with me.

Sri Krishna: Why are you thanking me, Partha? Have you forgotten it was me who voiced the last allegation?

Arjuna: It doesn't matter, Keshava. I will always remember what you said to me. Your advice has shaped my life, and I know you have nothing but love for me in your heart.

Sri Krishna: I am happy that you listened to my advice, Partha. I hope that generations to come will follow your example and learn to value their loved ones as much as their work and moral obligations.

Arjuna: Yes, Keshava. Whatever fate awaits me in my next life, I will remember your words and follow the path along which you have guided me.

5

ASHWATTHAMA

FLASHBACK

Ashwatthama: The birds in the sky harass the owl all day, showing off their prowess at flight and embracing the golden sunlight in a way the owl never can. But what happens at night? It is these birds that get preyed upon, for they are foolishly unaware of dangers hiding in the dark. Tonight, when all the Pandavas will be asleep, celebrating their victory in the war, I, the last soldier and Chieftain of the Kauravas, will rewrite destiny. Tonight will be the Pandavas' last night on Earth. I, Ashwatthama, will ensure victory for the Kauravas. I won't let my father's martyrdom be put to dust.

END OF FLASHBACK

In the Battle of Kurukshetra was a warrior who remained silent all his life. He fought for the Kauravas, and while he was skilled at warfare, he never attained the glory and fame that came to his peers and opponents. At the end of those eighteen days, however, he perpetrated a bloodbath. It was the bloodiest night Bharatvarsh had ever known—a pitch-black night that left the warrior and everyone around him reeling in pain. He never recovered from his heinous sin and was relegated to spending an eternal lifetime submerged in regret, agony and darkness. Today, in the Dharmakshetra, this warrior will have to account for his sin. No one can bypass the Assembly of Religion, for it is here that all differences cease to matter—apart from the one between the just and the unjust.

Chitragupta: I welcome all of you to today's Dharmakshetra. Everyone present in this assembly knows that my court is where you account for your deeds on Earth. It is the final step lying between Earth and your ultimate destiny. It is the courtroom where you arrive after death to either be granted the peace of Heaven or be condemned to the turmoil of Hell. But there is someone from Kurukshetra who committed a sin so revolting that he wasn't granted death at all. He did not reach *moksha*, but remains on Earth—stuck between life and death in an unbreakable circle. I know many of you nurture loathing for the one I talk of, but as the keeper of records, I have to call upon him and give him a chance to speak for himself. Keshava, do you agree with me?

Sri Krishna: Maharaj, you preside over this assembly; you can call whomever you feel must come on the stand. I agree with you—he must be given a chance; otherwise, we'd be committing an injustice.

Chitragupta: Ashwatthama, son of Drona, please come forward.

Drona: Come, son. You have got an opportunity to atone for your sins. Use it well.

Ashwatthama: Pitashree, it was not only me who sinned. Maharaj, please read aloud the allegations. I am ready for every question.

Draupadi: Ashwatthama, you aren't asleep, are you?

Ashwatthama: No, Devi.

Draupadi: So, this means your eyes are open—truly open—and you can see the people surrounding you. I am amazed that you have the courage to stand in this court while you're awake!

Ashwatthama: Devi, I request you to wait until it is your turn to accuse me. I don't find it necessary to address your taunts at the moment. Maharaj, what is the first allegation?

Chitragupta: Before reading aloud the first allegation, I want to summon Gangaputra Bhishma.

Drona: Pitamaha, my son already faces an insurmountable mountain of sin. I beg you not to fester his wounds or agonize him further. Please be merciful towards him.

Chitragupta: Gangaputra Bhishma, I have one question to ask you.

Bhishma: Yes, Maharaj.

Chitragupta: It was you who engaged Acharya Drona as the Guru of the Pandavas and the Kauravas when they were only children. Is that right?

Bhishma: Yes, it was me.

Chitragupta: Did you assume that if a battle was fought in the future, Drona too would participate in it?

Bhishma: Maharaj, why do you ask me this?

Chitragupta: Gangaputra Bhishma, please answer.

Bhishma: Well, no, Maharaj. Participating in battle is the duty of a warrior, not that of a Guru.

Drona: I agree with Bhishma, Maharaj. Whenever I was blamed for the injustice during the Kurukshetra War, it was this decision that haunted me—the decision to go against my religion and participate in the war. But I did it only because I wanted to be free from all my debts.

Chitragupta: Drona, I know why you participated in the war. But my question isn't to you. I want to know why Ashwatthama participated in the battle. Let me repeat something that Keshava once said: *Paradharma bhayavaha.* Do you know what this means, Ashwatthama?

Ashwatthama: No, Maharaj.

Chitragupta: It means: Performing someone else's duty while overlooking one's own can have dangerous consequences. And this, Ashwatthama, is the first allegation against you. Why did you discard your religion and embrace a role that wasn't yours, to begin with? You are not a Kshatriya, Ashwatthama, but a Brahmin. If you picked up a weapon, it should have been to teach, not to kill.

Ashwatthama: Maharaj, I too wanted to be free of my debts.

Bhishma: What debts, Ashwatthama? You did not owe anything to anybody. Dhritarashtra engaged your father as a teacher at a time when he was in dire need of money. But, to be honest, even he didn't have a reason to feel 'indebted', for there was neither an archer not a teacher in Hastinapur who could hold a candle to him. Even so, Drona chose to view his appointment as a debt and went on to participate in the war to repay this debt. I can still understand his point of view, but you? What obligation were you under that you felt compelled to pick up arms for the Kurukshetra War?

Ashwatthama: Pitamaha, my father was the best archer in Hastinapur. If his son could not become an archer, wouldn't that be a shame?

Bhishma: Who prohibited you from becoming an archer? You could have become a teacher and imparted your knowledge to others. What was the need to join the war? All the people sitting in this assembly had some reason or the other to pick up arms. Had the Pandavas moved far away, had they never built Indraprastha in their half of Hastinapur, Duryodhana wouldn't have had cause for jealousy. Yudhishthira and Duryodhana were both princes of Hastinapur, and they both wanted to ascend the throne. After Duryodhana rejected Keshava's peace proposal, war was the only option left; the throne couldn't be deserted, or there would be anarchy. But you did not belong to the Kuru clan. You had no connection with that battle. Then why did you take part in the war? Why did you commit the disgraceful act that will forever haunt every mother in Bharatvarsh?

Drona: Don't use such harsh words, Pitamaha. You know

him since he was a baby; he grew up in front of your eyes.

Bhishma: You are right, Drona, I did see him grow up. But it was my error in judgement that stopped me from recognising him for what he was.

FLASHBACK

Bhishma: Arjuna, tomorrow is the last day of your formal teaching. I am proud of you. You have learnt all the lessons supremely well, and I am sure you'll become the greatest prince of the clan.

Arjuna: Thank you, Pitamaha.

Bhishma: What is the matter? Why are lines of worry etched on your forehead? Worry doesn't suit you, my son, for you're the greatest archer in all of Hastinapur.

Arjuna: No, Pitamaha; I am not worried. It's just that I am confused about something.

Bhishma: What is it, son?

Arjuna: Pitamaha, you know that Ashwatthama, Acharya Drona's son, was a student in our batch.

Bhishma: Yes, I know.

Arjuna: He makes me uncomfortable. He always seems to be so competitive that it is almost unsettling.

Bhishma: Competition among students is good, Arjuna. Otherwise where is the fun? Did you lose to him in a contest?

Arjuna: No, Pitamaha, but he behaves strangely during practice.

Bhishma: Strangely? How so?

Arjuna: For instance, I was targeting a bird's eye during a practice session of archery. I succeeded in hitting the target. After the practice, he burned down the whole tree!

Bhishma: What? Why did he do that?

Arjuna: I don't know, Pitamaha. That is why I am confused. It seems his intentions aren't to learn but to achieve a hidden, dark motive. What do you think goes on in his mind?

END OF FLASHBACK

Bhishma: I should have noted the signs right from the start, Ashwatthama. You were envious of the Pandavas even as a young boy, and your envy increased in intensity as all of you grew up. It became poisonous. Duryodhana was also envious of his brothers, but, at least, he did not hesitate from displaying it publicly. Never did he hide his feelings as you did. You buried the poison in your heart, and it became so toxic that it turned you into a maniac who couldn't think straight.

Ashwatthama: I am a maniac, Pitamaha? Just look at your clan. Is there anyone here whose thoughts and motives weren't distorted? Two brothers of the same clan spent their entire lives battling against each other, and *my* motives are being questioned! What was I to learn when I grew up watching my princes fighting with each other constantly? I saw my father slaving day and night, working harder than any teacher ever has, only to please Maharaj Dhritarashtra. I wanted to help him repay his debts. I didn't want him to live under anyone's charity, but prove that he and his family were indispensable for the kingdom.

Chitragupta: You are lying, Ashwatthama; I can feel it in my bones. You were envious of the affection your father had for the Pandavas, especially for Arjuna. He hated fighting for the Kauravas, but he was bound by duty. He knew, deep down, that the Pandavas would win irrespective of how strong an army the Kauravas built. Before extending your hand of help to your father, did you ask him if he needed you at all? Your father adopted the Kshatriya caste because he had no choice. But if you hadn't followed suit, your father could have at least been reassured that his son was safe from the warfare. You didn't think of your father once, and you stand in front of me today, confidently lying about your motives!

Ashwatthama: Okay, Maharaj, I admit I lied. I did not join the warfare to help my father. I joined the battle so my father would cast one look in my direction! He watched the princes day and night, teaching them to defeat their enemies and achieve eternal glory, but not once did he think about his son, who sat in the corner of the Gurukul feeling neglected and unwanted. I would keep hoping that the sun would dawn on a day when my father would pat me on the back like he patted Arjuna. One day he would say to me: 'Good job, son!' But never did such a day come in my life. I was invisible to my father. Oh yes, he ensured that I had all the comforts I needed at home, but it wasn't riches I sought; it was my father's undivided attention.

FLASHBACK

Ashwatthama: Pitashree, look what I did! I may not have pierced the bird's eye, but I burned down the entire tree. When the tree is charred and dead, how can the bird survive?

Drona: What are you saying, son? Why did you do such a thing?

Ashwatthama: Why are you angry, Pitashree? This is my strategy to win the war: simply burn down the entire war arena! Isn't it a smart strategy, father?

Drona: No! It is a cowardly and unethical strategy. But why do you talk to me about war? What does it have to do with you?

Ashwatthama: Well, isn't that what your pupils are preparing for?

Drona: No, son. They are preparing so that there is no war at all. A warrior always endeavours to avert war to the extent possible. It is never a wise decision to embark on a move that will slay innocent people.

Ashwatthama: Really? I thought the religion of a warrior is—

Drona: I refuse to discuss this with you, Ashwatthama. You are not a warrior! You are a Brahmin, the son of a Guru. If there ever is a battle, you won't have anything to do with it. I am teaching you the art of warfare only so you can protect yourself. But it seems to me that you won't be much good with self-defence either. I have a low opinion of someone who believes in setting things ablaze instead of confronting challenges upfront. What you just did reflects a weak mind. As the son of a Guru, you, of all people, mustn't have a feeble mind.

END OF FLASHBACK

Ashwatthama: I accept my mistake, Maharaj. I abandoned my caste and took on the mantle of another. But I did it only to prove myself to my father. I wanted to outwit the Pandavas, especially Arjuna. But I see now that it would have been best not to harbour such intentions. In my thirst to be better than the Pandavas, I ended up being nothing at all. I wanted to impress my father, but look: he detests my actions, much like the entire world. Please forgive me, Pitashree.

Chitragupta: I have noted your acceptance, Ashwatthama. Your behaviour was inappropriate, and I second that this allegation against you is entirely true. I will now present the next accusation, for which I want to summon—

Ashwatthama: There are sure to be dozens of people, Maharaj. Who is it this time? Arjuna? Draupadi? I know she's dying to question me about that fateful night. I am ready to face her volley of insults and abuse.

Draupadi: No, Ashwatthama; I will not ask you anything. It appals me even to look at you.

Chitragupta: Rani Draupadi, you have to come forward. If you don't, who will cast the allegation?

Duryodhana: I will. Yes, Draupadi, I know what Ashwatthama did to you, and I also know you will be unable to control yourself. Maharaj, please permit me to cast this allegation on Draupadi's behalf.

Draupadi: Sure, go ahead, Duryodhana.

Arjuna: Draupadi! Why did you allow this man to speak on your behalf? I could have asked the questions. Who shares your pain more than I do?

Sri Krishna: Let him proceed, Partha. Duryodhana deserves a chance to prove that he wasn't to blame for the horrors of that night.

Duryodhana: I request you to please read out the allegation, Maharaj.

Chitragupta: It is alleged that Ashwatthama, on the last night of the Kurukshetra War, did something so heinous that it qualifies as the most irreligious act of the entire battle. Suyodhana, please tell the assembly about it.

Duryodhana: It was the day when Bhima had defeated me in the mace duel. I lay on the ground with my thigh bloodied and broken, counting the last moments of my life and recounting the tragedy that fate had designed for me. It was night-time when Kripacharya, the chief priest of Hastinapur and a fine teacher of warfare, Kritavarma, the leader of the Narayani Army, and Ashwatthama came in search of me. My army had been massacred; no warrior remained who could defeat the Pandavas. I admitted this to all three of them, for I knew it to be the truth. I begged Kripacharya to take on the post of the sole Acharya of Hastinapur, now that Guru Drona was no more. I requested Kritavarma, who was also part of Sri Krishna's Narayani Army, to devote the remainder of his life to Keshava's service. And to Ashwatthama, I said, 'Please look after the Gurukul of Hastinapur in place of your father.' Kripacharya and Kritavarma left, but Ashwatthama remained. He had an agenda of his own that he wanted to talk me into.

FLASHBACK

Duryodhana: What is it, Ashwatthama? Do you have something to ask me?

Ashwatthama: Yuvraj, please make me the head of your soldiers.

Duryodhana: What soldiers, Ashwatthama? The war is over. Everything is over.

Ashwatthama: No, it is not over! I am still alive, am I not? I will do what my father could not, what Karna could not. I will bring victory to you.

Duryodhana: Are you listening to yourself, Ashwatthama? What you say is impossible to do, so don't make hollow promises to a dying man.

Ashwatthama: My promises aren't hollow, Yuvraj; you'll soon see. I am leaving your side now but will return shortly and lay victory at your feet.

Duryodhana: May you be victorious, Ashwatthama.

END OF FLASHBACK

Duryodhana: Why did you do it, Ashwatthama? Why did you murder all five of Draupadi's sons in their sleep? What you did that night was a sin for which even hellfire wouldn't be adequate in punishment. Look up, now, and admit to the assembly that what you did was unforgivable.

Ashwatthama: Well, at least I *did* something! What did the 'valiant' warriors of the Kauravas achieve?

Duryodhana: That's beside the point. I did not order you to murder innocent children while they lay sleeping in their tents, oblivious to the disgusting and wicked monster lurking in the darkness! You killed five children and severed their heads out of the ugliness of your own heart, not mine!

Ashwatthama: Don't go all saint like on me, Duryodhana. You too had ordered my father to kill Abhimanyu, hadn't you? Wasn't he a child also?

Duryodhana: Abhimanyu was killed on the battlefield, in his full senses! I have already accepted that killing him was against religion, but what you did was not merely unethical but also a grievous, unpardonable sin. Draupadi, I beg your forgiveness for what my Chieftain did to your family. I know I have perpetrated many crimes against you, but my biting insults cannot have been as devastating as Ashwatthama's cold-blooded murders. His deeds shattered not only you as a woman but also your husbands and your entire family.

Draupadi: Ashwatthama, tell me: *how* could you do it? Did you not stop to think even for a moment?

Ashwatthama: No, I didn't. If I had been thinking straight, would I have done such a thing? When I went inside the tents, I didn't know that the sleeping figures in the dark were your sons and not the Pandavas. I wanted to slaughter the Pandavas for what they had done to me my entire life—for the brutal manner in which they had snatched my father from me. My father loved them more than he cared for me! Years of deeply embedded poison flowed straight to my sword, and I found I couldn't control it anymore. Trust me, Draupadi; I had no enmity against your sons. It was an honest mistake.

Bhima: You call it a mistake, Ashwatthama? When I saw my dead children, I felt utterly broken. I was more helpless than I had ever been in my life. As for Draupadi, I couldn't bear to see her agony. She was dying of pain; she was howling like a wounded animal. I could not feel anything, not even anger. I was so numb that I couldn't even find the head of my dead son Sutasoma.

Duryodhana: He brought his head to me, Bhima. That moment of shock was my last moment on Earth.

FLASHBACK

Duryodhana: What have you done, Ashwatthama? Oh, what have you done?

Ashwatthama: Why do you look upset, Yuvraj? Look, I have brought Bhima's head for you. I have killed all the five Pandavas. Victory is now yours!

Duryodhana: Ashwatthama, this is not Bhima; this is Bhima's son Sutasoma. Why did you kill that child?

Ashwatthama: I killed everybody. Everyone was sleeping,

and I killed them all. That Dhrishtadyumna too, how dare he kill my father? We have won the war!

Duryodhana: You are a maniac, Ashwatthama. We haven't won the war. I am defeated, and as for you, it's a defeat like no other man has ever met.

END OF FLASHBACK

Chitragupta: Is there anyone else in the assembly who wants to speak for or against this allegation against Ashwatthama?

Ashwatthama: Pitashree, please say something. Can't I expect your support even now? After all that I have said?

Drona: You have left me with no words, son. Maharaj, I entirely support this allegation.

Chitragupta: I have noted all your responses, members of the assembly. This allegation against Ashwatthama stands correct. I will now read the last accusation levelled against him, for which I want to summon someone. Please come forward, Arjuna.

Arjuna: Maharaj, am I permitted to address a few words to Duryodhana first?

Chitragupta: Yes.

Arjuna: Duryodhana, I know that I have always blamed you for every misfortune that fell upon us. I don't want to bring it all up again, but I am grateful for the way you supported Draupadi today. You have proved that some vestigial humanity lingers in your heart. Thank you, Duryodhana.

Duryodhana: Arjuna, my enmity was against you. Believe it or not, the loss of your sons pained me greatly. I am not as petty and self-absorbed a man as all of you assume I am.

Chitragupta: Arjuna, before I read out the last allegation against Ashwatthama, I need to ask you a question.

Arjuna: Yes, Maharaj.

Chitragupta: When Guru Drona taught you the art of using the Brahmastra, did you know that Ashwatthama also had knowledge of it?

Arjuna: No, Maharaj.

Chitragupta: That is what I wanted to confirm. The final allegation against Ashwatthama is that he misused the Brahmastra on the last night of the Kurukshetra War.

Ashwatthama: Maharaj, I have been quietly listening to all the allegations in my name. I have been taking in hatred from everyone. Standing here among these people who would like to see me dead is eating me from within. But Maharaj, this final allegation is absolutely unjust! I used the Brahmastra only after Arjuna had already fired it.

Arjuna: What was I to do? In front of me lay the corpses of my sons, my brothers' sons, and my brother-in-law. I was crazed! I had to avenge the tragedy that had struck my family only because of you. You heartless man! You cannot even imagine how I felt when I saw the anguished people around me and heard Draupadi's frantic sobs...

Ashwatthama: You didn't have to fire the Brahmastra to kill me. Aren't you a valiant warrior and a great archer? You could have shot me with your arrows.

Arjuna: Don't mislead the assembly! You well know that you hid in the forest, exactly like the coward you've always been inside. Didn't you once burn down the tree when you failed to hit the bird's eye? Well, I burnt down the entire forest so I could kill the man who had slain my sons!

Chitragupta: Ashwatthama, we aren't discussing why Arjuna fired the Brahmastra. You gave him reason enough to make one ill-thought decision, didn't you? But why did *you* do it? Were you not aware of what could happen if the weapons collided with each other?

Ashwatthama: I did, Maharaj. The entire universe would be destroyed.

Arjuna: You knew that and yet you fired the Brahmastra! Maharaj, my friend Sri Krishna advised me to take back the Brahmastra, and I immediately did so. But you, Ashwatthama? What did you do?

FLASHBACK

Sri Krishna: Ashwatthama, Arjuna has taken back his Brahmastra. Please recall your weapon too before disaster strikes. Don't stand there thinking!

Ashwatthama: I can't do that. I don't know how to recall it. Keshava, please tell me what to do.

Sri Krishna: Oh, you evil man! Ashwatthama, listen to me: You targeted Arjuna when you first cast the Brahmastra. Since you cannot retract it, you must at least change its direction. Immediately!

Ashwatthama: Keshava, I have done as you asked.

Arjuna: Oh, what did you do, Ashwatthama? You directed the Brahmastra in Abhimanyu's direction! It will hit Uttara, his pregnant wife! You wanted to destroy the entire Pandava clan, didn't you? First, you slaughtered Draupadi's sons, and now you will kill Abhimanyu's child who is still in the womb. No greater sin has ever been committed, Ashwatthama, for killing an infant in the mother's womb is punishable far more severely than death.

END OF FLASHBACK

Ashwatthama: But no one got killed, Maharaj! Sri Krishna saved the baby. I do not understand the meaning of this allegation when there were no casualties at all.

Sri Krishna: I did not save anyone, Ashwatthama. The child was born because it was his fate; he was destined to be born alive and grow up to be a fine young man. But that does not excuse your sin, Ashwatthama. When compared to your offence, the misdeeds of Duryodhana and Dushasana seem pale. You are the one who thought nothing of destroying the entire world only to fuel distorted motivations. No transgression can ever be greater.

Chitragupta: Guru Drona, when you taught your son the art of Brahma Shastra, did you also teach him how to take back such a weapon?

Drona: No, Maharaj.

Chitragupta: Why?

Drona: If someone is taught how to retrieve such a weapon, he might be tempted to use it over and over again.

Chitragupta: Ashwatthama, what can I say? Even your father does not trust you. Well, the allegations against you are now complete.

Ashwatthama: So, it is time for judgement, right? I am curious to hear your verdict, Maharaj, for what can I possibly suffer that I haven't already? For what I did to the Pandava clan, Sri Krishna has already punished me with a fate worse than death. My punishment will never end.

FLASHBACK

Sri Krishna: Ashwatthama, you'll be sad to hear that Abhimanyu's wife has given birth to a boy—a beautiful child called Parikshit. The Pandava clan lives on, despite your best efforts.

Ashwatthama: How did he survive, Sri Krishna? Didn't my Brahmastra kill him?

Sri Krishna: Do you know the meaning of Parikshit? It means one whose test has already been taken. The child passed his test, Ashwatthama, and it was your irreligious act that put him to the test in the first place. Do you know why he lived? It was because I had blessed the child with the power of every good deed I have ever committed on Earth. Remember,

Ashwatthama—evil can never win over goodness; it can only cloud things momentarily.

Ashwatthama: So, kill me, Sri Krishna. Kill me for trying to kill that child. I know you will.

Sri Krishna: No, Ashwatthama. You strew the ground with corpses, but your body will never join them. You will never be assimilated with the Earth.

Ashwatthama: What do you mean?

Sri Krishna: You wanted to kill someone who wasn't even born yet, who had never seen the Earth in all its glory. You have seen the Earth, haven't you? But you will never see death. If my words are true, then what I say today will be your eternal destiny. Ashwatthama, I condemn you to an endless life soaked in guilt, agony and loathing. You will long for death to free you of the pain, but death will never come to you.

END OF FLASHBACK

Ashwatthama: Ever since that day, I have been stumbling and suffering. I walk the Earth in no particular direction. Death is nowhere in sight, even though I cannot eat, drink or sleep. Sometimes I think I was fated to be punished right from birth. When I was a child, my father chastised me every day—all he could talk about was Arjuna and his great displays of skill at the Gurukul. Even as a warrior, among people like Duryodhana who concocted evil plans to kill the Pandavas, it was again I who got labelled as an irreligious man.

Duryodhana: You *are* an irreligious man, Ashwatthama. I had reasons to hate the Pandavas which is why I plotted to kill them. I wanted my kingdom back. But you had absolutely no reason for doing what you did. You are the son of Guru Drona, the beloved teacher of the Pandavas. Even after their victory, you could have lived on in peace. Sri Krishna may have punished you; your father may have chastised you. But why did you punish *me*? I hate to be connected in any way to your heinous offence, and yet, the world will always remember that it was I, Duryodhana, who agreed to make you my last Chieftain.

Chitragupta: Ashwatthama, I have listened to all the allegations against you, but today, I will announce no verdict. No decision will be taken in my court today nor will any punishment be meted out.

Ashwatthama: Why, Maharaj?

Chitragupta: You will return to Earth and continue the punishment that Sri Krishna meted out to you. It is well-deserved retribution, and I will not overrule it. As for my records, I am going to attribute to you the burden of the greatest sin committed during the Kurukshetra War. You are the only one in today's assembly against whose name I don't have a single redeeming deed.

Ashwatthama: I accept your decision, Maharaj. Pitashree, I am leaving now. I will embrace you only when I finally attain *moksha*—if that day ever arrives. I hope you will remember me if not as your son, at least as a reminder of the grudge you carried in your heart. Let me be the undying example of what a grudge can become if it isn't contained in time.

Drona: How do you know about that, son? Oh, please forgive me; I am responsible for the condition you find yourself in today.

Ashwatthama: Don't say any more, Pitashree.

Drona: Let me speak, son. A lot of allegations have been levelled against you in this assembly, and each was proved to be valid. Everyone who comes on the stand at the Dharmakshetra blames someone or the other for his offences. But you, like a neglected child, spoke only of the wounds of your heart. It is today that I have understood the sorrow you spent your childhood in, the angst that coloured your youth. Yes, I know you have committed grave offences that humankind will never forget, but behind each one of them was a callous, irresponsible father who failed miserably at his duties as a parent.

Ashwatthama: No, father; don't blame yourself. You did try to explain things to me, but I was wallowing in too much self-pity to listen to you. When you heard about my death on the battlefield, thanks to an untruth that the Pandavas circulated, you discarded your weapons in mourning. It was me who never listened to you when I should have, but overheard everything I shouldn't have.

Drona: What did you overhear, son?

FLASHBACK

Kripi: You look pleased, Acharya. What is the matter?

Drona: Yes, Kripi, I am thrilled. I always knew that Arjuna was the best at archery, but now the whole world agrees with me. Today was the final day of the princes' formal training and the show that Arjuna put up mesmerised everyone. I can't believe my students have grown up to become such adroit warriors.

Kripi: That's great, Acharya. You sure do look overjoyed. It seems as if your *guru dakshina* will be the entire kingdom of Hastinapur!

Drona: Oh, I will get my *dakshina*. But it won't be Hastinapur; it will be Panchal.

Kripi: You still haven't forgotten how King Drupad insulted you, have you? For how long will you harbour this grudge in your heart?

Drona: How can I forget, Kripi? I am a father, and no father can stand to see his young son deprived even of milk! I remember every detail of that day when Ashwatthama had come running home to me, declaring proudly, 'Pitashree, I drank milk today! I am delighted!' My little boy went to bed happily, but I stayed up crying all night. I didn't have the heart to tell him that what he had drunk wasn't milk but merely water mixed with flour. Drupad, my erstwhile friend, had promised that he would always be there for me. He had pledged to help me out if I was ever in financial difficulties. But Kripi, don't you remember what happened when I did approach him for help?

Kripi: I remember, Acharya.

Drona: That man insulted me! He refused to recognize me and threw me out of his kingdom! No, Kripi, I cannot forget this insult. I will harbour this grudge in my heart until the day Arjuna takes him prisoner. Drupad must understand what happens to people who break their promises.

Kripi: Why must it be Arjuna? Can't our son Ashwatthama avenge your insult?

Drona: No, Ashwatthama cannot do it; he is not gifted like Arjuna. Defeating Drupad, who is a skilled archer himself, is something only Arjuna can do. Moreover, I don't want our son to do anything against his caste. I have done everything I could to give him a happy life, and I want him to fulfil his duty as a Brahmin and the son of a teacher.

END OF FLASHBACK

Ashwatthama: I heard you say, father, that I wasn't gifted like Arjuna. It only worsened the jealousy in my heart and made me drift farther away from you. I could never understand that you did love me. Arjuna may have been your favourite disciple, but I was the son for whom you wanted all the comforts of the world. I ardently wish I had understood this before; perhaps I could have avoided my damnation. Forgive me, father, as I take your leave. My sins have caught up with me, and only Sri Krishna knows how much longer I have to live burdened under the grief of everyone in this room.

Sri Krishna: I promise you, Ashwatthama, that the day I feel you have atoned for your sins, I will grant you salvation.

6

BHIMA

FLASHBACK

Bhima: Panchali, you had pledged that you wouldn't wash your hair until I got you Dushasana's blood. You swore to wash your tresses with the blood of the man who had so disgracefully dragged you into a courtroom full of people and attempted to disrobe you. Look, my Panchali, I have brought his blood for you.

Draupadi: Bhima, history will remember me as the wife of the five Pandavas. But only I know the place you have in my heart.

END OF FLASHBACK

Bhima was the Pandava who believed in action, not thought. He was born to get things done—sometimes, without considering their consequences—and that's how he continued to live. The clouds thundered; the seasons came and went. But nothing changed Bhima's commitment to listening only to his heart. Today, in the Dharmakshetra, Bhima will have to answer for his actions. It won't be his heart that will help him defend himself; it will be the motives and the thoughts, albeit subliminal, that propelled him to behave as he did.

Chitragupta: Members of the assembly, I wish to tell you something today. When all of you were alive, getting your affairs in order on Earth, I would sometimes observe your actions. Some of you would be discussing politics while others would be manoeuvring through relationships. There were people engaged in diplomacy and preparations for war. But I didn't pay much attention to any of it. Even if I had, chances are that I wouldn't have understood your thoughts or motives. But there was one person to whom I paid close attention. And whenever I did so, I smiled.

In this Dharmakshetra, many of you have come to the stand and spoken in support of, or against, your friends, family members and foes. Your faces sometimes revealed regret; at other times, I saw disgust. It made me wonder: what is going on in the mind of that person whom I have never seen thinking before acting? Did he too reflect on his actions and experience regret or disgust?

Today, allegations will be levied against a person who inspires great passions—in some, emotions of love, while in others, fear and distaste. In my mind, however, there is only curiosity, and in my notebook is the list of charges. Vayuputra Bhima, please come to the defendant's stand.

Bhima: Pranaam, Maharaj.

Dushasana: Maharaj, I request your permission to leave the assembly. I cannot look at this monster. It might make me lose control, and I don't want to insult the honour of your court.

Bhima: What is the matter, Dushasana? Why can't you look at me? Forgive me for saying this, Maharaj, but my little brother seems too afraid to levy any charges against me. He has always loathed me. Even when we were both children, I urged him to let me join in play. But he refused. Tell me, Maharaj, what can I do? Should I return to my seat or will you call someone else to question me?

Chitragupta: Dushasana, you are not permitted to leave the assembly. This is not your home or even the Gurukul where you can come and go as you please.

Duryodhana: Don't worry, brother. Just watch what I do to this monstrous Bhima today.

Chitragupta: Vayuputra Bhima, Yudhishthira's younger brother, do you want to say anything to the assembly before I start reading out the charges?

Bhima: What can I say to anyone, Maharaj? My brothers know what is on my mind; they understand me even without words. As for Duryodhana and his brothers, they won't understand even the most coherent of explanations. I suggest you start reading your list, Maharaj. I am ready.

Chitragupta: I would like to summon Bhima's wife to the court.

Draupadi: But Maharaj, I have no allegations against Bhima. He has always loved and protected me.

Chitragupta: Rani Draupadi, I am referring to Bhima's first wife and Devi Kunti's first daughter-in-law, Hidimbi. Devi, please introduce yourself.

Hidimbi: I am the sister of Hidimba—the King of the Rakshasas, the wife of Vayuputra Bhima, and the mother of the great warrior Ghatotkach. I am Hidimbi.

Chitragupta: Bhima, all of us in the assembly today know that you have been an obedient son and brother. You were also an ideal husband. But the first allegation against you has been levied by your wife. It is for a deed that went unnoticed by everyone—perhaps even by you.

Bhima: I don't understand, Maharaj.

Chitragupta: Answer my question, Bhima: Where and how did you meet Devi Hidimbi?

Bhima: My brothers and I were stumbling about in the forest with our mother. After the Wax Palace of Varnavrat had burned down in the night, we were lost in the woods. It was then that I came face to face with Maharaj Hidimba, the king of the demons and Hidimbi's brother.

FLASHBACK

Hidimbi: Why did you kill my brother? How will I survive without him? Did you think about me even once or does the plight of a woman stranded alone in this forest not affect you at all?

Bhima: I had no choice, Hidimbi. Your brother wanted to

kill us all; I had to defend my family. But we will not leave you alone and helpless in the forest. Matashree, if you allow me, I would like to take Hidimbi as my wife.

Kunti: You have my permission, son. You are fulfilling the duty of a Kshatriya by taking her under your protection. Henceforth, Hidimbi is a bride of our family.

END OF FLASHBACK

Bhima: Hidimbi, since the day I first took you as my wife until now, I have always loved you. You are my first wife and have a special place in my heart. What are the charges you're pressing against me?

Hidimbi: I know, Bhima. I haven't ever doubted your love for me. But your love failed to reach out to the one person who meant a great deal to me. Why didn't you think before taking the decision that would leave my life hollow?

FLASHBACK

Yudhishthira: Karna is now participating in the war. Everything will change. I don't see this as a favourable turn for us at all. I am worried that it might alter the very course of the war.

Sri Krishna: You are right, Yudhishthira. Karna has in his possession the Indrastra—a weapon that's as powerful as Arjuna's Brahmastra and can decimate our entire army. As long as he has the Indrastra with him, it will be impossible for us to attain victory.

Yudhishthira: There is only one option. We must introduce to the war an unbeatable warrior who will compel Karna to use the Indrastra against him. It will have to be a warrior as outstanding as Abhimanyu, just as fearless, and as challenging to defeat.

Bhima: No, brother, don't make me do this.

Sri Krishna: Bhima, he is as dear to me as he is to you. I see him as my son. But we are left with no option. Take my word for it, Bhima: his sacrifice will never be forgotten. The day we attain victory, his contribution will be upheld as indispensable.

Arjuna: Bhima, you don't have to do it. I have lost my son in this battle, and I don't want to subject you to the same pain. I will sacrifice my life to keep your son alive.

Bhima: No, brother. I am going to bring my son right away. I know that Ghatotkach will never refuse.

END OF FLASHBACK

Hidimbi: You left us behind in the forest, Bhima. It is I who brought up our son. When he saw his father for the first time, he didn't hear any words of love and affection. No, he received a command to prepare for death! Bhima, do you know that your son was just like you? He was unafraid. He was willing to give away his life if it would help you in any way. But my son was naive and young. You were his father and should have thought about your decision. How could you be so heartless as to send your son, your flesh and blood, to a violent death?

Bhima: In the Kurukshetra War, some warriors were destined to have their names etched in gold in the annals of history. But Hidimbi, none of these people were afraid of dying. No one remembers the warriors who weighed each step they took, letting the fear of death cloud their minds. Did you want your son's name to be lost among those millions of people who lived and died in fear?

Hidimbi: I don't care, Bhima. Even if his name got erased from memory, even if no one looked up to him, he would be there with me! You wouldn't have had to light his funeral pyre! A mother aspires not for glories and fame, but for her son's long life and health.

Gandhari: Today, I feel like taking off my blindfold to witness this mother's sorrow. Her words ring in my ears! I can imagine how she lives her days, pining for her dead son. Dear daughter-in-law, don't weep. The person you are accusing has no consideration for anyone's life. Come, Devi Hidimbi, sit with me. I share your sorrow as a mother who lost her sons to this man. Even though my eyes are blindfolded, I am haunted by the dead bodies of my sons Dushasana and Duryodhana, both of whom were so mercilessly slaughtered by Bhima. Let him see how it feels to face two mothers from whom he snatched away the motivation to breathe.

Draupadi: Yes, Hidimbi, go and sit with her—the mother whose sons were fated to die in battle, the blood of whose sons was fated to turn the battlefield of Kurukshetra crimson. Or you can sit with me, sister, for I too am an ill-fated mother of Hastinapur. I too lost all my children. But unlike Devi Gandhari, my sons died for no fault of theirs. I feel sorrow—a pain so intense that it tears me apart. But at least I feel no shame.

Hidimbi: Devi Gandhari, I can understand your sorrow. Both of us have faced what no mother should: the untimely death of her children. But there is a sea of difference between us. While my grief is for the loss of my son, you mourn for your fate. Wasn't it your misfortune that you gave birth to sons who would commit grievous sins and deserve the horrors they would eventually experience? Maharaj, I take back my allegation. Whatever my husband did, he did it not because he didn't love our son, but because it was his duty as the father of a warrior. Bhima, I only have one last question.

Bhima: Ask, my beloved.

Hidimbi: When you asked our son to pick up arms in the battle, what did he say?

FLASHBACK

Bhima: My son, I have come to ask you for something. But I find myself unable to do it.

Ghatotkach: You can ask me to do anything you want, Pitashree. I know why you are here.

Bhima: You do?

Ghatotkach: Yes. You are worried that Karna might use

the Indrastra against Arjuna Chacha. If he is allowed to do that, you might even lose the battle. There will be untold destruction. We cannot let that happen.

Bhima: Indeed we cannot, son.

Ghatotkach: You want to compel Karna to use the Indrastra against someone who is as powerful and impossible to defeat as Arjuna Chacha, don't you? And you think I fit the bill?

Bhima: You do, son. You are the most fearless warrior I know and also the most selfless. But it is tearing me apart to send you to the battlefield—

Ghatotkach: Don't say that, father. I consider myself fortunate. I am delighted that like Abhimanyu's father, my father, too, finds me a worthy and dependable warrior. I would be proud to help you win the battle.

Bhima: My son, your name will live on forever not only as a brave warrior but also as a devoted son. Even in the future, whenever the black day comes when a father must send his son to war, incognizant of the outcome, he will think of you. Ghatotkach, you have redefined death, and there won't be another man quite as unafraid and obedient as you.

END OF FLASHBACK

Bhima: Our son was a true warrior, Hidimbi. I am proud to have fathered a man like him, who didn't blink once when I commanded him to sacrifice his life and attain martyrdom.

Chitragupta: Devi Hidimbi, I have noted that you have

recanted your allegation against Bhima. You may now take your leave.

Duryodhana: What big words you use today, Bhima! Words like sacrifice and martyrdom don't suit killers like you.

Bhima: Duryodhana, it is not your turn to speak, is it? Shut up and sit quietly in your place.

Chitragupta: Allow me to decide whose turn it is to speak. Bhima, we will now move to the next allegation against you.

Gandhari: Forgive me, Maharaj, but I want you to do me a favour. Can I please be permitted to levy the next allegation against Bhima? It's only him I want to interrogate. If you so desire, I can even leave the assembly after I am done.

Yudhishthira: Why, Badi Ma? What do you want to ask?

Arjuna: Maharaj, I don't think this is fair. She can question my brother when you ask her to do so.

Gandhari: Why, o great archer, are you scared? Are you afraid that this mace-wielding brother of yours will be dumbstruck at my questions? Duryodhana, my son, did you notice how these Pandavas who conquered you are afraid not of warriors but of women? What could be more shameful?

Yudhishthira: What are you saying, Badi Ma?

Gandhari: Only the truth, Dharmaraj! Why, aren't you scared of your mother and Draupadi, your wife? Your brother Arjuna is so afraid of women that when Urvashi, the most beautiful of all celestial beauties, approached him, he folded his palms and bowed respectfully before her! Nakula and Sahadeva emerged from their mother's womb and immediately proceeded to hide behind Draupadi's saree. This Bhima is no different. No matter how strong and well-built he might be, his mind is infantile.

Yudhishthira: Badi Ma, what you label as fear is only respect and affection. Throughout my life, I have treated every lady I know with honour. Arjuna bowed respectfully even before celestial beauties because it was necessary to do so at the time; he had to obtain weapons that would serve us well during the war. My little brothers Nakula and Sahadeva followed suit; they behaved as they had seen their elders do.

As for Bhima, please don't mistake his silence for fear. He stands there quietly today not because he is afraid of your questions but because he wants to protect you from painful memories. He may have killed your sons, but he understands the agony it brought to your heart. I have complete faith in my brother Bhima. Maharaj, I don't think Bhima will have any objections if Badi Ma wishes to ask him anything.

Chitragupta: Devi Gandhari, I know your heart is full of disgust for Bhima, the murderer of your sons. I can allow you to address him only if you promise to maintain the dignity of the court.

Gandhari: I promise, Maharaj. Son Dushasana, when Bhima came on to the stand today, you wanted to leave, didn't you?

Dushasana: Yes, Matashree. I could not endure the sight of this monster in front of me. Just looking at him made me think of—

Gandhari: Shh, my son, don't reminisce about those painful memories. You have nothing and no one to fear today. It is Bhima who should be afraid, for he's about to experience the fury of a wronged mother.

Duryodhana: Bhima, my mother is facing you today. Remember that while I can endure your vile words and misbehaviour, you will have to pay a hefty price if you direct the slightest insult in her direction.

Bhima: Tell your mother to weigh her words before directing them at me, Duryodhana. Anyone who tests my patience is only asking for trouble.

Chitragupta: Bhima, I warn you to stay in control. This is the Dharmakshetra, not Kurukshetra, and if you lose your composure in my court, I will have something to say. It won't be pleasant, I can assure you.

Arjuna: Keshava, I don't like what is happening here today. Who knows what Badi Ma is thinking? She could somehow trap Bhima with her words and prove him guilty of crimes he hasn't committed. I don't think it is wise to allow her to confront Bhaiya.

Sri Krishna: Arjuna, this is Bhima you are talking about, the man who is guided by nothing but the truth. There isn't another man in this court with a purer heart than his. His truth is stronger than even his mace. Have faith that it will protect him today.

Gandhari: So, tell me, Bhima: How much do you love Draupadi?

Bhima: I love her more than anything else in the world. I love her so much that even if you had a hundred more sons who had dared to insult her, I would send all of them to their funeral pyres.

Gandhari: Is your love for her so blind that it compels you to kill in cold blood? I am not even talking about what you did to my sons. No, Bhima, I am asking you about a slaughter that the world may have forgotten, but I haven't.

Bhima: What do you mean, Badi Ma?

Gandhari: Do you remember what happened after you lost the kingdom in the game of dice? How you had to go and live in the forest?

Bhima: How can I forget that? It was all because of your 'upright' and 'honourable' son! The last year of our thirteen-year-long ordeal was exceptionally difficult. We had to stay in hiding as, if we were discovered, Duryodhana could make us repeat the punishment for God knows how much longer! We went to Maharaj Virata's kingdom.

Gandhari: I must say, you spent quite a disgraceful time there, didn't you? While Dharmaraj Yudhishthira became the king's counsellor, the great Arjuna became a eunuch. Nakula and Sahadeva worked in the stables. The beautiful Draupadi became a maid, and you had to become the cook.

Bhima: Yes, Badi Ma. Besides hearing the agonized screams of your errant sons, food is the only thing that brings me great pleasure.

Gandhari: Correct me if I am wrong, but during this period of Agyat Vasa, no one knew that you were the Pandavas. No one guessed that the five of you were Draupadi's husbands.

Bhima: Yes, no one guessed. We blended pretty well with the rest of the king's staff.

Gandhari: So, since no one knew that Draupadi was a married woman or that her husbands lived in the same palace, there was nothing wrong if someone proposed marriage to her. Was there, Bhima?

FLASHBACK

Kichaka: Who are you?

Draupadi: I am Malini, Queen Sudeshna's maid.

Kichaka: Maid? You should be the queen of a large kingdom! Do you know who I am? I am Kichaka, Maharani Sudeshna's brother and the Chieftain of Maharaj Virata's army. Look here, Malini—don't you like me? Look me in the eyes, feel my skin, and then tell me—can you resist me? Well, I don't know how you feel, but you have surely won me over.

Draupadi: I don't think you know it, Senapati, but I am a married woman.

Kichaka: Really? Where is your husband then?

Draupadi: He resides in my heart.

Kichaka: And you reside in mine! Malini, I always get what I want. I don't care if you are married; you belong only to me. I will tell my sister tonight that I want her maid to serve only me—in some delicious ways! You will like that, won't you?

END OF FLASHBACK

Gandhari: That night, Panchali must have come weeping to you, demanding, 'Kichaka insulted me! Kill Kichak!' Hearing her wails, the soft little heart inside your giant-like body must have melted. Before thinking of the consequences, you dived in and murdered Kichaka. Do you know how serious an offence it is to attack the one who has given you food and shelter?

Draupadi: That is not what happened, Badi Ma. I am neither weak nor inconsiderate of those who help me. Yes, I did tell my husbands about Kichaka's behaviour, and all of them were enraged. But I forbade them to attack Kichaka. Do you know why? I did it because I didn't want Duryodhana to get wind of our whereabouts. Kichaka was a renowned wrestler, and only three people in the world had the strength to kill him: Duryodhana himself, his Guru, Balarama, and Bhima.

Gandhari: Don't lie, Draupadi. Kichaka *was* killed that night, and Duryodhana *did* come to know about it. If you had forbidden your husbands to attack him, why and how did he die?

Draupadi: Bhima did what he thought was right by me. He wanted to abide by my words, but he couldn't bear to see me humiliated.

Bhima: Badi Ma, nothing mattered more to me than the happiness of my wife. I wanted to see her safe and sound. Anyone who dared to insult her would have to pay with his life. Ask your son Dushasana about it.

Gandhari: I am not interested in the love that you and this woman share, Bhima. Tell me why you killed Kichaka even after she forbade you to. He had only expressed his feelings to her and, even though I accept that he was probably driven by lust, it wasn't a crime that deserved a death penalty!

FLASHBACK

Draupadi: You were right, Senapati. I find myself unable to resist you. Come to the dance hall tonight. I will be waiting for you there.

Kichaka: Malini, I knew you would come. How can a mere maid like you reject the valour and greatness of a Senapati? Tonight, I will do justice to this captivating beauty of yours and make love to you like no man ever has.

END OF FLASHBACK

Gandhari: It was Draupadi who called him to the dance hall, then? What passion both you and your wife share to indulge in pointless killing! Never did you think about his sister!

Bhima: I was helpless, Badi Ma. Kichaka would have dared to dishonour Draupadi had I not killed him. He had wanted to marry her and might have done so by force. But she was my wife, my Panchali!

Gandhari: Did she walk around with a sign plastered on her forehead that declared she was your wife? Does anyone who looks at your wife deserve to be killed like sheep? Shouldn't you have tried to talk to Kichaka or make him see sense? But no, like a mad elephant you will trample on people and crush them to death only because your darling Draupadi asks you to! Why are you like this, Bhima? Who gave you the right to take a human life? Did your mother never explain to you that life is valuable and it is only the Almighty who gets to grant or deny it?

Bhima: Kichaka deserved to be killed, Badi Ma. He was the epitome of all that is evil and unjust in the world. It is men like him who think they can control women and get them to do their bidding. For them, a woman's consent has no meaning. This was Draupadi he had dared to touch, but Badi Ma, I would have punished him had it been any other woman as well. How can men get away with manhandling women and assaulting them only because they assume their higher social standing makes it permissible? If a woman does not want to marry a man, he cannot get her to do so by force. What Kichaka did was an insult not only to my wife but also to every woman in Bharatvarsh.

All my life, Badi Ma, I have been angered at the sight of injustice. Sometimes, my mother held me back; at other times, my brothers forced me to restrain myself. But not one of them forbade me to kill Kichaka. All of them knew it was inevitable for that man to meet his death. There was a tornado in my heart, and it blew away Kichaka, destroying in its wake the false assumption that a woman of a lower social class must bow down to her masters and lose all her dignity. It was a lesson I had been longing to teach ever since brother Yudhishthira placed Draupadi as a pawn in that game of dice.

FLASHBACK

Duryodhana: Are you ready, Yudhishthira? If you win this time, I will return everything. But what will you stake? You have nothing left!

Vidur: Stop this game, Duryodhana. Yudhishthira, please listen to me.

Duryodhana: I have got it! You can stake a treasured possession you still own and, strangely enough, share with all your brothers. Your final pawn will be Draupadi.

Yudhishthira: Okay, Duryodhana, cast the dice.

Duryodhana: And I win again, Dharmaraj! Draupadi is now mine. Let me send someone to bring my new and beautiful maid here to the gambling room. I want her to behold her new husband.

END OF FLASHBACK

Bhima: During that game, an infernal fire was burning in my heart. If I hadn't controlled it, everyone would have burnt that very day—your sons, Maharaj Dhritarashtra, Pitamaha, Vidur, Karna, and yes, my brother too! There would have been no need for war, for no one would have survived to fight it.

Gandhari: You may not have burnt everything that day, Bhima, but you certainly set the fire going. The horrifying pledge you made rankles in my ears to this day.

FLASHBACK

Bhima: Duryodhana, Dushasana, look at me! From this moment on, whenever you see me, you will see not your brother Bhima but your death! I will never forgive you for what you have done to my wife. No, not even if you fall prostrate on the floor and beg for my forgiveness. Draupadi might forgive you; Maharaj Yudhishthira might embrace you, but I, Bhima, will not find peace until I cut open your chest and watch the blood oozing out. I will avenge every insult you have dared to perpetrate on my Panchali and make it my life's purpose to annihilate you. Henceforth, in every breath that I take, I will await the destruction of the Kauravas. This is a promise that I, Vayuputra Bhima, make today, and nothing will make me go back on my pledge.

Gandhari: It was Duryodhana and Dushasana who insulted Draupadi. Why did you kill all my sons? You didn't even know their names, Bhima. I couldn't even find their dead bodies or perform their last rites.

Bhima: Badi Ma, I don't have any answer for you but this: untimely death was written in the destiny of your sons. Even if they weren't born with this destiny, it became inevitable after my brothers and I came to Hastinapur.

Gandhari: What does that mean? Are you saying that you wanted to kill my sons the moment you caught sight of them?

FLASHBACK

Bhima: Matashree! Where are you? I have been looking for you everywhere.

Kunti: What is it, Bhima? Are you hungry again?

Bhima: No, Matashree. Someone has come to our village, and he keeps singing all the time. I don't like it!

Kunti: Why, son? What is he singing?

Bhima: He says that when I grow up, I will kill my brothers. How can I kill my brothers, Matashree? I love all my brothers! Yudhishthira Bhaiya, Arjuna, Nakula and Sahadeva are dear to me. Am I not your good son? Will I indeed become a killer?

Kunti: No, son. You will not kill your brothers.

END OF FLASHBACK

Bhima: That day onwards, Matashree, I didn't do anything to hurt the Kauravas, but they surely started trying to kill us. Duryodhana did everything in his capacity to try to kill me in particular. All his methods would be underhanded.

Duryodhana: Bhima, I have already responded to the allegation of trying to kill you and your brothers. Why are you wasting the court's time? We want to know why you killed my brothers and me, not hear about my nasty childhood all over again. Do you have any answer to my mother's questions or do you intend to keep screaming pointlessly?

Bhima: You were asking for punishment, Duryodhana. I have already declared that I found it just to avenge any insult to Panchali with murder.

Duryodhana: Yes, so it was I who deserved the punishment, not my brothers! I was responsible for what happened to you; it was me who hatched the conspiracies to kill you. Why did you slaughter all my brothers? Didn't I tell you, Dushasana, that this demon will have no answer to our mother's questions?

Dushasana: Mahabali Bhima, why are you quiet? What happened to the fury and fire you keep spouting everywhere? Has it all burnt out?

Chitragupta: Bhima, do you have an answer to the allegation? If Suyodhana was responsible for the insults heaped on Rani Draupadi, why did you pledge to kill Sushasana and all his brothers?

Bhima: Maharaj, Dushasana also deserved to be killed. He was the one who dragged my Panchali by her tresses and insulted her in front of the entire clan. He tried to disrobe her! How could I forgive him for daring to touch my wife?

Dushasana: Bhima, tell me: Have you always obeyed the orders of your elder brother Yudhishthira?

Bhima: Of course.

Dushasana: Have you obeyed him even when he asked you to do something disgusting and vile?

Bhima: My brother isn't like yours, Dushasana. He well knows the difference between the right and the foul.

Dushasana: Assume that he did ask you to do something you felt was in poor taste. Would you still follow his orders?

Bhima: Yes.

Dushasana: That is precisely what I was doing. It was why I insulted Draupadi! How can you punish someone who is following the injunctions of his elder brother? Tell me, Bhima, why did you kill me like a wild beast?

FLASHBACK

Duryodhana: What happened? Did the maid Draupadi refuse to come? What kind of soldier are you? Don't you know how to use your strength? Dushasana, I think the erstwhile Rani Draupadi finds it demeaning to obey a mere soldier. Why don't you go and bring her here? She is your sister-in-law, apart from now being my maid. Make her listen to you.

Dushasana: Come along, maid. My elder brother is calling you.

Draupadi: I won't go. You can't make me, Dushasana.

Dushasana: Oh, you think so, do you? I have several fascinating ideas about how to force you into going with me.

Draupadi: Dushasana, do not overstep the mark of decorum! I refuse to go; leave me alone.

Dushasana: This is hilarious! A maid is talking about decorum! Come with me and explain to the entire assembly what etiquette is about. If you don't cooperate, I will drag you there.

END OF FLASHBACK

Sri Krishna: Dushasana, your argument is flawed. You claim that you shouldn't have been punished because you were only carrying out the command of your elder brother. But, tell me, if the one who executes a vile and criminal order doesn't get punished, how will he ever understand the difference between good and evil? There will be nothing to distinguish between orders that must be obeyed and those that must be crushed.

Everyone in the assembly today acted upon somebody's orders: Draupadi obeyed Kunti Ma's orders and married all the five Pandavas. Didn't she get punished? Yudhishthira obeyed the orders of his creed. But look, even he is held responsible for the tragedy that eventuated. Your mother, who is perhaps the most devoted wife the world has ever known, was also punished with all-consuming grief. Tell me, Dushasana, why shouldn't you have been punished?

Dushasana: Keshava, what with your hypnotizing debates and Bhima's strength, my defeat has always been inevitable, hasn't it? But I will not be content until Bhima tells me why he killed my brothers. Forget my brother Duryodhana; keep my sins aside. But tell me, what felony did my other brothers commit that deserved a death penalty? Bhima, do you even know my brothers' names? Even one?

Bhima: Vikarna.

Dushasana: Ah, just the one brother who never obeyed his elders! No wonder you remember his name, for it must have delighted you to see discord among the Kauravas.

Bhima: Dushasana, I bet even your mother does not remember all the names.

Gandhari: Saam, Sudushil, Bheembal, Subahu, Sahishnu, Yekkundi, Durdhar, Durmukh, Bindoo, Krup, Chitra, Durmad, Dushchar, Sattva, Chitraksha... Do you want me to take the remaining names, Bhima? Don't forget, I am the mother of a hundred sons—sons that you killed. I know all their names; I remembered them until the moment I breathed my last, and never will I forget what you did to my family. Answer Dushasana, Bhima. Or have you no response?

Chitragupta: Bhima, Devi Gandhari and Sushasana's questions remain unanswered. Do you accept the allegation that, aside from Suyodhana and Sushasana, you murdered the remaining Kaurava brothers for no apparent reason?

Draupadi: I will answer this question, Maharaj. Bhima killed all the Kaurava brothers because they belonged to a family that could never respect its women. Had your brothers so wanted, couldn't they have tried to stop you from insulting me over and over? They could have talked you into stopping your irreligious acts! But all they did was support you in every crime you perpetrated. Anyone who is party to a crime as grievous as that is equally guilty! And Dushasana, didn't you know that Bhima's vengeance would be complete only when he killed you? Why didn't you step forward and confront him instead of using your brothers as shields, letting them all die on the battlefield? It seems to me that you didn't care for them as much as you're now pretending to!

Duryodhana: Enough, Draupadi! You and your husbands have continually been putting on the martyr act, trying to win everyone's pity with your admonishments and tears. I am the bad dog, am I not, so all of you unflinchingly give me a bad name and hang me! Admit the truth: Bhima has NO answer to this allegation. He killed all my brothers because he is a monster, period. You well knew that after Dushasana and I died, my brothers would be your slaves. They would be nothing compared to your strength. You didn't need to kill them, Bhima, but you did it nevertheless because you begrudged my mother even a few moments of peace. Even if I forgive you for what you did to me, I cannot forget the ocean of grief you submerged my mother into.

Sri Krishna: Hear yourself speak, Duryodhana. I agree that your brothers would have been left powerless after the Pandavas triumphed. But as time went by, they would have undoubtedly become enmeshed in feelings of rage. They would have craved another battle to kill those who had murdered their brothers. The Earth would never have been able to endure another battle like the Kurukshetra War. No, Duryodhana, poisonous vipers strike the members of their own clan; no member of such a clan survives.

Gandhari: I cannot refute you, Keshava. You are the supreme truth on Earth; you are cognizant of the righteous here in this transitory world.

Chitragupta: Devi Gandhari, while I agree with Keshava, the fact remains that Bhima was unable to answer your question. I request you to please take your seat now, for I will pose the next allegation.

Gandhari: Yes, Maharaj.

Chitragupta: Mahabali Bhima, do you consider yourself to be a great warrior?

Bhima: Yes, Maharaj. No warrior in the universe could equal me in strength.

Chitragupta: How does a great warrior behave with his enemies in battle, Bhima?

Bhima: For a warrior to be victorious, the foe must be killed. Once all the enemies have been vanquished, victory is attained.

Chitragupta: Bhima, your weapon of choice is the mace. Few, if anyone, can rival you in a mace fight. All those you killed in Kurukshetra succumbed to the injuries you inflicted with your mace, right?... Why are you silent, Bhima?

FLASHBACK

Gandhari: Karunesh, are these the corpses of my sons?

Karunesh: Yes, Maharani.

Gandhari: Karunesh, I was informed by Sanjaya that Bhima killed ten of my sons today. While narrating the events of the war to my husband, Sanjaya saw my sons' deaths in his divine vision. You have brought me the corpses of Saam, Subahu and Sattva. Where are the rest?

Karunesh: Their bodies could not be found, Maharani. I struggled profoundly even to find these corpses.

Gandhari: How can that be? Will a mother now be denied the right even to mourn her dead sons? How will I perform their last rites?

END OF FLASHBACK

Chitragupta: Where were the remaining corpses, Bhima? If you had killed them with your mace, their bodies would certainly have been found on the battlefield.

Bhima: I don't know what to say, Maharaj. I did kill them, and that's all I remember.

Chitragupta: When you first came here today, Bhima, I was curious to ascertain if you are mentally sound. I find it difficult to fathom how any warrior could use his strength so very heartlessly that he mutilates the bodies of those he kills! You murdered Devi Gandhari's sons so ruthlessly that even their corpses couldn't be located. Their heads were severed; their limbs were strewn in opposite directions. Isn't that right, Bhima? This is the next allegation against you: your behaviour during the battle did not befit a warrior. It was bestial, not human.

Draupadi: Maharaj, have you ever seen a forest fire? It seems tame and restricted at first, but with even the slightest gust of wind, the entire forest is set ablaze. Bhima is the Vayuputra, the son of the Wind God. If the wind is quiet and pleasant, you'll not find a more temperate man. But if the wind turns wild and untamed, Bhima is capable of complete annihilation. I am Draupadi, born of fire, and yet I couldn't have lived my days on Earth without Bhima by my side. He is a fiery man, Maharaj, but his heart is pure and true.

Dhritarashtra: Stop piling adulations on this beast, Draupadi. You are right in one thing: he did set my entire family ablaze! Maharaj, I cannot listen to this endless game of allegations and counter-allegations anymore. It seems obvious to me that it is meaningless to blame Bhima for anything in your court.

He will never be found guilty, for doesn't he belong to the hallowed, ever-so-righteous clan of the Pandavas? I seek your permission to leave, Maharaj, along with my wife and sons.

Chitragupta: None of you is going anywhere. What has happened to all of you today? I may be even-tempered, but I cannot endure anyone taking undue advantage of this in my Dharmakshetra! I have asked someone a question, but it is someone else who starts declaiming. The proceedings of the assembly are not over, but people stand up to leave. I cannot permit this ignominy! Where will you go anyway, Maharaj Dhritarashtra? You forget that it is here that your ultimate fate will be decided. You have left the mortal world far, far behind.

Dhritarashtra: I am sorry, Maharaj. Please proceed.

Chitragupta: Vayuputra Bhima, Rani Draupadi talked very philosophically in your favour. But I am afraid it isn't an adequate answer. I need to hear it from your mouth. Tell me, Bhima, why did you kill Sushasana and his brothers so brutally?

FLASHBACK

Bhima: As I stand in front of you today, Dushasana, I finally understand what the village bard in my childhood meant. I feared he prophesized I would kill my dear brothers Yudhishthira, Arjuna, Nakula and Sahadev. I was a child then and did not know anything about religion and irreligion. But today I realize he predicted that I would kill you. Dushasana, perhaps what I am about to do doesn't befit a Kshatriya, but I don't care. What you did to my Panchali didn't befit a Kshatriya either, did it? Which warrior, the protector of a woman's honour, drags his sister-in-law by her tresses and attempts to disrobe her? Today, you can feel the hellfire that burnt in my heart back then—can you see your death approaching?

I have lived with many demons, Dushasana. Why isn't Panchali mine and mine alone? Why don't I captivate her in a way that Arjuna does? Why don't I have Yudhishthira's wisdom? By killing you today, Dushasana, perhaps all the demons inside me will also die.

END OF FLASHBACK

Draupadi: Bhima—

Bhima: Don't say anything, Panchali. When I came to this assembly today, I knew many allegations would be levelled against me. I know that I have been cruel. But I have no complaints, no regrets; I accept everything that happened as part of my fate. Maharaj, I have never asked for forgiveness for any of my actions, and I will not do so today. Maharaj, perhaps I am a poor judge of what is ethical and what isn't, which is why I will accept whatever decision you take today.

Dhritarashtra: Forgive me for interrupting again, Maharaj, but I want to make a request. You have been meting out only minor punishments to the Pandavas—petty things that don't really affect their glory, do they? But I beg you to please punish this Bhima strictly. He annihilated my entire clan, and that surely deserves harsh, severe damnation!

Chitragupta: What are you talking about, Maharaj? Didn't you take the matter in your own hands and mete out punishment to Bhima while still on Earth?

FLASHBACK

Dhritarashtra: I remember the day when the five of you first came to Hastinapur. I had welcomed all of you with a tight embrace. I was delighted to see my brother's children finally come to me after years of turmoil in the forest. Bhima, I had heard the rumours that you would cause the destruction of the Kuru clan, but I never paid any attention to hearsay. Warriors bring their fate with them. Death was written in my sons' destinies, while your destiny was to become a prince of Hastinapur. I have one last desire, Bhima. Won't you fulfil an old and dying man's last wish?

Bhima: Of course, Maharaj.

Dhritarashtra: All those years ago, I had welcomed you to Hastinapur by embracing you. I want to embrace you one last time now that you and your brothers have returned victorious from the battle. Come forward, Bhima, allow me to hug you for one final time.

END OF FLASHBACK

Chitragupta: Do you remember what you did to Bhima, Maharaj? Had Sri Krishna not swiftly replaced Bhima with his life-sized statue, you would have crushed the Pandu prince to death! You played a nasty, hypocritical trick with the intention to kill, and you have the audacity to talk to me about punishment?

FLASHBACK

Dhritarashtra: Forgive me, Bhima, forgive me! I had lost my mind. I wasn't thinking straight—

Sri Krishna: You have been through a lot, Maharaj. After this last display of 'courage', I wouldn't recommend that you stay on in Hastinapur. Leave the royal palace, Maharaj, and try to seek peace in the forest. Here, in your royal bed, the pillows may be of the softest fabric and servants may fawn over you day and night, but you will find neither rest nor sleep.

END OF FLASHBACK

Chitragupta: Sri Krishna meted out just punishment to you, Maharaj Dhritarashtra. But that was your punishment for your remaining days on Earth. Here, in the Dharmakshetra, I will be the one to decide the eternal fate of both you and Bhima.

Gandhari: You will be the one to decide, Maharaj, and we will all have to accept your judgement. But to my eyes, this man in front of me is a monster. For his heartless killing of Dushasana and his use of deception to kill Duryodhana, I will never forgive him. Every shred of my being will curse him.

Bhima: Maharaj, I committed no deception in killing Duryodhana. Mata Gandhari assumes that I broke the rules of warfare because I struck Duryodhana on the thigh. I know that it isn't permitted to strike your opponent below the waist in a mace duel. But Maharaj, I had no choice. If I hadn't struck him on the thigh—the only vulnerable part of his body—he would never have been defeated. Isn't it also a rule of warfare that both opponents should be equal in strength? It was Duryodhana who was loudly declaiming this rule not long ago, trying to prove his greatness in not choosing Nakula or Sahadeva to compete with. But Maharaj, on the day of my mace fight with Duryodhana, we were not on the same footing. While I was a warrior with human strength, he was a demon in possession of unearthly powers. What was I to do?

Duryodhana: Don't spin yarns, Bhima. I had no unearthly powers. I merely had my mother's blessings and prayers. You had that too; hadn't Mata Kunti blessed you?

Bhima: It wasn't merely her blessing that Mata Gandhari gave you but magical strength! You too were aware of this, Duryodhana, or you would never have had the courage to confront me. You were convinced that you were invincible. If it hadn't been for the magic, I would have conquered you in a matter of minutes! I have always been a more powerful and skilled mace warrior than you, Duryodhana.

Duryodhana: Bhima!

Bhima: Am I lying, Duryodhana? Come on; tell the court how your mother prepped her son to face Bhima in a duel!

Chitragupta: Stop it, both of you! So many years have gone by; your families have been destroyed in the battle.

But neither of you has been able to forgive and forget. Why can't you see that it is this venomous enmity that went on to reap horrific results?

Devi Gandhari, is Bhima speaking the truth? Did you bless Duryodhana with magical powers that made him invincible?

Gandhari: Yes, Maharaj.

FLASHBACK

Gandhari: Duryodhana, my son, you know that I have never set my eyes on you. I have cradled you in my lap and allayed your wounds but never have I been able to see my child.

Duryodhana: Yes, Matashree. It has aggrieved me greatly too.

Gandhari: I have very little time left on this Earth, son. Before leaving this earthly abode behind, I want to look at you, my firstborn son, to my heart's content.

Duryodhana: Matashree, I have waited for this all my life. I have longed for you to take off your blindfold and behold the son who loves you a lot.

Gandhari: Go and have a bath, my child. Remember that when I set my eyes on you, you should be in the same state in which you were born. I want to behold you in your bare flesh, unclothed, just like an infant.

Duryodhana: Yes, Matashree.

END OF FLASHBACK

Chitragupta: What happened then, Suyodhana?

Duryodhana: I went to take a bath as my mother had instructed. I was just going to meet her when Sri Krishna arrived. He made his quintessential barbed remarks and planted doubts in my mind.

Chitragupta: What kind of doubts?

Duryodhana: He enquired how I could go to my mother in that condition. I wasn't a baby anymore, was I?

FLASHBACK

Gandhari: Are you here, my son?

Duryodhana: Yes, Matashree.

Gandhari: Son, I am about to remove my blindfold. I will look at you with all the meditation, devotion and strength I have garnered over the years. The strength of my love and affection for you will make you unconquerable. Your body will become a streak of lightning that vanquishes everything in its path but remains undefeated.

Duryodhana: Thank you, Matashree.

Gandhari: What is this you have done, son?! Why are you clothed from the waist down? Couldn't you have listened to me even once in your life? I cannot do anything to help you now, Duryodhana. I am going to lose you like I lost all my children.

END OF FLASHBACK

Chitragupta: It stuns me, it does, the magnitude of deception that went into that mace battle. While one warrior used deception, the other sacrificed his war ethics. Do you remember the rules of warfare, Bhima?

Bhima: Yes, Maharaj.

Chitragupta: Do you remember the rules of warfare, Suyodhana?

Duryodhana: I do, Maharaj.

Chitragupta: Okay. If that is so, then I, Chitragupta, am breaking the most stringent law of my assembly—the law of non-violence. Today, at this very moment, there will be a battle of mace between Bhima and Suyodhana. Nobody will strike below the waist, and neither will anyone be unconquerable. I want to see if you have learnt anything beyond physical prowess, if the etchings of fate hold any meaning to you in the light of the devastation that both of you have witnessed.

Bhima: Come, Duryodhana, do as Maharaj orders. Prepare for a duel right now!

Gandhari: No, my son!

Duryodhana: No, Bhima, not today. I will obey my mother. I had battled you in Kurukshetra to alleviate the rage and envy within me. But I will not fight you today. Perhaps we will meet again in another birth, and I assure you, neither of us will have any excuse when that day arrives.

Chitragupta: I wanted to see if either of you had learned anything from the past. Bhima, while Suyodhana has learnt to control his rage, you remain as wild and uncontrollable as ever. You cannot control your anger even when it threatens to bring about massive destruction in your family!

Bhima, after listening to all the allegations levied against you today, I have decided that you have been heartless and cruel to the degree that no human being ever has before. It is a blessing to have complete faith in one's strength, but, without a stronghold on ethics, it rapidly becomes a curse. For a true warrior, ethics are as crucial as physical strength, and you have sacrificed your faith to fuel your thirst for revenge. At the same time, it is also true that no one has loved as intensely as you have loved Draupadi.

Bhima, you are the wind—so pleasant on a hot and fiery day but so destructive when you blow up into a storm. The world will continue to remember you when they feel helpless and anguished. From you, they will draw strength, confidence and the courage to protect their beloved even in a catastrophe. But you are the one they will curse in the face of destruction. I adjudge that your name will not be included among the great warriors of Bharatvarsh. Bhima, henceforth you will be regarded as a man of great physical strength who knew how to love fiercely and loyally. But no one will see you as a skilled warrior ever again.

Bhima: I accept your decision, Maharaj. I have never been a warrior; I have let my physical strength and quick temper compel me to be brutal. If the world remembers me as a man who knew how to love, I will consider myself blessed. It will give me hope that I deserved to be born on Earth, for what is the meaning of a life that is devoid of love?

Draupadi: Bhima, you remember the promise you made to me, don't you?

FLASHBACK

Draupadi: Bhima, my end is close. Any moment now, I will take my final breath. Before I die, I want to ask you for something.

Bhima: Anything, Panchali.

Draupadi: If, in my next birth, I get married to the five of you again, I would like you to be the eldest brother. I would like you to have the greatest right over my heart and soul. Perhaps, in that new life that we will live together, all of us will truly be happy.

END OF FLASHBACK

Bhima: I remember, Panchali. I promised you then, and I repeat it now: I will always love you dearly. You will be in my heart forever, and it will be an eternity before my love for you fades.

7

GANDHARI

The eyes reflect a person's soul. It is by looking into a person's eyes that great psychics and soothsayers have predicted their motives and desires. But what about the woman whose eyes remained shut to the world, even though perfectly capable of vision? Today, in the Dharmakshetra, the blindfold will be taken off. The truths that have so far been concealed in the eyes of Devi Gandhari, the wife of Maharaj Dhritarashtra and mother of the hundred Kauravas, will cease being a mystery.

Chitragupta: I welcome all of you to today's Assembly of Religion. I summon Devi Gandhari to please take the stand. Devi Gandhari, you have already introduced yourself to the assembly, but before I start reading out the allegations against you, is there anyone in the court who would like to speak?

Duryodhana: Who could have anything to say? My mother has always lived a pure and chaste life. I have no clue what the allegations against her are, but I am sure they will be invalidated.

Chitragupta: I can sense restlessness in you, Devi Kunti. Do you want to say something?

Kunti: Maharaj, how can I, a mere maid, dare to speak about the Maharani of Hastinapur?

Gandhari: What are you saying, sister?

Kunti: Ignore me, Maharaj. There is nothing I wish to say.

Chitragupta: Devi Kunti, I know you are attempting to conceal something. But in my court, nothing can stand in the way of judgement; no mysteries can cloud that which is true. But never mind, if you don't want to speak up right now, you can wait for your turn. Devi Gandhari, if you wish, you can take off your blindfold. This is the Assembly of Religion, not the mortal world, and no vows made on Earth need to be regarded here mandatorily.

Gandhari: Maharaj, this is not an ordinary blindfold. It is the symbol of my chastity and piety as a married woman. It is an integral part of my being. If the blindfold is opened, it might burn to ashes numerous people in this assembly, and then you will hold me responsible. No, Maharaj, I implore you to let my blindfold stay put.

Dhritarashtra: Throw your blindfold away, Gandhari! Your blindfold decimated Hastinapur; what could be worse than that?

Gandhari: What are you saying, Maharaj?

Chitragupta: Maharaj Dhritarashtra, I have to ask you to come forth instead of lashing out at Devi Gandhari from your seat. Devi Gandhari, this is the first allegation against you. You were such a stickler for your vow of wearing a blindfold that you stood by the sidelines as Hastinapur got destroyed.

Gandhari: What kind of allegation is this, Maharaj? How can you say such a thing? How can my husband, for whom I took this vow in the first place, accuse me of such a grave sin?

Dhritarashtra: Why did you take such a self-sacrificing, meaningless vow, Gandhari? Did I ask you to do it?

Gandhari: No, Maharaj, but as your wife, I wanted to share all your joys and suffer every sorrow that touched you. I wanted every difficulty written on your fate to become part of mine. It is the duty of a wife to participate in everything that her husband faces—happiness and despair, trials and tribulations. I didn't want you to loathe yourself for your inability to see. Instead, I wanted to be the one person in your life who also knew how it felt to live in perpetual darkness. History is witness to the fact that no wife has ever made a sacrifice of this magnitude before. Why are you casting aspersions on me for fulfilling my duties as a wife?

Dhritarashtra: I repeat: I had never asked you to make this sacrifice. Gandhari, what you call a sacrifice and 'a wife's duty' was hardly as innocent as that. It was a curse that you bestowed upon my sons, my kingdom and me, wasn't it?

Duryodhana: Pitashree, what are you implying? Matashree has always loved and supported us.

Dhritarashtra: What help has she ever been to you or me, Duryodhana? All she wanted to do was satisfy her ego. She masked her true intention under a display of wifely devotion. Don't look so aghast, son, for I know I speak the truth.

FLASHBACK

Dhritarashtra: No, Gandhari, no! You cannot take this vow. I may be blind, but you are not. You can be my eyes. You can hold my hand and show me the wonders of the world. I don't know what a flower looks like or which colours paint the evening sky at sunset. I haven't ever seen lightning divide the sky in two, even though I have heard it in my darkness and been afraid. You can help allay my fears, my wife, and help me forget that I am sightless. When our son is born and runs about the palace, who will hold his hand? Who will pick him up when he falls? A mother cannot remain blindfolded, Gandhari, for she must look after her children. I forbid you to do this.

Gandhari: But Maharaj, my religion and wifely duties—

Dhritarashtra: Gandhari, your biggest duty as a wife is to obey your husband. I am pleading with you not to make such a terrifying vow. Look, I have put my hands together in a plea. Don't do this.

Gandhari: No, Maharaj. Today, in our chamber, you are consoling me and forbidding me from fulfilling my wifely duties. But in time, when the subjects of Hastinapur cast aspersions on my devotion and loyalty, I fear that you will remain silent. Please permit me to take this vow; it is the only path I can adopt to live out my remaining days. I may not be able to show you the colours of the world, but I will at least take heart in the fact that I have never deserted my husband. You won't be alone in the darkness, for I will be right by your side.

END OF FLASHBACK

Dhritarashtra: I begged you not to do it, Gandhari, but you were so absorbed in your piety and inflated ego that you went ahead anyway. There were only two people who should have kept an eye on our kingdom. While one was cursed with blindness, the other chose to blind herself. While you were so 'loyally' sticking to your vow, a war broke out and razed everything we owned to the ground.

Gandhari: Maharaj, how can you say that the Kurukshetra War wouldn't have been fought had I not been blindfolded? How can you hold my vow responsible for the horrifying course of events?

Dhritarashtra: You *were* responsible, Gandhari. Had you not been blindfolded, you would have seen the rancour and envy our son was growing up with. You would have seen that he brewed poison in his heart—the poison that would make him insult his brothers and their wife.

Gandhari, you cannot deny that our son indulged in disgraceful and irreligious activities, but neither of us could do a thing, because we were sightless. The day you made the vow, you pledged not to support your blind husband, but to plunge his life into deeper darkness. I could no longer hope that my wife would be my true companion, the virtuous mother of my sons who would make my children see sense.

In your silence and sightlessness, our children continued to sin. There was no one to tell them off for their wrongdoings or show them the right path. I was congenitally blind, but why did you purposely choose disaster for our entire family?

Gandhari: Have you finished talking? Don't you want to insult your wife further? Maharaj, today, in the presence of the entire assembly, my husband has held me culpable for the destruction of his entire dynasty.

Duryodhana: Pitashree, how can you blame mother like this? She did everything she could for both you and us. We lacked nothing while growing up; she brought us up as princes deserved!

Dhritarashtra: Oh no, you lacked quite a lot, son. You missed developing a sense of shame, the power to distinguish between right and wrong. If your mother hadn't blindfolded herself, she would have seen your transformation from a human being to a demon. She might have been able to stop it!

Duryodhana: I disagree, Pitashree. Matashree always taught me to differentiate between the good and the bad. What I grew up to be, or the crimes I committed, are entirely my fault, not hers. You misunderstand, Pitashree.

Dhritarashtra: I have fathered one hundred children, Duryodhana. You may not understand, but I do! The values a child imbibes forever remain the responsibility of his parents. As your mother, Gandhari was duty-bound to have kept a watch over you. But she adamantly stuck to her vow and ignored everything that came in the way of her false pride. Gandhari, I still haven't got my answer. Even after I commanded you to, why didn't you take off your blindfold?

Chitragupta: Devi Gandhari, do you have an answer to this question?

Gandhari: No, Maharaj, I have no answers. I am deeply hurt by his unjust allegation and too numb to respond. But Maharaj, I do have a question for my husband. Do you permit me to address him?

Chitragupta: Yes.

Gandhari: Maharaj Dhritarashtra, you make a great noise about how you were blind since birth and couldn't change anything that took place in Hastinapur. But I want to ask you, Maharaj, how then did you consider yourself capable of being the king? Shouldn't the one who had been entrusted to handle the affairs of Hastinapur have more foresight and gumption than needing to turn to his advisor Vidur for everything? You were present in the room when that fateful game of dice was played. You may not have seen Draupadi's insult, but you knew of it. You heard her wails! But what did you do as the ruler of Hastinapur? You remained seated on your golden throne, not even embarrassed enough to ask a servant to escort you out of the chamber. I was sitting right by your side; never did I sense the slightest agony at the foul treatment our sons meted out to their brothers and sister-in-law. Forget your position as the king; couldn't you, as the father, have commanded your sons to stop? Couldn't you have accepted Sri Krishna's peace proposal? Forgive me, Maharaj Dhritarashtra, not only are you sightless, but you are also deaf and dumb!

Maharaj Chitragupta, in front of you is the powerful king

of a huge kingdom who could not change a thing. And yet the blame rests on his wife's blindfold—a blindfold she had put on only out of love and devotion. It was my husband who never stopped our sons from becoming scoundrels. I, on the other hand, did everything in my power both as a wife and as a mother. His allegation is absolutely untrue.

Chitragupta: Devi Gandhari, I am afraid I have to agree with Maharaj Dritarashtra. I understand that you blindfolded yourself to fulfil your duties as a wife. But you also had responsibilites as a mother—duties that were equally important. Had you not blindfolded yourself, you could have taken an active part in raising your sons to become upright and honourable men. You could have protected the future of Hastinapur, but you chose to stick to your pride. I adjudge that you have undoubtedly been inadequate in bringing up your children.

Duryodhana: No, Maharaj, I maintain that she brought us up very well! We had an excellent childhood—at least until the Pandavas arrived. My father may have grudges against my mother, but as her eldest son, I can vouch that she never skimped on her responsibility as a mother.

Chitragupta: Devi Gandhari, your son continues to blame the Pandavas for everything that went wrong in his life. He doesn't stop to think that it was he who could have been at fault. Consider this an example of how your children were brought up. I have noted in my book that this allegation against you is true. Your sons have never shown ethical conduct, and the blindfold around your eyes has undoubtedly played a part. What happened to Hastinapur can, of course, not be wholly attributed to you. But I have to say that you, along with Maharaj Dhritarashtra, were both responsible in no small measure.

Gandhari: I accept your decision, Maharaj.

Chitragupta: I will now proceed to the next allegation against you. Your sister-in-law, Devi Kunti, has alleged that you misbehaved with her. You denied her what was rightfully hers.

Gandhari: What untruths! I have always taken great care of my sister.

Kunti: Yes, Didi, I will tell the whole assembly about how lovingly you cared for me.

Gandhari: Why are you speaking so bitingly to me, Kunti? When has there been any discord between us?

Kunti: Didi, do you remember the day I came to your palace with my five sons? I had just lit the funeral pyre of my husband, Maharaj Pandu.

Gandhari: Of course, I remember, Kunti.

Kunti: Do you also remember the grand welcome you gave me? Well, I don't know about you, but I have never forgotten my entry into that palace, which was as much mine as yours. I had been the wife of the King of Hastinapur, hadn't I, Didi? Can you recall the treatment you gave to a royal widow?

FLASHBACK

Kunti: This had been my chamber, Didi—

Gandhari: Could you help me be seated, Kunti? So, what were you saying? Oh, about the chamber—yes, I know it had been yours, but you see, it is close to my husband's courtroom. I figured it made sense to make this my chamber so I can be with my husband for the greater part of the day.

Kunti: It doesn't matter, Didi. I am fortunate that you chose to live in my chamber. So, should I move my things to your former chamber?

Gandhari: Oh no, I have given it to Duryodhana.

Kunti: Then where should my sons and I live?

Gandhari: Don't worry, Kunti. I have chosen excellent chambers for you quite close to the palace. It is a reasonably large room, and I am sure you and your sons will be happy there.

Kunti: Won't we live in this palace?

Gandhari: What kind of talk is this? Of course, the palace also belongs to you. It is your very own. I have been awaiting my sister-in-law's arrival for a long time! By the way, Kunti, did I tell you about the maids of Hastinapur? You won't believe how much they shirk their duties; not a thing gets done properly in the palace! Now that you are here, you will need to come to the palace every morning and show the maids how to work correctly. I will finally get to rest, for my sister will take over everything, won't she?

Kunti: Yes, Didi. May I take my leave now?

Gandhari: Wait, Kunti! It is almost lunch time. Why don't you go to the kitchen and see if the cooks are doing their work properly? Like the maids, our cooks are also big-time work shirkers!

Kunti: All right, I will go to the kitchen and check on them.

Gandhari: My dear Kunti, you are happy to have returned to Hastinapur, aren't you?

Kunti: Yes, Didi, I am happy.

END OF FLASHBACK

Kunti: It wasn't me who was happy, Didi; it was you! You were over the moon, weren't you, to have gotten a new maid? You ensured that I was hard at work in the palace for the entire day, day after day. Maharaj Pandu had already wrested from me the right of being the Maharani of Hastinapur. But you took away even my right of being the bride of a royal clan. Doesn't that qualify as misbehaviour, Didi?

Gandhari: I am shocked, Kunti. So much venom, so much hatred you nurture in your heart for me! When you came to Hastinapur, I was genuinely pleased I would get to spend time with my sister. I was always affectionate towards you. How thick-skinned are you that my love could never warm your heart?

Kunti: How *could* it, Didi, when behind your apparent affection was a thinly-masked insult? You made it clear from the very first day that my place in Hastinapur wouldn't be that of a queen. The message was that I shouldn't even dare to think of myself as your equal!

Gandhari: I now understand how Yudhishthira grew up to become so lustful for the throne. It was you, Kunti, who poisoned your son's ears! In your lullabies at night, you sang to them of greed and envy. Together you hatched plans to snatch the throne from my son!

Yudhishthira: Badi Ma, I urge you not to speak to Matashree in this manner. Please do not sully her good name, for she has never committed that which you accuse her of.

Gandhari: Indeed, Kunti, you have instilled excellent values in your sons. They cannot hear anything against you. But what this Dharmaraj Yudhishthira, this epitome of wisdom, doesn't realize is that you manipulated his mind since his childhood. You kept goading him to take over the throne; you continuously bemoaned the injustice I, apparently, had done to you. It pained you terribly to see me living in your former chamber—so much so that you wanted the entire palace for yourself! Listen to yourself, sister. Before blaming me for 'depriving' you of your rights, pause and assess the envy that has eternally plagued you and your family!

Chitragupta: Devi Kunti, do you have any evidence to support your allegations?

Gandhari: I am sure she doesn't, Maharaj. How can she have any evidence when what she is saying is grossly untrue?

Chitragupta: Devi Kunti, I am asking you for the last time: Is your allegation supported by any tangible evidence?

Kunti: Forgive me, Maharaj, but I was trying to recall something. Didi, do you remember Mrignayani, the maid who had come with you from Gandhar?

Gandhari: Of course, I remember her. But how is she connected to the proceedings of today's assembly?

Kunti: She didn't intend to be connected to anything that is going on here, Didi. But there was a day when she made a mistake. Her tongue slipped, and she told me of my real position in Hastinapur.

FLASHBACK

Kunti: Mrignayani, why haven't you prepared Didi's meal yet?

Mrignayani: What on Earth are you talking about? And who are you to inquire about my work?

Kunti: Mrignayani, watch your words. Go and prepare Didi's meal; she must be waiting for it.

Mrignayani: Go and prepare it yourself! Don't bother me.

Kunti: Maid, you forget whom you are addressing!

Mrignayani: Indeed I haven't forgotten. I am talking to a maid.

Kunti: Hasn't anyone ever taught you to control your tongue? Do you want me to show you? I am not sure you will like my methods.

Mrignayani: You might reprimand me how you like, Kunti, but how many people will you silence? All the servitors and maids of the palace know that you are nothing but another maid of our Maharani. If you hadn't been a maid, you would have been living in this palace and not in a hovel in the wilderness!

Kunti: Did Didi say all this to you?

Mrignayani: She's not doing anything wrong. She is the Maharani and is older than you. She can order about her widowed sister-in-law as she pleases. Quit staring, Kunti, and go to the kitchen to prepare her lunch. You wouldn't want the queen to be hungry, would you? She might throw you out of that dingy room you call your home!

END OF FLASHBACK

Kunti: That day, I clearly saw the crookedness that lay hidden beneath your show of love and affection. I was nothing more than your servant. You had become so used to being addressed as 'Maharani' that my very presence unnerved you. It was impossible for you to see me happy, for you constantly feared I would take over your coveted position as the queen of the land. Maharaj, I have nothing else to say. If you permit me, I would like to return to my seat.

Chitragupta: Devi Gandhari, do you have anything to say?

Gandhari: No, Maharaj. Perhaps Kunti's allegation is true. It never occurred to me that it would be so painful for a sister-in-law to perform her duties towards the household. I assumed ever so wrongly that it would bring her joy to serve her elders. But such values had never been taught to her, poor thing. It wasn't her fault but mine for making such assumptions about her character.

Chitragupta: Devi Gandhari, I can distinctly hear the mockery and disdain in your words. Your behaviour justifies Devi Kunti's allegation. This is the first time the assembly has seen someone prosecuting herself. I feel compelled to accept this allegation against you as legitimate.

Gandhari: I am not surprised, Maharaj. Today, every allegation levelled against me will be validated. No one remains to feel the slightest affection for me.

Dushasana: Matashree, don't say that! I am here for you, and so is Bhaiya Duryodhana. In this Dharmakshetra, you are the most genuine person I know. You have never hurt a fly; there is no venom in your heart.

Arjuna: Dushasana, do you even know your mother? Have you forgotten the unholy crime she committed driven only by the angst and the poison in her heart? No one on Earth has committed a greater sin than that, not even you and your brothers!

Gandhari: Arjuna, my son, I beg you not to remind the court of my single most damaging mistake. I am truly apologetic even though I know an apology can hardly suffice. Cast any allegations you want in my direction but pray, don't bring that up!

Arjuna: Why shouldn't I bring it up, Badi Ma? You admit that it was the gravest crime of your life. How can I let it go unpunished in this Dharmakshetra?

Chitragupta: Devi Gandhari, I know you are cognizant of the crime Arjuna is referring to. For everyone else in the assembly, I will read out the last allegation against you. Devi Gandhari is accused of cursing Sri Krishna and his entire clan with imminent death.

Duryodhana: What?! Matashree, is this true?

Arjuna: Yes, Duryodhana, it is wholly true. My friend Sri Krishna did not touch a single weapon during the Kurukshetra War. He strengthened your army with his Narayani soldiers. He brought you a peace proposal so the war could be averted in the first place. And yet, he was devilishly cursed by your mother.

FLASHBACK

Draupadi: Arjuna, you have returned from Dwarka! How is your friend? You told him, didn't you, that I am angry with him? It has been days since the battle, but he hasn't turned up even once to meet me!

Arjuna: He couldn't, Panchali.

Draupadi: Well, take me with you the next time you go to meet him.

Arjuna: There is nothing left there anymore. Nothing at all.

Draupadi: What?! What do you mean? Arjuna, please tell me; you are petrifying me!

Arjuna: Draupadi, the entire Yadu clan has been destroyed. All the men have died. The whole of Dwarka sank into the ocean and now rests in the abyss. Not even the ruins remain on the ground.

Draupadi: But how did all this happen?

Arjuna: I don't know, Draupadi, but I hear that the men fought amongst themselves and killed each other. Only the women and children remain; I have brought them with me to Hastinapur.

Draupadi: And what about Keshava? Please don't tell me he—

Arjuna: He has left us, Panchali. He went away, leaving us all alone and misguided. Who knew he would go away like this, never to return?

END OF FLASHBACK

Arjuna: Keshava lost his entire clan only because of you, Badi Ma. How could you do such a thing?

Duryodhana: Matashree, for once I agree with Arjuna. Why did you do this?

Gandhari: I did it because I am a mother! I had lit the funeral pyres of all my sons. I was desolate and heartbroken. I was sinking into an ocean of sorrow, and I wanted to do the same to the man responsible for it all.

Arjuna: But how was Keshava responsible for anything? How could you curse him for no fault of his? You were protesting against Bhima's destruction of the entire Kuru clan, and yet you did the same to Keshava's kith and kin.

Sri Krishna: No, Arjuna, Badi Ma did not curse me recklessly. She wanted to curse me, and she had concrete reasons for doing so.

FLASHBACK

Gandhari: So, you have arrived in Hastinapur, Keshava? How does it feel? Are you insane with happiness yet?

Sri Krishna: Badi Ma—

Gandhari: Don't you dare to call me 'Ma'! My sons who would call me 'Ma' are all dead. They have left me alone in this world. I could not even find the corpses of some of them.

Sri Krishna: I can fathom your pain.

Gandhari: No, Keshava, you can't. You will fathom my grief only when you experience it yourself. I curse you, Sri Krishna, that just like you have destroyed my entire family, you will also witness the destruction of your entire clan. Every man in your clan will pick up arms, striking each other and bloodying the fields of Dwarka. You did not pick up weapons in the battle, did you, Keshava? So, I curse you that while all your loved ones will die, you won't breathe your last on the battlefield. Your death will be an ordinary if sorrowful one. This is a mother's curse, Keshava, and it will soon begin to unfold in front of your eyes.

Sri Krishna: I accept your curse, Badi Ma.

END OF FLASHBACK

Gandhari: Please forgive me, Keshava. Please forgive me.

Sri Krishna: No, Badi Ma, don't apologize. What you did was just.

Arjuna: Keshava, what are you saying? She cursed your entire family even though they had committed no ill!

Sri Krishna: Partha, Badi Ma cursed me for what she thought I did to her family. She, who had once been a princess, had been married off to a blind king. All her life, she remained blindfolded, oblivious to the path of sin that her children had adopted. As a mother, she lost all her children on the battlefield. What is more heartrending for a mother than the untimely death of not one but all her hundred sons? Today, Maharaj Chitragupta is doling out punishments in the Dharmakshetra, but few have suffered as much as Badi Ma. She grieved over and over and faced one agony after another, while still on Earth. I cannot blame her for thinking I was at fault. After all, I have always sided with the Pandavas, even during the Kurukshetra War.

Gandhari: It was my mistake, Keshava. Forgive me.

Sri Krishna: I had forgiven you the very instant you uttered the curse.

FLASHBACK

Sri Krishna: Badi Ma, I know you are aware of who I am. I am Keshava of Kurukshetra. The wounds inflicted on the warriors were actually inflicted on my own body. I was the one to lie on Pitamaha's bed of arrows. I was Duryodhana's broken thigh, Dushasana's shattered chest. I was the drape of Draupadi's saree and the blindfold around your eyes. Any disaster that strikes this era happens to me and wounds my very being.

Now that the Kurukshetra War is over and justice has been delivered, my purpose on Earth has been fulfilled. It is now time for me to leave, and I am grateful to you for giving me my freedom.

Badi Ma, I don't know when we will meet again. But when we do, there is something I will ask you to do. For now, I ask you to leave Hastinapur. There is nothing left for you here but pain.

END OF FLASHBACK

Sri Krishna: Maharaj, I request you not to punish Devi Gandhari for cursing me. She has already suffered her punishment, and I now ask you to free her of this charge.

Chitragupta: Devi Gandhari, all the allegations against you have now been addressed. I have considered your responses and assessed the motives of your actions. I judge that you are guilty of failing to teach your children the difference between ethical and unethical conduct. You also misbehaved with your sister-in-law, driven by vanity and pride that were perhaps unknown even to you. The future generations of Bharatvarsh will always consider you an example of what *not* to do as a wife, mother and sister-in-law. As for the last allegation, Sri Krishna has already forgiven you. I uphold his decision.

Gandhari: I accept the judgement, Maharaj.

Sri Krishna: Badi Ma, do you remember I had told you that the day we meet again, I would ask you for something?

Gandhari: I remember, Keshava. Whatever you ask me to do will be my command.

Sri Krishna: Badi Ma, I only ask you this: Take off your blindfold. You don't need to hide from the world anymore, for this is the Dharmakshetra, and here you will find only the truth. Keeping yourself blindfolded to sin will not prevent it, but choosing to look out for your children might. Let no mother ever again turn a blind eye to her duties towards her children in her pursuit to be a loyal wife.

8

YUDHISTHIRA

FLASHBACK

Yudhishthira: Bhima, Arjuna, wake up! Why can't you hear me? Nakula, Sahadev, get up! Doesn't my voice reach your ears?

Yaksha: They won't get up, Dharmaraj.

Yudhishthira: What?! And who are you?

Yaksha: I am you, Dharmaraj. I am your inner being.

Yudhishthira: What do you want from me?

Yaksha: Don't you want to know how your brothers died? I can tell you.

Yudhishthira: They are not dead!

Yaksha: They are, Dharmaraj. And aren't you too dying of thirst? Don't you desperately want some water?

Yudhishthira: I do. But please tell me what happened to my brothers.

Yaksha: Well, I told your brothers that they could drink the water in this lake only if they answered my questions satisfactorily. But not one of them listened to me. What about you, Dharmaraj? Can you answer my questions? Only then will I allow you to drink this water. If you cannot, you too will die of thirst like your warrior brothers here. So, are you ready?

Yudhishthira: I am ready. There is no question I cannot answer.

END OF FLASHBACK

Yudhishthira: Please accept my respectful salutations, Maharaj.

Chitragupta: Welcome, Dharmaraj, to today's Assembly of Religion. Members of the assembly, let me warn you that today, you will witness something that hasn't happened here before. The court is about to experience something unprecedented. Dharmaraj Yudhishthira, you have been asked questions several times in your life, haven't you? But I am convinced that you remember that one day the best.

Yudhishthira: Yes, Maharaj. I'll never forget the day the Yaksha asked me questions at the lake. I had to answer his questions satisfactorily to bring my brothers back from their deaths. I was fortunate that the Yaksha was pleased with my responses.

Chitragupta: It is in the answers you gave that day that the allegations against you lie hidden.

Sri Krishna: Partha, in today's Dharmakshetra, allegations will be levelled against Dharmaraj—the man whose grasp over religious teachings cannot be rivalled by any human being. Listen carefully to the proceedings, for you will find a lot to learn.

Arjuna: But Keshava, what allegations could be levelled against Bhaiya? Anyhow, I am not worried. He is sure to have all the answers, for there's no man wiser than he is.

Sri Krishna: Knowledge is highly elusive, Arjuna. Sometimes it leaves you at the precise moment you need it the most.

Arjuna: I do not understand, Keshava.

Sri Krishna: Listen to the proceedings, Partha, and you will understand.

FLASHBACK

Yaksha: Here's your first question, Dharmaraj. Tell me: What is true forgiveness?

Yudhishthira: True forgiveness is to forget about the wrongdoings of your enemies in such a manner that you free yourself of inner conflict. Only when you forget the mistakes of your enemies—or the fact that mistakes were ever committed—have you understood the true meaning of forgiveness.

Yaksha: Dharmaraj, your answer is correct.

END OF FLASHBACK

Chitragupta: Yudhishthira, you had claimed that forgiving one's enemies was forgiveness in its purest form. In my court, the first allegation against you is that you lied while answering. Not only did you not practise what you preached, but it is also possible that you didn't understand the gravity of your own words. I call forth Maharaj Dhritarashtra to further explain this allegation to you.

Dhritarashtra: Pranaam, Maharaj.

Chitragupta: Maharaj Dhritarashtra, do you have any evidence to prove that Dharmaraj Yudhishthira does not know the meaning of the word 'forgiveness'?

Dhritarashtra: Maharaj, forgive me if I get incoherent, but answering questions during Duryodhana's trial drained my frail body and pained my heavy heart. It saddens me to stand here asking questions to Yudhishthira—

Chitragupta: Maharaj, Yudhishthira may be renowned the world over as Dharmaraj, but in this assembly, nobody can escape the need to account for all his earthly deeds. He will have to answer any question put across to him.

Dhritarashtra: Maharaj Chitragupta, I want to ask Yudhishthira only one question. Tell me, son, are you a Dharmaraj?

Yudhishthira: Yes, I am.

Dhritarashtra: That's what everyone believes. Even in your verbal match against the Yaksha, you turned out to be a genuine expert at religion. You declaimed that there is no greater form of forgiveness than forgetting the mistakes of your enemies. Dharmaraj, weren't my sons your biggest enemies?

Yudhishthira: Yes, Maharaj.

Dhritarashtra: Then why couldn't you forgive them, Yudhishthira? Why couldn't you abide by your teachings?

Duryodhana: Pitashree, what are you saying? There is no need to beg forgiveness for my brothers or me.

Dhritarashtra: Son, I am not begging for forgiveness now. I am referring to the period before the Kurukshetra War commenced.

Duryodhana: Do you mean that you had actually approached Dharmaraj before the war to beg for forgiveness? Did you prostrate before these lowdown people? Pitashree, I never knew you could be this weak! Now I understand why my soldiers were so cast down right from the start. If the Maharaj of Hastinapur himself wandered about in the enemy's tents, begging for forgiveness with his head down and his tail wagging, then how could the soldiers ever believe we could win the war?

Yudhishthira: Duryodhana, he is your father. Behave yourself.

Duryodhana: Dharmaraj, please focus on your trial. There is no need to tell me how I should behave towards my father.

Chitragupta: Dharmaraj, Maharaj Dhritarashtra has alleged that he went to you to ask for forgiveness, but you paid no heed. Is this true?

FLASHBACK

Yudhishthira: Pranaam, Maharaj. Why are you here so late at night?

Dhritarashtra: Tonight is the only night that is left. When tomorrow arrives, the rising sun will herald the destruction of my entire clan. Everything I hold dear will be burnt beyond recognition and lost to the world.

Yudhishthira: We don't want this war, Maharaj. You know we don't.

Dhritarashtra: But what are you doing about it? My sons are younger to you. They are your little brothers! Haven't you grown up playing together and fighting over toys? If they are pulling an infantile tantrum, shouldn't you, as the elder brother, understand and forgive them? I admit that Duryodhana hasn't ever been fair to you and your family. I also accept that it was a fatal mistake to reject the peace proposal—

Yudhishthira: The peace proposal?

Dhritarashtra: Don't you know about it at all?

Yudhishthira: I don't, Maharaj.

Dhritarashtra: Keshava had come to Hastinapur a few days back with a proposal of peace. But Duryodhana rejected it. It is a thing of the past, son, forget it. Today's reality is that the soldiers on both sides are ready for battle. My son and his friends are developing war strategies. Even though morning will soon be here, the night of my life gets darker than ever. No one cares about the devastating pain in the heart of a father.

Yudhishthira: Maharaj, my mother's plight is the same. But what can I do now? It is not possible to retreat from this battle.

Dhritarashtra: I don't know anything, son, except that I cannot endure this agony anymore. What is worse for a father than the prospect of his sons' imminent deaths? Try to feel my pain, Dharmaraj, and forgive Duryodhana.

Yudhishthira: Maharaj—

Dhritarashtra: Don't start this battle, son. Don't let this war begin, for it will obliterate everything.

Yudhishthira: Maharaj, please don't weep.

Dhritarashtra: I know, son, that my behaviour does not befit a king. Standing front of you today is not a monarch, but your father's older brother. I implore you to forgive my son Duryodhana. Your forgiveness can save my family from being wiped off the face of the Earth.

END OF FLASHBACK

Dhritarashtra: Yudhishthira, a helpless old man was begging in front of you. If you had even a shred of the forgiveness you taught the world about, you would have accepted my plea. Everyone believed that there was no one in the universe with a greater understanding of religion than you. Why didn't you accept my plea, Yudhishthira? Did you fail miserably when it came to applying your vast ocean of knowledge to decisions in your own life? Anyone can preach, son, but it is in embracing these teachings ourselves that true greatness lies. Why are you silent, Yudhishthira?

Duryodhana: Pitashree, I am severely disappointed in you. Did you feel no shame in demeaning yourself like a common beggar in front of this man? Yudhishthira, you know the elders of my family have always adored you. Couldn't you have done what my father requested so very humbly?

Yudhishthira: Duryodhana, I have always respected your father. He has the right to ask me anything, and I will be duty-bound to answer. My brothers and I fought a battle with you and your brothers; we never had any enmity with your father. I request you not to interrupt the proceedings while I respond to his allegation.

Maharaj Dhritarashtra, in front of you today is neither the Puru Samrat nor the son of your younger brother. I stand facing you only as a sincere servitor of religion. My answer to you today will be unaffected by social or familial relationships; it will emanate only from the truth. Maharaj, you alleged in front of the assembly that you came to me and pleaded for forgiveness. But what you did not reveal was my answer to you.

FLASHBACK

Yudhishthira: No, Maharaj, I am afraid I cannot help you today. I am left with no choice but to wage this war, not because it pleases me, but because it is the demand of my faith.

Dhritarashtra: What religion compels you to kill your family members? I am sure no religion dictates or supports murder.

Yudhishthira: Tell me, Maharaj—who is really my own? Mata Gandhari is my own, isn't she? But her sons have always conspired to kill my brothers and me. If brothers hatch murderous plans, can they be called your own? Did you know that your sons once plotted to have my mother killed? You didn't plead with Duryodhana when he rejected the peace proposal that I didn't know about, but would have willingly upheld. Don't you think it is too late for your plea of forgiveness?

Dhritarashtra: But son, haven't you always believed in forgiving your enemies? Doesn't your religion teach you that?

Yudhishthira: Yes, religion dictates that forgiveness is a virtue. But Maharaj, I also have to fulfil the diktats of an even greater religion: that of a son. I have to fight this war not because I covet the throne of Hastinapur or even Indraprastha. I would be content to live with the sages in a small cottage in the wilderness. But for the sake of my mother, who staked her own life—who could have breathed her last in the fire of enmity between the Pandavas and the Kauravas—I have to charge into battle.

Dhritarashtra: So, you are saying you will let your love for your mother overtake your true religion. I thought you didn't let anything come in the way of—

Yudhishthira: No, Maharaj, true religion is that which directs you towards true duty. For me, true duty is in fighting this war. It would be irreligious to retreat from a war that we are fighting to avenge what your sons did to me, to my brothers, to the kingdom that was rightfully ours, and above all, to my mother. I am powerless to commence or close this battle. If you want to plead for forgiveness, I recommend you talk to my mother. Her tent is close to mine. I promise, Maharaj, that if my mother forgives you, I will retreat from Kurukshetra at sunrise tomorrow. All my troops will go with me, and the battle will no longer ensue.

END OF FLASHBACK

Yudhishthira: Did you get your answer, Maharaj?

Dhritarashtra: I should have known, Dharmaraj. You were sure to spin your typical webs with words and persuade the assembly that you are innocent.

Yudhishthira: No, Maharaj, I don't intend to speak anything but the truth. I never have. When the Yaksha had asked me the meaning of forgiveness, I had told him that forgiving even the greatest sin of your enemies was forgiveness in its purest form. You could forgive completely only if you could extinguish all inner turmoil and forget that a sin had ever been committed. While all of you enthusiastically stuck to the first part of my answer, claiming that 'enemies must be forgiven', what about the inner turmoil that plagues both the sinner and the one who must pardon the sin? Maharaj, haven't you experienced this turmoil within your heart?

Dhritarashtra: I don't know what you mean, Dharmaraj.

Yudhishthira: You do, Maharaj. There were plenty of times when I could observe palpable tension on your face. You sat wondering: Should I stop the game of dice or let my sons continue the horrifying series of deceptions? Will I have to hand over Hastinapur to the Pandavas?

Breaking free from inner turmoil isn't straightforward; it is a task that even saints have struggled to achieve. For many years, turmoil haunted my mind and plagued my body. I had seen my little brothers lacerated by the insults they had to face; I had watched my wife sob quietly at night, her tresses loose and unruly, and tears flowing ceaselessly. But never had I done a thing to console them. Nothing at all had I done for those who loved me and obeyed every command I gave!

That night, too, when you came to meet me, I was struggling with my inner being. I asked myself constantly if this war must be fought. Wasn't there a righteous middle path that wouldn't involve warfare? But you know the truth; there wasn't. When you pleaded with me, the voice of my soul said: This is the only opportunity you will get to avenge your family's humiliation. Don't let it go. And so I didn't, Maharaj. Even if I had called off the war and handed over the kingdom of Hastinapur to the Kauravas, Duryodhana would have known no peace as long as all of us were breathing. Our clan was embroiled in hatred and envy to such a degree that only the rancour of chariots on the battlefield could douse the flames.

By fighting the war, Maharaj Dhritarashtra, I freed myself from the turbulence that had been wreaking havoc in my heart for many years. Perhaps I could have accepted your plea, but then, I would have failed myself. I found my pardon when I decided to fight, and history will agree that few were more in need of mercy than I was. True forgiveness comes when you can forgive yourself, for how can one who bears a load of guilt ever be light-hearted enough to forgive another?

Dhritarashtra: Well, I wish you the delight of a light heart, Dharmaraj. But I assure you, you and my son Duryodhana will always be held equally responsible for the Battle of Kurukshetra. No religion in the world will forgive you, even if Maharaj Chitragupta does. The battleground that you bloodied had perpetrated no sin, nor had it entrusted you with the right to punish the guilty. You will live with regret in every lifetime of yours, and the innocent people who died because of you will never let your inner self find the elusive peace it sought so eagerly.

Chitragupta: Maharaj, you may now take your seat. For the second allegation against Yudhishthira, I summon Devi Kunti to come forward.

Arjuna: Ma, you won't go anywhere. I won't let you.

Kunti: I have to, son. Don't assume that I am here to contest anything that Yudhishthira has done, for any mother would be blessed to have a righteous son like him. But I have to seek his pardon for something I once did—something he has never forgiven me for. I would hate to see my son carry a grudge against his mother even after leaving the mortal world.

Sri Krishna: Arjuna, you have no right to stop your mother. You are a spectator in this court today. Mata Kunti must divulge her truth, as there is no other path to find peace.

Chitragupta: Dharmaraj, do you remember the second question the Yaksha had asked you?

FLASHBACK

Yaksha: Which religion reigns supreme on Earth?

Yudhishthira: The supreme religion on Earth and beyond is kindness.

Yaksha: Dharmaraj, your answer is correct.

END OF FLASHBACK

Chitragupta: You had responded that kindness was the greatest religion on Earth and beyond. And yet, you have been unable to forgive your mother, Kunti. The next allegation levelled against you, Dharmaraj, is that you are a heartless son.

Arjuna: Matashree, why have you made this allegation? When has Bhaiya ever been anything but kind and loving towards you?

Kunti: Your brother knows, son. He also knows that my heart is heavy with the sorrow he caused me on the last day of the war. Since then, he hasn't even met my eyes; he avoids looking at me, let alone addressing a single kind word to his mother.

FLASHBACK

Arjuna: Bhaiya, do you know what Matashree is saying? She wants to leave Hastinapur and live in a forest!

Bhima: Yes, Bhaiya, she is leaving the palace now. Why don't you say something? Stop her!

Yudhishthira: Matashree, have you made up your mind? Won't you live here with us?

Kunti: I have made up my mind, son.

Yudhishthira: Matashree has always been firm in her decisions. If she wants to leave, we must not stop her.

END OF FLASHBACK

Arjuna: Matashree, I still don't know what made you decide to live in the forest. Did something happen that forced you to move far away from all of us?

Kunti: Tell your brothers, Yudhishthira.

Yudhishthira: I was upset with Matashree for hiding the truth about Karna, our elder brother. It is true that I had suspected it for some time, but my suspicions had no evidence to support them. If she had told me before the battle that he was the eldest Pandava, I would have ensured that he remained alive. Matashree would have all her sons with her after the war.

Karna: Dharmaraj, she did not tell anybody that I was her son. It wasn't just you from whom she hid this truth about her life.

Kunti: Yes, I had told no one, Yudhishthira. I can understand it must have disturbed you, but did you have to mete out such a harsh punishment? Couldn't you have shown pity towards your mother and forgiven her? Especially when you already suspected it? I was a heartbroken woman when you came to inform me of Karna's death, but you didn't stop to think about my sorrow before lashing out at me. Arjuna too had been disturbed when Sri Krishna himself lit Karna's funeral pyre. But his grief did not amount to forgetting his mother. Why were you so heartless, son?

FLASHBACK

Yudhishthira: Pranaam, Matashree! You will be happy to know that we are closer to victory than ever. In today's battle, Karna was killed. Isn't that splendid news?

Kunti: How can you be so calm? How can you break this news to me with a smile on your face? Don't pretend you don't know anything!

Yudhishthira: What, Matashree?

Kunti: Karna was my son, Yudhishthira. He was your elder brother, the eldest Pandava. He was my firstborn son, and today he lies dead on the battlefield.

Yudhishthira: What?! Matashree, you shock me. It is true that I had suspected a fondness in your heart for Karna; you always looked hurt whenever his name was taken. You were plagued by thoughts of the lonely, neglected life he led after his mother abandoned him. But I would tell myself that it was my imagination gone haywire. Why didn't you tell me, Matashree? How could you keep this from me?

Kunti: What else was I to do? You know Karna is the son

of the Sun God. He came to me in the form of a blessing when I was still an unmarried woman. How could I accept him as my son? The society would have despised both of us and treated us as outcasts. I would have brought great disgrace to the clan!

Yudhishthira: I don't want to hear anything, Matashree. I cannot even raise my voice in front of you because I am your son. But if only I could—

Kunti: What, Yudhishthira? Tell me. Come out with whatever is in your mind.

Yudhishthira: Henceforth, Devi Kunti, you are no longer my mother.

END OF FLASHBACK

Kunti: Your words cut through my skin, son. Never has any son punished his mother quite so severely. That day, I lost not one but two of my sons.

Bhima: Matashree, is Bhaiya's behaviour the reason you left Hastinapur after our victory?

Kunti: Yes, son, I could not stand facing him again. His words rang in my ears day and night. If the son I had loved with all my heart and guarded with my life could disown me, what remained in my life? Ask your brother if he even flinched when I left. I am sure he didn't.

Yudhishthira: No, Matashree. I didn't. But I never asked you to leave Hastinapur. That was solely your decision.

Kunti: You may not have asked me to leave in as many words, but you left me with no option. I could not live with you and face you every day, knowing that you despised me. Our relationship had always been one of love and affection; how could I watch it turn coarse and bitter with every passing day?

Chitragupta: Dharmaraj, it was you who had told the Yaksha that kindness reigned supreme over all other religions. But when you had to become the bigger person and forgive your mother with kindness, you failed to rise to the occasion. You did not understand her agony but left her writhing in pain. Didn't your decision to disown your mother go against your religion?

Yudhishthira: No, Maharaj. How could I garner forgiveness for a mother who kept me away from my eldest brother? I had grown up looking after my little brothers. I never knew my father; I had to grow up before my time so that my brothers could find a father in me. The idea of being sheltered by a father or an elder brother was my distant and impossible dream; the delights of childhood could never warm my heart. While my brothers would play about in the Gurukul, I would always be anxious about my duties and whether I was fulfilling them adequately. I had to keep a watch over Duryodhana, who started hatching plans against us even when he was only a young boy. I would console Bhima, Arjuna, my mother, but did anyone ever enquire what I was going through? No! My happiness was meaningless; my life's purpose was to fend for my family. Who cared if Yudhishthira ever got an opportunity to laugh and make merry?

All that could have been different, Maharaj, had my mother told me of Karna, my elder brother. Karna would have been there to look after me. Let me ask my brothers: have any of you ever come up to me and asked, 'Bhaiya, can we help you in any way?' No! When I was only a child, I was fed with notions of the royal palace, the throne, and how I would have to grow up and capture it. Had Karna been a part of my life, I too could have experienced what freedom and happiness meant.

When I disowned you, Matashree, it was not me talking; it was the thorn I had grown up with. The overwhelming burden of responsibilities had deeply embedded the thorn in my flesh, and that day, I pulled it out. Maharaj, I have nothing further to say in response to this allegation. I am ready to accept whatever judgement you decide is just.

Chitragupta: I will announce my judgement only after all the allegations against you have been heard.

Karna: I am curious. Don't you even look at your mother anymore?

Yudhishthira: Karna, I haven't solicited your advice on how to behave with my mother.

Karna: Yudhishthira, didn't you just give a long speech about how you would have loved to have an elder brother? Let me tell you: having an elder brother isn't only about freedom; it is also about obedience and respect. If you cannot learn to pay attention to my advice, perhaps you didn't deserve to have me as your elder brother.

Yudhishthira: Maharaj, I request you to read out the next allegation against me.

Chitragupta: Dharmaraj, I want you to think about the third question that Yaksha had posed to you. Can you recall it?

Yudhishthira: Yes, Maharaj. He had asked me, 'Who can truly be called wealthy?'

Chitragupta: What was your reply?

Yudhishthira: I told him, 'The one who has no desire can truly be called wealthy.'

Chitragupta: If you believe in what you say, Dharmaraj, you are stricken by poverty.

Yudhishthira: I don't understand, Maharaj.

Chitragupta: I summon Rani Draupadi to come forward to levy the next allegation against you. She has alleged that even though you knew she was the wife of all the Pandavas, you nestled desire for her in your heart. You wanted her to be yours alone.

Sahadeva: Nakula Bhaiya, I do not understand. Draupadi was Yudhishthira Bhaiya's wife; what was his crime in desiring her?

Nakula: Sahadev, Draupadi feels that Yudhishthira Bhaiya wanted her to be his wife alone. The fact that she was also our wife and had been won at the swayamvar by Arjuna Bhaiya agitated him.

Yudhishthira: Draupadi, I don't believe you. You are my wife, aren't you? What is wrong in desiring you?

Draupadi: I knew you would say this, Dharmaraj. But I am not talking about our marital relations. I am talking about a time when we weren't married—a time when you lusted after me from afar. You know what I mean, don't you?

Arjuna: Bhima, has Draupadi lost her mind? What made her feel that Bhaiya lusted after her? Did he ever propose marriage to her that we don't know of?

Bhima: I don't know, Arjuna. Panchali would always confide in me. I would be privy to all her secrets. But it seems there was a part of her that I didn't even know existed.

Yudhishthira: Please explain yourself, Draupadi. I am completely clueless.

Draupadi: Do you remember when Arjuna brought me home to Mata Kunti after winning me at the swayamvar? Matashree was cooking lunch, and her back faced all of us. Without turning, she ordered that whatever Arjuna had brought home should be divided equally among all five of you. Do you remember, Dharmaraj?

Yudhishthira: Of course, I remember.

Draupadi: Didn't your religion have any diktat that prohibited the division of a woman among five men as if she were a household commodity? You didn't say a word against Mata Kunti's order!

Yudhishthira: It was my mother's command, Draupadi. I couldn't go against it.

Draupadi: No, Dharmaraj. I will tell you why you didn't protest. It was because you wanted to marry me! You desired me ever since you saw me at the swayamvar. When Mata Kunti ordered all of you to share me, you were the happiest man alive.

Yudhishthira: That is untrue, Draupadi! I only married you because mother commanded it.

Draupadi: So, are you saying you did not desire me? Didn't you love me, then?

Yudhishthira: I did love you, Draupadi. But I fell in love with you after we got married.

Draupadi: I refuse to accept this, Dharmaraj. I am a woman, and women have excellent intuition when it comes to understanding emotions.

Chitragupta: Dharmaraj, do you have any evidence to prove that Rani Draupadi's allegation is untrue?

Yudhishthira: Maharaj, I have always obeyed my elders. I am a man who unfailingly respects his seniors—especially his mother. I cannot offer any evidence because this is part of my very being.

Chitragupta: Dharmaraj, in the Dharmakshetra, decisions are never taken without considering evidence—or the lack of it. Rani Draupadi, do you have any evidence for your allegation?

Draupadi: Maharaj, I have already said that I have sound intuition. I could sense his conflicted emotions from the way he looked at me. Arjuna never had any time for me, while Bhima's life revolved around my happiness. As for Nakula and Sahadev, they were always in awe of everything I said. But Dharmaraj would never be consistent in his behaviour towards me. Sometimes I would catch him staring at me, while at other times he steadily looked away even when I tried to meet his gaze.

Chitragupta: But didn't this happen after you were married to the five Pandavas? It doesn't prove Dharmaraj guilty of nurturing a selfish desire for you even when he knew you were the wife to all his brothers.

Draupadi: No, Maharaj, I can prove that his desire for me was selfish. I told you I take great pride in my intuition, and I have reason to believe that his feelings for me date back to before our wedding.

Chitragupta: Please explain at length, Rani Draupadi.

Draupadi: Maharaj, after I took all the five Pandavas as my husbands, we encountered a problem. Who would have rights over me and for how long? It was unthinkable that I could perform my wifely duties to all of them at the same time. Dharmaraj came up with a suggestion: each Pandava would be my husband for one year, starting with Dharmaraj himself, for he was the eldest brother. He further announced that anyone who broke the rule would have to miss his turn; the lost year would automatically get added to Dharmaraj's turn. Tell me, Maharaj: was this decision fair? Shouldn't Arjuna have had the first right over me because it was he who had won the swayamvar?

Chitragupta: I will pronounce my judgement after all the allegations are complete.

Draupadi: Anyhow, Maharaj, I accepted Dharmaraj's decision. One night during that first year, Dharmaraj and I were in our chambers. For some reason I cannot remember now, Arjuna had to enter our chambers. Dharmaraj was infuriated; he declared that Arjuna had infringed the law and would be banished from the house. He lost his time with me while Dharmaraj continued to be my husband. In fact, he did everything in his power to ensure that Arjuna and I did not spend time together. The next time it was Arjuna's turn, he sent him away to gather weapons! Am I lying, Dharmaraj? Is this not true?

Yudhishthira: Yes! It is true! I have loved you since the first time I saw you. I admit that it was not my place to feel envious of my younger brother, but what could I do? It pained me no end that Arjuna had won you over, not me. I wanted you to be my very own.

Draupadi: Thank you for speaking the truth, Dharmaraj. I will grant you that you took great care of me as your wife. You have always looked after my comfort. It was because of you that I became the Queen of Indraprastha, the Rani of Hastinapur. But your all-consuming desire turned around the direction of my life. If you had wanted, you could have explained to your mother how it was sinful to divide a woman in five portions. But your silence changed my life as I knew it.

Chitragupta: Dharmaraj, I need your statement for my record: do you admit that this allegation levelled against you is true?

Yudhishthira: Yes, Maharaj. Draupadi's allegation is true. But if you permit, I want my sentence for this crime to be delivered by Draupadi, not you.

Draupadi: What punishment can I possibly give you, Dharmaraj? All I desire is that men learn to understand a woman's emotions, that they consider her feelings before projecting their own over her life. While desire and love can bring great joy, they can also cause great destruction. I forgive you, Dharmaraj. Whatever your motivation might have been, your love for me was pure and true.

Chitragupta: Thank you, Rani Draupadi; you may now take your seat. Dharmaraj, to read aloud your next allegation, I want to summon Acharya Dronacharya, the Acharya of Hastinapur.

Drona: Pranaam, Maharaj. Arjuna, why do you look perturbed? I dislike seeing lines of anxiety on your forehead. Are you worried that I will ask your brother such questions to which he will have no answer?

Arjuna: No, Acharya. I am worried because I know that anyone who argues with my brother over matters of religion is certain to lose. I cannot bear to see you defeated.

Arjuna: Maharaj Yudhishthira, the next allegation against you is the sin of lying on the battlefield. Guru Dronacharya has alleged that in response to his question, you spoke an untruth. Your lie was the reason he gave up his arms, soon after which Dhrishtadyumna killed him. Guru Drona, you may now address Yudhishthira.

Drona: Dharmaraj, can you tell me how many kinds of questions one can ask?

Yudhishthira: That's an odd thing to ask, Guru Drona. There can be various types of questions.

Drona: For instance?

Yudhishthira: For instance, some questions intend to find something—

Drona: Say, someone was to ask me, 'Acharya Drona, what are the names of your wife and son?' My answer would be, 'My wife's name is Kripi, and my son's name is Ashwatthama.' Is that right?

Yudhishthira: Yes, Acharya.

Drona: Then there are questions that can be answered only by a yes or a no. Isn't that true, Dharmaraj?

Yudhishthira: Yes.

Drona: For example, if someone enquired whether I was your Acharya, my answer would be a resounding yes. There would be no doubts, whispers or hidden meanings. You are the Dharmaraj, the master of all things religious. Was it so trying for you to answer my straightforward question in Kurukshetra with a yes or a no?

FLASHBACK

Drona: Yudhishthira, has Ashwatthama been killed?

Yudhishthira: Yes—*(a conch shell is blown loudly in the background)*—but not the man, the elephant.

END OF FLASHBACK

Drona: Don't pretend that you told me the truth. Your truth was shrouded in deception! In that noisy, tumultuous battlefield, how could you expect me to hear your half-whispered afterthought? Would I, Ashwatthama's father, ask about my son's fate or that of an elephant? I was distraught at that time because I feared the worst for my son; I hadn't either the energy or the inclination to listen to anything you said after the 'yes'.

Maharaj, it was widely believed that Dharmaraj, my most 'pious' disciple, was so religious that his chariot always remained afloat, never touching the surface of the battlefield. He was the most truthful of all the warriors. But after this barely-concealed lie, his chariot must have come crashing to the ground. Do you have any justification for what you did? Or should I assume your silence is your acceptance?

Chitragupta: Dharmaraj—

Drona: Don't address him as Dharmaraj! This man is so shameful that he lied through his hat even to his supposedly respected Guru!

Chitragupta: Acharya, I well know how to address whom in my court. Dharmaraj, do you wish to respond to Acharya Drona's allegation?

Yudhishthira: Maharaj, Acharya Drona just said that some questions demand objective answers. I too want to ask him a question whose answer I would need in a yes or a no. Am I permitted, Maharaj?

Chitragupta: Yes, you may ask your question.

Yudhishthira: Acharya Drona, I am sure you remember the *Chakravyuha* that the Kauravas constructed around Arjuna's son Abhimanyu. Were you a part of the plan too?

Drona: I was, but—

Yudhishthira: Please answer in a yes or a no, Acharya.

Drona: Yes.

Yudhishthira: All right. I have another yes-or-no question for you, Acharya. Arjuna is your disciple; some would say he is your favourite disciple. Does that mean you taught him everything you know?

Drona: Yes.

Yudhishthira: So, I assume there's nothing in the realm of warfare that remains unknown either to Arjuna or to you.

Arjuna: Keshava, what is Bhaiya talking about?

Sri Krishna: Your Bhaiya is winning.

Drona: Yudhishthira, I am failing to see your point. Where is your interrogation headed?

Yudhishthira: Acharya, you alleged that I spoke an untruth— that my delay in speaking the truth amounted to lying. I predicated my 'yes' with a subtext that you did not need. In response, I have one final question for you, Acharya.

Drona: What is it?

Yudhishthira: Do you know what the Brahmanand weapon is? Ah, you are silent. Let me direct the question to someone else. Arjuna, do you know about the Brahmanand weapon?

Arjuna: No, Bhaiya.

Yudhishthira: What about you, Duryodhana? I have a hunch you know which weapon I am referring to.

FLASHBACK

Drona: Look at this weapon, Duryodhana. It is called the Brahmanand. When I shoot it from my bow, Yudhishthira is certain to be captured.

Duryodhana: But Acharya, are you sure Arjuna won't have an antidote for this? In your teachings, you must have imparted Arjuna with the knowledge to counter all kinds of weapons.

Drona: That is between Arjuna and me, Duryodhana. I recommend you get some rest before the sun dawns on a new day. Tomorrow, I assure you, will be the final day of the war.

END OF FLASHBACK

Yudhishthira: Acharya, I don't need to tell you this, for you are our Guru and know everything there is to know about the art of warfare. The Brahmanand is not permissible in war, yet you wanted to use it to capture me. No warrior can counter the Brahmanand. If I hadn't spoken a delayed, whispered truth, I would never have been able to defeat you. You would have captured me, and that would have meant victory for the Kauravas. Not answering your question in a yes or a no was the only way to defeat you on the battlefield while remaining within the boundaries of truth. Maharaj, I have nothing further to say in response to Guru Drona's allegation. I can only implore you to thoroughly consider the motives behind my action before making your judgement.

Chitragupta: Dharmaraj, it is my duty to consider all the arguments presented in my court. After listening to you, I have concluded that what you said to Guru Drona on the battlefield was not an untruth. However, neither was it the truth. If you had wanted, you could have answered Dronacharya's question objectively, in which case you claim it would have been impossible to defeat him. I have noted the outcome of my consideration in my notebook: this allegation against you is not legitimate. Neither is it invalid. You spoke neither the truth nor a lie. Acharya, you may now take your leave.

Drona: Yes, Maharaj. I hope that the proceedings in your court today will teach our future generations to voice their truths clearly and succinctly. A truth without a voice is not very far from an untruth.

Yudhishthira: Maharaj, I request you to read out the next allegation against me.

Chitragupta: To announce the last allegation against you, Dharmaraj, I would like to call upon Maharaj Shalya.

Maharaj Shalya: Pranaam, Maharaj.

Chitragupta: Maharaj Shalya, I welcome you to my Assembly of Religion. Please introduce yourself to the attendees.

Maharaj Shalya: I am Shalya, the king of the state of Madra, the brother of Maharaj Pandu's wife Madri, and the maternal uncle of the Pandu princes Nakula and Sahadev.

Chitragupta: Maharaj Shalya missed sharing a key aspect of his introduction. On the seventeenth day of the Kurukshetra War,

Maharaj Shalya became the Chieftain of the Kaurava soldiers. He was killed during the battle by Maharaj Yudhishthira; his was the only death at the hands of Dharmaraj. And yet, before he became the Chieftain, Maharaj Shalya was only a charioteer; he drove the chariot of Angaraj Karna.

Shalya: Indeed I did. For days on end, I drove Karna's chariot like a man from a lowly caste, even though I should have been participating in the war!

Chitragupta: Angaraj, please come forward and tell us why you chose Maharaj Shalya as your charioteer even though he was the king of a large kingdom like Madra.

Karna: Maharaj, in any battle, the charioteer is a warrior's closest friend. Arjuna's charioteer was Sri Krishna himself! We too wanted someone as skilled as Sri Krishna to take on the important role of a charioteer.

Shalya: Important role, indeed! You and your best friend Duryodhana did it only to insult me. Maharaj, I was a Samrat; this low-caste son of a charioteer should have driven *me* around the battlefield!

Karna: I am displeased to see that the bitter sting of your words remains intact. Even during the Battle of Kurukshetra, all you did was shatter my confidence with your jibes.

Shalya: They weren't jibes. I only spoke the truth.

Chitragupta: I can see that the two of you know no better than to waste the time of my court with your verbal spats. I will tell Dharmaraj about his next allegation while you continue to quarrel like children.

Dharmaraj, the next charge against you is that you conspired with Maharaj Shalya to continually discourage Karna during the war. It was because of this conspiracy that Angaraj Karna kept getting more demoralized with each passing moment. Dharmaraj, you may not have killed anyone but Maharaj Shalya during the war, but it was your mental battle of nerves against Karna that changed the very course of history.

Karna: What?! All this while I was under the impression that Maharaj Shalya's barbed remarks emanated from his frustration. After all, Duryodhana and I had virtually forced him into becoming a charioteer.

FLASHBACK

Shalya: Karna, I heard that you used the Indrastra weapon against Ghatotkach. If this is true, I believe there is nothing that can now defeat Arjuna. It might be easier on you if you face him straight up and embrace your fate of certain death. It was Arjuna who laid Pitamaha on a bed of arrows, who single-handedly killed innumerable soldiers. Without the Indrastra, you have neither the ammunition nor the skill to defeat him in battle.

Karna: Are you suggesting I turn my back and flee?

Shalya: Well, I didn't suggest it, but it surely is an alternative to death. Sometimes I am incredibly proud of you, Angaraj. With what bravado you charge further into battle and march towards your death! I see no worry lines on your forehead, no tension headache wreaking pain on your temples. I admire you for being so nonchalant in accepting your imminent martyrdom!

Karna: Maharaj, I have heard enough!

Shalya: Angaraj, your charioteer begs your forgiveness. Come along; let's go. Kurukshetra awaits a great and honourable martyr.

END OF FLASHBACK

Chitragupta: Angaraj, it wasn't Maharaj Shalya who truly uttered remarks like that. It was Maharaj Yudhishthira speaking through him.

Karna: I am appalled! When you figured you couldn't defeat us or our forces, you tried to weaken us mentally? You made a man who had promised to be on our side double-cross us in times of need? Maharaj Chitragupta, I don't think the court needs to hear any more. Dharmaraj should lose his pious title; he is nothing but a sick fraud whose true nature is cheating!

Yudhishthira: Watch your words, Karna. What happened to you wasn't because of any conspiracy I hatched. You only have your friend Duryodhana to blame.

Karna: Don't speak gibberish. My friend would never hatch such evil, underhanded plans against me.

Shalya: How gullible you are! Let me tell you what this so-called friend of yours did. Do you remember how, after Duryodhana rejected the peace proposal and war became inevitable, both the Kauravas and the Pandavas started inviting friends and family members to join hands with them? I didn't need an invitation. I was the Pandavas' uncle; was there any doubt which side I would take in the war? But Duryodhana could not rest until he had embroiled me in quicksand. To help my nephews, I had to extend my support to the Kauravas instead! Surprised, aren't you?

FLASHBACK

Shalya: What a grand welcome my nephews have arranged for me! Go and tell them that I am pleased with all their arrangements of food and dwelling. I will do whatever they need me to do in the Kurukshetra War.

Servitor: Yes, Maharaj.

Duryodhana: Maharaj Shalya, I am glad that you appreciate the arrangements I made for you. I figured that since you have come here all the way from Madra, you must be tired. As your nephew, it is my duty to look after you, isn't it?

Shalya: Duryodhana! What are you doing here? Did you make all these arrangements?

Duryodhana: Of course it was me, Maharaj. Who did you think it was? That self-absorbed Yudhishthira? He couldn't care less about you! But it does not matter, Maharaj. You can sit back in this comfortable tent and enjoy the liquor I have got specially distilled for you.

Shalya: Duryodhana—

Duryodhana: What? Oh, were you going somewhere? Were you headed to the tents of the Pandavas? But didn't you just tell the servant that you promised to support the one who had made all these arrangements? I know you are one to keep your word, Maharaj. I welcome you to my army! With your help, we will take such good care of the Pandavas that even their corpses will shiver at my sight.

END OF FLASHBACK

Yudhishthira: Angaraj Karna, do you now see the scheme your friend hatched against the Pandavas? Would you call this swindling acceptable? Anything I did was merely in response to Duryodhana's connivance.

FLASHBACK

Yudhishthira: We have lost Mama Shalya's support. He will now fight for Duryodhana.

Arjuna: Not just him, Bhaiya, but his armies are also on Duryodhana's side. The Kauravas will now have eleven armies—that's a lot more than we can say for ourselves!

Yudhishthira: What worries me the most is that the Kauravas now have a charioteer as skilled as Mama Shalya. Everyone knows that few can match his skills at manoeuvring through the battlefield—perhaps no one but Keshava can rival him. Look, there's Mama Shalya.

Shalya: Yudhishthira, I am here to speak to you. I know you are worried because of that sly scheme Duryodhana somehow managed to pull off against me. He has my armies too; I have nothing left to give you, my dear nephews.

Arjuna: No, Mamashree, Bhaiya and I are not as anxious about losing your army as the fact that Duryodhana now has a skilled charioteer like you. You know how critical a charioteer is on the battlefield; he can be the difference between triumph and defeat.

Yudhishthira: Yes, I have a strong hunch that Duryodhana will ask you to be Karna's charioteer.

Shalya: What! I will NOT be the charioteer of that lowborn!

Sri Krishna: Maharaj, you have promised to help Duryodhana. You cannot refuse anything he asks of you.

Shalya: Yes, that is true. What should I do? Can't we do anything at all?

Yudhishthira: Mamashree, if Duryodhana asks you to be Karna's charioteer, go ahead and do it. Do not protest.

Shalya: But Yudhishthira—

Yudhishthira: Listen to me. Your soldiers might be with Duryodhana, but your words are more powerful than any army. They can inflict more damage than dozens of weapons put together.

Shalya: What do you mean?

Yudhishthira: Mamashree, you know that Keshava is going to be Arjuna's charioteer during the war. His words and support will make a tremendous difference to Arjuna, helping him plod along even when times are adverse. What you say to

Karna can also have a similar effect.

Shalya: Or they can have a devastating effect. I think I understand you now, Dharmaraj.

END OF FLASHBACK

Shalya: Anything I did to you during the battle, Karna, was merely in retaliation to how your friend cheated me. My nephew Yudhishthira cannot be blamed for it.

Chitragupta: Maharaj Shalya, I can understand the motives behind your biting words to Angaraj Karna. But today, it isn't you who is on trial; it is Dharmaraj. It seems evident to me that he manufactured the entire conspiracy to wage a mental battle against his enemy. His action transgressed the ethics of warfare.

Yudhishthira: No, Maharaj, I disagree. What I did wasn't a conspiracy; it was a war strategy. To win the war against evil, Arjuna's Gandiva and Bhima's mace weren't enough; we also needed intelligent planning. To be victorious, a king must vanquish his enemy both physically and mentally. My decision wasn't trickery; it was the duty of a monarch.

Maharaj, to date, no one has been able to prove that I have indulged in deception. Do you know why? It is because I *never* have! If anyone in this court wants to accuse me of being wily and fraudulent, I challenge him to come forward and attempt to prove it. I, Dharmaraj, have always walked along the path of *dharma*; it is my *dharma* that I wear as an amulet and hold in front of me as a shield.

Chitragupta: Maharaj Shalya, you may now leave the assembly.

Karna: Yes, please leave, Maharaj. It doesn't matter what your reasons were; you betrayed the duty of a charioteer. With the Pandavas was Sri Krishna, who always helped and guided them. But whom did I have? A charioteer who constantly found faults with me and dragged me deeper into despondency! You drove me to my death! Keshava, if I am a warrior in my next birth, I beseech you to be my charioteer. Please bless me with this honour.

Sri Krishna: Stay blessed, Angaraj Karna. It will be my honour.

Chitragupta: The allegations against Dharmaraj Yudhishthira are now at an end. Before I announce my judgement, is there anyone who wishes to speak? Come forth now or acquiesce to be silent forever.

Sri Krishna: Partha, there is only one thing that the Dharmaraj hasn't answered to in today's court. It rests deep within Bhima's heart.

Arjuna: But Keshava, what can Bhima Bhaiya possibly have against him?

Chitragupta: It seems no one wishes to address Dharmaraj with any further questions. It is now time for judgement.

Bhima: Please wait a moment, Maharaj!

Yudhishthira: Bhima?

Bhima: Bhaiya, there is something I have to ask you. It has been troubling me for a long time, and I will never get the opportunity to bring it up again.

Yudhishthira: Really, Bhima, now you too have allegations against me! There could be nothing that's sadder—

Bhima: No, no! The allegations against you are at an end. Didn't you hear Maharaj Chitragupta say so? I want to ask you something that I did once before. Remember, Bhaiya, I asked you a question right before I breathed my last? I don't know if you gave an answer and I didn't live to hear it, or whether you only had silence in response.

Chitragupta: Please tell the assembly what your question was, Bhima.

Bhima: Maharaj, I speak of the time when Dharmaraj decided to leave the kingdom and our subjects behind and pursue *nirvana*. Draupadi and the four of us followed him without asking any questions.

Yudhishthira: But I never told you to come with me. It was your independent decision.

Bhima: It was, Bhaiya, but we had been with you all our lives. How could we possibly let you leave and stay behind in a world where you no longer existed? We started walking and continued to walk day after day, our feet becoming weary and blistered. Fearful forests and turbulent rivers lay in our path, but we did not stop. Great mountains could not slow us down—at least not until we finally caught sight of the Himalayas. We did not have adequate clothing to shelter us from the cold winds. My dear Panchali found it almost impossible to walk by then, and soon after, her body gave up the fight. I came to you with my hands folded in prayer and begged you to stop. But you refused. In a few days, Sahadev, Nakula and Arjuna—the little brothers we had looked after with so much love—also gave up their bodies. But you continued walking. I walked by your side until my death came to me. I was horrified all the while at your steely resolve. You had left your brothers and your wife behind; their bodies froze in the chilling winds of the Himalayas, but the thought didn't even furrow your brows. These were people who had always obeyed you, brothers who had never raised their voices to you, a wife you had pawned at a game. But even when you saw them visibly struggling for life, you couldn't allow them a few moments of rest. Why, Bhaiya? Why did you not stop when your entire world and all your loved ones had fallen along the way?

Sri Krishna: Draupadi, isn't that the question you too have been longing to ask? You can admit it, Draupadi, for Bhima has already voiced it.

Draupadi: Yes, Keshava. Forgive me—

Sri Krishna: Don't ask for forgiveness, Draupadi. It isn't only you who wanted to ask Dharmaraj this question. Arjuna did too, and Nakula and Sahadev...perhaps the entire world has been plagued with the question ever since Yudhishthira commenced his walk to *nirvana*.

Dharmaraj, answer Bhima's question. Your response is decisive for the future of the world. Whatever you say will be the ultimate truth, for I will be answering with you in spirit, if not in words.

Yudhishthira: Bhima, I will answer your question today.

Bhima: I am listening, Bhaiya.

Yudhishthira: When all of us were walking towards *moksha*, we were gradually finding release from all our mistakes on Earth. In the pursuit of *moksha*, it is essential to give up everything you have attained on Earth. It is a cleansing that begins with material desires and goes on until nothing but your soul remains. No one can carry baggage of any kind to the land of eternal rest—not physical objects like ornaments, nor emotional bonds of marriage or kinship. We gave up our kingdom first and all our royal glories; we lost our comforts, our riches, and also our clothes until we only remained in spirit. It was then time to part with baggage of another kind— the baggage of relationships. Tell me, Draupadi, how long have you known me?

Draupadi: Since we got married, Dharmaraj.

Yudhishthira: That means our relationship was the newest. Draupadi and I had known each other only for a few years. We were, therefore, the first to be released from our bond of marriage. Bhima, you are my first brother; our relationship was the oldest, which is why we stayed together even when Arjuna, Nakula and Sahadeva had departed.

I had embarked on the pursuit of *moksha* alone. Not once had I asked anyone to accompany me; they came of their free will. To attain my goal of *nirvana*, it was inevitable that I sever my bonds with them—one by one. That is what happened, Bhima, and that was the reason I could not stop. Keshava, I trust that my response is adequate.

Sri Krishna: Thank you, Dharmaraj. You spoke a timeless truth, and I am glad it has been voiced in this assembly. On your way to salvation, you couldn't have held on to your loved ones even if you had endeavoured to. It is important that humankind remembers this: nothing that is acquired on this Earth can ever transcend to the beyond.

Maharaj Chitragupta, I request you to please announce your judgement now. Today, a sincere guardian of religion was on trial—what do you adjudge his final destiny to be?

Chitragupta: In the Dharmakshetra today, many allegations were levelled against Dharmaraj Yudhishthira. True to his name, Dharmaraj responded to all the accusations with honour and truth. This assembly negates all the charges levelled against him.

Yudhishthira: I am grateful, Maharaj.

Chitragupta: There is only one allegation that you were unable to refute—the one levied by Rani Draupadi.

Yudhishthira: Yes, Maharaj. I am grateful to her for having forgiven me.

Chitragupta: Yes, she has forgiven you, but that does not protect you from the punishment that the Dharmakshetra must mete out to you. It is a crime to exercise your rights on your wife without regarding her emotions or desires. You sinned when you attempted to own her, well knowing that she was the wife to all the Pandavas and that she nurtured a special place in her heart for Arjuna.

Yudhishthira: I accept my offence, Maharaj. I will respectfully take whatever punishment you choose to give me.

Chitragupta: Dharmaraj, your name will forever be etched in the chronicles of history for your righteousness and honour. You emerged victorious in the Battle of Kurukshetra without losing your sense of piety. But in the annals of love, Dharmaraj, you'll be considered defeated.

Yudhishthira: I accept your punishment, Maharaj.

Sri Krishna: Thank you, Dharmaraj, for being an example for generations to come. Those who tread the path of religion will always be protected by religion. Some decisions may be hard, others may tear your heart apart, but staying true to your sense of honour and justice will never let you down.

9

KARNA

FLASHBACK

Sri Krishna: Duryodhana, it is I who will light Karna's funeral pyre. People like him are rarely born on Earth, and I too am deeply saddened at his demise.

Arjuna: What are you doing, Keshava?!

Sri Krishna: Partha, Karna was an exceptional human being. Never has there been one as generous as him, nor as valiant and selfless. He might have fought for the Kauravas, but he was the eldest Pandu. It should have been Yudhishthira who set his funeral pyre alight.

END OF FLASHBACK

In the Battle of Kurukshetra, many great men and warriors were put to the test. It wasn't their might or valour that was truly tested; it was their righteousness, honour, and ability to abide by religion even in extreme circumstances. While some emerged successful at the test, others failed. Some became victims on the battlefield; others voluntarily surrendered their lives. But there was only one warrior who lost more than anyone else did; there was only one valiant young man who was more victorious than anyone could hope to be.

After the Kurukshetra War, one final test remains for Karna: the Assembly of Dharmakshetra. He was born of the Sun; then how could his intentions be shrouded in the black clouds of allegations? Will the Suryaputra succeed in overcoming the darkness?

Chitragupta: Today, I am summoning to the assembly someone who has several allegations levelled against him. I hope that none of you will dishonour the dignity of the assembly but let me patiently consider all arguments and make a weighted decision.

Dushasana: Bhaiya, who do you think is coming here today?

Duryodhana: I know who it is, Dushasana. And I am ready to decimate any allegations that get levied.

Chitragupta: Suryaputra Angaraj Karna, please come forward.

Karna: Pranaam, Maharaj. I am grateful that you did not add 'Kuntiputra' to my name.

Chitragupta: When Devi Kunti was at the witness stand earlier, you made it adequately clear that you didn't want to be addressed as Kuntiputra. The proceedings of this assembly get written in stone; no one forgets anything here. Angaraj, before I start reading aloud the allegations against you, you are free to address the members of the assembly. Of course, it is entirely your decision.

Karna: Maharaj, what can I say to anyone in the assembly? Everyone who has been on the stand before me—everyone but Duryodhana—has regarded me as a bitter enemy. It is perhaps only Sri Krishna who nurtures the slightest hint of affection for me. No, Maharaj, there is nothing I can say that will make a shred of difference to these people. My existence has only caused them pain; they have always wished to see me dead. Please read out the first allegation, Maharaj. It is my duty to answer every question you ask.

Chitragupta: It is ironical that you should say that, Angaraj, because the very first allegation claims otherwise.

Karna: I don't understand, Maharaj.

Chitragupta: The first allegation against you is that you failed to fulfil any of your duties on Earth.

Duryodhana: That is untrue, Maharaj!

Chitragupta: Suyodhana, did I ask for your opinion? Angaraj Karna hasn't had a chance to respond and you, in a state of great agitation, are negating an allegation you don't know about. Please take your seat and remain silent until I ask you to speak up in favour of your friend.

Angaraj Karna, I will now explain the allegation. Let's take the first instance. Do you remember the day you came to know that you were not Radhey, the son of Radha, but Kaunteye, the son of Devi Kunti? Do you recall what you did when you found out?

FLASHBACK

Kunti: Come with me, my son. Come and be with your brothers. What belongs to them also belongs to you. Indraprastha, Hastinapur, my love—all this is your right by birth.

Karna: It is too late. I have always been called lowborn, and so I wish to remain. It is not possible for me to accept that I am a Kaunteya, the eldest brother of the Pandavas. It is beyond me to retreat from this war and disappoint my friend. If I go with you, I would be breaking the hearts of those who raised me and looked after me. Please leave, Devi Kunti. This is the camp of the enemies of your sons. It is inappropriate for you to be here.

Kunti: I have lived away from you for years, my son. I have been plagued with the immense guilt of having abandoned you. Please come with me now and free your mother of this sorrow.

Karna: I cannot. So much of my life has gone by alone; I haven't the strength to aspire for a family. We will meet after the war when I have vanquished the Pandavas.

END OF FLASHBACK

Chitragupta: Devi Kunti told you that you were the eldest Pandava. But even so, you did not leave the side of the Kauravas; you fought against your brothers. If that isn't neglecting your duty as a son and an elder brother, what is? Why are you laughing, Angaraj? Is that some convoluted answer to my question?

Karna: Forgive me, Maharaj, I am merely laughing at the strange turns of my life. When Rani Kunti came to my tent before the war, I alleged that she had wronged me; she had failed to fulfil her duties as a mother. Today, in your court, the situation has somehow boomeranged, and I am being portrayed as the villain who neglected his duties as a son. I call that a proper riddle of ethics!

Chitragupta: The allegation is not a riddle, Angaraj. Sometimes, it so happens that both the accused and the one casting the accusation are equally guilty. Devi Kunti was at fault because she abandoned you, her firstborn son. But by neglecting her maternal overtures when she finally came through for you, you too made a mistake.

Karna: So, you are saying that Devi Kunti and I are both guilty, is that so? Well, Maharaj, the allegation against me is that I failed to fulfil my duties as a son and a brother. But these duties never existed at all! I was raised by a charioteer and his wife; I have fulfilled all my duties towards my adoptive parents. They are the only ones I consider truly my own. I had a brother too—a fine man called Shone. Never did I hesitate to be there for him. If you want, you can question my family members, Maharaj.

Yudhishthira: But Karna, when Matashree told you of your real lineage, all your duties became entwined with our lives. You should have supported us and our mother, not our foes.

Karna: Dharmaraj, the assembly has already seen that you are an expert at religious matters. Do you mind if I ask you a simple question?

Yudhishthira: No. Please ask what you have to.

Karna: Dharmaraj, do duties stand alone in the universe? Or do rights also accompany them? Do affection and bonding coexist with familial duties?

Yudhishthira: Yes, Angaraj.

Karna: I thought so. Duties and rights are tightly bound together; one cannot exist without the other. You had no rights over me, and I had no duties towards you. Didn't you admit that you were suspicious of a relationship between Devi Kunti and me? Didn't you find it odd that her eyes brimmed over when someone took my name? But you didn't find it necessary to make enquiries. You only used me as a shield to defend your stand, telling the assembly of how you would have loved to have an elder brother. Maharaj, my only duty was towards the parents who had brought me up and towards my friend Duryodhana. God knows I have fulfilled my duties towards them with complete sincerity.

Bhishma: It wasn't 'duty' that you fulfilled towards Duryodhana as much as it was your attempt to repay his debt. He had made you Angaraj, and you spent your entire life vainly trying to rise from that mammoth favour.

Karna: Pitamaha, you are free to assume whatever pleases you. Duryodhana turned my life around when he bestowed upon me the title of Angaraj. I will be eternally grateful to him.

Bhishma: Yes, your gratitude compelled you to overlook all your duties but the duty towards your friend. Do you know, Karna, that title of Angaraj that Duryodhana won you over with was merely a ruse?

Duryodhana: Pitamaha!

Bhishma: Don't interrupt, Duryodhana. You were a prince when you bestowed the title upon Karna; not the king. Without consulting your father, you had no right to make anyone the king of any land! No one becomes king merely because a kingdom has been bestowed upon them; they must invest in the kingdom as a Rajkumar first. Karna, Duryodhana did this 'great favour' to you only because he wanted your expertise. He could sense that if anyone could defeat Arjuna, it was you. The truth is, you were neither the rightful King of Anga, nor did you have any obligation to serve Duryodhana.

Duryodhana: Pitamaha, I didn't expect this from you. Didn't you say in this very assembly that Karna and I were true friends? That our friendship was genuine even if nothing else was?

Bhishma: Your memory is as weak as your morality, Duryodhana. When I had lauded the friendship between you and Karna, it had been you on the stand. You had been charged with befriending Karna only to defeat Arjuna. But today, I am not commenting on you and your intentions. I am questioning Karna and his duties towards a friendship that had no foundation.

Karna: Pitamaha, they don't call you a wise man for no reason. How succinctly you have labelled Duryodhana's friendship as genuine and mine as opportunistic! You have only bolstered what I said earlier: no one cares about me or my happiness; you are willing to support even the Duryodhana you usually bash if it will help malign my name.

Chitragupta: Angaraj Karna, Gangaputra Bhishma, and Suyodhana, I request you to pause for a while. From what I have heard until now, it is clear to me that Angaraj Karna had no duties towards Devi Kunti and the Pandavas. Devi Kunti had always kept him at a distance; indeed, she had abandoned him when he was only an infant. Therefore, the allegation that he failed to perform his duties as a son and a brother is untrue.

However, Gangaputra Bhishma has brought something else to light—something that takes me to the next allegation against Karna. Gangaputra Bhishma correctly stated that Suyodhana had no right to declare Karna as the Angaraj. Then why did Angaraj Karna, who is renowned for his knowledge of ethics and protocol, accept this title? Did he accept Suyodhana's friendship for reasons beyond emotion? The second allegation against you, Karna, is that you accepted Suyodhana's offer of friendship because you wanted an opportunity to confront and defeat Arjuna.

Karna: No, Maharaj, I refuse to accept this allegation. It is untrue.

Bhima: It is true, Karna! Accept it! I distinctly remember your behaviour during that ceremony in Hastinapur where all of us displayed our skills at warfare. You challenged Arjuna in front of the whole of Hastinapur. Maharaj, Karna had only one objective in his life: to defeat Arjuna. He could get to do that only if he sided with Duryodhana, Arjuna's diehard enemy. Duryodhana, I am sorry to say that your 'friend' took unfair advantage of your friendship.

Duryodhana: Bhima, I have warned you not to jeer at the friendship between Karna and me. It is a relationship that your fat head cannot comprehend!

Gandhari: Son, Bhima is speaking the truth.

Duryodhana: No, Matashree. Bhima is heartless; how can he understand what friendship means?

Gandhari: Let me prove it to you, son. Karna, you claim to be my son's best friend, don't you? Will you answer a question that his mother wants to ask?

Karna: Yes, Devi Gandhari.

Gandhari: When you agreed to fight for Duryodhana in the Kurukshetra War, you knew that the Kauravas would lose. I know you did. You aren't mindless; you well understood that only they could win who had Sri Krishna's support. With Sri Krishna rests the truth and ultimate triumph. Tell me, Karna, didn't you know Duryodhana would lose?

Karna: I did.

Gandhari: Then why didn't you stop him? Why didn't you urge your friend not to enter into the final battle he would ever fight? Answer my question! Maharaj, please ask Karna to answer my question.

Chitragupta: Angaraj Karna, if you don't answer Devi Gandhari's question, it will imply that you wanted the war to break out. It will prove that you befriended Suyodhana only to get a chance to defeat Arjuna. It was your obsession with overpowering Arjuna that mattered, not the need to protect your friend from impending doom. Answer her question, Angaraj.

Karna: I did not stop him because I didn't want to lose him! Forgive me, Maharaj, but it is tearing me apart, to contain my emotions at Devi Gandhari's unjust allegation.

Duryodhana: Speak, my friend. I will see to it that nobody here stops you from speaking your mind.

Karna: Maharaj, all the luminaries present in your court know of and feel connected to their roots. There isn't anyone who will grow hesitant or feel embarrassed if asked for an introduction. Behold the son of Ganga, the sons of Pandu, the daughter of Drupad! With their roots also became apparent the direction their lives would take. I have never been that fortunate. I grew up as the lowborn son of a charioteer who struggled with the traits of a Kshatriya. I faced a perpetual identity crisis that only got exacerbated when someone told me I had been found on a riverbank. Can anyone in this assembly even begin to fathom how that must have felt to me? To know that my mother had discarded me and left me to die in a basket that she set afloat on a river? I admit that my parents—Anirudh and Radha—loved me a lot, but they knew I wasn't truly theirs.

When I became old enough to start learning the art of warfare, I went to Guru Drona. But he refused to take me as his disciple. I learned archery from Guru Parashurama, who was kind enough to impart to me excellent teaching in warfare, especially in archery. When the time came to prove myself, I tried to enter the Dikshan Ceremony at Hastinapur. But I was turned away once again. Neither Guru Drona nor Kripacharya permitted me to enter the ceremony. How could they allow a lowborn man to compete with the princes in public? It was only my friend Duryodhana who came forward like my messiah and infused new vigour into my desolate life. I finally experienced what it was like to be loved and needed. The very thought that my friendship towards Duryodhana was tainted with selfish motives fills me with disgust.

Duryodhana: It *is* disgusting that these people should think so, my friend! Pitamaha, have you got your answer now? Have you understood why Karna became my friend?

Karna: Devi Gandhari, you asked me why I didn't stop Duryodhana from fighting the battle. How could I, Devi? I had only one friend on Earth. He had never asked me for anything in return for his friendship and support. How could I refuse to do as he asked?

Duryodhana: Karna, I know you didn't want me to bring this up, but today I have to reveal something you said to me before the war. I think everyone in the assembly should know the truth about you so they can never again question the sincerity of your friendship.

FLASHBACK

Dushasana: Why do you appear worried, Bhaiya?

Duryodhana: I am thinking about how Keshava had come with the peace proposal today. I rejected it outright.

Dushasana: It was the right thing to do, Bhaiya. The Pandavas and Sri Krishna assume we are afraid of them, that we would tremble in fright on the battlefield. You made the right decision by refusing that patronizing proposal.

Duryodhana: What about you, my friend? Do you think I made the correct move?

Karna: My friend, you don't need to hear it from me. The anxiety on your face clearly shows that you too are uncertain about whether or not you took the best step.

Duryodhana: Everyone is advising me not to enter into the battle. Are they correct? Am I missing something? Never has a decision been quite so difficult to make. Had you been in my place, Karna, what would you have done?

Karna: That is beside the point, Duryodhana. I am not you. I am Karna, and Karna only does what his friend Duryodhana wants.

Duryodhana: I know that you will always side with me. But assume that it was you on whom the onus of this decision rested. Tell me, what would you have done?

Karna: My friend, a lot has transpired in Hastinapur that has been nightmarish, to say the least. But what is in the past cannot be changed.

Duryodhana: And the future? Will the future be rendered black if I fight this war?

Karna: Duryodhana, I can only tell you this: if brothers go to war against each other, no good can ever come of it. Warring brothers weaken the foundation of the family, and how can a bright future be built on a tremulous foundation?

Duryodhana: Karna, do you know what will happen if I don't wage this war? You will never be able to fight Arjuna, let alone defeat him.

Karna: My friend, I hold you above everything in my life, including my bow. If you have second thoughts about going to war, don't hold back on my account! I am convinced that I am a more skilled archer than Arjuna and no battle is essential to prove this.

Duryodhana: Karna, if I make peace with the Pandavas, we will have to live a life of unending agony, envy and watchfulness. Our defeat in the battlefield of life would be certain. On the other hand, if we choose to go to war, there is a possibility that we might win. No one can predict who the victor will be until the battle is fought. So, should we carry on? Would I have your support?

Karna: Everything I own is yours, Duryodhana. My body, my bow and arrow, and my soul are yours until my last breath. You only have to command, and I shall obey.

Duryodhana: I only want one thing, my friend: Don't leave my side. Be with me in this war, for I cannot fight it without you.

END OF FLASHBACK

Chitragupta: Suyodhana's statement proves beyond doubt that this allegation against Angaraj Karna is false. He did not befriend Suyodhana to further his ends, but was committed to fulfilling every duty that friendship entailed.

Karna: Thank you, Maharaj.

Chitragupta: Angaraj, we have established that you were a true friend to Suyodhana. But is your friendship strong enough to disprove the next allegation?

Karna: Maharaj, I don't know what the next allegation against me is. But yes, whatever it may be, nothing will stand in the way of the friendship that Duryodhana and I share.

Chitragupta: Well, we will see. Maharaj Dhritarashtra, please come forward to voice the next charge against Angaraj Karna.

Duryodhana: Pitashree, I wonder what it is that you want to accuse my friend of. But I hope you will remember that every word you utter will be as good as raising questions against your son. I value Karna as an integral part of my life; he is part of my being.

Chitragupta: Suyodhana, was that a warning to your father?

Duryodhana: No, Maharaj. I was only reminding Pitashree that his son has few friends in life. Karna is the only one who has stood by me unwaveringly; he is the one exception in my life full of fair-weather friends. I hope Pitashree will remember that.

Chitragupta: This is the Dharmakshetra, Suyodhana. Only the truth is spoken here; only the truth is adjudged victorious. However, I grant you that Angaraj is unlikely to be prepared for the truth I am now about to divulge.

Karna: I am ready, Maharaj. I am not a man who is scared to face the truth.

Chitragupta: Angaraj, the next allegation against you is that you betrayed your friend Suyodhana during the Battle of Kurukshetra.

Duryodhana: How many times will my friend have to prove his innocence, Maharaj? He sacrificed his life for me; what more evidence could there be that he is not a traitor?

Chitragupta: Be patient, Suyodhana. I have someone here to substantiate this allegation: your father, Maharaj Dhritarashtra.

Duryodhana: But Maharaj, how can my father give testimony to what did or didn't happen in Kurukshetra? Have you forgotten that he wasn't a part of the battle?

Chitragupta: Suyodhana, it is not me who has forgotten anything, for I never forget. *You* seem to have overlooked how your father had a constant, vivid view of everything on the battlefield through the eyes of his charioteer, Sanjaya. Through his divine powers to visualize that which was miles away, Sanjaya showed your father everything that went on during the war. Maharaj Dhritarashtra, tell the assembly about the incident that made you suspicious of Angaraj Karna. When did you feel that he was betraying your son?

Dhritarashtra: Pardon me for being blunt, Maharaj, but when did Karna do anything at all during the battle? Not once did I see him help my son in any way!

Duryodhana: Pitashree, Karna was the third chief soldier of my army. He waged a terrifying fight against the Pandavas, killing entire legions of soldiers. Eventually, as the Chieftain, he sent to their deaths giant chunks of the Pandava armies—

Dhritarashtra: Son, don't be naïve. If the killing of soldiers was adequate to win the war, why wasn't Guru Drona able to do it? Why was Pitamaha unable to do it?

Duryodhana: Pitashree, quit talking in riddles.

Dhritarashtra: It was me was who riddled, son. When Sanjaya narrated to me the proceedings on the battlefield, I was plagued by the most disturbing riddle of all: what was the matter with Karna?

FLASHBACK

Sanjaya: Maharaj, Angaraj Karna and Sahadeva are now confronting each other on the battlefield.

Dhritarashtra: Ah, it is impossible for Sahadeva to survive. What can a mere child do against a mighty archer like Karna?

Sanjaya: With one arrow, Karna has succeeded in breaking Sahadev's bow. The flag of his chariot has been ripped in two.

Dhritarashtra: Tell me, Sanjaya—what is happening now? Has Sahadeva been killed?

Sanjaya: No, Maharaj, Karna has left the spot. He muttered something to Sahadeva before leaving, but I couldn't quite catch the words.

Dhritarashtra: Did you say that Karna left the place? Well, perhaps what he did was correct. He should not have killed an innocent young man like Sahadev. Sanjaya, where is Bhima now? Is Karna heading towards Bhima?

Sanjaya: Maharaj, Bhima and Karna are engaged in a violent spat; they are shooting insistent arrows at each other.

Dhritarashtra: Karna and Bhima in a battle of archery! That must be some sight! I had no inkling of Bhima's prowess with the bow and arrow; I always figured that all he could fight with was the mace.

Sanjaya: Well, it does seem that Prince Bhima is not competent with the bow and arrow; he looks far less adroit than Karna. One of Karna's arrows severed both the legs of Bhima's chariot and also broke his bow in two.

Dhritarashtra: Bhima has had it today! He will never be able to match Karna's valour and skill. The next arrow will hit his heart. Bless you, Karna. Sanjaya, is there any way you can send my blessings to Karna via telepathy?

Sanjaya: No, Maharaj, it is too late. Karna has left the spot again. He muttered a few words to Bhima too, but again his words were lost in the racket of the battlefield.

Dhritarashtra: I don't understand what Karna is up to. Why does he keep moving away when he is so close to defeating those darned Pandavas? Bhima is Duryodhana's sworn enemy; Karna should have killed him when he had the chance! What is he doing now, Sanjaya?

Sanjaya: Maharaj, Karna is now facing Dharmaraj Yudhishthira.

Dhritarashtra: Ah, now I understand. The smart man! He

doesn't want to waste time and energy on the other Pandava princes; he wants to kill Dharmaraj Yudhishthira directly. When the leader of the enemies is no more, my son will automatically win the battle.

Sanjaya: He has left, Maharaj.

Dhritarashtra: Who? Yudhishthira? Do you mean he is no more?

Sanjaya: Oh, no, Maharaj. I meant that Karna has moved on from the spot.

Dhritarashtra: What?! Why did he go away, Sanjaya? Why did he let go of the opportunity to kill not one but three Pandavas?

Sanjaya: Maharaj, this time I managed to hear what he said to Yudhishthira.

Dhritarashtra: What? What did he say?

Sanjaya: He said, 'Don't forget to thank your mother.'

END OF FLASHBACK

Dhritarashtra: It was only after the war was over that I came to know Karna was a Pandava too. He had promised his mother that he wouldn't kill any Pandava but Arjuna. Tell me, Maharaj, doesn't that amount to betraying his friend and my son Duryodhana?

Kunti: No, Maharaj, it was not betrayal. It was the highest sacrifice a son and warrior could make.

Arjuna: Matashree, what are you saying? You know that he wanted to kill me and yet you are labelling his actions as 'sacrifice'! Does he even know what a pure and selfless connotation the word sacrifice has?

Kunti: Trust me, Arjuna; if anyone knows what sacrifice truly means, it is only Karna. I was his mother, but I had denied his existence all my life. I never embraced my son or even revealed his identity to the world, letting him be insulted every day. But, selfishly, I chose to tell him about his family only when war was imminent. The memories of that day will be with me in every birth I take.

Karna was in his camp, eager to support his friend Suyodhana and achieve victory in the war. I went up to him and begged him not to kill my sons, for they were his younger brothers. I cannot even imagine the pain he must have felt at the revelation, but he didn't let me return empty-handed. He promised me that he wouldn't kill any of my sons except Arjuna. He wanted to battle only with Arjuna to prove that he was a superior archer, but he pledged that I would still have five sons after the war was over.

Duryodhana, he didn't betray you by not killing my sons; he was bound by his promise to his mother. Even in this painful decision, he considered you, as once Arjuna was defeated, the Pandavas would find it almost impossible to win the war.

Dhritarashtra: Well done, Kunti. Quite a show of motherly love you have put up today! I admire Karna for his temperament; few men can 'protect a mother's honour' as he did.

Karna: Maharaj, do I sense sarcasm in your words to Devi Kunti? I can assure you: she did not stand up for me today out of motherly love. She was only trying to repay the debt she owes to me. Duryodhana, my friend, please forgive me. I had no choice.

Duryodhana: Karna, there is no need for you to apologize to me. You tried to kill Arjuna at the very least! But most of my other warriors were such cowards that far from killing the Pandavas, they were afraid even to face them.

Gandhari: Son, Karna and Kunti have managed to fool you with their emotional extravaganza. But it is hardly the truth. They may have succeeded in disproving your father's charges, but I too have evidence of Karna's blatant betrayal. Maharaj, if you permit me—

Chitragupta: Go ahead, Devi Gandhari.

Gandhari: Karna, you have answered this question before but let me ask you again: which powerful weapon did you possess that Arjuna did not?

Karna: The Indrastra.

Gandhari: Yes, the Indrastra—the weapon named after Indra Dev, widely believed to be Arjuna's true father. If this weapon belonged to Indradev, how did you get it? How did it land in the hands of Suryadev? Doesn't it seem natural that as Arjuna's father, Indradev would have given this special weapon to his son?

Karna: Yes, Devi Gandhari.

Gandhari: All right, forget about the Indrastra. Tell me about the *kavach* and *kundal* you were born with. No infants are born with gleaming armour and golden earrings, so they were certain to be special in some way. What do you say, Kunti?

Kunti: Yes, Didi.

Gandhari: I will need to hear more than just a 'yes'. What did the amulet do?

Karna: It was impenetrable.

Gandhari: Impenetrable? How can that be? Karna was killed on the battlefield; Arjuna penetrated his body with a deadly arrow. Does that mean you were without your amulet, Karna?

Karna: Yes.

Gandhari: Where was it then? Where did it go? If you had it on, no arrow would have been able to pierce your heart. You would have been unconquerable. The outcome of the battle would have been altered dramatically. Well? Maharaj, since Karna does not seem keen to answer, let me reveal the whereabouts of the amulet. Karna gave it to Indradev, Arjuna's father! Didn't you, Karna? Didn't you gift the father of your enemy a neat package of guile disguised as 'friendship' with my son?

Karna: I did.

FLASHBACK

Sage: I have heard great things about your generosity. Won't you give me a donation?

Karna: Of course, I will give you anything you want.

Sage: You should think before you speak. You might find it impossible to part with that which I have come to seek.

Karna: You don't know me. I never go back on my word; neither do I let anyone leave my home empty-handed. Ask, and it shall be given.

Sage: Excuse me for enquiring, but isn't there a golden glow underneath your white clothes? Where does it emanate from?

Karna: That comes from my amulet. It has been around my chest since birth. The *kavach* and my *kundal* are both parts of my body.

Sage: I want both the *kavach* and the *kundal*. I await your response: will you give them both to me?

END OF FLASHBACK

Gandhari: You so casually gave away the *kavach* and *kundal* that could have made you invincible. Why, Karna? I see it as clearly traitorous!

Chitragupta: Angaraj Karna, do you have any response to Devi Gandhari's accusation? Who was that sage?

Karna: Devi Gandhari, you asked me a short while ago how the Indrastra came to be in my possession. You wondered how a weapon that belonged to Indradev could be with the son of Suryadev. I will tell you now—it came to me because of that Brahmin. While he took away what was most precious to me—the *kavach* and *kundal* that had protected me since birth—he also gave me something in return.

FLASHBACK

Karna: Who are you? Are you who I think you are?

Sage: I can't read your mind. I am only a simple Brahmin!

Karna: Then why do you need my *kavach* and *kundal*?

Sage: One should never ask a Brahmin the reason behind his request. True charity does not require rationales.

Karna: I agree with you, Indradev.

END OF FLASHBACK

Karna: Maharaj, that Brahmin was Indradev, Arjuna's father. He could not stop himself from doing his best to ensure his son's victory. He knew that I never refused any mendicant who came begging at my doorstep, and exploited my generosity.

Gandhari: No, Karna, Indradev did not snatch away only your *kavach* and *kundal*; he also eliminated all chances of my son's victory. And you, who had said that your heart and soul both belonged to Duryodhana, did not flinch before cutting off parts of your own body and presenting them to the enemy's father! You are indeed wonderfully charitable, Karna, and wondrous is your friendship!

Duryodhana: Enough, Matashree! What Karna did that day was not hidden from me. He did what his religion commanded him to do. Moreover, he gained something in return. Indradev gifted him the Indrastra; isn't that right, Karna?

FLASHBACK

Indradev: Today, you have proved that there is no one more charitable than you in the entire world. No one can ever present a greater gift.

Karna: I hope it has made you happy, Indradev.

Indradev: Karna, I am not cruel. Your generosity has indeed pleased me, and I want to offer you something in return.

Karna: What?

Indradev: I appeared in front of you today in the guise of a simple Brahmin. Exactly like that, one regular arrow that you shoot from your bow will turn into an Indrastra if you will it to. It will be a weapon of such might that nothing will be able to withstand its power.

Karna: Nothing at all?

Indradev: Nothing and no one!

Karna: Not even Arjuna?

Indradev: Not even Arjuna.

Karna: Thank you, Indradev. Before you leave, I have one request to make to you.

Indradev: Tell me, Karna.

Karna: I hope you will not speak of today's incident to anyone. If you do, no one will ever trust an impoverished, needy man again.

END OF FLASHBACK

Gandhari: Well, he did get the Indrastra, but a fat lot of good that was! Yes, he managed to kill Ghatotkach with it, but could he win the war for you? No! If he had retained his *kavach* and *kundal*, you would have triumphed, my son. My question to Karna remains the same: why didn't you refuse? Was your obsession with charity so overpowering? Was the need to prove that you were the most generous man in the world above your loyalty to Duryodhana?

Karna: I couldn't have refused, Devi Gandhari. I may have grown up as a lowborn man and been continually insulted for my social standing, but I was a true Kshatriya. No Kshatriya can ask a mendicant to leave empty-handed from his doorstep. The gift that is demanded is immaterial; it must be given at all costs.

Gandhari: Your pining to be recognized as a Kshatriya and the obsession with rising above the 'insult' of your low-caste compelled you to do some great misdeeds, Karna. Do you know how frantic Duryodhana was when he heard about your great act of altruism?

FLASHBACK

Dushasana: Bhaiya, for how long will you continue to pace about restlessly? Please tell me what the matter is. It is driving me wild.

Duryodhana: Dushasana, Karna did something so unbelievable today that I cannot have a moment of peace. If you heard about it, you too would be pulling your hair out in agitation.

Gandhari: What has Karna done?

Duryodhana: Matashree, Karna has given away his *kavach* and *kundal*! Donated them to a Brahmin!

Gandhari: I always knew that friend of yours was good for nothing. Grand words don't win battles, son.

Duryodhana: Matashree—

Gandhari: You will now stop me from insulting your friend, right? How do you think he will win against Arjuna? How will he help you become victorious?

Duryodhana: Matashree, I hadn't befriended Karna because he was invincible. What he did today doesn't make him any less of a friend to me.

Gandhari: Son, you are naive. Don't you realize that had Karna not committed this inane act, he would have been able to repay the debt of your friendship?

Dushasana: Bhaiya, I agree with Matashree.

Duryodhana: So what do you suggest I should do? Tell him that he is of no further use to me? Throw him out of my house?

Gandhari: Yes!

END OF FLASHBACK

Gandhari: It is the greatness of my son that he didn't discard Karna that very day. Anyone else in his place would have done so.

Karna: Duryodhana, you know that I have perpetually lived in regret since that day. I stayed up night after night, filled with anguish for giving away what could have helped you win the war. But again, I had no choice. I begged you for forgiveness then, and I am doing it again today.

Duryodhana: It does not matter, my friend. I will always maintain that we are both true Kshatriyas. Do you know that I had once asked Arjuna to ask me for anything? That man asked me for a weapon that Pitamaha specially designed for me! The Pandavas were afraid of us and had to employ such disgusting tactics to defeat us. I am sure both you and I have learnt a lot from their cunning ways—all of which will serve us well in our next lives.

Maharaj, I want to reiterate that this allegation laid against my friend is untrue. No matter what my parents claim, my friend has never betrayed me. Not on the battlefield, not in any moment that we spent together.

Chitragupta: Angaraj Karna was accused of betraying his friend by promising not to harm any Pandava but Arjuna. He was also accused of weakening Suyodhana's chances in the war by donating his protective *kavach* and *kundal*. After considering all the viewpoints and the evidence, I have concluded that this allegation is invalid. The friendship between Suyodhana and Karna was not based on anything remotely selfish; it was pure and true. Karna's actions stemmed from his sense of duty, for which he deserves to be lauded, not blamed.

I will now proceed to the next allegation against Karna. Guru Parashurama, I request you to come forward.

Karna: Pranaam, Acharya.

Guru Parashurama: No, Karna, don't touch my feet. I will be unable to bless you.

Chitragupta: Guru Parashurama, thank you for coming to the assembly. I request you to introduce yourself to all the attendees.

Guru Parashurama: I am the son of Renuka and Jamadagni, the disciple of Mahadev Shiva, and the spiritual mentor of Drona and Bhishma.

Karna: Gurudev, I am also your disciple.

Guru Parashurama: I don't deny it, Karna, but you have done nothing worthy enough to have your name included in my introduction.

Chitragupta: Gurudev, in today's court, Karna has braved one allegation after another. In the Dharmakshetra, everyone must take stock of his deeds; there is no scope for mercy on emotional grounds, if I adjudge that a sin has been perpetrated. But Gurudev, I have to say, it pains me to see such a strained relationship between a Guru and his disciple.

Guru Parashurama: The strain that you sense is not

unfounded. Karna duped his Guru; he did not tell me the truth about himself only because he wanted to trick me into teaching him archery.

Karna: I knew the day would come when this allegation would be raised against me.

Guru Parashurama: You did, didn't you? Why then did you cheat me?

Chitragupta: Gurudev, please tell the assembly how it was that Karna cheated you.

Guru Parashurama: Everyone in today's assembly knows that I have fought many wars. I have won each time too, for no warrior can defeat me in battle. But I gave it all up because I realized that it is not a Brahmin's place to engage in warfare. I gave up fighting and concentrated only on teaching the art of warfare.

Nakula: What is Gurudev saying? How is this connected to Karna?

Sahadeva: I am sure there is a connection.

Guru Parashurama: Maharaj, the day I decided to dedicate myself to teaching, I made a promise to myself: I would never teach archery to a Kshatriya.

FLASHBACK

Guru Parashurama: How long have you been standing here?

Karna: I have just arrived, Gurudev.

Guru Parashurama: Gurudev? I am not your Guru; neither are you my disciple.

Karna: How should I address you then?

Guru Parashurama: Call me by my name. I wish to know why you have come to see me.

Karna: Guru Parashurama, I want to learn the art of archery from you.

Guru Parashurama: I told you not to call me 'Guru', and you forget my command in only a moment. How will you remember what I teach? Who are you?

Karna: My name is Vasu. I have come from Hastinapur.

Guru Parashurama: What does your father do?

Karna: He is the *purohit* at a small temple.

Guru Parashurama: You said you are from Hastinapur. My student Drona is the Acharya of Hastinapur. Why didn't you approach him?

Karna: I did. But he refused to accept me as his disciple.

Guru Parashurama: Oh yes, he only teaches princes.

Karna: What should I do, Sri Parashurama?

Guru Parashurama: To start with, call me Gurudev!

END OF FLASHBACK

Guru Parashurama: That was the beginning you made with

me, Karna. Everything you said to me right from the start was a lie.

Karna: But, Gurudev—

Guru Parashurama: You have lost the right to call me that, Karna.

Karna: I beseech you not to be so harsh on me. Wasn't I a good student? Didn't I obey all your commands? Didn't you look upon me with pride?

Guru Parashurama: Yes, you were a good student. If Drona is the best archer in Bharatvarsh, you were right after him. Any Guru would have looked upon you with pride. If I hadn't believed in you, I would never have taught you the art of using the Brahmastra.

Bhima: Bhaiya, did you hear that? Karna also had the Brahmastra. Why didn't he use it against Arjuna?

Yudhishthira: We will soon find out.

FLASHBACK

Guru Parashurama: Why are you waiting, Vasu? Cast your aim.

Karna: But Gurudev, how can I aim without chanting my prayers?

Guru Parashurama: Vasu, it is the Brahmastra that I have given to you. If one is thoroughly conversant with the incantation to invoke it, it is not essential to voice it. Your soul knows the prayer, doesn't it? Pick up your bow and aim! Remember only this: if you ever need to use the Brahmastra, it must only be against a Kshatriya. Do you promise?

Karna: Yes, Gurudev, I promise.

END OF FLASHBACK

Gandhari: Karna, now that it has come up, I feel compelled to ask you about it. I knew that you possessed the Brahmastra. But it always defeated me why you never used it. Wouldn't it have guaranteed you victory against Arjuna?

Drona: Devi Gandhari, I can tell you why Karna was unable to use the Brahmastra. It was because anything that has been learned by guile and trickery can never be useful in times of need. Arjuna received the Brahmastra through perseverance and meditation. He was successful in invoking it when he had to. But Karna had tricked his Guru to receive the gift. When he needed to use it, the knowledge escaped him!

Karna: Devi Gandhari, I couldn't use the Brahmastra because Guru Parashurama took it back from me.

Guru Parashurama: What else could I do but take it back, Karna? You had lied to me! How could I let lies go unpunished? I had told you that I considered all the Kshatriyas of the world my enemies. It was the Kshatriyas who murdered my helpless, innocent father! You too were a Kshatriya and manipulated me to become my student. I couldn't endure blasphemy of that sort!

Chitragupta: Guru Parashurama, how did you find out that

Karna was a Kshatriya and not a Brahmin? Did he confess?

Guru Parashurama: Oh, no, Maharaj, that would have been too much to expect from this cheat! I found out one afternoon when I was resting. Karna came up to me and said, 'Guru Dev, don't sleep with your head on the ground. Allow me to sit beside you so you can rest your head on my lap.'

Chitragupta: What happened then, Angaraj?

Karna: Maharaj, while Sri Parashurama was sleeping, a scorpion appeared out of the blue. It stung me on my thigh and latched itself to my skin. It kept sucking my blood, but I did not move because Sri Parashurama was asleep. It felt as if I was frozen. When my Guru finally woke, he was fully rested. I thought my devotion to him would please him. But how wrong I was!

FLASHBACK

Guru Parashurama: Who are you? Tell me at once before I lose my temper completely!

Karna: I am a poor Brahmin.

Guru Parashurama: You are lying once again! You have been lying to me right from the outset.

Karna: No, Gurudev.

Guru Parashurama: Don't playact! The scorpion kept stinging you for as long as I was asleep, but you didn't even flinch. No Brahmin can tolerate so much pain; it is only Kshatriyas who can stand it.

Karna: Gurudev—

Guru Parashurama: I want to hear the truth and nothing else.

Karna: Gurudev, my name is Vasusena. I am an orphan. Adhiratha, a charioteer in Hastinapur, brought me up.

Guru Parashurama: Such deceit! Hadn't I told you I only teach Brahmins? You knew this, but you went ahead and deceived me nevertheless.

Karna: No, Gurudev, I didn't mean to—

Guru Parashurama: Henceforth, you won't address me as Gurudev. You lose the right to call me your Guru. I am also taking back the Brahmastra that I gave you. On the day you are in the greatest need of the Brahmastra, you will find yourself unable to use it. You will forget everything that I have taught you.

Karna: No, Gurudev! Please forgive me.

Guru Parashurama: Vasusena, you have insulted the relationship between a Guru and his disciple. I can forgive every sin in this world but that. Please go away for I refuse to have you as my disciple for a moment longer.

END OF FLASHBACK

Karna: My Guru's curse is the reason I could never use the Brahmastra. It turned out to be the bane of my existence.

Drona: Whatever he did was completely justified. You had deceived your Guru, and it was inevitable that you be punished.

Karna: I would prefer it if you don't comment on this, Guru Drona. I blame YOU for everything that happened. Your refusal to teach me is the reason I had to resort to deception. You were the reason Arjuna was able to kill me in the battle. My curse was the result of the malice you bore in your heart.

Guru Parashurama: Karna, why are you blaming my student? Don't project your mistakes on to others!

Karna: He is deserving of blame, Sri Parshuram. Guru Dronacharya is a teacher only in name; in spirit, he has always focused more on politics. He nurtured enormous aspirations for himself. He wanted to achieve great glory by teaching the princes of Hastinapur. When I approached him, I didn't know about his true temperament. I went with high hopes. With my hands folded, I pleaded with him to accept me as his student. I told him, 'Gurudev, my life is full of misery. If you teach me archery, I will feel that I have redeemed my life. Please take me under your wing. I promise to do exactly as you say and forever remain indebted to you.' But no, the grand Guru Drona only taught princes. How did a lowborn man like me have the temerity to step inside the threshold of the Gurukul? I was humiliated and heartbroken, but I promised myself something that day. If Guru Drona wouldn't teach me, I would learn from his Guru. Little did I know that his Guru was just like him! If Guru Drona had a clause that he would only teach princes, Sri Parashurama taught only Brahmins. What was I to do? From whom was I to learn?

Maharaj, if I was pushed towards untruth, it was only my longing to learn archery that drove me to this sin. If I failed to find a Guru to teach me archery, the fire inside me would continue to burn, reducing me to a cinder.

Drona: Cut out the emotional drama, Karna. The bottom line is that you resorted to trickery only to quell the fire inside your heart.

Karna: I would not have needed to lie, Guru Drona, had my Gurus been true to their *dharma* and refrained from discriminating on the grounds of caste and prejudice. What you and Sri Parashurama did to me affected every aspect of my life, including my decisive battle with Arjuna. Had I not been as accursed as I was, Arjuna too would have delighted in battling with me. His victory would have been one he could proudly own. Arjuna, am I not speaking the truth? Or did you desire the victory you did receive, so shrouded in dubiety?

Arjuna: Karna, you have always talked about your obsession with confronting me in battle. I haven't ever said so before, but I too longed to face you on the battlefield. When the opportunity finally came, our face-off remained incomplete. If you had still been in possession of the Brahmastra, had you not been cursed but had been able to recall everything you had learnt, our combat would have truly been unmatched. It would not only have quenched the obsession both of us nurtured in our hearts, but would also have been a confrontation the universe would remember for aeons to come.

Karna: I agree, Arjuna, I wanted to face you as a warrior. I wanted neither of us to exploit the undue advantage of our lineage or crow over being Indraputra or Suryaputra. But look what happened! Look what my Gurus did to me! While one refused to teach me, the other snatched away all the learning he had imparted to me. When I faced Arjuna on the battlefield, my mind was in a fugue state: I could not remember how to invoke the Brahmastra or recall the tactics of winning an archery duel. Even the fundamentals of warfare escaped my memory.

Arjuna: Forgive me for saying this, Gurudev, but I beg to disagree with you today. All my life, I have obeyed every command you have issued to me. Sometimes, I have unthinkingly gone along with what you instructed me to do. But today, I must say that what you did to Karna was unfair. He too had the right to learn from you. He suffered a great deal because of your refusal to take him as your student.

Karna: Arjuna, I didn't know you had it in you to come forth in support of the truth like this. Thank you, Arjuna.

Drona: Arjuna, whatever I did, I had only you in mind. My only intention was to support you and make you the greatest archer in Hastinapur.

Arjuna: I know, Guru Drona. I will eternally remain grateful to you for supporting me throughout my life. But your behaviour did bring me a regret I will never be able to overcome: the biting truth that while I defeated Karna, he was fighting under a curse. He was unable to face me like an equal, and this will always render my victory hollow.

Chitragupta: Guru Drona and Arjuna, please take your places. The allegations against Angaraj Karna are now at an end. Before pronouncing my judgement, I want to ask you, Karna: is there anything you want to say to the assembly?

Karna: Maharaj, I would like to address Devi Gandhari. Do I have your permission?

Chitragupta: Yes, Angaraj.

Karna: Devi Gandhari, I want to apologize to you. I desperately wanted to help your son. But I was accursed. Despite my best efforts, I could not help Duryodhana. But it wasn't my fault; I blame the Guru of Hastinapur for my failure in helping your son.

Duryodhana: There is no man like you, Karna, no friend who is as generous and selfless. Blessed was the day you came into my life! It was Guru Drona who was cursed, for he lost a student like you. If he had taken you as his disciple, the fame he so keenly coveted would have been his in the blink of an eye.

Karna: Thank you, friend. Your words mean the world to me. I grew up lonely and was always looked down upon. The mother who gave birth to me calmly discarded me in the river. I grew up being chastised for being a lowborn man. No Guru was willing to teach me the art of warfare. Even when I finally got an opportunity to prove myself and repay my debt towards the friend who had been the only one ever to have affection for me, a curse destroyed everything. Sorrow was written in my destiny; chastisement was my fate.

Chitragupta: The final allegation against Angaraj Karna was that he had deceived his Guru. He had lied to secure a place in Sri Parshuram's Gurukul. But after considering all the arguments made in favour of and against the allegation, I have concluded that this charge isn't justified. It was the

Gurus whose behaviour was in violation of their ethics as teachers. The code of a teacher requires him to impart knowledge to every student irrespective of caste, colour or creed. Both Guru Drona and Guru Parashurama violated this crucial tenet of a teacher's religion. Angaraj Karna, I negate this charge against you as your behaviour did not break any norm of religion.

Karna: Thank you, Maharaj. I feel as if this is the first time someone has understood my pain.

Chitragupta: I am sure many in today's court have felt your pain before, but never have they tried to understand your point of view. Angaraj Karna, as the allegations against you are now complete, I will pronounce my judgement.

Sri Krishna: Maharaj, before you declare your final judgement, can I address Karna? There is something I need to ask him.

Chitragupta: Keshava, you don't need anyone's permission, not even mine. Please proceed.

Sri Krishna: Karna, who are you?

Karna: What do you mean, Keshava?

Sri Krishna: I mean: Are you Suryaputra, Kuntiputra, Sootputra, Vasusena or Angaraj? Who are you?

Karna: I don't know, Keshava. I don't know what to say.

Sri Krishna: How long will you continue to feel pity for yourself? What is holding you back from facing the world as who you are?

Karna: What do you mean, Keshava? My life *has* been a ceaseless series of traumatic events. Whenever I tried to prove myself, I sank deeper into ignominy.

Sri Krishna: Karna, today I find it essential to tell you the source of your misery in life. It was your endless quest of self-discovery! While it is vital that we find ourselves while on Earth and identify our real purpose, it mustn't become a quest with no end in sight. Let me explain this to you, Karna.

It was in adolescence that you realized you weren't the lowborn son of a charioteer, but a warrior. You were also undeniably connected to the Sun God in some mysterious manner. You started questioning yourself: Who am I? Eventually, you found a path that could perhaps lead you to some answers—the path of archery. When you saw Arjuna, you were hit by a wonderful realization: if you could somehow prove that you were a better archer than Arjuna, the entire universe would be forced to accept you as the greatest archer. Your identity of a lowborn man would be forgotten. When Guru Drona refused to teach you, you lied to Guru Parashurama and became his disciple. But your quest to find yourself was unabated. You might have become Angaraj, but it wasn't an identity you could rely on. You stuck to your generous nature, bloating it beyond all human endurance, for it would give you one reliable identity: that of being the most charitable person in the universe.

Did you ever stop to think that in this bid to find yourself, you lost a great deal? Had you accepted the social status that your destiny had brought to you, you could have focused on archery without the undercurrents of competition. Guru Drona might have turned you away, but you could have tried to tell Guru Parashurama the truth. If he too had refused you, you could have adopted Ekalavya's style of learning. Do you know Eklayvya, Karna? He was the son of a tribal man; the forest was his home. Like you, he too wanted to become Guru Drona's disciple. But when Guru Drona turned him down, he built a mud statue and learned archery by practising in front of his virtual Guru every day.

You are a great archer, Karna. You know that archery is an art that needs both focus and practice. When you aimed an arrow, did you consider the direction it was headed in? I have a feeling you only cared about assuaging the fire inside you. Your arrows aimed to destroy, but victory can never be achieved by those who propagate destruction.

Karna: Keshava, I was helpless. What could I have done?

Sri Krishna: You could have done a great deal. You could have stopped Draupadi from being insulted. You needn't have taken part in killing Abhimanyu. You could have accepted your mother's apology and accompanied her to your brothers.

Karna: But what about my friend? How could I have deserted him?

Sri Krishna: He would have forgiven you, Karna. I am certain.

Karna: He may have, Keshava, but I wouldn't have been able to forgive myself.

Sri Krishna: Yes, Karna, you wouldn't have forgiven yourself. Forgiveness doesn't come naturally to you. You could never get over what your mother did to you or forgive Guru Drona's prejudiced behaviour. You held on to grudges against Arjuna and Draupadi. You did everything in your power to 'repay your debt' to your friend, but you could not forgive yourself for being unable to secure his victory in the Kurukshetra War.

Karna: I accept whatever you say, Keshava. Perhaps I was incapable of forgiveness.

Sri Krishna: Karna, I recommend that you stop wallowing in self-pity. Yes, your mother discarded you, but she had no choice. You were called lowborn, but your parents showered you with love. You became the Angaraj. You had a friend like Duryodhana who trusted you all through. You met your death at the hands of a warrior like Arjuna. You lived a fulfilling life, Karna. There is nothing more you could have received, for no man gets more than what his destiny chooses to hand out to him.

Karna: Yes, Keshava.

Chitragupta: Thank you, Keshava. I will now announce my judgement as I am sure Angaraj Karna is eager to know the outcome of my considerations. Karna, your life has been speckled with obstacles and challenges. You have encountered numerous problems in life, but you have faced them with admirable courage. You were loyal to your friend with a steadfastness that no man can beat. This friendship will always be cited as an example in the coming generations to demonstrate how pure and selfless friendships should aspire to be. While you did not speak the truth to your Guru, it was because you spoke an even greater truth: the desire to learn.

I adjudge that every allegation against you is invalid. Keshava mentioned that you went overboard in supporting your friend, permitting many irreligious acts along the way.

But you have already suffered the punishment for those crimes. Your suffering on Earth was adequate punishment; you don't need to suffer anymore.

Angaraj Karna, I declare you the paragon of charity, loyalty and friendship. While you and Arjuna the mightiest archers of the world, your name, by virtue of your birth, will always be taken before Arjuna.

Karna: Thank you, Maharaj. I am grateful to you. In your court, I have got everything I could want.

Duryodhana: My friend, I am happy for you because you have got your heart's desire—your name will always be taken before Arjuna's. But remember, regardless of the brothers, friends and glories that become yours in your next life, I will always have the first right over you. You will always be the friend I value and love with all my heart.

10

NAKULA–SAHADEV

FLASHBACK

Sahadeva: Pranaam, Duryodhana. Why are you here?

Duryodhana: I have come to meet you, Sahadeva. Of all of you here in Indraprastha, you are the first person I have come to greet.

Sahadeva: Please take a seat.

Duryodhana: No, Sahadeva, I don't have the time to sit. I have come to consult with you about something. You know I have always—

Sahadeva: Yes, you have always consulted with me before beginning any new venture in life. You want to know what the stars hold for you, isn't that right?

Duryodhana: You are the only Pandava who can understand what goes on in my heart. Yes, Sahadeva, I have one question for you.

Sahadeva: Ask, Bhaiya.

Duryodhana: Who will be the King of Bharat?

Sahadeva: Only he will become the King of Bharat who is worthy of the throne and convinced that he is destined for it.

Duryodhana: Thank you, Sahadev. You always read what's on my mind and voice the very words that rest in my heart. I am now going to explore the mystic palace that you and your brothers have constructed together. Nakula, take good care of your youngest brother for he is my favourite.

Nakula: Sahadeva, what was he doing in your chamber?

Sahadeva: He had come to ask about his fate.

Nakula: I am surprised at you, Sahadeva. You know he is our bitter enemy, and yet you keep showing him the way! As you are so conversant with the stars, why can't you implore the celestial bodies to side with us for a change?

Sahadeva: Fate does not listen to me, Nakula Bhaiya. It listens to no one as it moves along steadily and unceasingly. All that I can do, sometimes, is hear fate speaking.

Nakula: Well, what does it say about us? What lies ahead in our fate?

Sahadeva: I haven't been able to hear it. I don't think anyone has.

END OF FLASHBACK

Chitragupta: I welcome all the attendees to today's Assembly of Religion. Today, the stand will have not one but two defendants. Even though the charges against them are different, their names will always be taken together. So, I have decided that they will respond to the allegations collectively. I ask Nakula and Sahadev, the sons of Madri, to come forward.

Nakula: Pranaam, Maharaj. Please accept my greetings, Keshava.

Sahadeva: Keshava, I trust that you have forgiven me.

Sri Krishna: Yes, Sahadev, I have forgiven you. I can understand the reason you did what was unthinkable at the time.

Arjuna: Keshava, what did Sahadeva do? He is my youngest brother and has always lived an innocent, pure life. Why is he asking forgiveness of you?

Sri Krishna: He doesn't need to ask for my forgiveness, Partha. He only did what was destined for him.

Nakula: Maharaj, if you forgive me, could I ask you a question?

Chitragupta: You may ask, Nakula.

Nakula: I have been following the proceedings of your court closely. You have been calling my brothers to address the allegations; you have called Draupadi, my uncle, and even people who are unrelated to us. But Maharaj, why didn't you ever call us to testify?

Chitragupta: Nakula, in my court, everyone must answer the questions raised against them. But no one can do so before their time. Now that your turn has finally arrived, I hope you will respond to all the charges with honesty and straightforwardness. Before I begin reading from my notebook, the forum is open for anyone who wishes to address the defendants.

Sahadeva: Maharaj, before anyone can say anything, I want to bring up a concern I have with our introduction. I am sure Nakula Bhaiya agrees with me. You called us the sons of Madri. But we would like to register our names in your records as the sons of Kunti. Whatever we have become in life has only been because of Mata Kunti. She is our rightful mother, and we wish to include her in our introduction.

Chitragupta: I accept your plea, Sahadeva. Now, since no one has come forth to speak, I will commence reading aloud your charges. Nakula, my first question is for you. As a prince of Hastinapur, you were trained in the art of warfare. While Suyodhana and Bhima were skilled at mace fighting, Arjuna mastered the art of archery. At which art were you skilled?

Nakula: Maharaj, I am skilled at swordplay. I can assure you that no one in this assembly can defeat me at a battle of swords.

Karna: Oh yes, Nakula, all of us know very well. Who can forget the 'valour' and 'skill' with which you brandished your sword and killed three innocent children? Why do you look dumbstruck? Is your gift of the gab not as sharp as your sword?

Nakula: Maharaj, I have answered your question. I request you to read aloud the first allegation against me.

Chitragupta: Nakula, I believe you already know the first charge against you: it lies hidden in Angaraj Karna's furious words. But let me put it straight for you. Tell me, what happened on the fourteenth day of the Kurukshetra War?

Nakula: The fourteenth day was an agonizing one for us, especially for Bhima Bhaiya. It was the day his son Ghatotkach was killed at the hands of Karna.

Chitragupta: So, after Karna killed Ghatotkach with the Indrastra, only two weapons of unmatched power remained with Arjuna and Karna—the Brahmastras, right?

Nakula: Yes, Maharaj.

Chitragupta: Sahadev, you were considered the most intelligent among all the princes of the Kuru clan. Can you tell us what was expected to happen now that Karna had already used the Indrastra?

FLASHBACK

Nakula: Sahadeva, Karna used the Indrastra against Ghatotkach today. While I am deeply aggrieved at Bhima Bhaiya's loss, I am also relieved that Arjuna Bhaiya is now safe. With the power of the Indrastra gone, Karna will be unable to defeat Arjuna.

Sahadeva: Yes, I too am relieved. I think Karna will now maintain a distance from Arjuna Bhaiya. Nevertheless, we need to defeat Karna as soon as we can. As long as he continues to fight for the Kauravas, it will be impossible for us to triumph.

Nakula: Do you have a plan to defeat Karna? You are the most intelligent among us; your war strategies are sound.

Sahadeva: Well, I do have a plan. But to execute it, you will have to do something atrocious on the battlefield tomorrow.

Nakula: No! Sahadev, please don't ask me to do anything that goes against religion. This war has already been a hideous series of unethical acts; I don't want to add to the outrage.

Sahadeva: If you don't execute this plan, I fear that the war will never come to a close.

Nakula: What are you asking me to do?

Sahadeva: Do you know the sons of Karna?

END OF FLASHBACK

Karna: Perhaps you don't even remember their names, Nakula, so let me refresh your memory. My sons' names were Chitrasena, Sushena and Satyasena. They were as young and guiltless as Abhimanyu. Maharaj, I request you to announce the allegation. Let the entire assembly know the devious faces these brothers hide, behind their façade of innocence.

Chitragupta: Nakula, you are charged with breaking the rules of war when you killed the three sons of Karna.

Arjuna: Maharaj, I beg to disagree. Karna's sons may have been young and innocent, but they were fighting in the war, weren't they? How did it amount to breaking the laws if Nakula killed them?

Chitragupta: Arjuna, as one of the greatest warriors of your time, don't you know that it is unethical to attack an unarmed warrior? A sword-wielding warrior cannot fight one who is without a sword.

Karna: Maharaj, why are you surprised? No one in their clan knows the rules of war. If they had known the meaning of ethics, do you think Kurukshetra would have been tainted with such enormous sins?

Yudhishthira: Karna, rules have been infringed by all of us—including you. I don't think you have any right to point fingers in the direction of my brothers.

Karna: Dharmaraj, I am not the one pressing any charges; it is Maharaj Chitragupta's job to do so. All I am doing is speaking up against the gross injustice done to my sons; I am fulfilling a father's duty! So, my brave warrior brothers, why did you do it? Didn't your inner voice warn you against deceiving three children out of their lives?

FLASHBACK

Nakula: This doesn't seem right, Sahadeva; it is grossly unethical. Karna's sons are archers while I am a sword fighter. How can I fight against them?

Sahadeva: We cannot afford to think like this, Nakula Bhaiya. It is the only way to get Karna furious enough to challenge Arjuna Bhaiya to a fight. Only when they confront each other will Arjuna Bhaiya succeed in defeating him; otherwise, Karna might keep slinking away, wasting time on Kurukshetra as we lose more men every minute. It is imperative that we kill Karna to deprive the Kaurava army of an able warrior and Chieftain.

Nakula: It is against religion, Sahadeva.

Sahadeva: No, it is the voice of our destiny.

END OF FLASHBACK

Karna: My sons pleaded with these brothers, trying to make them see reason. Chitrasena chastised Nakula for breaching the rules of warfare. My brave sons were not afraid; they were ready to face Nakula if the Pandu prince was willing to contest them at archery. But this sword wielder showed neither mercy nor honour.

Sahadeva: It was their fate, Angaraj Karna—

Karna: Shut up with your gibberish about fate! If my sons were fated to die at your hands, then you too are fated to be severely punished in the Dharmakshetra. Maharaj, they have no response other than a meaningless drone about fatalism. I think they accept that this allegation is true.

Yudhishthira: No, Maharaj, it isn't true.

Karna: Dharmaraj, how can *you* deny this charge? I understand they are your brothers but doesn't your honour stop you from supporting this unforgivable transgression?

Yudhishthira: Angaraj Karna, why did you kill Ghatotkach?

Karna: How is this relevant? If I hadn't killed Bhima's

demonic son, he would have wiped the Kaurava army off the face of the Earth.

Yudhishthira: But you killed him with the Indrastra, shooting it straight at his heart from your bow. Didn't you know that he was a mace wielder just like his father? It was you who committed a transgression, Angaraj. What my brothers did was in retaliation to your felony.

Chitragupta: Dharmaraj's statement proves that it was Angaraj Karna who broke the laws of warfare, compelling Nakula and Sahadeva to retaliate. They were indeed fated to do what they did, or there would have been no end to the war. I negate this allegation.

Karna: Maharaj, I don't think you are making a just decision. If it wasn't Nakula and Sahadeva who transgressed, it wasn't me either. Ghatotkach was the first to break the rules of warfare. I had to respond to—

Chitragupta: Yes, Angaraj, you responded by killing Ghatotkach. It isn't you who is on trial; you have accounted for all your deeds already. However, I have adjudged that Nakula and Sahadeva aren't guilty in this situation. You have to respect my judgement, Angaraj.

Karna: Forgive me, Maharaj.

Chitragupta: I will now proceed to the second allegation against Sahadeva. To press charges, I request Shakuni, prince of Gandhar and brother to Devi Gandhari, to step forward.

Shakuni: Maharaj, it disgusts me to face these two brothers. While one killed my son Uluka, the other murdered me.

Nakula: You were destined to die, Mama Shakuni. It was your scheming and plotting that catalysed the terrible war. As for the death of your son, wasn't he fighting in the battle? What was irreligious about his death?

Sahadeva: I agree with Nakula Bhaiya. Neither you nor your son was killed with the remotest deception. Our minds are not as corrupt and convoluted as yours.

Shakuni: Nakula, Sahadev, patience was never your virtue. I am not claiming that you killed my son or me with deception. I have come here to accuse you of something else. You just claimed that it was me who catalysed the war, didn't you? Are you incredibly thick-skinned or do you merely have a poor memory?

Sahadeva: We are heartily tired of your riddles, Shakuni. Talk straight or leave the court.

Shakuni: Maharaj, please tell these innocent children about the allegation.

Chitragupta: Sahadev, I talk of the day Sri Krishna went to Suyodhana with the peace proposal. We all know that Suyodhana rejected it and the battle became inevitable. But what few members of the assembly know is the reason Suyodhana rejected the proposal. They assume it was only his pride and envy that stopped him from consenting to the proposal, but the real reason was different. Sahadeva, the second allegation against you is that you stopped Suyodhana from accepting the peace proposal, thereby triggering a war that would kill thousands of people.

Yudhishthira: Maharaj! What are you saying? And why did

you invite Shakuni to bolster this unfair allegation?

Shakuni: Let me answer that, Dharmaraj. The one who stopped Duryodhana from accepting the peace proposal was the most intelligent among the Pandavas. It was necessary to invite the most intelligent among the Kauravas to vanquish him. Tell me, Ashwiniputra Sahadev, wasn't it your craftiness that stopped Duryodhana from accepting Keshava's peace proposal? Wasn't it your guile that affected a war that went on to destroy the entire Kuru clan?

Nakula: What is Maharaj saying, Sahadev? Is this allegation true?

Yudhishthira: Sahadev, this is the first time I have heard of it! It is outrageous that you should have influenced Duryodhana in some way and convinced him not to accept the proposal of peace. I had no knowledge of the proposal until Keshava returned from Hastinapur and told us about it. What have you been hiding from us?

Sri Krishna: Tell them, Sahadev. It is time for you to reveal the truth that you have been concealing in your heart for all these years. Let their reaction not make you anxious.

FLASHBACK

Sahadeva: Pranaam, Keshava.

Sri Krishna: Pranaam, Sahadeva. What do the stars tell you today? Do they reveal why I have come to meet you?

Sahadeva: Keshava, your thoughts are unfathomable;

the constellations are powerless to decipher or alter your intentions. Do you know what will happen if I ask them, 'What does Keshava want?' They will laugh at me uproariously!

Sri Krishna: I see you have learnt a lot from Dharmaraj. But Sahadeva, while the stars may have hidden my motives, you're no stranger to what your eldest brother wants.

Sahadeva: Yudhishthira Bhaiya? No, Keshava, I don't know what he wants. But I do know what he does *not* want: war.

Sri Krishna: Yes, Sahadeva. I have come to tell you that I am now heading to Duryodhana with a treaty of peace.

Sahadeva: Really? Keshava, you know that Duryodhana won't agree to any peace treaty.

Sri Krishna: I do know, Sahadeva. But it is essential to give Duryodhana one last chance to stop the war. I am going to propose that he grant Yudhishthira only five villages in Hastinapur in exchange for peace.

Sahadeva: Yudhishthira Bhaiya will be content even with five villages.

Sri Krishna: I agree. But now Sahadeva, we must take a decision on an urgent matter.

END OF FLASHBACK

Shakuni: In his peace treaty, Keshava had demanded five villages from Duryodhana. Do you remember, Sahadeva?

Sahadeva: Yes.

Yudhishthira: But you couldn't part with five villages, Duryodhana. You held on to everything with such a maniacal possessiveness that we had no choice but to pick up arms.

Duryodhana: I would have given you five villages, Dharmaraj, had they been ordinary ones.

Yudhishthira: What? Keshava, I cannot make head or tail of anything he is saying.

Duryodhana: Tell him, Keshava. Tell him now! Aren't you always explaining something or the other to everyone in this court? Today, clarify to Dharmaraj what his little brother did.

Sri Krishna: Dharmaraj, Sahadeva did not do anything wrong. I asked him a question, and he answered. That is all.

FLASHBACK

Sahadeva: What do we have to decide, Keshava? And how can I help you? All the knowledge that exists in the world is yours already.

Sri Krishna: Sahadev, you correctly observed that Yudhishthira would be content with only five villages in Hastinapur. But which ones should they be? You are familiar with Hastinapur like the back of your hand. Tell me, which five villages should I ask for?

Sahadeva: How does that matter, Keshava? We would be fortunate if Duryodhana even listens to the peace treaty; expecting him to bargain with us over the choice of villages is too much to ask! Keshava, do you hope for peace? Or do you want the war to ensue?

Sri Krishna: Your answer lies in the constellations that you read. I only abide by what the stars foretell. Tell me, Sahadeva, which villages should I ask for?

END OF FLASHBACK

Duryodhana: Let me tell the court which villages Sahadeva recommended: Paniprastha, Sonprastha, Indraprastha, Bahatprastha, and Tilprastha. Villages that were in the heart of Hastinapur! If I gave the Pandavas these five villages, it would be as good as installing my sworn enemies right at the centre of my kingdom!

Shakuni: Yes, Bhanje. Sahadeva demanded, through Sri Krishna, the only five villages that Duryodhana would find impossible to give. Do you know what this means, Dharmaraj? It was your youngest brother's scheming that affected the war, not my dice.

Yudhishthira: I am shocked, Sahadeva. You knew that Keshava's peace proposal was the last opportunity to stop the war. Why did you do such a thing? Did you will for the destruction to happen?

Nakula: Answer, Sahadev. Bhaiya is asking you a question.

Chitragupta: Sahadev, if you don't answer, I will have no option but to assume that you intentionally picked the very villages that Suyodhana would be unable to part with. You did it because you willed the war to begin.

Sri Krishna: Maharaj, with your permission, I will answer this question for him.

Chitragupta: You are permitted, Keshava.

Sri Krishna: Sahadeva is my dear brother, the youngest of all the Pandavas, the one who never received the glories and the attention that came to his elder brothers. He was a man of few words who remained lost to the mortal world, absorbed instead in the world of stars and constellations. More than the other Pandavas, it was Duryodhana who paid attention to everything he said. Duryodhana trusted in his abilities to converse with the celestial bodies that decide our destinies. Over time, Sahadeva developed an excellent understanding of Duryodhana. He knew that the eldest Kaurava prince was certain to refuse any peace treaty offered to him. He also knew that the final punishment for Duryodhana's life of irreligion could come only after his death. For Duryodhana and his brothers to confront their ultimate fate, the Kurukshetra War was inevitable.

When I approached Sahadeva to pick the five villages, I did it because I trusted in his intelligence. I respected his knowledge of that which is to come. He was the only Pandava unaffected by an all-consuming pledge, the only one not obsessed with revenge or aspirations to ascend any throne. Of all those present in the assembly today, only two people knew the inevitable: Sahadeva and me. Both of us also knew that the inevitable, by its very essence, could not be averted. It was as certain as the sun rising on the horizon every day or the Earth rotating on its axis. What Sahadeva did was on account of the inevitability of war. He merely carried out a sentence that destiny had already inked in his fate.

Shakuni: I should have known that Sri Krishna would protect the little Pandava prince with his circuitous words. But I am convinced he will have no answer to what I am about to ask.

Nakula: You won't ask anything! What rights have you to question my brother?

Shakuni: Oh, so I haven't the right to address my nephew, the one who killed me in cold blood?

Sahadeva: Let him ask his question, Nakula Bhaiya. I am neither scared of him nor incognizant of what he's going to say.

Shakuni: Since when did you become prescient? What other gifts do you have, Sahadeva?

Sahadeva: You are curious to know why I resolved to kill you. Isn't that right, Mama Shakuni? Well, I will tell you.

Shakuni: Out with it, Sahadeva. Curiosity is pestering me.

Sahadeva: Mamashree, you will remember how Duryodhana always came to me for advice. I was one of the Pandavas and therefore his enemy, but that didn't stop him from consulting with me on important decisions. On my part too, I never let anything distort the advice I gave you or Duryodhana. Irrespective of the strained relationship between the Pandavas and the Kauravas, I sincerely read what the stars foretold. It is tragic that you never heeded the message; you failed to see how you were orchestrating your destruction through your irreligious acts.

Shakuni: Whenever I come to this court, I hear nasty things about myself. Now, apparently, my fate was villainous from the start! Sahadeva, how does my fate have anything to do with your resolution? What did I ever do to you that you resolved to kill me?

Sahadeva: When two people come together, their fates merge too. Your misdeeds tainted your fate, rendering your future bleak and horrifying. But you also took Duryodhana down with yourself. Had you not poisoned Duryodhana's ears since he was a child, had you not let the horrors of your fate find their way into Duryodhana's, his life could have chartered a different course.

Shakuni: If that is so, my nephew, you could have killed me much before the battle. Why wait until the war to kill an evil man like me who tarnished the fates of anyone in his proximity?

Sahadeva: No one can be killed before it is time for him to die. You had to remain with Duryodhana until the end of the battle so he could realize his grave mistakes.

Chitragupta: Shakuni, I have attentively listened to all your arguments. I see no point in retaining you in my court any longer. You may please take your leave.

Sahadeva: Maharaj, are the allegations against Nakula Bhaiya and me at an end?

Sri Krishna: Karna, if you harbour any angst against Nakula or Sahadeva, now is the time to speak. No actions must go unaccounted for in the court of Maharaj Chitragupta. The Dharmakshetra is the last step before you step on to your ultimate destiny. It is here that all grudges must be released, all sins punished.

Karna: I have nothing to say, Keshava. I have already asked them everything I wanted to.

Sahadeva: And I have pleaded for his forgiveness, Keshava.

Sri Krishna: No, Sahadeva, you are keeping something from the court. If you don't tell Maharaj Chitragupta about it, I will have to.

Sahadeva: Yes, Keshava.

Sri Krishna: Mata Kunti, after the Battle of Kurukshetra ended, five of your sons were with you. You lost one son in the course of the battle.

Kunti: Yes, Keshava. Karna had promised me before the war that he wouldn't kill any of my sons except Arjuna. It would be either Karna or Arjuna who remained alive after the war. I was destined to lose one son in the battle; there was no way around it.

Karna: Yes. It was because of my promise to Devi Kunti that I didn't fight against any of you in the battle; no one could I kill except Arjuna. Not even you, Nakula, despite what you had done to my children.

Sri Krishna: Karna, I know you blame Mata Kunti for the unfair promise she extracted from you. You were restricted by your promise and could not do your bit to support Duryodhana in the battle wholeheartedly. But it wasn't only Mata Kunti who's deserving of your anger; it is also Sahadev.

Karna: What? How could that be?

Sri Krishna: Yes, Karna. Even before the war started, even before you faced Arjuna in battle, Sahadeva had already written death in your destiny. If he hadn't, destiny might have taken a turn that we cannot predict anymore. But who can tell? You might have defeated Arjuna. Both of you might have been alive after the war. The history of Bharatvarsh would have been drastically different from what it has turned out to be.

Arjuna: Keshava! What are you saying?

Sri Krishna: Arjuna, before the war began, Sahadeva did something that ascertained Karna's death. If it hadn't been for him, it is possible that all of you—including Karna—would have survived.

Yudhishthira: What did he do, Keshava?

Sri Krishna: Few are as skilled as Sahadeva at deciphering the movement of stars. He has always chosen his words with great consideration. But that day, he erred.

Sahadeva: Yes, Keshava, I made a huge mistake.

FLASHBACK

Sri Krishna: Sahadeva, have you picked these five villages because Duryodhana will never agree to give them to the Pandavas?

Sahadeva: Yes, Keshava.

Sri Krishna: I am pleased with you, Sahadeva. Today, you have shown great intelligence that belies your age. Tell me, what do you want in return for the favour you have done to me? It was because of you that I was able to make this decision.

Sahadeva: I don't want anything except your support, Keshava. I am glad that you are with us.

Sri Krishna: Don't hesitate, Sahadev. Ask, and I shall give it to you.

Sahadeva: All right, Keshava. When the war comes to an end, I want all four of my brothers to remain alive.

Sri Krishna: Four of your brothers?

Sahadeva: Yes, Keshava, four of my brothers.

END OF FLASHBACK

Sri Krishna: That day, you asked me to protect all four of your brothers and not all the sons of Kunti. Had you only asked that all your brothers survive the war, Karna too would have been alive. Mata Kunti would have all her sons by her side.

Karna: Your ill-chosen words cost me my life. Sahadeva, I didn't know that you too wished me evil.

Sahadeva: No, Bhaiya, forgive me. I didn't know that you were my eldest brother. My words betrayed me, and it was you who had to suffer the punishment. Trust me; I have never wished evil upon you.

Sri Krishna: Sahadev, you don't need to ask for forgiveness. The words you chose to voice that day saved your family. It was your birth in the Pandavas' household that turned out to be the secret of their great fortune; your knowledge and purity of heart saved them all. I don't know whether Karna, Shakuni or the other attendees of the assembly forgive you. But I most certainly do.

Karna: Keshava, I too forgive Sahadeva. Had he chosen his words more carefully, I might have survived the war, but I would have foregone the chance to live an eternal life.

Duryodhana: Blessed indeed is the Pandava family! First, they interrogate each other—which, I think, is only a ruse—and then they forgive each other in only a blink. But I am not a Pandava, and I am afraid I lack this overwhelming sense of forgiveness. Maharaj, when I was on the stand, everyone blamed me for refusing to accept the peace proposal. But now it is clear that the treaty was so designed—thanks to this conniving Sahadeva—that there was no way on Earth I *could* have accepted it!

Moreover, I was also reprimanded for trying to imprison Keshava after the war. And yet, here stands this fine young man who barely did any better! Won't anyone in this court unmask this cunning Sahadeva?

Chitragupta: Hold your horses, Suyodhana. The charges aren't over yet. Sahadeva, the last allegation against you is that you tried to imprison Sri Krishna.

Kunti: Maharaj! You cannot be serious. That was only a childish tantrum! Sahadeva didn't seriously mean to imprison Keshava.

Chitragupta: Devi Kunti, in my court, accusations are levied on the basis of action and not motivation. I have to fulfil my duty by questioning every questionable act. Sahadeva, is this allegation true? Judging by the silence around me—

Sri Krishna: Maharaj, is the supposed victim of this questionable act permitted to speak?

Chitragupta: You don't need anyone's permission, Sri Krishna.

Sri Krishna: Maharaj, throughout their lives, the Pandavas have encountered numerous tests. Arjuna's tests began with targeting the eye of the bird perched on the topmost branch of a tree. He didn't flinch when he had to target the eye of the fish at Draupadi's swayamvar. His were tests of skill, focus and concentration. Dharmaraj was tested by the Yaksha through a volley of questions so telling, that his brothers' lives were at stake. At every test they faced, the Pandavas were successful. But Sahadeva's tests required not strength or knowledge, but truth. He was tested on the supreme truth—the kind that no one in this assembly can shake.

FLASHBACK

Sri Krishna: Dharmaraj, the war now seems imminent. Can you think of any plan that would stop the impending carnage?

Yudhishthira: Keshava, if you cannot suggest a plan, it is unlikely that I will be able to. Bhima, what do you say? Arjuna, Nakula, do you have any idea that can stop the war from being fought?

Sahadeva: I have an idea, Bhaiya.

Yudhishthira: Really? You?

Sahadeva: Yes, hear me out: cut Draupadi's tresses, throw Bhima Bhaiya's mace into the ocean, and break Arjuna Bhaiya's Gandiva.

Arjuna: What?! Have you lost all sense, Sahadev?

Sahadeva: No, Bhaiya. Look, if Draupadi does not have her tresses anymore and you and Bhima Bhaiya are without your powerful weapons, no battle will be fought. I assure you.

Yudhishthira: Sahadev, you are insulting all of us. I urge you to be quiet.

Sri Krishna: Sahadeva, I am curious: why are you carrying this long rope?

Sahadeva: It is for you, Keshava. If Bhaiya agrees to do as I say and decides to retreat with our troops, you will still want the war to be fought. If I capture you, it is possible that no prospect of war will remain.

END OF FLASHBACK

Sri Krishna: Maharaj, it is true that Sahadeva tried to capture me. But he did it only to safeguard the welfare of his loved ones. On the other hand, when Duryodhana tried to capture me, his motive was to force me into siding with him. His mind was clouded with thoughts of victory; he was willing to fall right into the abyss to conquer his foes.

Sahadeva has always sided with truth, and this is also why his place in my heart will forever be irreplaceable. When I asked him what could be done to stop the war, his response was the supreme truth. If Draupadi shaved off her tresses,

Bhima would not need to slaughter anyone for vengeance. If Arjuna did not have his Gandiva, neither Pitamaha nor Karna would meet their deaths. But one roadblock remained in Sahadeva's strategy: me. He knew that I was the charioteer in the battle between good and evil. Even if Arjuna, Bhima and Draupadi agreed to do as Sahadeva said, I would still recommend war, because how else could religion triumph? The darkness on Earth had reached massive proportions; it was a sight that charred my heart and suffocated me every day. For religion to be victorious, war was imperative.

Maharaj, in trying to capture me, Sahadeva sided with truth and debate. He understood truth as no other Pandava did—for him, as for me, truth was greater than religion. The one who has known and recognized truth can never take a step that deviates from religion. Sahadeva, while cognizant of the ultimate truth, was unwilling to accept it until he had tested it with debate. For his gumption and intelligence, he deserves admiration, not animosity.

Chitragupta: Thank you, Keshava. The allegations against Nakula and Sahadeva are now complete, and it is time for judgement.

Nakula: We are both ready, Maharaj.

Chitragupta: In the course of today's proceedings, Nakula was blamed for killing Karna's son through deception. Sahadeva was blamed for manipulating the peace treaty in a manner that would render it unacceptable to Suyodhana. He was also accused of trying to capture Sri Krishna—an allegation that Keshava has argued against. After listening to all the arguments, I have concluded that neither Nakula nor

Sahadeva purposely arbitrated any act of irreligion.

In the Kurukshetra War and the history of Bharatvarsh, Nakula and Sahadeva have frequently been overlooked; their role in the scheme of things has either been criticized or ignored completely. But I adjudge today that both of you were, to a large extent, responsible for the victory of the Pandavas. It was your commitment to the truth, Sahadeva, and your loyalty to your family, Nakula, that steered the Pandavas towards victory. Henceforth, the history of your clan and the chronicles of our times will both be incomplete without you.

11

SRI KRISHNA

The Mahabharata was an epic of mammoth scale, a saga of fantastic valour, heart-rending and heartwarming relationships, machinations that humankind has never known before or since, and the struggle of the eternal truth to shine through. In the previous sessions of the Dharmakshetra, allegations were leveled, and questions were asked to various participants of this grand epic. Maharaj Chitragupta performed his responsibility of accounting for everyone's deeds and meting out the last judgement. While some defendants embraced a happy ending, moving on to their final place of peace and rest, many failed to find closure. But today, in the very last session of the Dharmakshetra, allegations will be levied, and questions will be asked to the one who is perceived to be above reproach, justification and interrogation. Sri Vasudeva Krishna represents the ultimate truth, but unless some truths that are embedded in his heart come to the fore, the Assembly of Dharmakshetra will remain incomplete.

Chitragupta: I welcome all of you to today's Dharmakshetra.

At the very outset, I want to announce: it won't be me who will conduct today's proceedings, for I wasn't the one who called today's assembly.

Arjuna: You didn't? Then who did?

Chitragupta: It was Sri Vasudeva Krishna. Pranaam, Keshava. Please come forth and occupy my seat. Since it was you who called today's assembly, you should be the one to preside over it.

Sri Krishna: No, Maharaj. Today, as always, you will preside over the assembly, and I will answer every question you raise against me.

Chitragupta: But Sri Krishna—

Sri Krishna: Please allow me to explain. When I stepped down on Earth, it was because a clan awaited my presence. There was great turbulence in the clan—about which all of you now know. While there was great love, there was also great hatred. Envy, loathing and untruths mounted in scale with every passing day until it became almost impossible for the Earth to sustain the burden of evil.

I could not sit back and watch; I had to fight for the ultimate truth and put to an end the irreligion that had come to rest in the hearts of innocent-faced children, valourous youth, loving wives and devoted mothers. I orchestrated the destiny of the clan to lead the truth to victory. While sometimes, I steered the wheel of fate myself, at other times, I drove it through others. When the time came, I put an end to the saga, burying many unanswered questions deep under the ground.

Today, years since that epic battle, families in Bharatvarsh continue to be the same. Wars are still fought; brothers vie for riches and glories, sometimes stepping on each other's toes. But in all their actions, they remember the lessons that the Mahabharata taught them. They know that if the Earth ever again loses its sense of honour and righteousness to the extent that evil is triumphant, I will step down and vanquish the darkness. Maharaj, to ensure that the lessons of the Mahabharata are never forgotten, it is imperative that I ferret the skeletons I buried under the ground and divulge the truths that only I know of. Like everyone before me, I too have several questions to answer. If these questions go unasked, the lessons of the Mahabharata will get limited to the Pandavas, the Kauravas, and their kith and kin. But the Mahabharata is not the story of these two clans or the enmity between them; it is not the narration of what happened to the kingdom of Hastinapur or the saga of a fearsome battle. No, Maharaj, the Mahabharata is the story of our society—a glimpse of the past and a foretelling of what can come in the future if humankind deviates from the truth.

Maharaj, you have been kind enough to let me participate in your court so far. One last time, I request you to extend your support and preside over the assembly.

Chitragupta: No, Keshava, I cannot do it. How can I raise allegations against you?

Sri Krishna: Maharaj, you only have to do your duty. And, in turn, I have to do mine.

Duryodhana: Karna, is Keshava doing what I think he is?

Karna: No, my friend, that is impossible.

Sri Krishna: So, Maharaj? Are you ready to preside over this final assembly of the Dharmakshetra?

Chitragupta: Yes, Keshava.

Sri Krishna: Excellent! I will now take my place at the defendant's stand.

Arjuna: Keshava, please don't do this! Your place is not there but in the hearts of everyone present in the assembly today.

Sri Krishna: Arjuna, I have to stand here today and face the allegations against my name. If I don't, the Assembly of Religion will remain incomplete. Generations to come will be plagued by doubt and unrest that will keep them from abiding by the truth.

Draupadi: No, Keshava. I will not let it happen. I cannot see you standing there at the defendant's stand, allegations lashing at your heart. You can consider this my devotion or my love, but I will NOT let it happen.

Sri Krishna: Draupadi, if you consider me your own, don't stop me today. There are answers I must give—

Duryodhana: No, Keshava, you don't have to give any answers. Excuse me for interrupting, but I don't think anyone in this assembly has the capability to ask you anything. You might find it odd that I stand here talking in your favour. Yes, I may have been a lifelong enemy of the Pandavas, but it is evident even to me that you are beyond reproach. Who among everyone present here can dare to cast any allegation against you?

Yudhishthira: Keshava, I agree with Duryodhana. If you so desire, I will apologize to Duryodhana and everyone else for any wrongdoing I may have committed against them. I know that they won't deny me forgiveness. Keshava, if you want, even Bhima will embrace Dushasana in front of your eyes. Whatever you desire will unfurl here today, but please refrain from punishing us like this.

Sri Krishna: Dharmaraj, you are the one who has mastered religion. All your life, you stood by your ethics and didn't let anything shake your truth. But you too had to endure the brunt of allegations, hadn't you? Today, it is my turn. Don't think too much about it.

Chitragupta: I still find myself unable to do this, Sri Krishna. How will I forgive myself for raising doubts about your intentions and actions?

Sri Krishna: Maharaj, please begin reading out the allegations against me. Look in your notebook, and there you will find a list. I have known many people during my time on Earth; some of them I have befriended, others have despised me. Nonetheless, today, I have to be answerable to one and all. Nobody who has spent a lifetime on Earth can meet his final fate without going through your court. Don't deny me this destiny; don't deprive me of this opportunity to lighten my heart.

Chitragupta: For what I am about to do now, I hope that everyone in the assembly will forgive me. Keshava, the first allegation against you is that if you are God, fully aware of both the past and the future and equipped with the power to alter fate, why did you allow such grievous destruction to happen?

Sri Krishna: Let me try to understand the meaning of this allegation. Do you mean to ask why, if I am Vishnu, did I not reveal my divine powers and appear in front of all in my Virat-Swaroop, instantly eliminating the hatred, enmity and disgust in Hastinapur? Why didn't I come to Earth sooner and prevent the macabre events instead of letting the bad blood between the Pandavas and the Kauravas become poisonous? Have I understood it right?

Chitragupta: Yes, Keshava. That is the allegation.

Sri Krishna: Tell me, Dharmaraj, did this question plague you too?

Yudhishthira: Yes, Keshava. The question did come to me, but it did not plague me. I knew the answer to the question and, with the permission of Maharaj, will repeat it today.

Chitragupta: Go ahead, Dharmaraj.

Yudhishthira: Maharaj, Keshava did not stop the events from unfolding because destruction was imprinted in the destiny of Hastinapur. The loathing that always existed between the Pandavas and the Kauravas was fated; Keshava did not want to intervene.

Sri Krishna: Yudhishthira, if I had wanted to, I could have changed the destiny of Hastinapur. But I did not. Maharaj, I wish to respond to this allegation myself for Dharmaraj's response is both inadequate and incorrect.

Maharaj, every era dawns to set an example for generations to come. For instance, the Satya Yug or the Era of Truth taught the world about Rama and Ravana. The world learnt the importance of loyalty, duty, and complete devotion. Every era has its virtues and faults, and this is what makes it an indelible example in the annals of history. If I had altered the destiny of this era, its purpose would have been lost. No one would have learnt what it had intended to convey. I am the only one at fault for prioritizing this lesson over the great sorrow that came with the destruction.

Yudhishthira: Yes, Sri Krishna.

Sri Krishna: Dharmaraj, I advise you not to accept what I say quite so soon. Belief that shies away from questioning is blind, but true faith must never be blind.

Yudhishthira: I will remember that, Keshava.

Gandhari: Keshava, Prabhu, I now know that whatever happened to us was a lesson we had to learn. You strove only to help the truth be victorious. The lessons you helped us learn will serve our future generations in good stead.

Sri Krishna: Yes, Badi Ma.

Chitragupta: Sri Krishna, I hope that you aren't offended by what I am saying, but I fail to understand one thing. You are an *avatar* of Vishnu; you are Narayan, right? But all the attendees of my court address you with different names. You too have built a plethora of relationships with the people on Earth. You call them your beloved friends, Kakashree, Pitamaha, and now Badi Ma. Why did you need to do this, Keshava? What was the need to pretend?

Sri Krishna: Maharaj, it is the nature of man to disregard the words of the one who preaches from a higher moral ground. The advice gets portrayed as an order; it doesn't seep into the heart and become a lesson. People need the support and guidance of someone who is their own. Times may change, but this never will. Human beings will always listen to those whose words touch their hearts. Emotions can overrule everything, even the divine.

Arjuna: Yes, Keshava, isn't that why you always explained things to me like my truest friend? Never was there a hint of command in your voice. I could only sense affection and friendship.

FLASHBACK

Arjuna: They surrounded my child from all sides and killed him! Those 'brave' warriors of the Kaurava army slaughtered an innocent child with such deception!

Sri Krishna: Arjuna, Abhimanyu's loss agonizes me no end. He was a son to me too.

Arjuna: They had better watch out. Tomorrow, I will show them the price of murdering my son.

Sri Krishna: Arjuna, you cannot bring him back.

Arjuna: They killed him! He was my dear son, a braver man than any of those cowards, and they killed him like beasts!

Bhima: Control yourself, Arjuna. Nothing you do can bring back Abhimanyu. But we will avenge his death. Those disgusting men will have to pay for it.

Yudhishthira: Yes, Arjuna! The Kauravas will be defeated in tomorrow's battle.

Arjuna: Oh no, Bhaiya. Tomorrow would be too late. The image of my son's corpse lying on the ground of Kurukshetra will haunt me until I avenge his murder. I will destroy the Kauravas right now. Tonight will be their final night!

Sri Krishna: Arjuna, will anything you do bring Abhimanyu back? If you have a plan to revive Subhadra's son and bring him back to us in this camp, I will not stop you from executing it at once.

Arjuna: No, Keshava, but destroying the Kauravas will assuage the fire that is burning my heart to ashes. He was my son—

Sri Krishna: No, Partha, he was first a warrior. He lived like one and breathed his last with more courage than the bravest of warriors put together. He deserves your salute, Partha.

Arjuna: Yes, but he also deserves to be avenged.

Sri Krishna: I can understand your thirst for revenge. The Kauravas deserve to face the ire for the sin they committed on the battlefield today, and I will ensure they get what they deserve. You will be the one to deliver it, Arjuna. But refrain from attacking anyone right now. Hold on until tomorrow. I am your friend, aren't I? Please trust me on this.

Arjuna: Yes, Keshava.

END OF FLASHBACK

Arjuna: You kept your word, my friend. You helped me avenge the murder of my son, and for that, I am eternally grateful to you. If it hadn't been for you, I might have attacked those undeserving of blame while the real culprit evaded me, hiding in the shadows, never to be found.

Sri Krishna: Yes, Arjuna, the ones who had surrounded Abhimanyu were not responsible for his death. The real culprit had been Jayadrath, the King of Sindhu, for it was he who stopped you from reaching your son and helping him. It is curious that Jayadrath was able to stop you, really, for he is no match for you at archery. But it was his divine boon from Lord Shiva that saw him through. He could have chosen any one day in his life when he would be able to contain any warrior—even you. That was the day he picked.

Chitragupta: Forgive me, Keshava, but the list reflects that herein lies the next allegation against you.

Sri Krishna: Do not hesitate, Maharaj. Remember that you are merely doing your duty. So, let me clarify the next allegation for the understanding of everyone in the assembly. It accuses me of resorting to magic to change the course of the war. Is that right? The allegation is that Arjuna was able to kill Jayadrath and therefore avenge Abhimanyu's death only because I resorted to trickery.

Chitragupta: Yes, Keshava.

Sri Krishna: Well, Arjuna had resolved to kill Jayadrath the day after Abhimanyu breathed his last. He had pledged that if he failed to do so, he would give up the war and step into his funeral pyre. All through the day, the Kauravas ensured that Jayadrath maintained a safe distance from Arjuna. Not once did Arjuna get to confront Jayadrath, let alone defeat him!

Evening soon came, and the warfare for the day drew to a close. Arjuna had failed to keep his resolve and stepped towards his pyre. Suddenly at that moment, a miracle happened: the clouds cleared, and the sun came up. Hey presto! The war wasn't over after all! Arjuna did not lose a moment and shot the fatal arrow that pierced Jayadrath's chest. I think all the attendees of the court believe that I conjured the miracle. Arjuna, you believe it too, don't you? Maharaj, the truth is that nothing that happened that day was a miracle. I did not pull any magic tricks. Not one!

Arjuna: Keshava, it was certainly a miracle. I was about to give up my life when, all of a sudden, I got the chance to fulfil my resolve. If you hadn't conjured that miracle, the outcome of the Kurukshetra War would have been unimaginably different.

Sri Krishna: No, Arjuna, it wasn't a miracle. If you insist on calling it a miracle, perhaps you may call it a natural wonder. It was nature who was the magician that day, not me.

Arjuna: So, this means the sudden clearing of the clouds was completely natural?

Sri Krishna: There was nothing natural or religious about Abhimanyu's death. When such a grossly irreligious act is committed, the entire universe is shamed. In return, the universe plans its revenge. Frequently, the juncture to seek revenge comes in ways that thoroughly surprise us. After Abhimanyu was killed, the very firmament of the Earth shook. The repercussions were felt even in the divine lands, and Suryadev was in great turmoil. He couldn't believe that his son Karna had also been party to an act so very heinous.

The Agnidev couldn't allow you to walk into the flames and give up your life. The 'miracle' happened because nature willed it to, Arjuna; nature wanted to help you fulfil your pledge. I admit that I knew the Heavens would help you, but—

Arjuna: You did? Why didn't you tell me, Keshava? I was looking for Jayadrath all day! I grew more frantic by the minute and dreaded the evening.

Sri Krishna: If I had told you, Arjuna, wouldn't you have been tempted to wait until the evening? It would make you forget your duty. Nature does not side with the one who overlooks his duty but bends over double to be of assistance to the truth.

Maharaj, since we are on the subject of my apparent penchant for wiles, I want to talk about another significant incident.

Karna: Keshava, you have already explained your actions abundantly even when you didn't need to. None of us here believes that any of your actions were ill-judged or misplaced, let alone unethical.

Sri Krishna: Angaraj, do you know what I am talking about? I want to accept something I did that can be called unethical; indeed, it has been the subject of a serious allegation earlier in this court. Maharaj, I think you know what I mean. I am accused of tricking Guru Drona by using his son Ashwatthama as a pawn. When Guru Drona asked Yudhishthira if Ashwatthama was dead, and Dharmaraj mouthed the first part of his answer, I created a loud interruption. Guru Drona never got a chance to hear how an elephant called

Ashwatthama had died, not his son Ashwatthama.

Chitragupta: Yes, Keshava, the next allegation against you is that you intentionally blew the conch shell when Yudhishthira was talking, so that Guru Drona would hear only a half-truth.

Sri Krishna: I agree, Maharaj. I blew the conch shell because I did not want Guru Drona to hear Dharmaraj in full. Today, I will tell the assembly why I was compelled to do what I did.

Duryodhana: No, Keshava, we don't need explanations for you. It would have been to everyone's benefit had Ashwatthama truly been killed that day. Perhaps, the monstrous crime he went on to commit would have then been averted.

Sri Krishna: No, Duryodhana, just as no one can be born before their time, it is impossible to leave the Earth before all dues have been paid. Maharaj, the reason for Guru Drona's suffering on the battlefield and outside it is something else altogether.

Chitragupta: Please tell us, Keshava.

Sri Krishna: Maharaj, Gurudev Drona lived a life of quiet repression. He never had the courage to express the true emotions in his heart. When Ekalavya came to him and pleaded to become his disciple, Guru Drona felt the pangs of truth. He wanted to allow Ekalavya to become a student in the Gurukul, but he was too afraid to go against the façade he had built around the truth. 'I only teach princes,' he tried to convince himself, and also refused Karna, who deserved to become his student like few other men of his times.

When the conch shell was blown to announce the commencement of the Kurukshetra War, Guru Drona was once again hit by the voice of religion. 'It isn't your religion to fight in a war,' said the voice. 'It is irreligious to kill Abhimanyu in this evil, unfair manner,' the voice grew louder. But not once did Guru Drona listen.

Truth couldn't survive in a heart so charred; it left his body and disappeared. On the battlefield, when the truth came out in the open from Yudhishthira, it failed to reach Guru Drona, who had resisted the truth all through his life, on all the opportunities he had received for redemption. Maharaj, Guru Drona had lost the right to hear the truth in its purest, most sonorous form. What happened to him was not a 'war strategy' I designed, but merely the vengeance of truth.

Guru Drona: I respect your explanation, Keshava.

Sri Krishna: Maharaj, please read aloud the next allegation in my name. I have a feeling the charges will now progress to a murderous degree of deception.

Duryodhana: Yes, Keshava, once again, you are correct. Let me explain the next allegation against you as it is one that has troubled me deeply. Do you remember that last mace battle between Bhima and me? Of course, you remember! I don't have any great respect for Bhima's overrated skill with the mace, but I did believe that he was honest and sincere about keeping the rules. But you gestured to him to strike me on my thigh! Didn't you, Keshava? You knew that my thigh was my weakest spot; you were also aware that it was not permitted to strike below the waist. But you did it only so Bhima could shatter my thigh and realize Draupadi's vengeance. Why did you do something so grossly unjust? You don't have to answer if you don't want to, Keshava, but I am convinced that you *have* no answer at all.

Sri Krishna: Duryodhana, you have answered your question correctly. It *was* essential for Bhima to shatter your thigh during that final mace battle you fought with him. When you pointed to your thigh and asked Draupadi, the wife of your brothers, to be seated on it, you insulted not only her but also all the women in Bharatvarsh. However, it is also true that Bhima broke the rules of warfare to fulfil his pledge, and I was the one who led him to it. Why did I have to stoop to deceitful measures like that? Duryodhana, go and take your seat for I will now tell the assembly about a truth that only you heard.

FLASHBACK

Duryodhana: What have you done, Keshava? How could you have the heart to compel Bhima to defeat me with such deceit? Didn't your ethics stop you from inflicting such agony on a warrior like me through disdainful and unforgivable tactics?

Sri Krishna: Your agony is your answer, Duryodhana.

Duryodhana: What do you mean? I am in too much pain to decipher your riddles, Keshava.

Sri Krishna: Duryodhana, you have lived a life of sin. So severe and unforgivable were your mistakes that they became pointed, acerbic questions in your heart. It is these questions—with heads as sharp as spears—that now cause you the agony you are in.

Duryodhana: But—

Sri Krishna: Your time is at an end, Duryodhana. You have sinned more than a lifetime could contain, and you're not permitted any more questions in these final moments of your life. Where was your sense of ethics when you vied blindly for the throne of Hastinapur, well knowing that it rightfully belonged to Yudhishthira? Where was your judgement of morality when you insulted Draupadi in front of all your elders and ordered your younger brother to disrobe her?

Duryodhana: I admit it, Keshava. I sinned. But what about the deceit you and Bhima perpetrated against me today? Wasn't that a sin too? Isn't it sinful for a Kshatriya to overrule the tenets of his religion of warfare?

Sri Krishna: No, Duryodhana. What happened today was intended to let religion triumph over irreligion. It wasn't only your thigh that was shattered today but also the bastions of all those who side with irreligion and evil. Today, when religion confronted irreligion on the battlefield, both exuded great might and confidence. But what you forgot, Duryodhana, was that no matter how promising things appear for irreligion, the victory of religion is inevitable. If it is to ensure that the good is eternally triumphant, all means will justify the end.

END OF FLASHBACK

Duryodhana: I beg your forgiveness, Sri Krishna. I will not forget the truth again.

Sri Krishna: Duryodhana, you accepted your mistakes only in the final moments of your life. By then, you were beyond redemption. However, I applaud you for your final, if delayed, acceptance. Acknowledging your sins is the first step towards a spiritual existence, and I am happy to see you past the first rung of the ladder.

Maharaj, I know that the list of allegations against me is now complete. However, I can still see a question writ large in the hearts of two attendees of your court. Why are you hiding the question? Is it because you are afraid to voice it, afraid that I will take offence? If you don't speak up, I will have to.

Chitragupta: Please proceed, Sri Krishna.

Sri Krishna: Maharaj, I am referring to Partha and Bhima. Tell me, Pandava brothers, isn't there something you are hesitating to ask me?

Bhima: No, Keshava.

Sri Krishna: Bhima, I was not present when you and Arjuna had this conversation before the Kurukshetra War. But do you really think it has remained concealed from me? I can see the question loud and clear in your heart: WHY did Keshava do such a thing?

FLASHBACK

Bhima: Tell me, Arjuna, why did Keshava ask you to promise that you will never ask him to pick up weapons during the war?

Arjuna: I don't know, Bhima. But believe me, it is making me anxious.

Bhima: Why didn't you say something? You should have asked him why he made you promise such a thing.

Arjuna: Bhima, I don't want Keshava to feel that he must do something for me. I don't want him to be burdened by expectations. Who are we to demand anything from him?

Bhima: What do you mean?

Arjuna: You know Keshava is omniscient. He can read anyone's mind—motives, intentions, aspirations. Did he know that I was expecting him to help us in the war by fighting for us? Was that why he proactively brought up the subject and extracted such a promise from me?

Bhima: It sounds possible, Arjuna. But it is a pity, isn't it? Had Keshava agreed to pick up arms even once during a battle, it would have been the end of the war.

END OF FLASHBACK

Sri Krishna: I never discussed it with you, Bhima, neither did I talk about it with Partha. But today I will quell the doubts in your hearts. I did not arm myself for if I had, how would you have got the opportunity to kill Dushasana and Duryodhana? How would Arjuna root Pitamaha down to a bed of arrows or lead Karna to his death? For the epic of Mahabharata to teach the world a lasting lesson, it was essential for you to fight with honour and valour. I couldn't have taken on the onus of something that was destined to be the responsibility of the heroes of the epic. The era needed its heroes and villains, and to ascertain this, it was imperative that I remain unarmed.

Duryodhana: Then I expect, Keshava, that it was also imperative that you spend time only with the heroes. Why suffer the disgrace of dining with the villains?

Chitragupta: Suyodhana, what is the basis of your statement?

Sri Krishna: Thank you for bringing this up, Duryodhana. Maharaj, Duryodhana is referring to the day I had gone to Hastinapur with the peace treaty. It was a historic day—the last stop before destruction was unleashed in its complete fury. But I remember the day also because it was the only time that I lied.

Chitragupta: That is impossible, Keshava! You have never lied.

Sri Krishna: Yes, I have. Once. It was almost lunch-time when I reached Hastinapur, and Duryodhana had arranged a hearty meal for me. But I refused to eat in the palace. I lied that I wasn't hungry and went over to meet Vidur Kaka at his house. Duryodhana, I did not do this to insult you.

Duryodhana: Well, it sure looked like it.

Vidur: Keshava, the meal we shared was perhaps the happiest of my life.

FLASHBACK

Vidur: Welcome, Keshava! It is my great fortune that you have stepped into my house.

Sri Krishna: Kakashree, are you going to ask me for lunch or not? I am starving!

Vidur: Forgive me, Keshava, the meal will be ready in a trice. My wife is preparing it in the kitchen. I had assumed that you would dine in the royal palace—

Sri Krishna: Oh no, Kakashree, Yuvraj Duryodhana did not find it necessary to invite me to a meal. It is only you and Kaki who look after me so well.

Vidur: Keshava, I am afraid the meal might seem scanty. But this is all we could put together.

Sri Krishna: It looks delicious. I know Kaki has outdone herself to cook this meal for me. Please allow me some moments of silence as I dig in.

END OF FLASHBACK

Sri Krishna: That reminds me, Vidur Kaka, I forgot to thank you for the meal that day. I was absorbed in its deliciousness and love.

Duryodhana: I too had a meal prepared for you, Keshava. I bet it was more delicious than what Vidur Kaka could put together.

Sri Krishna: Duryodhana, you felt insulted when I refused to dine at your house. But it wasn't me who insulted you. Tell me, what is the meaning of a meal that is served with neither love nor affection? If you invite someone for lunch and expect them to eat because they are indebted to you in some manner, then that, in my opinion, is the perfect example of an insult.

Duryodhana: I understand, Keshava. Please forgive me.

Sri Krishna: Maharaj, one last question remains before you can declare the Dharmakshetra complete. It is a question that my dear friend Draupadi will ask.

Draupadi: No, Keshava, I have nothing to ask you. You were my closest friend and companion. I never thought of you as God; I always believed I had a right over you. Don't close friends have the authority to demand things of each other? There were times when I was stubborn and mean and argued with you to get my way. If anything, I want to express my gratitude to you for making my tumultuous life worth living.

Sri Krishna: You are dear to me, Draupadi. I always wanted to be by your side and protect you. But there was a time when I almost failed you. I left you fearing that I had deserted you just like everyone else you called your own.

Draupadi: Yes, Keshava. I was desolate.

Sri Krishna: Maharaj, the last question I want to answer in today's assembly pertains to my absence when a grave crime was being committed against my dear friend, Draupadi. Dushasana was attempting to disrobe her by pulling at her saree. She was being subjected to an insult that would haunt her to her grave, but I did not show up to help her.

Dushasana: But Keshava, you *were* there! Draupadi was calling out your name all the while I was pulling at her saree.

It must have been your divine power that made her saree infinite. I kept pulling, but you continued to drape her, never letting her be dishonoured. Wasn't it you, Keshava?

Sri Krishna: No, Dushasana. That day, I wasn't with Draupadi. But she was with me.

FLASHBACK

Draupadi: What do I do, my friend? I cannot bear this pain. I don't know whether to let my anger ravage my insides or allow my agony to make me numb. Should I do something, Keshava? *Can* I do something or will fate run its course?

Sri Krishna: Fate will run its course, Draupadi, but destiny isn't unchanging. We make our destiny with our deeds and misdeeds. It doesn't do to become fatalistic and quit taking action. Do you know what happens when man surrenders himself to destiny, not even attempting to write his future? His life goes astray and becomes purposeless, meandering like a muddy stream.

Draupadi: I did not understand, Keshava.

Sri Krishna: Vent your anger, Draupadi. For the insult you have faced, announce the beginning of the end.

Draupadi: I was born of fire. All my life so far, I have endured everything I have encountered, battling against all the odds without complaint. But today, I have been humiliated in a manner that I refuse to accept quietly. I will not let history forget the humiliation of a pious, devoted woman! The Earth will be littered with corpses; Duryodhana's thigh will be shattered; Dushayasan's chest will be torn apart! Blood will flow like turbulent rivers, and in the blood, I will bathe my tresses.

END OF FLASHBACK

Sri Krishna: The rage of a woman can bring about great destruction. It can also teach an entire era the greatest lessons it must learn. I only helped you fulfil your life's purpose, Draupadi. It was your faith in me that protected you on the day of the game of dice. The one who believes in me with all his heart and abides by the truth will always find me right beside them.

Draupadi: Keshava, I don't care what you mean to anyone else. But for today and always, you are my greatest friend.

Sri Krishna: Draupadi, your love and friendship mean more to me than the prayers and offerings of the most devout of devotees. There is no purer bond than friendship, and I promise to be true to it until the world exists no more.

Chitragupta: Keshava, now that all the allegations against you and the questions you wished to answer are at an end, please permit me to disband the assembly.

Sri Krishna: No, Maharaj, the questions and allegations may have been quelled, but an important matter remains to be addressed. Without it, everything that has transpired in your court may be forgotten. The purpose of my incarnation would be unfulfilled.

Chitragupta: What is it, Sri Krishna?

Sri Krishna: Maharaj, everyone present in your court today has accounted for his or her deeds on Earth. They have responded to the charges against them and accepted the judgement you meted out. But what did they learn from the experience? Now that this era has come to an end and we are on the brink of welcoming a new one, please ask everyone what they have learnt from the Dharmakshetra. What are the lessons they will carry forward to their next births?

Chitragupta: Yes, Keshava. Gangaputra Bhishma, as you are the oldest of all the attendees in my court, so we will begin with you. Please announce to the assembly, one by one, the lessons each of you have learnt from this Assembly of Religion.

Bhishma: I have learnt to be careful about what I promise. During my time on Earth, I believed that a promise could never be broken. But now I know that no matter how unbreakable a promise might seem, never can it be greater than a woman's honour and dignity.

Dhritarashtra: I have understood that true blindness does not lie in the eyes but in the inability to comprehend and understand religion. I was truly blind because I let my congenital blindness define my life, never attempting to allow the path of truth to illuminate either my life or the lives of my sons. Maharaj, I have also understood that it doesn't do to shower your children with mindless and absolute affection if you fail to teach them how to distinguish between right and wrong.

Gandhari: Maharaj, I have learned that nothing should exceed its limits, not even your piety and loyalty as a wife.

Sri Krishna: No, Badi Ma, you have understood not the limits of wifely duties but the meaning of being a life partner in the truest sense of the word. A wife must not follow her husband along the blind alleys of irreligion; she must be his strength and hold his hand, so he doesn't get sucked into the pit of darkness.

Vidur: Maharaj, I have learnt that it is best to understand and establish the lessons of religion as soon as possible. Irreligion, in its own right, can grow to become as powerful as religion. If it is allowed to rule, life can become as helpless as I felt in the palace that day, watching Rani Draupadi being insulted while Maharaj Dhritarashtra, whom I was supposed to counsel, remained unmoving and silent.

Kunti: Maharaj, I have learned that I must accept whatever fate has in store for me.

Karna: Maharaj, I too have learned this. I have accepted that I mustn't allow self-pity to overpower me if I am displeased with what fate has doled out. It is possible to live a fulfilling life with courage and the acceptance of who you are.

Yudhishthira: Maharaj, I have learned that religion is not the ultimate guide to human behaviour. It cannot be deemed complete and infallible until all its faults have been eradicated. It is important to keep the truth in view as religion might err or be inadequate at times, but the truth is complete and unmovable.

Duryodhana: I have learnt never to leave anything incomplete. I must remember to commit to any task with all my heart. And yes, I must remember to listen to my elders.

Even if it is true that my elders might be mistaken, I should respect their experience and, at the very least, hear them out.

Dushasana: Maharaj, I have understood that a man who judges himself poorly and has a low opinion of himself is likelier to be driven towards heinous, disgraceful activities. I have to develop my own identity and not hide behind that of my elder brother. Only when I learn to think on my own and discern the good from the evil can I live a life worth remembering.

Bhima: Maharaj, I have learnt to develop a balance between my mind and my heart. One must exercise caution and restraint, as action without due thought can trigger the greatest of tragedies. But I maintain that if the mind is quiet and non-committal, one must listen to the heart.

Draupadi: Keshava, I have learnt to remember my rights and never allow anyone to snatch them from me. I am not a pawn that anyone can stake at a game of dice; I am a woman who can be controlled only by herself and her destiny.

Arjuna: I have realized that in my quest to achieve my goal, I must consider not only my duty to myself and to religion but also to those who love me. Religion dictates that man must be true to all his duties, and this includes his responsibility towards his wife.

Nakula: I too have learnt to be righteous. Abiding by the truth reigns supreme over all religions.

Sahadeva: Maharaj, I have overpowered the stifling feeling of being inconsequential because I was the youngest. I have learnt that whatever one does to ensure the victory of religion is an important step; no endeavours made to let good triumph over evil are meaningless or puny.

Sri Krishna: Maharaj, I am happy to see that all the attendees of your court have learnt their lessons well. It means that I too have been successful at instilling the stalwarts of this era with lessons that will make the new era happy, progressive and righteous. It is now time for your judgement, Maharaj.

Chitragupta: Keshava, I don't need to pronounce any judgement. Every allegation against you has been proved invalid. In answering all the questions, you have taught lessons that humankind will always hold close. My court decrees that Sri Krishna is innocent of all charges. However, he will still be punished.

Karna: What? Maharaj, all the allegations against Keshava have been refuted. You said so yourself. Why then must he be punished?

Arjuna: Moreover, Maharaj, it wasn't you who called today's assembly. It was Keshava himself. How can you punish him if he wasn't even listed as a defendant in your book?

Chitragupta: Arjuna, Karna, it isn't me who owns this assembly. This assembly is part of the universe that Sri Krishna carries in his soul. Today, it won't be me who will sentence him to punishment; it will be Sri Krishna himself.

Sri Krishna: Being trapped in the circle of life and facing the challenges of the Earth, day after day, is a tremendous challenge. I admire all of you for doing it with so much courage and acceptance. During my time on Earth, I had an opportunity to experience what you go through every day.

Now that I have listened to all of you in the Dharmakshetra and watched you recount the lessons you have learnt, I have faith that the next era will be peaceful and just. But time is an unpredictable entity; no one can predict the turn it might take or the precise moment evil starts building new roots in the Earth I so love.

Today, I promise that whenever the evil in the world starts overpowering the good, when envy, hatred and anger become deep-seated in the hearts the people, when religion seems to shake in fright and has to bow down to irreligion, I will come to you. Whenever you call me to redeem your life, protect the good, destroy the evil-doers, and establish righteousness all over again, I will come to you, from age to age. And that is my punishment.

यदा यदा हि धर्मस्य ग्लानिर्भवति भारत ।
अभ्युत्थानमधर्मस्य तदात्मानं सृजाम्यहम् ॥
परित्राणाय साधूनां विनाशाय च दुष्कृताम् ।
धर्मसंस्थापनार्थाय सम्भवामि युगे युगे ॥

THE END